A RUTHLESS
PROPOSITION

ALSO BY NATASHA ANDERS

The Unwanted Series

The Unwanted Wife

A Husband's Regret

His Unlikely Lover

A RUTHLESS PROPOSITION

NATASHA ANDERS

Montlake
Romance

Text copyright © 2016 Natasha Anders
All rights reserved.

Published by Montlake Romance, Seattle
www.apub.com

Amazon, the Amazon logo, and Montlake Romance are trademarks of Amazon.com, Inc., or its affiliates.

ISBN-13: 9781503951068
ISBN-10: 1503951065

Cover design by Laura Klynstra

Printed in the United States of America

For Lorinda and Chevon with so much love.
The best friends a girl could ask for.

CHAPTER ONE

"Freshen up, Miss Knight, and meet me back in the living room in forty-five minutes. We'll have to work through dinner," Dante Damaso commanded as he tugged off his tie with one hand and poured himself a brandy with the other.

Cleopatra Pandora Knight stared at her boss with a simmering resentment that she hid behind a mask of impassivity. She was exhausted. They had landed at Narita airport that afternoon and had hit the ground running, with one meeting after the next, as they attempted to deal with the bureaucratic red tape that had delayed the start of construction on Dante's new hotel. All she wanted was a hot shower and a good night's sleep since she knew that she had to face more of the same frenetic pace tomorrow.

Sadly, that was not to be; the boss wasn't done working, and that meant no sleep for Cleo until he said so.

"Yes, Mr. Damaso," she said demurely, keeping her voice low and emotionless. He didn't acknowledge her response, picking up a newspaper and perusing the headlines with the intense focus he gave whatever activity he happened to be engaged in at any given moment. Recognizing the dismissal, Cleo turned and headed for her room.

When Cleo realized that she would be sharing the penthouse suite of one of the most exclusive hotels in Tokyo with her boss, she had a moment of panic. Until she'd seen the suite. Her entire apartment back in Cape Town could fit into this place several times over. It had three huge bedrooms, two full bathrooms, and a living room. Nothing but the best for Dante Damaso. Until *his* hotel was built, he would stay in what would soon be the second best hotel in Tokyo.

Cleo rolled her head on her shoulders and listened to her neck creak with the movement. God, she felt like she could sleep for a week, whereas the boss barely looked winded. It was a little infuriating how indefatigable he was, especially since it impacted Cleo directly. She sighed and allowed herself a moment of self-pity before rummaging through her suitcase for a change of clothing, and padding to the bathroom.

She was back in the living room exactly forty minutes later, dressed in a modest blue slip dress in which she felt a lot more comfortable than the suits she was required to wear for this job. Her short bob was still damp from the shower, and she hadn't bothered with makeup. She hoped that the boss wouldn't mind her lack of formality and was relieved to note that he'd removed his tie, unbuttoned the top two buttons of his white shirt, and folded back his shirtsleeves to reveal extremely masculine forearms. Her favorite kind—strong, lightly dusted with hair, with raised veins mapping a path to his capable-looking hands.

He looked up and grunted when she entered the room.

"Good, you're back. We have to go through today's minutes and compile a list of the most pertinent facts. Then take care of the day's correspondence. You get started on that; I have to make a few phone calls."

He turned away from her and lifted his phone to his ear. Cleo stared at his broad back for a moment before trudging over to the laptop with a muffled sigh. She wondered if he'd ordered room service yet; she was starving. She glanced around the room and gasped in outrage when she saw the room-service cart standing off to the side of the room, with the uncovered *empty* plates precariously stacked one on top of the other. Another quick look around the room told her that there was definitely no other food around. Had he actually *forgotten* to order something for her? Was the man wholly incapable of thinking of anybody but himself? She picked up the room telephone to order her own meal, but he had finished his call and cast her a sharp look.

"Stop wasting time, Knight," he growled, tapping away at the screen of his phone. "We have a lot of work to do. I didn't bring you along to sit around looking pretty and doing nothing."

The injustice of that statement left her fuming, and she bit back a sarcastic retort, knowing that she had no alternative but to swallow down the anger she felt toward him. Cleo knew that—due to the last-minute nature of this trip—she'd been his only choice as assistant. And since the man had avoided testing her full potential in the office up until now, he didn't trust her to get anything done competently. Still, Cleo had jumped at the opportunity to join him. The heady excitement of a trip to Japan combined with the desire to prove herself capable of doing this job to both Dante Damaso *and* to herself had proved hard to resist. Yet now, feeling completely overwhelmed, all she wanted was to run back home with her tail between her legs.

All because her boss was doing his level best to be an ass.

Don't respond! Don't respond! She repeated the two words over and over to herself. No mouthing off at the boss, no matter how much he deserved it.

An hour and a half later, after they had powered their way through a series of e-mails and memos and had pored over her notes from the day's many meetings, Cleo was starting to feel cross-eyed from staring at the computer screen too long. Her brain was scrambled, and she was practically drooping with exhaustion. Even though she hadn't eaten since the flight—a decade ago—she was too damned tired even to think about her stomach.

Dante Damaso peered at her when she stopped tapping at the keys and frowned over the top of his black-rimmed glasses.

"Let's take a five-minute break," he suggested, and Cleo almost melted into a puddle of gratitude. She stretched lavishly and enjoyed a jaw-popping yawn at the same time. A quick look at her boss told her that while he had suggested a break, he wasn't taking one himself—his head was once more bent over zoning ordinances and blueprints. The man really was tireless, a trait that she found both admirable and frustrating at the moment. She supposed years of international travel and frantic work schedules had inured him somewhat to the effects of a forty-eight-hour-long day, one that had started on a completely different continent.

She padded over to the huge floor-to-ceiling window that overlooked Tokyo in all its sparkling glory. She had never seen anything remotely close to this spectacular view. The city was vast, and its lights sprawled as far as the eye could see. Despite being forty floors removed from the heaving excitement of the city, Cleo could feel it calling to her like a seductive siren.

She turned away from the allure and found herself inadvertently appreciating a spectacular view of a different kind. Big, sexy Dante Damaso as she had never seen him before, ruffled, stubbled, and completely disheveled. The look suited him and gave him an edge that the normally smooth, urbane man kept hidden beneath layers of intimidating sophistication and flawless tailoring. It was an image of the man she really preferred not to have in her head, because it made him seem a lot more human—more approachable—than he usually was.

He looked up and happened to catch her eye, and even from across the room, she could see something spark and smolder in his gaze. It was gone in a flash, and she wondered if her tired brain had tricked her into seeing things. She wandered over to the exquisite coffee table where she had left her cell phone to charge and checked her messages. A couple from her brother, Luc, and her best friend, Cal, and one informing her that she could very well have won five hundred grand already! Fantastic. She allowed herself a moment of pure whimsy— with her "winnings" there'd be no further need to spend her mornings making coffee, watering Dante Damaso's precious ficus, or sending the polite equivalent of "Thanks for the sex. Let's never see each other again" notes with flowers to her boss's random lady friends. In the nearly four months that she'd been working for him, she'd already sent five notes accompanying equally polite, pretty floral tributes. It was sickening.

Her nose wrinkled at the thought, and she jumped guiltily when the object of her thoughts called her name curtly.

"Yes, sir?"

"Ready to get back to work?"

Not really.

"Of course, sir," she said, proud that she managed to keep her voice relatively emotionless.

She sat down at the antique secretary that she had claimed as her workstation and tried to hide her wince when her butt and back hit the hard, unforgiving surface of the ornate high-back chair. She rolled her shoulders and sighed quietly as she closed her eyes and kneaded the tightly knotted muscles in the back of her neck.

"Tired?"

She jumped when Damaso's voice came from behind her, and she looked up over her shoulder to meet his dark, enigmatic gaze. He'd come up to within half a yard of the back of her chair and had his hands shoved into his trouser pockets. He was staring down at her, his eyes narrowed and intent.

"A little," she admitted.

He nodded, never taking his eyes off hers, and seemed to weigh his next words before speaking.

"Would you like a neck rub?"

Cleo blinked, shocked by both the question and the heat that flared in his eyes. She knew very well what that neck rub would entail, where it would lead, and he meant for her to know that. Until that very moment, she would never have guessed that the man had even noticed her as a female, yet the way he was looking at her right now told her that he very much appreciated what he was seeing. He kept his hands to himself and his expression—despite everything going on in his eyes—impassive. If she refused his offer and all it entailed, she imagined he would simply shrug it off, and they would carry on as if this crazy moment had never happened.

The question was . . . did she *want* to refuse him? She was tired, frustrated, and his offer could be a fantastic way to let off steam and unwind after a hard day. Who would it harm? They were both consenting adults. There was no romance or love or hearts and flowers here. She might dislike him, but she'd be lying to herself if she didn't admit to feeling sexually curious about him. Maybe just this once? Just a taste. This was sex, plain and simple, and sometimes that's really all anybody needed.

Dante Damaso watched the play of emotions on his assistant's ridiculously expressive face. Shock and confusion, followed by intrigue, trepidation, and definite interest. He couldn't have surprised himself more with that damned question. She was a tempting little thing, which he'd been trying damned hard to overlook in light of their personal connection through her brother. To that end, he limited the amount of time he spent with her as much as possible. But right now he was as human as the next guy. He was irritated by the way his day had gone, and his frustration built as the hours wore on with little progress being made. Now, after seeing this woman in her distracting blue dress, he was also horny as hell. He could do something about at least one of those things, but if she wasn't interested, they'd move on. It would probably be for the best anyway, considering the spur-of-the-moment nature of his proposition. He should withdraw his offer and leave it at that. After all, he couldn't think of a more inappropriate—

"Yes, thank you." Her whispered words brought his commonsense train of thought to a screeching halt, and his jaw dropped as he watched her dip her head, allowing the sharply defined points of her sleek bob to swing forward and hide her face. His throat went bone-dry, and all sound judgment fled as he watched his hands reach for that vulnerable nape. He hesitated just shy of touching her and inhaled deeply, catching a whiff of the fresh, floral scent that had tantalized his senses all evening. When his fingers finally made contact with her soft, exposed flesh, his breath shuddered out of his chest in tandem with hers.

He was instantly, painfully, and immutably hard, and he allowed himself to deepen his touch, even though every instinct in him was screaming that this was a mistake.

This is a mistake. The thought—which had been buzzing around in Cleo's head from the moment of initial contact between them, through their first stunning kiss, into the shedding of her clothing, and then when his mouth latched onto her breast for the first time—was getting ever more insistent. But Cleo had more interesting things to focus on, like the way his large, assertive hand was making its way down her body to . . .

"Oh God!" she moaned as that hand did magical, sinful, *unimaginable* things. Her back arched, and his smoldering gaze fell to the beaded tips of her breasts. She uttered another breathless little cry when his hot mouth fixed on one hypersensitive nub. Her fingers curled into his silky hair as she tried to keep him there.

"I can't . . ." Her voice tapered off into a high-pitched whine when his supremely talented mouth left her breast only to lavish the same treatment on the other mound.

She could feel his hot hardness poised at her entrance, and her hands left his hair to claw at his back and tight buttocks, trying to pull him toward her. He lifted his head to stare down at her, his eyes feverish as they pinned her with single-minded concentration.

"You want me?"

God, his sexy voice, roughened with desire and strain, nearly made her come right on the spot. She couldn't quite believe how much he was making her feel, how very much she wanted him inside her. She couldn't remember wanting any other man half as much as she did this one. And yet . . .

This is a mistake!

The words had grown shrill and insistent, but Cleo pushed them away as she reached up for another one of those drugging kisses.

He complied, but only for the very briefest of seconds. Her frustration reached new heights when he took himself in hand and deliberately ran his blunt, sheathed tip down her slick, sensitive channel. From the tight bundle of nerves at the apex, slowly back down to her entrance, where he came to rest for a long, aching moment.

"You want this? Yes?" He pressed forward slowly, and she hissed when she felt him breach her, so much thicker and harder than she had ever had before.

MISTAKE! The clamoring was incessant, but she ignored it again and arched toward him.

He refused to comply, remaining still, not even breathing, giving her just that one small taste of what was to come.

"*Sí?* Yes?" His voice remained annoyingly steady, but the fevered gleam in his eyes told her he wasn't as indifferent as he seemed.

"Yes! Damn you." She truly hated him in that moment, and a bit of venom seeped into her voice. "Yes, I want you. I crave this. I need . . . *oh.*" This last as he inched forward with such slowness and care that it felt like forever before he was buried from tip to hilt. He was almost uncomfortably large, and it took her out of the moment for a brief second. Sensing her discomfort, he rested there and gave her time to adjust to his size while he lowered his head and focused his lavish attentions on her breasts again. He braced one of his hands on the bed beside her head, keeping his weight off her, and allowed his other hand to go roaming. When that hand finally dawdled its way down to where they were joined, Cleo was already arching her hips toward his. He grinned and slid his free hand under her to palm her butt and adjust her position. He sat upright, knelt between her spread thighs, and dragged her even closer.

It was a seriously sexy position, sprawled flat on her back while he feasted his eyes on her uninhibited nakedness. He lifted her higher, forcing himself even deeper inside, and then, with a wicked grin, finally began to move again.

"Play with your breasts!" he commanded, his voice sounding a little breathless. She complied, rolling the distended nipples between her thumbs and fingertips, then flicking at them. He grunted in approval and moved his hands to her hips, angling her upward while he continued his assertive thrusting. *God, he is magnificent.* Sweat beaded on his forehead, dampened his hair, and added a fine sheen to his bronzed skin. He kept his focus on where they were joined, watching intently as he plowed into her tightness. His brow furrowed and his chest heaved, the first real signs that he was as affected as she was.

"Give me your hand," he growled, and she reluctantly released one taut nipple and lifted her right hand toward him. He didn't release her hips. Instead, he leaned down, captured her middle finger in his hot mouth, and sucked it inside. After one final seductive lick, he released her finger.

"Touch yourself," he said, and she groaned before obediently doing as he had commanded. "Good." The word was so gruff it was barely recognizable.

Cleo was unbelievably turned on by the picture she presented to his lascivious gaze. She had never been sexually shy, but this was . . . this was way beyond anything she'd ever experienced. Her back arched off the bed, her thighs lay sprawled across his, and she was quite unashamedly pleasuring herself for his—and her own—gratification. This was complete abandonment with the least likely man in the world, and she wasn't at all sure how she'd gotten here.

She was well past the point of no return and the inevitable was but a heartbeat away, and then . . . it was there and so cataclysmic that her whole body simply clenched. The sharp cry that she uttered died in her throat as every single atom of her being focused inward on an explosion of pleasure so powerful it tore her apart and left her feeling vulnerable and emotionally raw.

His orgasm finally took him. She watched in fascination as his eyes slid shut, his head flew back, and every cord in his neck stood out in stark relief. He gritted his teeth, preventing even the faintest of sounds from emerging. Only the sharp catch and gradual release of his breath gave any indication of how much the climax had affected him. She resented his control. Hated how she had given herself so completely while he, for all intents and purposes, had kept a cool head from that first kiss to this last lazy thrust.

His grip on her thighs finally loosened, and she imagined she'd have bruises in the shape of his fingertips on her butt and thighs by morning. She could barely move as he smoothly extricated himself from her, tugged off the condom, and fell flat on his face on the bed beside her, his long, muscular legs still entangled with hers.

"Thanks, Chloe. I needed that." His voice was slurred. He sounded like a very drunk or very tired man, and the gentle snore that followed a mere second later confirmed the latter fact. Cleo sighed, trying not to be completely demoralized by the fact that this man, whom she had known for nearly four frickin' months, had just called her by the wrong name. She maneuvered her way completely out from beneath him, sat on the side of the bed, and pushed herself up onto unsteady legs, feeling like a newborn calf. She knew she should probably get back to her own room, because she very much doubted that he would appreciate waking up with her still beside him.

She hunted around the room for her dress and underwear but couldn't find her panties. Why did it have to be her panties? She dressed hastily and was thankful that her walk of shame would span only the length of his room to the connecting door that led to her room. Nobody else would see her.

When she had the door firmly shut behind her, she wobbled over to the bed, where most of the contents of her suitcase were chaotically strewn all over the duvet cover, and sank down in relief. Her entire body still shook in the aftermath of the best sex—and the biggest mistake—of her life.

She buried her face in her hands.

"It's just sex," she told herself, and was embarrassed by the unsteady pitch of her voice. And by the lie. She was definitely embarrassed by the blatant lie, even if the only person she was trying to deceive was herself. That wasn't *just* sex. That had been the most mind-numbing, bone-melting, awe-inspiring forty-five minutes of her life, and there was no getting around that. The irritating man certainly knew his way around a woman's body. Her nipples ached just thinking about it, and to be frank, everything else was still tightening and convulsing in the aftermath of the soul-shattering orgasm she'd just had.

But to sleep with Dante Damaso? She shuddered in a way that had nothing to do with the microexplosions still tingling all over her body and everything to do with the fact that she could barely stand the man. So what if he was mouth-wateringly gorgeous? He was still an obnoxious, misogynistic jerk with a smug self-assurance that rubbed her the wrong way every time he spoke. Then there was the way he practically sneered every time he said *Miss Knight*, or the way he couldn't seem to look at her when he talked to her, or seemed incapable of a single *please* or *thank-you*. And—horribly—after one stupid mistake on her very first day of work, he now insisted on painstakingly checking every single letter she typed for him before she was allowed to e-mail it. It was humiliating, and while the mistake hadn't been repeated since then, he made it absolutely clear that he did not trust her to do anything more challenging than make coffee, water the plant, and send his kiss-off notes. Of course, he didn't micromanage the rest of his staff the way he did Cleo, and she knew if he weren't one of her brother's buddies, Dante would probably have fired her within the first week. But she was damned if she'd quit, the way he obviously expected—*wanted?*—her to.

And she had slept with him. She couldn't even blame alcohol, exhaustion, or temporary insanity . . . hold on. Maybe she *could* blame temporary insanity. She must have lost her mind. Why else would she have slept with the condescending, arrogant bastard?

She headed toward the en suite bathroom, tugging off her hopelessly wrinkled dress as she went. She fumbled with the complicated bells and whistles in the shower cubicle. *It's a shower; why is it so damned difficult anyway?* She finally got the water going and gratefully stepped beneath the powerful spray before swearing and fumbling with the knobs and buttons to set it to a temperature less than scalding.

"Damn it." The words were mild but heartfelt. She didn't know if she was sophisticated enough to be cool about a one-night stand. With her boss. Whom she despised.

She rested her forehead on the cool tiles before thumping it softly and rhythmically against the unforgiving surface. This was a disaster. She enjoyed sex, but she had never previously indulged outside at least a semicommitted relationship. This was uncharted territory for her. Where did they go from here?

Of all the stupid . . . She shook herself. She wasn't achieving anything with the self-recriminations. It had happened. Now she needed to figure out how the hell she was going to get through the rest of their time here and what she would do if she had to find a new job once they got back to Cape Town.

It would suck if it came to that, because she really enjoyed the challenge of this job. Back in South Africa, Dante regularly swapped her for other executive assistants in the upper echelons of his global, multi-billion-dollar leisure industry conglomerate, and it was on those days Cleo truly liked her new job. None of the other executives seemed to doubt her competence and rarely gave her the mind-numbingly boring and simplistic tasks Dante liked to saddle her with.

Cleo finished her shower and wrapped herself in the warm terry-cloth robe provided by the hotel. She sauntered over to the huge floor-to-ceiling window and stared out at the sprawling nightscape. She had always dreamed of visiting Japan—had hoped to dance here someday. She allowed herself a small, wistful smile and a momentary pang at the thought of all she'd lost before shoving the memory of what she'd once been able to do—what she still yearned to do—back into a box and placing it into a mental drawer. She could never fully shut that damned drawer; it was always slightly open, and every so often something—the dream of a different life—would escape from it and haunt her reality. She drew in a long breath and released it shakily. She had way too much else going on right now. She couldn't allow the coulda/shoulda beens to intrude on what was already an emotionally impactful night.

She tried to empty her mind of everything and focus only on the view. From her fortieth-floor vantage point, the shimmering lights looked as pretty as a Christmas tree, but she wondered at the constant frenetic activity in this crazy city that didn't seem to have slowed down at all, despite the lateness of the hour. She knew she should try to get some sleep. It was after three in the morning, and Dante Damaso would undoubtedly be up, dressed, and disgustingly alert by seven. She crawled into the king-size bed, which was positioned so she could still see the skyline. She curled up on her side and stared down at the blinking lights of the traffic far, far below before drifting into a restless sleep.

Dante woke as he usually did, fully aware of his surroundings and not the slightest bit groggy despite the lack of sleep and jet lag. For once that ability wasn't a blessing, not when he was immediately bombarded by the memory of the colossal error in judgment he had made the night before.

"Shit," he hissed beneath his breath, wasting a brief moment of his very precious time on a twinge of regret before shrugging that smidgen of conscience away. Instead he attempted to focus his attention on a solution to what could definitely become a problem. The sex had been quite good, really, and just what he'd needed to blow off the frustrations of the day. But the girl was his employee, a very junior employee—and Dante hardly ever went there. Plus, she was his friend's sister, and Dante for damned sure *never* went there. And yet he'd gone there last night and had no one to blame but himself.

To give Chloe her due, she had never looked at him in that way, never hinted at wanting any form of sexual relationship with him. If anything, until last night, she had been indifferent toward him and even seemed to dislike him at times. He snorted at that last thought, dismissing it as unlikely. When women pretended indifference, they were usually playing hard to get, and she was definitely the type to play ridiculous games like that. Look how easily she'd fallen into his bed last night. Surely that was proof she'd been harboring some sort of attraction for him all along.

He just hoped she didn't think it would be the start of something; he really didn't need the complication of breaking Luc's sister's heart. He liked the guy and they had been friends for a long time—and even though Dante had known of her existence, he had never actually met Luc's sister until she applied for this job. He hadn't been too enthused by the idea of giving her the position—especially in light of his unexpected physical response to her presence. But he wasn't about to offend one of his few real friends by refusing to give the man's precious sister a job— no matter how woefully underqualified she was on paper.

He shook himself impatiently, irritated that he had already wasted this much time on the incident when he had to figure out how to approach the precarious situation with the Shinjuku metropolitan government. He resented having to devote any of his time to considering the possible ramifications of his ill-advised sexual encounter with a woman. Not when he had so many other pressing issues to deal with.

He shook his head as he rose from bed and crossed to the bathroom for a quick shower. He had the utmost confidence he would handle this incident in the best way possible; it was just sex, after all. By the time he was dressed and ready to face the day, he had already dismissed the episode and was focused on other, far more important matters.

When Cleo joined Dante in the living room, he greeted her with his usual morning grunt, keeping his focus on his laptop.

"Miss Knight, I need you to send an urgent e-mail to Miles Kinross for the Phase One original blueprints," he said without looking up.

"Right now?" she asked, and he lifted his gaze from the computer screen to frown at her.

"Yes, *right now*. I wouldn't use the word 'urgent'"—he used mocking air quotes—"if I didn't want it right now."

Cleo gritted her teeth, bit back the sarcastic retort hovering on the tip of her tongue, and settled for saccharine sweetness instead.

"Well, I only ask, *sir*, because it's midnight in South Africa, and Mr. Kinross may not be checking his e-mails. I thought you might prefer the direct approach of a phone call instead."

"Then make yourself useful and get him on the line. Be proactive for a change."

She lifted her brows and picked up her company phone. She *really* wished she hadn't fallen into bed with this man so easily. But having regrets now—while she still sported patches of stubble burn on her inner thighs and her breasts tingled tantalizingly—was a waste of energy. His sultry mouth had trailed over every inch of her skin, and his heavy stubble had left a pale pink trail in some of the places he had lingered. There was even a faint sting in the small of her back, telling her she probably wore the same naughty stubble burn just above her butt.

Cleo endeavored not to dwell too much on the unwelcome and intimate physical reminders of her lapse in judgment last night. But that wasn't an easy thing to do when she could barely suppress a shiver as she recalled how masterfully he had flipped her onto her stomach and dragged his wicked lips down from the nape of her neck to—

"Miss Knight?"

Whoa. She snapped out of the raunchy daze and stared blankly into his impatient face.

"The phone call?"

"Yes, of course," she sputtered, feeling foolish as she dialed the number.

Miles Kinross, as she had suspected, had already retired for the night and not alone, if the sultry feminine voice in the background was anything to go by. Kinross was a handsome man and—if office gossip was to be believed—like Dante Damaso, he rarely dated the same woman for longer than a month or two. Cleo was in the middle of explaining what they needed when the phone was yanked rudely from her hand and Dante took over the conversation.

She straightened her shoulders, determined to ignore his boorish behavior, and headed over to the lavish buffet breakfast he must have ordered from room service. At least he'd remembered to order enough for two this time.

She allowed herself another flash of aggravation at the memory of how he had completely overlooked her need for a meal last night. Inconsiderate bastard. No wonder she'd been so susceptible to his dubious charms; she'd been suffering from impaired judgment due to starvation. Dying of hunger now, she heaped her plate with scrambled eggs, crispy bacon, and toast before sitting down to dig in.

She barely managed more than a mouthful before he concluded his call.

"There's no time for breakfast. We're running late as it is. Our first meeting is in forty minutes, and the driver has informed me that it'll take at least half an hour to get there in rush-hour traffic. I don't want to be late. It's unprofessional and considered extremely rude in Japan."

"Oh, but . . ." She stared longingly down at her still-full plate.

"If you'd been up earlier, you would have had more time to eat," he pointed out as he picked up his briefcase.

Yeah, right. Cleo had dawdled over her morning prep, gathering her courage to face him. She had tried to anticipate every possible scenario: he'd sweep her up into his arms and propose a torrid affair, he'd be unable to meet her eyes and unsure of what to say to her, he'd explain how their indiscretion had been only a passing thing, never to be repeated.

She hadn't expected *this*. This complete lack of acknowledgment of what had been a huge breach of office conduct. In fact, he was so completely normal and unaffected she wondered if he even remembered their little *oopsie*.

She shoveled down one last forkful of eggs before getting up with a resigned sigh. She smoothed her black, pin-striped pencil skirt down over her thighs and glanced up in time to catch a smoldering look in his dark eyes.

Oh . . . my.

"Let's go," he growled, stepping aside and allowing her to precede him.

For one glorious moment, that look helped her push aside her insecurities and made her feel powerful and feminine enough to add a deliberate little shimmy to her walk as she sidled past him.

Dante bit back the stream of profanity threatening to escape his lips and focused instead on internalizing his annoyance. A resurgence of sexual tension was the last thing he needed right now. He'd believed he had successfully put the whole incident firmly behind him, but the way that no-nonsense skirt clung to her pert little ass was more than a little distracting. Especially now that he knew she was probably wearing cute little cotton cartoon-character panties—similar to the ones she'd worn last night—beneath the pin-striped twill. He ground his teeth as he followed her out, forcing his eyes up from the tight curve of her butt to her narrow back, and tried to regain his focus. He was only marginally successful, distracted by the light, fresh scent of her shampoo as it wafted back toward him, and the sassy bounce of her silky hair.

He battled with his hormones all the way down to the car, where the stifling humidity and heat outside displaced his infuriating horniness with discomfort of a different kind.

"Wow, this humidity is crazy," his distracting little assistant said as they settled into the air-conditioned black luxury sedan.

Dante grunted noncommittally and yanked out his tablet to check his notes for the meeting.

"Is it always like this in Tokyo?"

Why the hell was she still prattling on? She rarely made small talk with him, and he preferred it that way. When they did speak, it was strictly work related.

"I've never been to Japan before, so I didn't know what to expect. Weatherwise, I mean. I knew it was summer and knew it would be hot, but I really wasn't expecting this humidity. I mean, it's like a sauna out there."

He sighed before putting his tablet aside. "Chloe," he said, keeping his voice low so the driver couldn't hear them. "Last night was just to relieve some of the stress of the day; you know that, right? I don't usually fuck my employees. Too damned messy." And quite frankly, he didn't relish the potential sexual-harassment lawsuits from disgruntled sexual partners in the workplace, but he didn't tell her that. God knows he didn't need to plant that idea in her head. And then, of course, there was the fact this had happened so unexpectedly he hadn't gone to the usual legal lengths to protect himself. He was generally a hell of a lot more careful and more discreet when it came to choosing his sexual partners. He cleared his throat before continuing.

"We were both tense and in need of some stress relief. It's not necessary to make this awkward."

She muttered something beneath her breath, and he frowned. "What?"

"Cleo. It's Cleo," she said, meeting his gaze head-on, her ridiculously beautiful green eyes brimming with defiance. "My name's Cleo, not Chloe."

Shit.

"Right. Of course." He cleared his throat. Of course he knew her name was Cleo. He even remembered thinking *Cleopatra Pandora Knight* was a damned stupid name. But for some reason, after months of calling her nothing but Miss Knight, that pertinent fact had completely slipped his mind. He felt his cheeks heat up as he recalled using "Chloe" during and immediately after sex the night before. What kind of asshole forgets a woman's name while he's naked in bed with her?

"And don't worry, I wouldn't dream of making anything *awkward* for you. I'm just curious about the country. I'm not fantasizing about some happily-ever-after love affair with you or anything. The thought of that is as distasteful to me as it probably is to you."

Distasteful? Who the hell did she think she was? Better women than she would kill for the chance of a love affair with him . . . and why the hell was he even offended? She was nothing more than his employee. His very annoying and very temporary employee. So they'd had a little lapse in judgment. So what? Shit like that happened all the time. Not to him, but there was a first time for everything.

"Let's just keep our focus on work," he stipulated. "The sooner we get this delay sorted out, the sooner we get out of here and on with our lives."

"Amen to that."

༄

Cleo was proud of herself. Proud that she had managed to keep her temper in check and her mouth shut. And definitely proud that she had managed to curb the impulse to slap the stupid man right across his handsome, smug face.

Just do the job, Cleo. Keep doing the job, and when something more interesting comes along, you can move on with your head held high.

This wasn't going to be another one of her failures. Another lost opportunity because she couldn't hold her tongue or restrain her impulsive nature and uncertain temper. Working for Dante Damaso had tested her to her limits, even though—thankfully—she'd rarely had to deal directly with him until this trip. She wasn't going to let him ruin this career opportunity for her. The potential for growth in this company was huge; Dante had hired her as a temporary replacement for his pregnant assistant, with the assurance that after Donna returned, they would find a permanent position for Cleo within the company. And while Cleo still wasn't entirely sure this was the kind of work she wanted to do for the rest of her life, it was what she'd fallen back on when her true vocation had slipped beyond her reach. It didn't light up all the empty spaces in her soul the way dance did, didn't inspire her or make her want to leap out of bed in the mornings even when every muscle in her body protested the slightest of movements, but it was something. And she was relatively good at it. So it would have to do.

Up until this job she'd been drifting from one temp position to the next, but this was the first one offering job security, benefits, and all the other good stuff grown-ups aspired to. Cleo, who had felt like a total failure up until that point, had jumped at the opportunity. God knows she had to stop depending on her big brother to help her out every time she failed at something.

Luc was getting married soon, and while his fiancée, Blue, was a sweetheart, Cleo couldn't keep staying with him every time she lost an apartment because she was unable to pay the rent. Luc had never minded; he insisted that the house, which had once belonged to their grandparents, was half hers anyway and she had as much right to stay there as he did. But with Luc probably starting a family soon, Cleo just wouldn't feel right running to him every time life dumped an obstacle on her path. She already felt like a loser. And sleeping with the boss— just another thing in a long line of really bad decisions—intensified that feeling times infinity.

Cleo had been good at only one thing in her life: dancing. And after years of hard work and countless personal and physical sacrifices, she had been well on her way to establishing herself as a talent of note before an accident just after her twenty-fourth birthday had robbed her of that career path. Doctors told her she would never dance professionally again, and it was a fact Cleo had difficulty accepting. She still *felt* like she could dance; it was still there in her heart and soul. How could they tell her she couldn't do the one thing she loved above all else? Without dance in her life, she had found herself rudderless and devastatingly average. Now all she had left were her brain and a sharp tongue that kept getting her into trouble at the worst possible times. That tongue had been responsible for most of her past workplace failures, but her intelligence was what kept her constantly employed, even if she couldn't quite keep the jobs.

She glanced at Dante, who was poring over his iPad again, and managed, barely, to keep from rolling her eyes in derision. She watched him covertly and tried to keep her appraisal objective. He was sickeningly good-looking. Dante Damaso was all gorgeous golden skin, topped with black-as-night wavy hair he kept clipped ruthlessly short and combed back with a conservative side part. There was barely enough of the luxurious, thick and silky mass for a woman to run her fingers through. His honey-brown eyes were framed by lush, long lashes that curled slightly at the ends and stern, straight eyebrows. His mouth had a full, curved bottom lip and a thin, perfectly bow-shaped upper lip, and it would have been beautiful if not for the cynical sneer perpetually twisting his lips whenever she was in his general vicinity. And, of course, he had the straight nose and high cheekbones to go with his perfect looks.

It was nauseating, really; a crooked nose would have made him more approachable, more human. It was almost obnoxious for him to be *this* good-looking! And now that she knew what he looked like beneath his expensive, bespoke dark-gray suit, it was even worse. At thirty-three he was in his prime. He had washboard abs, a butt you could bounce a coin off, gorgeously muscled arms, and—her personal weakness—killer thighs and calves. And he certainly knew exactly how to use that perfect body to please a woman. No wonder his gorgeous lady friends were always hanging around even after he ended things with them—mind-blowing sex and multiple orgasms could become dangerously addicting.

While Cleo could definitely empathize with those women, amazing sex wasn't enough to make her moon over a guy or she'd be in serious trouble right now. Dante Damaso epitomized masculine perfection; it was a damned crying shame such good looks were wasted on a nasty specimen like him.

To distract herself from the awkward situation with her boss, Cleo turned her attention to the city just a window's breadth away. She couldn't remember ever seeing this many pedestrians in one place, hustling and bustling and going about their daily lives. She craned her neck and couldn't prevent a giggle from escaping when she spotted a guy in a panda suit crossing the intersection in front of their car. She scrambled for her phone and managed to catch his back as he walked away, his gigantic panda head towering above the other, completely unconcerned pedestrians. Nobody even stared. She absently started taking a few more pics and then several selfies, trying to get as much of the city in the background as possible and adding the really good ones to Facebook, Twitter, and Instagram. She positioned herself with her back to the window and took a few duckface selfies while they were stopped at a particularly busy intersection.

Dante was so engrossed in his reading that it took a while before the annoying clicking sound penetrated the heavy fog of statistics eddying in his brain. When he finally became aware of it, the click that followed was almost jarring as it jerked him fully aware of his surroundings. He looked over to where Chl—*Cleo*—was sitting on the far end of the backseat and blinked when he saw her sucking in her cheeks, plumping up her lips, and lowering her chin as she held her phone slightly above face level and snapped a photograph. Well, that explained the annoying clicking. She shifted her chin slightly to the left and took another picture. Then another and another.

"I hate to interrupt this narcissistic little lovefest you've got going on with your phone, Miss Knight, but surely you have something a little more productive to do with your time?"

She jumped and dropped her phone, which bounced off the seat and landed right between his shoes. She swore beneath her breath and bent over to retrieve it. He gaped as she squirmed her way between the front passenger seat and his knee, her round butt sticking up and wriggling temptingly right within cupping range of his hands. He held said hands up and away from her body in case they were tempted to do something stupid, like explore the silky smooth skin of her thighs, which was being revealed one tantalizing millimeter at a time as she maneuvered her way a little farther down.

He wasn't quite sure what to do with the provocative, twisting bundle of femininity half draped over his lap, but when one sharp little elbow missed his groin by just an inch, he cursed and took hold of that same elbow and dragged her up onto the seat beside him.

"What in the ever-loving hell are you *doing*?" he asked, sounding livid even to himself.

"My phone . . ."

"Yeah. I know. And I would have retrieved it for you. You didn't have to drape yourself all over me to get to it."

"I didn't." God, her cheeks were flushed, her usually sleek hair was a mess, and two of her mother-of-pearl blouse buttons had come undone to reveal the pretty blue-lace edge of her bra. She looked like a woman who had just been soundly kissed, and because it aroused him to the point of pain, it brought his suspicious nature to bear.

"Are you coming on to me?" he hissed. "Wasn't one night enough for you? If you want more than that, you need but say it. But don't expect anything other than sex from me. Just because you're Luc's sister doesn't automatically entitle you to more than that. Once we get this deal out of the way, we can fuck again if that's what you want, but it will never be more than that. *Entender?* Understand?"

"Oh, I *entender*," she said, her voice trembling slightly, making him wonder at the extreme emotion he could sense just beneath the surface. "I *entender* that you're a smug, arrogant butthole who thinks the sun revolves around him. I don't *like* you. But then I don't have to like you; you're just my boss. And while I may have had a moment's weakness last night, it just makes me human. And trust me, one night was enough to last a lifetime. It was great, but I'm not looking for an encore."

Cleo let her words sink in, knowing she had just kissed any future with this company good-bye. She allowed herself a moment's regret before clearing her throat and pointing to the floor between his feet.

"Now, would you mind fetching my phone for me please, *sir*? I'd hate for you to get the wrong idea if I went fishing for it again."

He kept his gaze level with hers, and the grim set of his mouth told her he wasn't at all impressed with her. Well, to hell with him. His opinion mattered not at all.

"Just because we have shared some level of intimacy does not give you the right to speak to me so," he said after a long and unnerving moment of silence. His voice teemed with barely restrained menace. "We are not contemporaries, we are not friends, and we are certainly not lovers."

"No, we're employee"—she touched her chest and then lifted the same hand to point at him—"and employer. You're my boss, and as I very much doubt I'll have a job after this anyway, I should probably voice my opinions now, while I have you here."

"Why would you not have a job after this? You think I am so lacking in morals I would fire you because we spent a mutually pleasurable night together? That was last night, and we were done with work. In this car, right now, I *am* your employer, and I *will* be spoken to with respect."

"Oh, does that mean I get to call you an arrogant butthole after hours?" She watched his face tighten and knew she was pushing every single danger button he possessed.

"What you call me in the privacy of your thoughts is of no concern to me. Just keep those thoughts to yourself."

"So, you're basically placing a gag order on me," she clarified.

"If that is how you wish to perceive it, then so be it."

He reached down to retrieve her phone—a clear indicator he considered the conversation closed—and glanced at the screen before handing it over.

"This isn't exactly what I would call professional behavior," he said, nodding down at the ridiculous pouting picture of her on the screen.

Embarrassed, she cast her eyes down, hating to feel so completely wrong-footed.

"It was meant to be ironic," she attempted to explain even while she knew he would never understand the intended humor behind the picture.

"I trust you will conduct yourself appropriately at this meeting?"

Damn it. So much for trying to impress the man with her professionalism and ability to do the job. She tried her best to keep her reply humble.

"Yes, sir. I apologize if my earlier lack of professionalism caused you to think otherwise, *sir*," she said in her best no-nonsense voice, although she couldn't quite disguise the sarcasm dripping all over that last word. He raised his eyebrows, indicating he hadn't missed the acerbity, then raked her body from top to toe with his gaze.

"You might want to run a comb through your hair," he said, the words dripping with disdain. "Maybe reapply your lipstick while you're at it. Oh, and I'm sure you'd like to adjust your skirt and button your blouse before we get there as well."

Bastard.

She scooted back to her end of the seat and quickly straightened her skirt and fumblingly fixed her blouse, flushing a little when she noticed her bra was showing. A quick check of her hair and makeup confirmed the former was sticking up a bit and her lipstick was smudged at one corner of her mouth. Wait, how on earth had she managed to smudge her lipstick while trying to pick up her phone? Who *did* that? This day just got worse and worse and it wasn't even eight o'clock yet. She reapplied it and quite pointedly turned her back on him to stare out the window.

She wasn't going to let him dampen her excitement of being here, and if this was all she got to see of the city, then she was damned well going to soak it in while she could. She heard him snort softly behind her but ignored it, willing him to go back to his oh-so-critical preparation. He only needed her here to take notes, write his correspondence, and do all the other menial crap that required little to no thinking.

She knew Donna, his executive assistant, had a very challenging and intellectually stimulating job—she handled projects, ran the office in his absence, and had all manner of other important and interesting duties. But Dante didn't trust Cleo to do even a small percentage of what his precious Donna did, and she didn't expect him to. She was nowhere near as qualified. He gave her the basic secretarial stuff to do while designating the more important tasks to other personal and executive assistants. The little he did entrust to her was always gone over by the man himself with a fine-tooth comb.

Naturally the other assistants were already swamped with their own regular duties and were starting to resent Cleo for not doing the job she was being so handsomely paid for. They knew Luc and Dante were friends because Cleo had foolishly mentioned it to one of the younger admin assistants in an aborted attempt to make friends. The woman had wasted no time spreading rumors that Cleo had been hired because of the relationship between the two men. Nobody would ever accuse Dante of nepotism to his face, of course, so Cleo bore the brunt of their hostility. After that, Cleo had been a lot pickier about whom she spoke to at work. Luckily there were a number of other people who didn't give the rumors any credence. People like Florence, the lovely tea lady; Solomon, the cheerful company driver; Dante's personal protection guys; and some of the junior staff members who didn't get saddled with her extra work. Despite the short time she'd been working there, she had no shortage of new friends.

But the irony was that Cleo hadn't for even a second realized the Dante Damaso of Damaso International, Inc., was the same "Dan" whose name Luc casually dropped into conversation on occasion. Luc and Dante had met in college and had become friends but were hardly the type of guys to invite each other to family gatherings, so Cleo had never had the opportunity to meet the man. She had also been way too involved with her own life and her dancing—too wrapped up in herself—to care about Lucius and his boring friends. So it had come as a shock to learn Luc's "Dan" was *the* Dante Damaso of the renowned Damaso International chain of five-star hotels and resorts.

Only after Luc had gone all stern and disapproving big brother on her for using his relationship with Dante to get a job, did the penny drop. That's when she'd understood that she'd probably gotten the job because she was Luc's sister. A favor neither Luc nor Cleo had actually asked for. By that time it had been too late to back out, and Cleo had been determined to make the best of the chance she'd been given. Of course, if she had actually *met* Dante Damaso during the interview process, she may very well have told him to shove his job. But his minions had conducted the recorded interviews, and Dante had—supposedly—made his decision after watching the recordings.

Cleo didn't know what she'd expected of Dante Damaso, but from the very first day he had made it clear he merely suffered her presence, and just half an hour into her first day—after asking her to make him a cup of coffee, photocopy some documents, send two e-mails (one of which she had messed up by leaving off a zero in a seriously huge number), and water his frickin' ficus—he had sent her downstairs to a junior executive. Once there, the junior exec's assistant had patronizingly ushered Cleo to a desk and instructed her to answer the phone if it rang, before the woman checked her makeup and swanned off with a breezy "Mr. Damaso needs me to assist him today."

The memory still made Cleo seethe—four months later—and she clenched her teeth when she thought of how consistently after that first encounter the same thing had happened. She began every day in Damaso's office suite, and after half an hour—during which she had the dubious privilege of making his coffee and watering that stupid ficus, or sometimes sending one of those loathsome little "Thanks for the sex" notes—she got shipped off to a different exec. Luckily the other executives had stopped giving her mundane tasks to do, and she'd started enjoying her daily little soirees away from the boss's office. Still, the half hours in the mornings had become almost unbearable. Dante was scathing, brutally frank in his dismissal of her skills, and almost unbearably rude. He never greeted her, never used common courtesies like "please" and "thank you" when he spoke with her, and Cleo was convinced a smile would crack his perfect face.

Dante was still grimly focused on his iPad, and Cleo went back to greedily watching the passing scenery, trying to commit as much of it to memory as she could while longing to be out there exploring the wonderful mix of old and new. She loved the wooden buildings that looked as if they'd been around since the Middle Ages, tucked away down alleys and overshadowed by aggressively modern monolithic skyscrapers. Nothing escaped her attention, and she tried to file away the interesting bits, wanting to research and read up on buildings, museums, and shops that captured her interest. All of which helped keep her mind off Dante's disturbing presence.

CHAPTER TWO

Praise Jesus! They had doughnuts! Cleo barely noticed all the bowing and talking around her as her senses homed in on that single, all-important fact. By now she was so hungry she actually felt faint, and if she could only get her hands on one of those gorgeous hoops of sugary goodness, all would be right with her world. She nodded dazedly at the half circle of somber-looking businessmen in dark suits bowing to her and was barely aware of the tall, dark presence looming beside her as her eyes drifted again and again to the tempting display of coffee and pastries set up over to the side.

The painfully prolonged polite greetings finally over, she stealthily drifted over to the table of goodies. She was just a finger's length away from a chocolate-glazed *precious* with her name written all over it when a firm hand clamped down on her elbow. Her empty stomach sank to the bottom of her sensible shoes, and she stared up at her boss with what she knew was the most effectively pathetic hangdog expression in her arsenal. But he was having none of it; his jaw was clenched so tightly she was amazed his teeth didn't crack. She gave one final forlorn look at the doughnuts before he led her to the long conference table in the center of the room.

"Try to pay attention," he muttered in her ear as he planted her into a seat that, cruelly, faced the delicious spread just a table's breadth away from her.

What followed was the longest, most *boring* and torturous three hours of Cleo's life. The meeting was conducted entirely in Japanese, which Cleo didn't speak but Dante most certainly did, and quite fluently too from what she could tell. She didn't know why she was there. He had a Dictaphone recording the meeting, so even if she'd been able to understand what was going on, she wouldn't have had to take notes anyway. All she could do was stare at the doughnuts and other delicious goodies in front of her and imagine how they tasted. At one point a fly landed on *her* doughnut. It took everything she had not to jump up with a primal scream and chase it away. Instead, she watched in revulsion as it crawled over every inch of her beautiful doughnut. She nearly sobbed in disappointment, gave up on the chocolate one, and shifted her attention to a gorgeous éclair on a different platter. But when that bastard fly, which she had now named Damaso Jr., landed on her éclair as well, she slumped back in her chair and stared glumly down at the blank notebook in front of her.

She picked up her pen and started scribbling. Hoping to at least look busy, she composed truly awful haiku and observations about the people seated around the table.

Her attempt at describing Dante:

> Hard of abs he is
> Beautiful to look at sure
> My God what a dick

Okay, maybe that last line was a little ambiguous. Was it an insult or a compliment? Even Cleo wasn't sure.

After several even worse attempts, Cleo gave up on the haiku. She segued into doodling, occasionally looking up and nodding to make it seem like she was listening to every incomprehensible word being spoken. She glanced over at Dante and was delighted to note that he'd perched his dark-rimmed spectacles on the tip of his nose. She'd seen them before, of course, but loved how truly nerdy they made him look. Sexy-nerdy, but it was a flaw and she'd take it.

The only other woman present, Ms. Inokawa, also slanted surreptitious glances at Dante and smiled demurely every time he spoke with her. If not for the calculating gleam in her pretty eyes, Cleo would have thought the woman sweet and slightly shy, but beneath all that saccharine sweetness beat the heart of a scheming seductress. And she had her sights on Dante.

Well, she was welcome to him. All Cleo wanted was a doughnut. Maybe that caramel one, it looked like the fly had skipped—*damn it*. Sure enough, as if drawn to it by her thoughts, the fly landed on that one too. By the time the meeting was over, the damned thing would have—

"*Miss* Knight?" She jerked upright, realizing Dante had been trying to get her attention.

"Uh . . . yes?"

"I asked if you got that?"

That? What? Wait, had they finally said something in English and she'd missed it? Damn it.

"Yes. Yes, I did." She tapped the page of her open notebook as if to confirm her words, and when his eyes followed the movement, she hastily closed the book, not wanting him to see her scribbles. His brow lifted and his head tilted as his eyes burned into hers, and she smiled breezily up at him. She'd just check his Dictaphone later to figure out what it was she'd missed. No problem.

"Well?" he asked. *Crap. Now what?*

"Yes, I got it," she repeated slowly, as if to an inattentive child. His eyes narrowed dangerously. God, he was scary when he did that. Okay, so maybe this was something he wanted done right away. That wasn't good at all. She'd have to cop to the truth. She leaned in toward him and was a little offended when he leaned in the opposite direction.

"I didn't *quite* get the last bit," she confessed, and his eyes flared with what looked like disgust. How was she supposed to know they'd suddenly switch to English? Okay, so she should probably have been paying closer attention, but after three hours of nothing but Japanese, she was bound to have zoned out at some point.

"I want you to arrange a meeting with Craig, Josh, Ryan, Tanaka-san, Inokawa-san, Watanabe-san, and myself for three thirty this afternoon." Cleo ducked her head as she quickly scribbled the information on a blank sheet in her notebook.

"You may use this conference room for the meeting, Knight-san," Ms. Inokawa said in her breathy little voice, shocking the hell out of Cleo with her English. Could they all speak English? If so, how rude of them to not once acknowledge her lack of Japanese. Then again, she was just the assistant, who couldn't even do the *only* thing that had been required of her at this meeting efficiently.

The meeting was apparently adjourned, because the men bowed and shook hands, Ms. Inokawa was speaking in that charmingly girlish voice, all the while smiling sweetly, while Cleo was left to her own devices, alone at the table. She got up—ostensibly to stretch—and finally made her way over to the fly-tainted, stale-looking pastries.

"Knight, get on those phone calls," Dante growled from the other end of the room. Cleo swallowed down her resentment before fishing out the company phone to contact the architect, the contractor, and Ryan Blake—the company's legal representative—all of whom were staying at the same hotel as Cleo and Dante. After a series of meetings with the three men the previous day, the boss had wanted to meet with the Japanese alone this morning in order to straighten out the mess he believed the other men had created. So if he was calling them back in, it must mean he'd made some headway in that morning's meeting.

The speed at which they all answered their phones attested to the fact that they'd probably been anxiously awaiting her call, and Cleo set up the meeting within minutes. Dante was still amicably chatting with the Japanese trio, but the moment she disconnected the second call, he looked at her with a raised brow. She nodded in response to the question she could see in his eyes, and he went back to his conversation without acknowledging her affirmation. Stifling her irritation at his rudeness, she started compiling a list of all the documentation they would need for the second meeting. She was well engrossed in that task when Dante's voice, coming from directly behind her, startled her back into the present.

"Are you coming? Inokawa-san has arranged lunch for us," he informed her, and Cleo bit back a groan of relief. She jumped up quickly before he could revoke the invitation, and swayed slightly as the lack of food and jet lag hit her. His hand caught her elbow and steadied her.

"What's going on with you?" he hissed.

"I haven't eaten much of anything since the in-flight meal yesterday morning," she hissed back. "So excuse me for feeling a little light-headed."

"Nonsense. You had dinner last night and breakfast this morning." He waved his hand dismissively, refuting her claims with innate arrogance.

"No, *you* had dinner and breakfast. You told me we'd have a dinner meeting and ordered only enough for yourself, and if you consider that one piece of bacon and mouthful of eggs I gobbled down this morning breakfast, then you and I have seriously different ideas of what constitutes a healthy meal."

His brow lowered as he considered her words; then he tilted his head toward the pastries on the nearby table.

"And this is why you've been staring at that table like an addict eyeing her next fix?" *Okay, is that a glint of laughter in his normally enigmatic gaze? That was . . . different.*

"I'm starving," she said flatly, unamused by his amusement.

"We'll remedy that immediately," he assured her, squeezing her elbow briefly before letting her go completely.

⁓

Cleo tried not to cry while she stared down at the minuscule serving of sushi in front of her. Ms. Inokawa had reserved a trendy sushi restaurant for lunch, and though Cleo wasn't a huge fan of Japanese food, she'd eat it if she was desperate enough. However, she hadn't been expecting a child-size portion of food. She wasn't the biggest of women—dancing kept her lean, and her frame was ideally petite for a dancer—but she had a healthy appetite, and the prettily decorated plate in front of her barely contained enough food to feed a gnat.

She was about to dig in when a hand clamped down on her thigh and squeezed painfully. Her shocked gaze flew to Dante's impassive face, and he turned his head to glare at her before nodding toward Mr. Watanabe, who was speaking. She belatedly recalled the cultural etiquette booklet she had speedily read through on the plane, and remembered eating or drinking before your hosts was considered extremely rude. Apparently Mr. Watanabe was going to ramble on for a while before giving the go-ahead to eat.

She stared at her sushi glumly and took solace in the fact that at least it wouldn't get cold, and her little friend Damaso Jr. was probably still back in that stuffy boardroom gorging himself on stale doughnuts and éclairs and therefore unable to ruin this meal for her. Mr. Watanabe finally stopped talking, and everybody picked up his or her chopsticks and proceeded to eat with great gusto.

"Damaso-san, you use chopsticks very proficiently," Cleo heard Ms. Inokawa, seated on Dante's left, say in her breathy voice. *Seriously?* Like the man wasn't arrogant enough, she was going to stare at him with those big brown eyes and fawn over him because he could use chopsticks? He modestly thanked her for her compliment, and Cleo choked down her sushi, trying very hard not to be sick.

A few minutes later she nearly *was* sick when she stared in horror at the plate of sashimi that had just been placed in front of her. Her hand fluttered to her mouth as she swallowed back her nausea.

"Don't you *dare*," Dante warned, leaning toward her and keeping a pleasant smile on his face to disguise the warning.

"But they're *alive*," she practically wept in reply. The sashimi shrimp on her plate were writhing weakly and had quite effectively killed her previously ravenous appetite.

"You don't like *odori ebi*, Knight-san?" Mr. Tanaka, who had been chatting shyly with her in broken English, noticed her reaction. "It's very fresh."

"It's not fresh," she said from behind her hand. "It's alive."

"Yes." Mr. Tanaka nodded, smiling encouragingly as he made an eager go-ahead gesture with his hands. "Fresh. Taste. Taste."

"I don't think . . ." She was on the verge of tears, horrified at the thought of the shrimp dying in her mouth. It was hypocritical, sure, but if they'd died even just seconds before being served to her, she would happily have eaten them. But the thought of them dying between her teeth or on her tongue or as they slid down her throat totally grossed her out. She turned pleading eyes on Dante, whose face was completely expressionless. "I *can't*."

He turned to their companions, said something in Japanese, and they all roared with laughter.

"Oh, Damaso-san, you are so funny," Ms. Inokawa chortled.

"Yeah. Hilarious," Cleo muttered beneath her breath. A slanted glance from him confirmed that he'd heard her. She directed another distressed look down at her plate, and a pair of chopsticks swooped into her line of vision and grabbed one of the poor creatures.

"Don't worry, Miss Knight, I'll save you from these creepy crustaceans," he mocked, before dipping the poor thing in soy sauce, hopefully drowning it, and popping it into his mouth. "You're just prolonging their suffering by letting them writhe like that."

She was ridiculously grateful to him for handling the situation even though he had made her the butt of the joke to do so. The incident was soon forgotten, but as the dishes grew progressively more unappetizing—*gah!* sea urchin—her queasiness and exhaustion made her feel more ill with every passing moment. Lunch stretched on for ages, and when it finally ended, Cleo, who had barely touched a morsel, had a huge headache and felt a little punch-drunk.

"Miss Knight, contact the driver and head back to the hotel to draft those e-mails we discussed earlier," Dante said as the group got up from the booth. She stared up at him blankly, wondering what she'd missed this time. He waved the other three ahead of them, and Cleo tried to focus on his face and what he was saying, which was difficult when she felt like a zombie.

"I'm sorry, I don't recall the e-mails you're referring to," she said, hating to reinforce his already low opinion of her.

"There are no e-mails, Knight. Go back to the hotel, take a shower, order room service, and get some sleep. The jet lag, combined with the busy evening and"—his eyes darkened and his voice lowered sexily— "exhausting *night* you had yesterday, has taken a toll on you. Rest up. I need you to be more alert tomorrow."

Oh, thank God.

"Thank you, sir," she whispered, for once feeling something akin to affection and gratitude toward the man.

"Go on now, Knight," he said, the words brusque and the tone businesslike. "Before I change my mind."

She resisted the impish urge to salute, and after he'd followed the other three people out onto the humid, bustling sidewalk, she got out her cell phone to contact the driver.

Half an hour later, she was back in the air-conditioned splendor of the car and happily chatting with the driver, Daisuke. He spoke fluent English and very sweetly pointed out a few of the interesting sights to her, giving her a brief history lesson while he was at it. Cleo was disappointed when they arrived back at the hotel. She was tempted to venture out on her own, since she had this unexpected free time, but hunger and exhaustion had really taken their toll on her, and by the time she got back to her room, she was dragging so badly that eating didn't even occur to her. She discarded her clothes on her way to the bed and fell facedown onto the covers. She was asleep seconds later.

"Miss Knight?" The regrettably familiar masculine voice resonated through Cleo's pleasant dream. She frowned and turned away from it, happily rejoining the cotton-candy sheep she'd been frolicking with just moments before. The sheep were cute, friendly, and delicious . . . she took a bite out of a particularly friendly fellow's sugary-pink fleece and relished the sweetness. The sheep baaed and—"Miss Knight!"

"Sheep can't talk," she muttered.

"What?" the voice asked impatiently. Cleo sighed and reluctantly opened her eyes.

"Oh. It's you," she groused when she met her boss's intense gaze. She blew her hair out of her face and pushed herself up, only to realize she was wearing just a pair of panties and no bra and didn't have so much as a sheet covering her. She squeaked and grabbed a pillow to cover her front. She scampered back against the headboard and pulled her knees up to her chest, sandwiching the pillow between her lap and torso. She glared at Dante, who stared back at her impassively from his position at the foot of her bed.

"I've seen it all in exquisite detail before," he reminded her, and she blushed.

"What are you doing in my room?"

"The concierge told me you didn't order any room service, and Daisuke informed me that you didn't stop for food en route to the hotel."

"And?" she asked belligerently, despite the fact that his words brought her hunger screaming painfully back.

"I ordered you a late dinner. I figured you might want to freshen up or something before it got here."

"A late dinner?" she repeated, trying hard not to be charmed by that sweet gesture. It was the least he could do, after all, since he was the reason she was starving in the first place. "What time is it?"

"Just after midnight. I got in about half an hour ago."

"The meeting ran that late?" she asked, surprised.

"No, but we got a lot done, and the Japanese wanted to celebrate with a night on the town followed by some . . ." He grimaced and then shook his head. "Never mind."

Intrigued by the slight flush darkening his cheekbones, she leaned forward, forgetting momentarily that only a pillow shielded her from his view.

"Followed by some what?" She pictured strip clubs or those hostess bars she'd read up on, maybe something even kinkier. What else could make him look so uncomfortable?

"Nothing. It's none of your business," he dismissed rudely, but sitting there nearly completely nude, groggy from hours of sleep, and with the room only half-lit, Cleo lost all inhibition and sense of self-preservation and refused to heed the warning in his voice.

"It can't be that bad. I mean, everybody knows about the hostess bars and stuff over here. Was it something like that? Did you have some pretty young thing sitting on your lap all evening telling you how handsome and strong you are?"

"I don't need to pay a woman to tell me I'm handsome and strong."

"True, I'm sure Ms. Inokawa was happy to do that for you," she said snidely.

"Jealous, Knight?"

She laughed incredulously at the question and waved a hand, the pillow slipping dangerously low.

"Hardly."

"You're having a bit of a—how do you say this?—wardrobe malfunction?"

She gasped when a quick look down confirmed one of her nipples was indeed peeking up above the pillow. She hastily adjusted before looking back up to meet his avid gaze.

"Stop staring at me like that," she snapped.

"Like what?"

"Like you're hoping it'll happen again."

"But I *am* hoping it'll happen again." She gasped again, sounding, even to herself, like some outraged Victorian maiden.

"That's a highly inappropriate thing to say," she pointed out, and he covered his mouth with his fist and coughed slightly, making her wonder if he was hiding a laugh behind the cough.

"And me standing here in your bedroom while you lounge around in only your panties *isn't* inappropriate?"

"There are levels of inappropriate behavior," she informed him primly, not even sure herself what the hell she was talking about. How could she be rattling on about appropriate behavior after everything they'd done the night before?

"Oh?" He sat down at the foot of her bed. "Please do educate me. Sitting on your bed, how inappropriate is this? On a scale of one to ten? Ten being highly inappropriate."

"Uh. Five . . . maybe?" she whispered.

"And if I moved a little closer?" He shifted up until his butt rested beside her feet.

"Five and a half." The words were barely audible, but he nodded before running the back of his large hand over her feet, then her slender shins, before turning his hand over so his palm did the downward stroke back to her feet.

"What about that?" he rasped as his breathing got a little heavier. He cupped her small feet in his hand, his thumb caressing the instep of the top foot. She fought to gather her scattered thoughts so she could respond.

"Six and a half."

"A full point up?" he mused. "Impressive."

He shifted even closer, and before she knew it, he tugged the pillow away, leaving her without the precious barrier. She yelped in protest, but he paid her no heed, and Cleo's heart slammed into her rib cage as he slid his broad chest into the space that had just been occupied by the pillow. And he was nowhere near as soft and comfortable. He was hard and hot and smelled *much* too good. Suddenly all Cleo could think about was last night and how fantastic he had felt above her, inside her, all around her . . . and all she wanted was more of the same.

He dropped his head and nuzzled the sensitive spot on her neck, just below her ear, his lips grazing against the rapid pulse there. He sucked lightly, then bit, and when she groaned, he licked away the sting.

"I don't like doing things by half measure," he muttered into her ear, his hot breath sending goose bumps careening across every inch of her skin and tightening her nipples painfully. "I want a perfect score."

With that he lifted his head and planted a deep, hungry kiss on her lips, and Cleo happily opened up for him, drinking him in, wanting him desperately. Every hot, hard, sexy, arrogant, unlikeable part of him.

She whimpered, once again fighting with that reasonable part of her that kept trying to insert itself into her business. She dragged her lips from his, a little shocked she could get this turned on from just one kiss.

"I thought we weren't going to do this again," she whispered, and for a moment, while he continued to nuzzle and suck on her neck, she thought he hadn't heard her.

"But that would be a waste of some perfectly good sex, *dulzura*." He ran his large hand down her naked back as he said the words, and Cleo found herself purring like a kitten in response to the caress.

"It was pretty good, wasn't it?" She hummed, doing a bit of her own nuzzling. She loved the feel of his expensive silk shirt against her pebbled breasts and lost all inhibition, blatantly rubbing them against his chest, wanting him to start focusing on the important stuff now. He complied, shifting until she was flat on her back and he was sitting on the side of the bed, with the upper half of his body bent over hers. His hot gaze traveled from her face down to her breasts, and with a shaky groan he lifted his hands to cup and caress the pretty little mounds. He plumped one up to receive his mouth, and when he tugged at the aching nipple with his lips, Cleo nearly came out of her skin. She'd always had unbearably sensitive breasts, which Dante hadn't paid much attention to the night before but seemed to be taking great delight in now.

"Can you come from just this?" he asked huskily. "From someone playing with your breasts?"

"I haven't yet," she managed to wheeze out, and he gave her a rakish little smirk.

"Ah. Another challenge," he said, before bending back down to her breasts. "Well, *dulzura*, allow me . . ."

More than an hour later, Cleo lay on her back, chest still heaving, body still shuddering, and an arm draped across her eyes to block out her embarrassment at how completely uninhibited she had been with the man snoring gently beside her. She could now check the whole "orgasming from just breast play" thing off her bucket list. He had certainly risen to the challenge there. He hadn't cheated once, no sneaky hands drifting south, and when she'd attempted to hasten things along with her own hands, he had firmly moved them back up to his chest.

After all that delicious foreplay, she had been more than ready for him to move on to the main event, but nope, he had made it his duty to find as many of her erogenous zones as possible before *finally* claiming her body. As before, once he finished, he simply rolled off her and fell asleep. This time in *her* bed, which was a little annoying and meant she would have to retreat to the spare room. She got up and tugged on the huge, white fluffy robe the hotel provided and padded toward the door. She didn't really know what the protocol was in this situation, but knew he wasn't the type to sleep through the night with a woman.

She threw a resentful look back at the inconsiderate ass sprawled across her bed and then sighed a little at what a fine ass he actually had. He lay in absolute naked magnificence, facedown, one leg bent at the knee and the other straight. His arms were up above his head, and his face was buried in a marshmallowy pillow. As she watched, he turned his head toward her so he could breathe easier. She paused, riveted by how vulnerable he looked in his sleep, how much younger.

She reluctantly admitted to herself that he was a remarkable man. To take his family's ailing hotel brand and turn it into this multi-billion-dollar corporation in less than ten years was an almost unheard of feat. He was only thirty-three, and to achieve so much at such a young age, he would have had to be ruthless and cutthroat.

"Play hard, work harder" was his motto, or at least that's what the newspapers and tabloids often quoted him as saying. Even if she wanted more from him, Cleo knew she didn't stand a chance of being much more than a lay to this powerful, handsome man. But that was fine; she didn't want more from him since he was nothing more than a *fantastic* lay to her. As long as they both understood that, everything would be fine.

She turned away from him and slipped into the huge, elegantly furnished living room that spanned the distance between their rooms. Her eyes immediately fell on the service cart standing in the middle of the floor. She moaned, her appetite roaring to life with such ferocity that she almost swayed with hunger. She lifted the domed lids off each dish and almost cried at the congealed mess that was all that remained of what had once been a beautiful dinner. She padded over to one of the ornate sideboards and reached for the telephone to call room service and order another meal.

It was nearly one thirty, and she felt invigorated after all that glorious sex—not tired in the least—and as she stood at the floor-to-ceiling window and stared down at the sparkling city lights below, she wondered what adventures were to be had out there. A reckless desire to go exploring surged to life and she tamped it down, knowing that wandering around in a huge city like this on her own, in the middle of the night, would be stupid. She sank into one of the massive Bakokko armchairs angled toward the window and folded her legs up in front of her, wrapping her arms around them and resting her chin on her knees.

"What are you doing in here?" A few minutes later, Dante's sleep-roughened voice startled her, and she squeaked slightly before turning her head to watch him enter the room.

"I didn't think you were the type of guy who liked to wake up next to the night's casual shag, so I retreated. Since you were passed out in *my* room, I thought I'd take the spare room tonight."

"Still doesn't tell me why you're in here," he pointed out, a sweeping arm indicating that he meant the living room.

"I'm waiting for room service," she said. "And don't you dare distract me again! I can't go much longer without food."

His lips quirked and he sat down in one of the other chairs, angling his body toward her. She averted her eyes when she comprehended that he was still *naked*. How had she not noticed that immediately?

"Do you mind covering up?" she asked, not as comfortable with his nudity as he clearly was.

"Why? Is it inappropriate for me to walk around like this?" he asked, and she clenched her teeth.

"You know it is."

"But after last night and what we just did in the other room, I think we have probably gone way off the scale by now. This can't be much more than a four, surely?"

"I'm not playing this game with you again," she gritted out. "Just put on some clothes before room service gets here."

"I don't think this is about room service, I think you find me . . . irresistible."

"Get over yourself," she muttered, hating that damned smug look on his face.

He yanked one of the chair cushions out from behind his back and placed it neatly over his crotch, folding his hands over the top of the embroidered pillow.

"What?" He challenged at her dubious look. "This worked for you earlier."

It hadn't really worked that well, considering the events that followed, but Cleo wasn't about to bring that up now.

The doorbell chimed and she jumped up, grateful for the distraction. She could have hugged the waiter when he pushed the cart into the room.

"Tip him," she ordered Dante, already lifting the lids off the bowls and dishes, her knees almost buckling at the divine smells.

"Bossy little thing, aren't you?" he murmured directly into her ear as he came to stand behind her, close enough for his body heat to penetrate the thickness of her robe. The waiter kept his eyes averted as Dante signed for the meal and added a generous tip. The waiter thanked them and beat a hasty retreat.

"You're naked again, aren't you?" Cleo asked without turning her head. He didn't respond immediately. Instead, his hands dropped to her shoulders and kneaded gently. He was pressed to her body, and his growing erection started to make its presence known against her back, even through the thickness of the robe.

"Not naked *again*," he denied. "More like . . . *still*."

His lips dropped to her earlobe and he sucked it into his mouth, giving it a little nip in the process. Cleo moaned, and as he ground his substantial erection against her, she pushed back until he groaned appreciatively. His hand reached around and slid into the front of her robe, finding her breast with unerring accuracy. Cleo allowed him a squeeze before looking down at the food in front of her and stepping away from him.

She turned around to face him and dropped a quick glance down at his huge, straining penis, which had her salivating for a completely different reason.

"Put that thing away," she said softly, nodding down at it decisively. "You and your insatiable penis will *not* be distracting me from my food this time."

He turned away from her and she could have sworn she heard a chuckle, which just about melted her heart because Dante Damaso was *not* prone to humor.

"Eat your food, *florecita*; you'll need the energy for later."

He really was a cocky sonofabitch. But Cleo was beyond caring about that right now, and she carried her food—a salad, penne carbonara, and cheesecake for dessert—over to the expensive-looking coffee table in front of her chair by the window. Dante followed her and sat down, with his pillow thankfully shielding his impressive package from her again. His eyes were intent as he watched her eat, and after satisfying her immediate hunger by scarfing down the first half of her meal with great gusto, Cleo grew more and more self-conscious beneath that relentless gaze.

"Please stop staring at me," she finally said around a mouthful of penne.

"I like looking at you." Well, that was completely out of left field. She felt her mouth gaping, knowing that with the half-masticated pasta in there, she probably looked like a drooling idiot. She recovered quickly and shut her mouth, barely bothering to chew the rest of the mouthful before swallowing.

"What?"

"I like looking at you," he repeated. "You're interesting."

Well, at least he hadn't lied and called her pretty. She knew she had a weird face. For one thing, her lips were too big in a too-narrow face. Her schoolmates had nastily called her "Juicy Lips" throughout primary school, and in high school the boys had started making all kinds of offensive suggestions about the things she should be doing with those "juicy lips." Then there was her crooked nose, broken when she'd fallen during a dance rehearsal years ago. It wasn't horrendous, and after the surgery to fix the damage had failed, Cleo resigned herself to accepting her slightly off-center nose. And finally there were her ridiculously big green eyes, which had people likening her to a baby doll for most of her life. Cleo hated her bug eyes; she thought they made her look continually surprised.

Her ridiculous face, combined with the petite body, often led people to underestimate her. That had been an asset while she was pursuing her dance career; she had wanted to be underestimated before "wowing" her competitors and choreographers with her talent. Choreographers and directors loved that unexpected quality about her, had raved about her "freshness" and her "quirkiness." But now, in the real world, being underestimated led to fewer opportunities and greater frustrations.

"What's going on in that head of yours?" Dante's voice intruded upon her troubling thoughts, and she focused her attention back on him.

"I was thinking . . ." She cleared her throat before affecting a cocky grin and reaching for her dessert. "I was thinking you still haven't told me what you did after dinner tonight. Did you go to one of those *onsen* places?" She was referring to the public hot spas that were so popular in Japan. "Did you have to get naked with Mr. Tanaka and Mr. Watanabe?"

He winced at the question.

"*Dios*, no."

"Then it really can't be that bad, can it?" She enjoyed needling him; his embarrassment made him seem a little more approachable. "Anything my imagination dredges up will probably be a lot worse than reality."

"We went to karaoke," he said, finally relenting, and Cleo choked on her first bite of cheesecake.

"You're being overly dramatic," he scoffed as she waved her hand in front of her face to cool her skin after her coughing fit.

"Karaoke?" she finally managed on a wheeze, and he nodded. "Seriously?"

"Yes. Can I have some of that cheesecake?" he asked casually.

"No," she replied equally casually, deliberately sticking another forkful in her mouth and chewing slowly before asking her next question. "Did you actually sing?"

"*Sí.*" His eyes dropped to the remaining cheesecake on her plate. "Just a bite?"

"No," she said as she took another teasing forkful. "What did you sing?"

"A bit of Queen, some Rolling Stones, a little Nirvana, Red Hot Chili Peppers, Blondie . . ." he recited. "You don't seriously mean to eat that entire piece of cake, do you?"

"I do," she affirmed. "*Blondie?* Seriously?"

"And Cyndi Lauper." He grimaced. "Ms. Inokawa really likes their songs but can't sing them because the English is a bit too fast-paced for her."

"But they're so *high-pitched.*" She laughed.

"I know. Can we stop talking about this now? And I warn you, this remains between us. Now give me some of that cake."

"No, it's *my* cake. Get your own dessert!"

"Okay."

"Oh my *God*, what are you doing?" she asked seconds later when he knelt in front of her chair and ran his hands from her knees to her thighs, parting her robe as he did so. She hurriedly put her cake aside as she stared down at him in shock.

"Getting my dessert," he mumbled, moving his hands beneath her butt and dragging her to the edge of the chair until he had her spread wide open in front of him. The corners of his lips quirked upward before he hummed in contentment, bent his head, and feasted.

Cleo, her own dessert forgotten, stared down at the top of his dark head in disbelief until his very talented tongue started to work its magic on her. She arched back in the chair and entangled her fingers in his hair as her eyes drifted shut.

"Oh. My God . . ."

CHAPTER THREE

The rest of their time in Tokyo sped by. Dante didn't micromanage Cleo as much as before, solely because he didn't have the time to oversee her every little move. She did her work efficiently and gave him no cause for complaint.

Their nights were equally busy. They never spoke about it, never gave what was happening between them a name, but they spent every night together having mind-blowing sex. And when it was over, Cleo always retreated to her room, and Dante never made any attempt to call her back. And if she ever had any doubts as to the nature of their "relationship," his indifference and distance during the day when he was focused on work certainly made things clear. He never, by word or by deed, let on that theirs was anything more than a working relationship. Yet he had a chocolate-glazed doughnut waiting for her at whatever conference room they happened to find themselves in on any given day, and he always ensured that her plate was full at lunchtime and that the menu would be palatable for her. When they headed back to the hotel in the evenings, Daisuke always took a different route so she got to see a bit of the city, which she suspected was Dante's doing as well. It was all so sweet, Cleo didn't know how to respond to it.

By their last day, the zoning problem had been completely ironed out, and everybody was in a celebratory mood. They would break ground on the new hotel in less than a month.

"Tonight, we will have an *enkai* to celebrate this wonderful occasion," Ms. Inokawa stated happily. "This is a very formal Japanese event, so there will be many speeches, but after that we will all enjoy drinking together and have many after-parties."

Her pretty eyes slid to Dante in clear invitation, and Cleo pretended not to see the smile he slanted the woman in return. Of course she wasn't jealous. Dante Damaso meant nothing to her. Just a bit of fun. A casual fling.

So that evening as they were preparing to leave the hotel, Cleo suggested she stay behind. After all, she told herself magnanimously, he might feel a bit awkward flirting with Ms. Inokawa while Cleo was hanging about.

"You're not staying behind. You've read enough of those etiquette books to know that it's damned bad manners," he snapped. He'd been in a pretty foul mood most of the day, despite the news that his new hotel had gotten the green light.

Cleo sighed and checked her appearance in the mirror one final time. She was wearing yet another variation of the same boring skirt, jacket, and blouse combo that she had rocked the entire week. She truly hated her work wardrobe; it wasn't at all to her taste. She was more at home in torn jeans and T-shirts, or slip dresses with long bohemian skirts, than in these horrendous suits that made her feel like a trussed-up pigeon. She didn't know who she was when she wore these clothes.

Because this was a work-related *enkai*, everyone would be dressed in business suits. Dante looked his usual dashing self in a three-piece, pin-striped, navy-blue, bespoke Desmond Merrion suit with a white shirt, red tie, and Tanino Crisci Lilian shoes, all of which she knew were ridiculously expensive because she had seen his personal bills. The man looked gorgeous and smelled luxurious. Cleo, on the other hand, just felt frumpy in her department-store knockoff gray pencil skirt, matching blazer, and pink cotton blouse. Ugh, and the sensible black pumps she was wearing were completely hideous too.

"Let's go." Dante ushered her out of the suite and to the elevator, and Cleo tried to drum up some enthusiasm for the event. At least she would get to see someplace other than a boring conference room in a bleak building.

"I hope the food's good," she said once they were in the elevator. He stood beside her, close enough for her to feel his body heat without physically touching him. His hands were clasped in front of him, and his feet were braced shoulder-width apart. He looked like a soldier ready for battle.

"Hmm," he merely grunted, and she raised her eyebrows. So it was going to be like that, was it?

Right, then.

She didn't say another word until they were seated in the car. Daisuke greeted them enthusiastically, like he hadn't seen them just hours before, and Cleo smiled warmly at him before continuing the fascinating conversation about Japanese pop culture that they'd been having earlier. He was entertaining and genuinely funny, and it wasn't long before Cleo was laughing at some of his anecdotes.

"My girlfriend loves *purikura*, and she has many hundreds of tiny pictures of herself and her friends." He told Cleo about something called "print club"—specialized photo booths found in most malls—that took tiny airbrushed pictures, which could be Photoshopped before being printed.

"Do you have any pictures, Dai?" Cleo asked curiously.

"I only go to *purikura* with Miki," he explained. Miki was his girlfriend. He flipped down the sun visor and retrieved the pictures he had stashed behind the mirror. He handed them back to her, and

Cleo exclaimed in delight over the colorful, brightly decorated little photographs of Daisuke and a pretty girl. She turned toward Dante to share the images with him, but he was staring out the window, ignoring them, his jaw tightly clenched as he glared at the passing scenery. Her smile slipped a little as she stared at the back of his head, wondering what was going on with him.

She handed the pictures back to Daisuke.

"They're really cute. I wish I'd had time to take a few myself." She could hear the wistful note in her voice and told herself to snap out of it. She was here for work, not vacation. "Miki is really pretty, Dai. How long have you guys been dating?"

"Two years." He beamed proudly. "She is studying to be a teacher."

"Fabulous. What will she teach?" He looked stumped for a moment as he considered her question.

"Uh . . . she will be a *shodo no sensei*. A penmanship teacher?" He looked uncertain. "She will teach the art of Japanese writing."

"Oh?" Cleo was not quite sure what he meant but didn't want to embarrass him.

"Every stroke must be correct. It is almost artistic. Very difficult." He glanced around before pointing to an incomprehensible sign written in bold black Japanese. "Like this!"

"You mean like in cursive?"

"*Christ,*" Dante suddenly said beneath his breath. "He means Japanese calligraphy."

"Oh," she breathed, feeling like a complete idiot for not realizing that immediately.

"You know it?" Daisuke asked eagerly, and Cleo nodded.

"Yes, I read about it. I should have known when you said artistic writing," she said apologetically.

"It's okay. My English is very bad," he said with a diffident grin. That was such a staggering untruth that Cleo's mouth dropped open.

"Your English is *great*, Daisuke," she said firmly, and he waved a hand in front of his face.

"No, no, very bad."

"But . . . it's not bad at all."

"Thank you. Thank you," he said so abruptly she blinked.

What?

The whole exchange left her feeling a little confused and flustered. She hoped she hadn't offended him by implying his English was bad.

"Let it go, Knight," Dante muttered, clearly not as oblivious to their conversation as he had appeared to be earlier.

"But . . ."

"It's the Japanese way to be self-effacing. Just leave it."

She nodded, even though it went against every instinct she had to just comply with what could only be described as a command. She changed the subject, asking Dai a question about the relatively new Tokyo Sky Tree. It was obviously a subject he took great pride and passion in, and by the time they reached their destination five minutes later, Cleo knew exactly how tall the building was, how long it had taken to construct, how many men had worked on it, and how people from all over Japan flocked to come and visit the tallest tower in the world—a point of pride for most Japanese people.

Cleo was still thinking about how much she would have loved to see the views from the observation deck of the Sky Tree while they were being ushered into the restaurant by Ms. Inokawa, who'd been waiting for them at the entrance. Their party was being held in an extremely traditional Japanese room. It had straw mats called tatami on the floor, and rice paper—or shoji—doors and panels. The décor was very minimalist, featuring only one long, very low table in the center of the room, with flat cushions known as *zabuton* on the floor beside each place setting. There were no chairs.

Cleo immediately felt intimidated by the room, not sure what would be expected of her and not wanting to offend in her ignorance.

"Knight-san, please." Ms. Inokawa gestured toward a spot close to the end of the long table before she ushered Dante up to the pride of place, dead center of the table. She bowed, left him there on his own, and rejoined Cleo.

Other somber-suited people filed into the room, while Ms. Inokawa gestured for Cleo to sit down beside her. Wondering if there was any graceful way to sit on the floor in a tight skirt, Cleo clumsily sank down flat on her butt with her legs folded to the side.

"Knight-san." Ms. Inokawa leaned over to whisper abashedly. "Because this is a formal party, we will sit in *seiza*."

"In what?"

"Like this." Ms. Inokawa sat beside Cleo, folding herself up delicately on the way down. Cleo grimaced, already dreading what was to come because there was no way in hell she could sit like that. The other woman was on her knees with her legs folded beneath her thighs and her feet tucked neatly beneath her bum.

"How long will we have to sit like that?"

"It is usually proper for women to sit this way for the entire party."

"Really? And the men?"

"They too will sit in *seiza*, but after a while they will probably cross their legs."

"I can't sit like that," Cleo whispered urgently. Ms. Inokawa's perfect brow furrowed ever so slightly, and she affected a lovely look of helpless distress. Dante, who could see everything from his central position on the opposite side of the table, got to his feet and ambled around to their end of the table.

"Is there a problem here?" he asked, and Ms. Inokawa bowed gracefully before shaking her head.

"There is no problem, Damaso-san." Rather surprised that the other woman didn't rat her out, Cleo slanted her a shocked glance before meeting Dante's eyes.

"I can't sit like this." She gestured to where Ms. Inokawa sat like the perfect epitome of modesty and beauty.

"Everybody will be sitting in *seiza*," Dante pointed out. Cleo nodded and tried very hard not to react to his impatience.

"So I've heard," she said. Dante sighed and glanced up as several important-looking men—some of whom she'd never seen before—entered the room.

"I don't have time for this, Knight. Stop playing childish and attention-seeking games and don't embarrass me," he growled, before striding away, leaving Cleo humiliated. She was absolutely—and unexpectedly—shattered that he had spoken to her like that in front of Ms. Inokawa, who was very discreetly keeping her gaze focused on her place setting. Cleo blinked hard when she realized that her eyes had actually gone misty, and she was annoyed with herself for letting him get to her. Still, after a week of sexing her up, surely he'd noticed the extensive scarring on her right knee. Surely he'd wondered about it. She knew every single detail of his body, every little imperfection—of which there were few—every nook and crevice, and he hadn't noticed the huge and ugly vertical scar on her knee? Well, wasn't that just a much-needed reality check for Cleo? She had to be careful around this man; she had to guard her heart, because while she had started to soften toward him, he hadn't ever seen her as more than a casual hookup.

"We can start in *seiza*," Ms. Inokawa leaned over to whisper conspiratorially, "but after everybody has had a few drinks, no one will notice if we move our legs to the side and sit on our behinds."

Surprised by the sympathy and camaraderie in the other woman's voice, Cleo looked up and saw genuine warmth in her eyes. *Great.* As if the whole situation with Dante wasn't bad enough, she'd gone and completely misjudged Ms. Inokawa as well.

"I'd like that," she said with a watery smile. "I have a bad knee. I don't know how long it'll hold up if I were to sit like that for too long."

"Don't worry," Ms. Inokawa said with a swift pat on Cleo's hand. "It won't be long before the beers start to take effect."

Cleo giggled when the other woman winked dramatically, and started to think that maybe this entire evening wouldn't be too much of an ordeal after all.

Fifteen minutes later her knee was screaming in agony, she could no longer feel her lower legs, and *yet* another man had started yet another long-winded speech. She suppressed a moan and wished there was some discreet way to shift her legs out from beneath her thighs without drawing everybody's attention to the movement. She was very much aware of the glances Dante was throwing in her direction and fought to keep her face impassive even while she felt like weeping.

Finally, everybody raised their small glasses of beer and held them aloft. The speaker said a few more things before ending with a word Cleo was happily familiar with.

"Kanpai!" He yelled the Japanese version of "Cheers," and everybody followed suit.

"Kanpai!" There was loud and manly laughter—Cleo and Ms. Inokawa being the only women present—as everybody clinked glasses and started drinking.

"It's okay for you to move your legs to the side now," Ms. Inokawa whispered, obviously sensing her distress.

"I don't think I can move my legs," Cleo whispered back, while she painfully tried to shift her position without crying out.

"Daijoubu?" the woman asked, and Cleo recognized the question—which she'd heard often over the course of the week—as "Are you okay?" She shrugged miserably.

"I'll probably be okay once I get the feeling back in my legs. They've fallen asleep." Although her knee was a different matter entirely, she wasn't sure if she'd done some damage to it, but it definitely didn't feel all right. She tried to placate the woman with a smile and picked up the bottle of beer placed in front of her and held it up to Ms. Inokawa. "May I?"

It was traditional to pour for the people seated closest to you and considered poor form to allow your neighbor's glass to run dry. The guy on her right, whom she didn't know at all, was holding a bottle up and smiling expectantly, and even though she pretty much hated beer, she managed a smile and a nod while he added the drop of beer that would be needed to fill the glass to the brim again. If she didn't stay alert, she would probably wind up extremely drunk, because it was almost impossible to monitor one's alcohol intake in a situation like this.

Things got rowdy quite quickly, and it was a little shocking to watch the previously somber Japanese businessmen get wasted and exceptionally loud and cheerful in pretty short order. Nobody remained seated—pouring etiquette went out the window—and soon people were crawling about on the floor from one person to the next, chatting and topping up each other's beers. She noticed that quite a few of the men had immediately moved toward Dante and were all vying to pour his drinks. He took the time to chat amicably with each and every man, looking sober as a judge but cultivating a jovial manner that Cleo didn't believe for a second was genuine.

A few of the younger men made a point of talking with her, some in great English, others a little less fluently. Cleo forced aside her pain, kept smiling, and delighted the men when she butchered a few of the standard Japanese phrases she'd learned over the course of the week. They were ridiculously flattering of her bad Japanese, and remembering Daisuke's reaction in the car earlier, she modestly waved off their compliments.

She turned to say something to Ms. Inokawa, but the woman was gone. Cleo cast her gaze toward Dante, expecting to see the woman fawning over him, but she wasn't there. Dante, however, met and held her eyes for a few long moments. His face was completely inscrutable, almost grim. Cleo frowned and wondered if he was pissed off with her yet again. She was the first to break eye contact, still looking for Ms. Inokawa, and she was surprised to see the other woman blatantly flirting with Craig Templeton, the contractor for the hotel build. The handsome older man was smiling and flirting back.

Well, that was new.

Cleo turned her gaze back to Dante to see if Ms. Inokawa's shift in romantic attentions bothered him, but he was still watching Cleo intently. His complete focus was starting to make her a little hot under the collar, and she shifted restlessly. Unfortunately, the inadvertent movement caused a shaft of pain to shoot through her knee, and she flinched. Dante's entire body went still, and his head tilted slightly to the left as he watched her quizzically. In that moment he reminded her of a wild animal on the scent trail of something small and wounded, and Cleo desperately tried to throw him off that trail with a casual grin and a careless wiggle of her fingers. As expected, the frivolous and flirtatious wave did the trick, and he gave her a frown before returning his attention to one of the many sycophants huddling around him. Cleo heaved a relieved sigh and gave her knee a surreptitious little massage before focusing on one of the earnest young men trying to have a conversation with her.

It was going to be a long night.

At around two the following morning, Cleo was more than ready to call it quits. The merry group had dragged Cleo and Dante from one night spot to another and was now insisting on karaoke.

"I have to get back to the hotel," she whispered to Dante, who didn't look as drunk as the rest of their loud group. In fact, he looked much too sober for a man who'd been drinking all night, and she wondered about that for a few moments before he distracted her with a glare.

"You have to do no such thing," he snapped, keeping his voice low. By now her knee was radiating almost constant pain, and all Cleo wanted was a hot bath, pain medication, and a long, long sleep.

"You don't need me here. This isn't part of my job description, and you can't force me to stay."

"One of your unofficial duties is to accompany me to business lunches and dinners."

"Unofficial as in not contracted," she pointed out, and he rubbed the nape of his neck before switching tactics.

"Okay, then, what about coming along in a personal capacity, as my . . ." He struggled to find a definition, and she raised a brow and folded her arms across her chest.

"Girlfriend?" she supplied, and he blanched.

"God, *no*."

"Mistress?" If possible, he went even paler.

"Absolutely not." He hesitated a few moments longer before shrugging and continuing, "As my friend."

"We're friends?"

"Of a sort."

"Well, be a pal and let me go to bed. I'm tired and in pain." Okay, she hadn't meant to reveal that last bit; it just slipped out. His eyes narrowed.

"In pain?"

"Yeah. My knee hurts," she confessed.

"This is why you have been limping since we left the first restaurant?" He had noticed that? She had tried very hard to disguise the slight limp.

"Damaso-san," one of the other men called from a few meters away, "you are coming?"

"*Chotto matte,*" Dante snapped back. "Give me a moment!"

Cleo still stood with her arms crossed and her bad knee bent so that her other leg was taking most of her weight.

"Explain!" he commanded, pointing to her knee.

"I have a weak knee, and sitting in *seiza* made it flare up a bit."

He swore colorfully in about three different languages before running an agitated hand through his hair.

"What's wrong with your knee?" he asked after a moment, and she huffed impatiently.

"You've seen every inch of my body," she said. "I assumed that, over the course of the week, you'd have noticed the great, ugly scar on my knee?"

"Of course I did," he admitted. "And I've been meaning to ask you about it. Only—"

"Only you've never had the time?" she completed. Where would he find the time? At night he was fully occupied with seducing her, and his days were dominated by back-to-back meetings required to get his precious hotel built. And then there was the obvious fact that he simply didn't care enough to delve into personal details. They didn't speak about anything other than superficial nonsense when they were alone at night, and once the sex started, the conversation dwindled down to what felt good and where.

"I was aware of the scar. I just never really appreciated that your knee might have been weakened by it. Which was foolish considering the extent of the scarring. But in my defense, it never seems to bother you, you usually walk without impediment, and you're quite limber— as I can personally attest."

His comment flashed her back to two nights before, when they'd had sex in the middle of his room, his hands supporting her butt and her legs wrapped around his waist, without even a wall to bolster them. It had been quite a testament to his strength and her flexibility. Only their mutual orgasms had finally sent them sinking down to the carpeted floor. She flushed at the memory and felt uncomfortably hot as she remembered how intense that session had been, the fear of falling combined with the excitement of maintaining rhythm and balance.

"Anyway," she said, hoping to divert them both back to the point at hand, "the knee doesn't really bother me unless I'm testing it, and, trust me, that *seiza* thing tested it sorely."

"How old is the injury?" he asked, looking deeply uncomfortable with the question, and she knew it was because he felt compelled to ask her a personal question to make himself look—and possibly feel—like less of an uncaring dick.

"I injured it about three years ago," she recalled, her lips twisting as she remembered the catastrophic fall that had killed all of her dreams.

"What happened?" Again, the question sounded torn from him. He clearly hated asking and probably had no real interest in the answer.

"I had an accident and needed knee surgery. The end. You don't have to ask me any more questions, *sir*. You've shown an interest. Noted."

He said nothing, merely watched her for a very long moment, that handsome face maddeningly blank.

"So be it." He shrugged dismissively. "We will return to the hotel."

"You don't have to go back. I can make it back on my own."

"Undoubtedly," he agreed. "But I find myself rather tired."

"Do you?" she asked on a whisper, and his lips quirked in that sexy, dreadful cat-that-got-the-cream grin.

"—ish."

"What?" she asked, although she knew exactly what he meant by that.

"I'm tired-*ish*," he clarified, even though the expression on his face suggested he knew he didn't really have to. "I may find my second wind by the time we return to the hotel."

Of course he would.

And did.

Breakfast felt different. Usually the meal, which was always delivered to their suite, was eaten in a rush while Dante rapid-fired a list of the day's requirements at Cleo. Today, with the urgency of the week behind them and the memory of the previous night's fantastic sex still throbbing between them, everything felt odd. Different. *Wrong.*

They would leave for the airport in under an hour, and they were in this weird space of nothingness where everything had been arranged and there was no more to be done other than enjoy the rare moment of peace and quiet.

Only it wasn't peaceful and it was much too quiet.

Cleo swallowed a piece of toast that felt like sandpaper as it slid down her dry throat. She chased it down with some acidic orange juice and wondered at her nervousness.

She got up and restlessly made her way over to the huge picture windows beside the Bakokko armchairs, which now had some pretty raunchy memories attached to them. There was a layer of smog hanging over the city that did nothing to detract from Tokyo's vibrancy. She had voraciously read her guidebook from beginning to end, diligently folding over the pages dedicated to places that she had longed to see, promising herself she would come back and visit someday. She knew that it was unlikely to happen and considered herself lucky to have seen this much of it at least, from way up in her glass tower and the claustrophobic confines of the car.

"Miss Knight." Dante's quiet voice intruded upon her thoughts, and she couldn't help but wonder if he'd called her Miss Knight because he'd forgotten her name again. The absolute ludicrousness of a man who knew her body better than she did addressing her so formally caused a tiny burble of hysterical laughter to rise in her chest. She swallowed it back down, instinct telling her he wouldn't appreciate her humor right now.

She turned to face him, hiding a grimace when her still-sore knee twinged in response to the movement. Sure enough, the grim set of his jaw and the tense line of his mouth confirmed that he was ready to have a Serious Discussion.

"Wait." She held up a hand and he paused. "Don't tell me. Let me guess. It was fun while it lasted but now *it*—whatever *it* was—is over, and we will never speak of it again. How did I do?"

"I will require you to sign a nondisclosure agreement," he said stiffly, and the words stole the breath right out of her. She felt so outraged, insulted, and—shockingly—*hurt*.

"And what if I don't sign it?" she asked through stiff lips. "I mean, aren't you supposed to sign those things *before* we do the stuff we're not supposed to disclose?"

"Usually, yes, but we were in bed together before I had a chance to consider the possibility that something sexual might happen between us. We don't suit. You're not my usual . . ." His voice petered off as he grasped that his next words would be in bad taste. Still, he might not have said them, but they hovered between them like an offensive odor.

"I'm not your usual type," she finished for him. "And because of that, you never thought we'd wind up screwing each other's brains out. So you didn't protect yourself the way you normally would have.

"Do you make all of your lovers sign nondisclosure agreements before you sleep with them?" she asked combatively, and his jaw clenched.

"Usually." The tight one-word answer surprised her.

"You do? *All* of them?"

He seemed to have no shortage of female companions, and the thought of him going through this same distasteful scene with all of them was a little revolting.

"I don't trust many people," he admitted, and his broad shoulders shifted uncomfortably.

"That's not a very romantic way to start a relationship," she noted absently, still a bit taken aback by his admission.

"The women I usually associate with understand the need for privacy. Nobody wants their private lives smeared all over the papers for the titillation of the masses."

"And you think that's something I would do?" she asked, stung.

"I don't know you, Miss Knight. I don't *want* to know you. We enjoyed each other and that's the end of it. What you are or aren't capable of doesn't interest me. I want you to sign the agreement so that I no longer have to consider the possibility that you may one day decide to do a cheeky little *sexposé* on your 'tryst with Dante Damaso.'" *Tryst* was such an un-Dante-like word for him to use that for a moment she could only gape at him before his words sank in properly.

"How do I know that *you* won't be the one to brag to your mates about screwing your secretary?"

"First of all, you're not my secretary, and secondly, this agreement would protect you from such an eventuality. It works both ways."

"So what happens if I don't sign your agreement?" she asked again, trying very hard to disguise the tremble in her voice. "Do I lose my job?"

"Your job has never been, and will never be, at stake because of our personal association," he said, the answer coming so quickly that she didn't doubt its veracity. "But this gesture would go a long way toward convincing me of your integrity."

"And yet it does nothing for yours." She could see that he didn't like the idea of his integrity being called into question. He tugged at his cuffs and straightened his already immaculate tie before launching another volley at her.

"You sign it and you have the comfort of knowing that none of this ever gets out. That your brother and friends never discover how very quickly you fell into bed with me." He played dirty, and for a second she almost fell for his bluff.

"Why would you tell anybody about this when you just admitted that you don't want it to come out?" she asked skeptically. "Also I'm a consenting adult, and you're not my first sexual partner. I'm pretty sure my brother and friends don't have any misconceptions about me."

"But they don't think you're an easy little slut either, do they?"

She could feel the blood draining from her face at the question. She struggled to breathe as the emotional impact of that sucker punch nearly caused her to double over in shock and pain. Why did this hurt? It shouldn't hurt. He meant nothing to her. He didn't have the power to hurt her. And yet . . . there was pain. An awful lot of pain.

"You think I'm a slut?" For a fleeting instant, she saw an expression almost like regret flash across his face.

"I could make it look like you are." He didn't answer her question, not really, but the failure to give her a yes or no was more of an indictment than an actual reply. "I could make you look like a scheming, manipulative, money-grubbing little tramp, while I come out smelling like a rose. But if you sign this agreement, you'd be protected from that. We could both go back to our lives none the worse for wear. Failure to sign would force me to play dirty. To go on the offensive, and neither of us wants that."

She hated him so much in that instant that she was shaking with it. He had to know how she felt, had to see it in her eyes, but he didn't even flinch, merely held the document out with a steady hand until she took it from him. Cleo tried to read it, but her eyes were blurred with tears she hadn't even known were there. She took the pen from him and signed in the allotted space beside his sprawling signature.

She handed both pen and paper back to him with violently shaking hands, wanting nothing more than to get out of his presence and take another shower.

"This is for the best, Cleo," he murmured gently, almost regretfully, and she laughed bitterly as she turned away from him.

"I would rather you didn't talk to me unless it's work related, sir. I don't think I could stomach your empty platitudes right now." She retreated to her own room without a backward glance.

The return journey to Cape Town felt endless. Dante and Cleo barely exchanged a word between Narita airport and Cape Town International.

They separated in Dubai for much-needed showers in the first-class lounge, and Cleo picked listlessly at some fruit while waiting for the boarding call of their next flight. She didn't see Dante at all between disembarking and boarding in Dubai, and she preferred it that way. The privacy of their first-class suites, which had been new and exciting to Cleo on the way to Tokyo, had merely made the flight back to Cape Town tolerable because she didn't have to see him and could actually manage to squeeze in a few hours of sleep.

The cold, windy, and gray weather of Cape Town suited Cleo's mood perfectly. She was moody, exhausted, her knee still hurt, and she just wanted to get home. Dante caught up with her after they had both cleared customs and baggage claim, just before they stepped into the arrivals lounge. He grabbed hold of her elbow and turned her toward him.

"The car will take you home first. I'm sure you must be tired."

"Car?"

"My driver, James, will be picking us up. Remember?"

"I assumed I would have to find my own way home from here."

"Don't be ridiculous. We'll drop you off first." He steered her toward the door to the arrivals lounge, and she jerked her arm from his grip before coming to a standstill. The other first- and business-class passengers gave them curious looks as they streamed by.

"There's no need for that. I've made alternative arrangements."

His jaw tightened. "You didn't have to do that."

"It's done."

He looked like he wanted to argue, but after a brief hesitation, he shrugged and strode away from her without another word. She watched him go, hating how conflicted she felt. She should feel relief that their messy little interlude was over and that he was gone, not regret and longing and pain.

She followed him out into the arrivals lounge and saw her best friend almost immediately. Cal—her ex–dance partner—was easy to spot because, aside from Dante, he was one of the tallest men she knew. He stood head and shoulders above everyone else in the crowd. She saw his tousled blond hair before he saw her five-foot-one frame and black hair, which wasn't as easy to spot in a crowd of people. When he did finally see her, his handsome face broke into a huge grin, and he waved enthusiastically. Cleo fought her way past the jostling mass of people and flung herself at him. She was just so relieved to see a friendly face that she couldn't help herself. He lifted her clear off the floor—it had always been so easy for him to pick her up—and hugged her warmly, enfolding her completely in his arms. Cal was the best hugger.

She clung to him, feeling safe and cocooned in his embrace, and her urgency and desperation must have been obvious because his arms tightened.

"Hey, sweetheart," he muttered. "What's going on? Are you okay?"

She shook her head and kept her nose buried in his neck. She loved the familiar smell of him. He put her down and gently removed her arms from his neck, wanting to see her face.

"What's happened?" Damn him, he knew her too well. And everything she felt was still too fresh to hide from him.

"I don't want to talk about it right now." A surreptitious glance around informed her that they'd attracted a bit of attention from passersby, and she knew that Dante was probably close by as well.

"Okay." Bless him, he was always so understanding. He looked around for her bag—a single medium-size roller suitcase—and raised a dubious brow when he saw it.

"You're such a miserly little packer. How did you survive a week in *Tokyo* with just that little bag?" he asked as he grabbed her elbow with one hand and the suitcase handle with the other.

"I didn't exactly have time to socialize. This was sufficient."

"I would need a bag that size for hair product alone," he said dismissively, and she giggled, surprising herself.

"Don't I know it?"

"Magnificence like this"—he tossed his hair for emphasis—"doesn't come easily."

Another giggle. Cal was exactly what she needed right now. She hooked her arm through his and rested her head on his shoulder and let his nonsense chatter wash over her like a soothing balm as he led her toward where he'd parked.

Dante watched Cleo leave with that blond behemoth; she was clinging to the man's arm and staring up at him adoringly as they walked away. So much for thinking he'd hurt her back in Tokyo. He'd had an uncharacteristic flash of conscience when he'd said the things necessary to get her to sign that nondisclosure agreement. It had been dirty and unfair, but it had gotten the job done. Still, Dante wasn't a complete monster. He felt moved by her tears and even a little *guilty* in the face of her obvious distress. But to see her now with that guy was like watching an entirely different person, and he was glad he hadn't been completely taken in by her little-girl-lost act back in Tokyo. He always protected himself: condoms and nondisclosure agreements without exception. No unwanted pregnancies and no unwanted scandals. It kept things clean and uncomplicated, which was exactly the way he preferred his life. Women served a purpose, and until Cleo they had all known exactly what they were getting into with him. He was on shaky legal ground getting her to sign it the way he had, but without it he felt naked and vulnerable. Feelings he would never admit to out loud.

Still, despite the fact that his bullying tactics had left a bad taste in his mouth, he couldn't regret the fact that he had stooped to them. It was over now. The document was safely signed and would be notarized as soon as possible.

He had a *very* brief flash of regret that he wouldn't experience Cleo Knight in his bed again before he put her firmly out of his mind.

CHAPTER FOUR

"I don't think I've ever actually *hated* someone before," Cleo confessed as she licked the salt off the rim of her margarita. She paused for a moment and thought about what she'd just said. "But God, I hate that man so much. The thought of seeing him again on Monday turns my stomach, and I'm so tempted to quit this job."

"You can't quit, hon." Cal tut-tutted. "Who'll pay the rent or buy the food? Until I find a job, you're the only one keeping this boat afloat."

"You'll find something soon, Cal." She patted his broad shoulder a little drunkenly before going back to contemplate her curiously unsatisfying frozen margarita again. "Now, can we please focus on my predicament?"

"Okay, so the guy is a world-class asshole," Cal recapped. "He treated you shabbily, which would earn him a well-deserved punch in the face if he were here right now, and you hate him but still have to work with him."

Cleo nodded morosely, the pit in her stomach increasing with every word. She put aside her half-finished drink, wishing she actually felt like getting rip-roaring drunk. It might have helped a little.

"Now, what I really want to know"—Cal leaned forward conspiratorially—"is he any good in the sack?"

Cleo sighed.

"He's fantastic, and that just makes me hate him more. Should I even be telling you all of this? I mean, I feel like I'm breaking that stupid contract with every syllable I utter."

"You probably are." Cal shrugged. "But if I can trust you to keep all my sordid secrets—you could sink me if you wanted to and you know it—then you can trust me with this."

And she did trust Cal; he was like a second brother to her. Her dance partner for years, he had seen her through all her trials and tribulations. He felt responsible for her fall and had been her emotional support while she'd tried to come to terms with everything she'd lost after the accident. He was the only one who truly understood. Luc didn't get it, her nondancing friends didn't get it, but Cal got it. Cal knew what it was like to feel alive only when you were dancing, and he recognized that she felt like the most important part of her had died after the accident. He was the one who'd gotten her out of bed in the mornings, had taken her to physical therapy, had bossed her into dancing again, even though she was just a shadow of her former self. He had helped her understand that while she would never again be the supremely talented dancer who had once had dance companies vying for her attention, she could still dance. It was in her blood, a part of her physical makeup, and she would never lose it completely.

"All I'm saying is that the man is *seriously* hot," Cal said. "And if he wasn't so obviously and uncompromisingly hetero, I would happily make a play for him."

"You're way too good for the likes of him," Cleo said.

"As are you," he said, completely serious.

"You're the best, Cal." She sighed and leaned in for a hug. He complied and she sagged against him, letting him support her slight weight.

"I'm so glad we're roomies," she crooned, and when he laughed, the sound had a bitter edge to it.

"Not exactly roomies," he corrected. "More like freeloader and working stiff."

"You're not a freeloader, Cal. We've all been through rough spots, and you've done so much for me . . ." She had difficulty talking around the lump in her throat. "So don't you dare denigrate yourself like that in front of me again, okay?"

"Yes, miss," he teased, making an effort to shake off his obvious depression, even though she could tell that it lingered just beneath the surface. "Now tell me more. I want to know everything—length, girth, angle. Pointing downward, straight ahead, or kissing the navel?"

"Seriously?" She choked back a laugh.

"Well, if that thing points down, it just looks flaccid and . . . I dunno, *incapable* somehow."

"I'm not discussing this with you."

"Why not? You told me all about Frank Whatsisface's, remember?"

"I did *not*. This is the first time I can recall us discussing the angle of any guy's erection."

"True," he conceded, after some thought. "But that Frank guy was really boring. I wasn't interested in hearing about his antics in bed."

"Come on, he was nice."

"And boring."

"He was always really sweet to me."

"And super boring."

Cleo sighed. She really couldn't argue with him. Frank Sharp, whom she'd dated for two months and slept with twice—in the same night—had been a regular snoozefest. Both in bed and out of it. Cleo had actually fallen asleep during the sex act, *both* times. Not her finest moment. She had broken it off with him immediately after that and hadn't dated anyone else in more than a year. Dante was the first man she'd slept with since then, and poor Frank couldn't compete with that. Most men would have difficulty competing with a guy like Dante Damaso.

"I'm not going to discuss the matter any further," Cleo said decisively. "I've probably broken a dozen of his stupid nondisclosure rules just by telling you about it. Best to let the matter rest and pretend it never happened."

Cal gave her a long, level look and she dodged his gaze. He could look as skeptical as he liked, but Cleo was going to pretend it never happened if it *killed* her!

Cleo had all weekend to think about what she would say and how she would act when she saw Dante again on Monday. She practiced her cool, slightly disdainful looks in the mirror, and her professional "Good morning, sir," "Yes, sir," "No, sir," and "As you wish, sir" out loud every morning and evening. Yet, she was still a bundle of nerves when she walked into the office Monday morning. He must have come to the office at some point over the weekend, because even though he clearly hadn't arrived yet, there was a Dictaphone full of e-mails she had to get ready, and two A4-size manila envelopes with her name sitting in the middle of her desk. She frowned at the envelopes before picking up the flatter one. She took a deep breath and stuck her finger beneath the flap to open it. The sheaf of papers inside was exactly what she'd been expecting to see: her copy of the nondisclosure agreement, officially notarized. She shook her head and shoved it back into the envelope and then into her desk drawer. Well, so much for being cool, calm, and collected this morning. One stupid envelope and she was feeling anxious and angry at the same time. Her gaze shifted to the other envelope, which was slightly bulkier than the first. She picked it up cautiously, having absolutely no clue what could be inside it. It was ridiculously light, lighter than the first envelope, and Cleo ripped it open with less care than she had the first one. She upended it and watched as a piece of paper fluttered to the desk, followed by a scrap of white cotton. She blinked at it uncomprehendingly for a few seconds before her eyes widened in recognition.

She gasped, blushed, and grabbed up the Hello Kitty boy shorts in a lightning-fast move, terrified that someone would see them. Only after they were safely tucked away in her bag did she shift her attention to the paper that had accompanied the panties.

Sure enough, Dante's bold, masculine writing was scrawled across the small square of paper. All it said was:

These got mixed in with my stuff. —DD

Cleo crumpled the paper up in her fist and tossed it in the wastepaper basket. Lovely. Just when she'd resolved to never again think of their encounter in Japan, he had to bring it all back in graphic detail without even having to be physically present.

She sat down behind her desk after getting the fancy coffee machine up and running, and watering her old enemy, the ficus. She was well into the e-mails when Dante finally sauntered in, nearly an hour later.

Completely focused on her work up until that moment, Cleo was aware of his presence almost immediately. She tensed, all her practice and preparation instantly forgotten in the face of his overwhelming presence.

"Uh . . ."

"Good morning, Miss Knight," he inserted smoothly, before she could get a single word out. "I trust the jet lag isn't too bad?"

"It's . . ." Damn. Why couldn't she speak? He waited for a moment, but when it became clear that she had nothing to offer other than that one strangled word, he cleared his throat and gestured toward the computer.

"Are you nearly done with those?"

She nodded mutely.

"Good." He shoved his hands into his trouser pockets and rocked back slightly on his heels. "Great."

Why was he just standing there, staring at her? Why didn't he say something? Or leave? Or tell her to go to so-and-so's office for the rest of the day?

"Peter Whitman's secretary has resigned," he said abruptly. "And I feel that the position would be more in keeping with your skill set."

"Oh."

"It's a slight dip in salary, but you knew that you'd eventually have to take a step down, right?"

"I did," she said, finally finding her voice. She stared down at her hands, spread on the keyboard in front of her, like they were the most fascinating things in the world.

"Right, then. That's settled," he said a little hoarsely.

"I'm not sure who Peter Whitman is," she admitted. "And when do I start?"

"You'll spend the rest of the week here, but you'll start with him next Monday. He's the head of HR. I was vacillating between HR and accounting, but I thought that, since you seem to be such a people person, you'd find HR more interesting."

The comment astonished her, and she raised her eyes to meet his surprisingly intense gaze head-on. His penetrating stare was a little unnerving, but she was quite touched that he had considered her personality before making his decision.

"Thank you."

"Look, you know that this job is way beyond your actual capabilities, right?" Why was he still talking about this? He sounded like a man who was determined to justify himself.

"Well, if I didn't before, I certainly know it now," she said dryly, and his frown told her that he didn't appreciate her flippant comment.

"This transfer has nothing to do with what happened between us in Tokyo." Ooh, he went there. She hadn't expected him to actually go there. "It was inevitable."

"I know it was," she said. "But it's rather sudden. After all, Donna is still on maternity leave."

"And she'll be gone for another six months. I can't have you here for another six months. You've proven yourself quite capable, but I need someone who can actually handle every aspect of the job."

"Of course." Weirdly, it felt like she actually had *him* on the back foot, and that made her feel a little more in control. "Would you like your coffee now, sir?"

He didn't reply for the longest time, before nodding curtly and swiveling on his heel to head to his office. After the door shut behind him, she dropped her head to where her hands still rested on the keyboard and just sat there for a few minutes, trying to recover her poise.

"Right," she said to herself as she pushed away from the desk and started to go slowly about organizing his urgent mail and pouring the extremely bitter dark-roast coffee he preferred.

She gave a perfunctory knock on the intimidating double doors that led to his massive office before pushing her way inside. Dante sat behind his exquisitely crafted bird's-eye maple-and-walnut antique desk and stared broodingly at his huge computer screen. He had his elbows on the desk and his hands steepled in front of him, the tips of his forefingers pressed against his lips. Her entry drew his gaze from the computer, and he stared at her over the top of his fingers.

She rounded the desk, placed the coffee mug beside his right elbow, and centered the mail in front of him. He didn't say a word while she was doing that, and she was acutely aware of his closeness, of the scent of him, the *heat* of him, and couldn't get back to the other side of the desk fast enough. She stood there, her hands clasped in front of her and her eyes downcast, waiting to hear where he would parcel her off to this morning, but when he said nothing for the longest time, she dared a glance up at him. He still stared at her, his eyes narrowed and his lips pursed. He was slowly moving his mouth back and forth across his fingertips, looking lost in thought at he watched her.

"Will that be all, sir?" she asked expectantly. Maybe he'd send her to HR to meet her future boss. It would do her good to apprentice with his current secretary. Frankly, she couldn't wait to get away from the top floor and its high-powered, frenetic pace.

"Did you get my package?"

She cleared her throat and shifted restlessly at the unexpected question.

"Yes, sir. Thank you, sir. I'll have a proper read-through later, since I didn't get a chance to check the finer details on Thursday before I signed it." She couldn't resist the dig, and she watched him closely for his reaction. But he revealed nothing, keeping his face completely passive, even while his gaze darkened.

"That's not the package I meant," he said after a few minutes of awkward silence. His deep, husky voice sent shock waves reverberating through her body as the words registered, and she felt a blush starting from her breasts and sweeping right up to the top of her head. She clamped her mouth shut and glared at him, refusing to respond to his words.

"I meant, did you get your panties?" he prompted perversely when she said nothing. "They were sweet. Not my favorites, mind you. That honor belongs to the blue Daisy Duck pair with the little white-heart polka dots all over them. Do you know which ones I mean?"

Of course she knew which ones he meant; he'd removed them with his teeth that last night in Tokyo. He'd been so absorbed with what was being revealed beneath the underwear that she hadn't for one second considered that the design would register with him.

"I wish you wouldn't talk like this," she said shakily. "It's—"

"Inappropriate," he completed. "I know. The problem is that when I'm around you, all thought of appropriate behavior completely flees my mind. Now why the hell do you suppose that is?" He sounded angry as he said the words, and Cleo shared his frustration. He was like an addictive drug that she couldn't flush out of her system. Every time she got in his general vicinity, she turned into mush and her brain stopped functioning.

He got up and rounded the desk until he stood behind her, close enough that she could feel the heat emanating off him in waves and his breath in her hair.

"I took one look at you behind that desk this morning, all—how do you say—prim and proper? And I wanted this," he said, his voice low. He didn't have to explain what *this* was; they both knew and they both accepted it even though they both hated the inexplicable need.

He moved, wrapping one strong arm around her torso and gripping her jaw with his hand as he tugged her back against his hard body. She could feel his iron-hard erection grinding into the small of her back. He sucked her earlobe into his mouth for the briefest of moments before moving down to nuzzle the sensitive area just below her ear.

Her knees buckled, and his other hand came up to cup the nape of her neck and gently but inexorably exert enough pressure to let her know exactly what he wanted. She complied, bracing herself on her elbows as she bent over his desk.

His hands went roaming, tugging her blouse from her skirt and burrowing their way beneath the silk chiffon until they found and cupped her small breasts through the lace of her demi bra. The slightest of tugs and he had the bra tucked beneath her breasts and his thumbs flicking away at her sensitive nipples. He played there for a while, knowing that very little more than that was required to get her going, before his hands trailed down over her flat stomach and then around to the small of her back, his fingertips skirting along the sensitive skin above the waistband of her skirt. When his thumbs met in the center of her back just above the slight swell of her behind, he shifted the position of his hands until he had her backside cupped in his palms.

Cleo whimpered, unbelievably turned on by being spread out on his desk in his office in broad daylight.

His hands grabbed a couple of fistfuls of twill and dragged her skirt up, up, ever so slowly up, until—after an excruciatingly long time—she felt cool air on the backs of her thighs. Dante—who'd been silent up until this point—groaned when he finally had her skirt up over her back and her panties revealed to him.

"Hell, yes, I want some honey," he ground out, and Cleo dimly apprehended that he was responding to Winnie the Pooh's "Hunny?" question on the back of her boy shorts. He hooked a thumb into each side of the shorts and dragged them down to her knees, before kneeling behind her. Cleo held her breath, hoping his intention was what she was anticipating, and sure enough . . .

"Oh *God*," she moaned when his tongue immediately went to work. She'd gotten so used to him doing this for her that she no longer felt self-conscious about the act, which had always embarrassed her with other guys. She curled her fingers against the surface of his desk and blindly stared at the rapidly cooling mug of coffee about a foot in front of her. She moved her upper body lower and lower until her torso and chest were flat against the desk and her cheek was pressed to the coolness of the surface. She spread her arms out on either side of her and just surrendered herself completely to him. She was on the verge of coming when he stopped, and she cried out in frustration until she felt him step between her thighs. She heard the sound of his zipper, the crinkle of a condom wrapper, and then . . . dear God—complete bliss when he finally penetrated her. He had her so primed that he barely had the tip in before she went up onto her toes, her back arching like a cat's, as her orgasm took her.

His hands on her hips held her still, and he waited until her climax had waned before resuming his slow and thorough conquest of her very willing body. She was building up to her third orgasm when the phone rang, adding a reckless sense of exhibitionism to their excitement that had only been hinted at before. The complete and utter inappropriateness of the setting added a titillating edge to the sex that rushed her headlong into another climax so intense that she actually blacked out for a couple of seconds. She came to moments later, in time to hear him groan, the first time she'd ever heard a sound from him during one of his climaxes. He was usually completely silent, just a catch of the breath followed by a long exhale. This soft groan was new, as was the whispered expletive that accompanied it. He went completely limp, his full weight descending onto her back for a few short moments before he stepped back and removed himself from her both physically and emotionally in one smooth movement. He gently pulled her panties back up and lowered her skirt, covering her up with such care that Cleo felt almost cherished. The feeling disappeared when he moved away hastily, leaving Cleo to push herself up with arms that felt like jelly. Her entire body felt wobbly, and she sank into the chair opposite his desk, not sure how to cope with this.

Dante staggered back to his side of the desk, lowered himself into his chair, and immediately swiveled it around until he faced the window. She stared at the back of his head, feeling wounded and completely rejected by the unmistakably dismissive gesture. If he wanted her to leave, he'd have to wait a few moments until she got her breath and motor functions back.

Neither of them said a word as their breathing gradually returned to normal. Cleo, her body still feeling like it could go back up in flames any second, moved gingerly in her chair, wondering if she would ever be capable of leaving the room again.

"I guess you're going to need another nondisclosure agreement." She quickly grasped the horrific consequences of their stupidity. His shoulders tensed and he shook his head, still not turning to look at her.

"The other one has it covered. Past and future sexual encounters, if I remember the wording correctly."

How terribly optimistic of him, she thought caustically.

"Not optimistic," he countered, and she grimaced when she realized that she'd spoken aloud. "Realistic. We have some crazy chemistry. A bit of backsliding was inevitable."

"No more after this, though," she said adamantly, and she watched his shoulders rise and fall in a sigh.

"No. I didn't mean for this to happen. It's probably just a remnant of our . . ." He paused, unable to find the correct word.

"Affair?" she suggested.

"No. Our . . ." Another pause.

"Relationship?"

"*No*, will you stop trying to complete my sentences?" He sounded wholly exasperated, and he spun his chair around to glare at her. "Our *thing* in Tokyo."

Cleo was too busy taking in the state of him to harangue him for his weak choice of words. How had his hair gotten so messy when she hadn't run her fingers through it? And his tie was undone, another thing he must have done himself. His shirttails were out and . . . *God*, he had another impressive hard-on. The damned thing was tireless.

"I think you should transfer me to Peter Whitman's office tomorrow. I could apprentice with his current secretary and learn the ropes from him or her."

"What should I do in the meantime? I don't have a replacement for you." He sounded annoyed and put out by her suggestion.

"All I ever do is water your plant, make your coffee, and send your e-mails. Any idiot can do that."

"But I don't want any other idiot, I want *you*, until I find a more qualified person for the job."

"Is this because of my special uh . . . skill set?"

He looked confused by her question.

"We have already established that your skill set is not suited to the job," he reminded her.

"Not *that* . . ." She leaned forward and waved a hand back and forth. "*This*. Us."

"There *is* no us."

"Okay, sure . . . but—"

"Cleo, if you're suggesting that I'm trying to keep you here so that I can have you around to fuck on demand, then I have to tell you, you're mistaken."

"Good, because that's not even an option for you."

He snorted scornfully and gave her a pointed and scathing once-over, not missing a single detail of her dishevelment.

"This was different," she said defensively. "You didn't demand anything I wasn't willing to give."

"I would never ask for anything you're not willing to give, because, fortunately, I know exactly what you want." The arrogant proclamation was so typically Dante that it took everything she had not to chuck something at him.

"I don't think either of us tried very hard to resist temptation today," she said, and he nodded his agreement. "But I want you to know that as of this very moment, this *thing* between us is over, and if I'm really not here to simply service you while it's convenient, then prove it by allowing me to start at Mr. Whitman's office tomorrow, *sir*."

He took an excruciatingly long moment to respond. He straightened his tie and ran a hand through his hair, making it worse. He reached for his desk phone and dialed.

"Whitman," he barked into the mouthpiece after a moment, keeping his eyes glued to hers. "Miss Knight will be starting in your office tomorrow morning. Have your current secretary show her the ropes."

He hung up without so much as a good-bye, still holding her gaze captive.

"Happy?"

"Yes."

"The rest of your day will be spent finding an adequate replacement for Donna, someone who will last the entire six months. Look in-house, but if that doesn't work, call a temp agency. You do not leave this office today until you have someone to replace you tomorrow. *Entender?* If she's incompetent, you'll be answerable for that."

She raised an eyebrow at his staccato commands.

"Yes, sir."

She finally managed to lever herself out of the chair, their conversation having killed any residual desire she might have felt toward him. It wasn't exactly sexy to go from the most intense and intimate lovemaking experience of her life directly back to discussions about nondisclosure agreements, office dynamics, and displays of colossal male ego. Thankfully, it seemed to have had the same effect on him. She had just reached the door when his voice stopped her.

"Miss Knight."

She paused, her hand on the doorknob. She didn't turn to face him, merely waited for him to say whatever was left to say.

"I would prefer someone older. Someone less like you."

Now what the hell did that mean? Someone less like her?

"You know," he said lamely when she turned to face him quizzically. To his credit he looked as confused as she felt.

"Nope. Don't have a clue." Her voice was so icy that her words practically froze as they left her lips.

"Someone with more experience. With less *personality.*"

"What?"

"You talk too much," he said pointedly. "Your attitude is too familiar and too sarcastic."

She opened her mouth to say something, and he held up a finger to stop her.

"And that was *before* everything that happened in Tokyo. You're completely irreverent and have a bizarre sense of humor. I also have no wish to hear about reality television shows, pop music, manicures,

Brangelina, *Star Trek*, or anything that's trending on Twitter—not even secondhand through whispered telephone conversations when my assistant thinks I'm not paying attention."

Well, he'd certainly been a lot more attentive during those half hours in the mornings than she'd given him credit for. But one thing struck her as odd.

"*Star Trek?*" she repeated. She loved the new movies but hardly ever publicly discussed them.

"You're constantly talking about how sick you are of the Cardassians," he elaborated uncomfortably. Her eyes widened and she stifled a laugh.

"Different kind of Kardashian," she corrected. It would be hopeless to explain it to a man who clearly had no interest in pop culture— even while every model or actress he was publicly photographed with inserted him into the very scene he was so scornful of. Quite frankly, she was impressed that he even knew about the Cardassians in *Star Trek*, which attested to a level of geekdom that she would never have suspected of him.

"So you're looking for the anti-me?"

"It shouldn't be so hard to find the complete opposite of you. You are quite . . ." His brow lowered as he tried to find the correct word. "Singular."

"Thank you," she said, ridiculously flattered until a closer glance at his straight face told her that it hadn't been a compliment. Her fledgling smile died, and she once again—as she often did in his presence— fought the urge to roll her eyes.

"Okay, so you're looking for an old, boring, and competent assistant," she itemized, and his lips thinned but he said nothing. "I'll get on that right away, *sir.*"

The hot sex of earlier was all but forgotten beneath the surge of dislike and irritation she currently felt. She was determined to find him the best assistant she could because she would be perfectly happy never to see him again.

Dante watched her leave, waiting for the door to swing shut behind that tight little ass before throwing his head back against the chair and groaning. What the hell had he been thinking? Fucking her in the office was completely unacceptable and—for him—completely unprecedented. He had been so cool and collected when she'd walked into his office that morning, but all the excruciatingly polite *sirs* had started to annoy him, and then when she'd brought his coffee and mail around the desk, she'd smelled fantastic—her shampoo, soap, perfume, and her unique musk had combined into an irresistible cocktail designed to lead a man straight into temptation. Added to that, her skirt clung to her every curve, and that soft blouse draped over the barely there mounds of her breasts—he had gone from zero to rock hard in less than thirty seconds.

Impulse control had gone straight out the window, and he had bent her over his desk and had lost complete control right there in a place that should have been sacrosanct. No personal complications had ever dared intrude in here before. Now he would never again look at his desk without picturing her bent over it, legs spread, skirt up over her back and adorable little panties down around her knees. He groaned again and stared down at his ridiculously keen cock, which once again stood at attention, begging for more.

"Never going to happen again," he said out loud. Asking her to find an assistant by the end of the day was nearly an impossible request, considering his exacting standards, but really anybody would be better than Cleo right now. He just didn't trust his ability to stick to his resolve not to touch her again if she was working in close proximity to him. He knew this *weakness* was only because he hadn't gotten her out of his system yet, and they should probably allow this *thing* to run its course between them—but he also knew that if he went cold turkey, it wouldn't take long to forget about her. She wasn't irresistible, just the flavor du jour, so to speak. She was there, he was horny, and they were good together . . . when they weren't forced to make conversation.

But it was over now. Time to move on.

Cleo found Dante's "old, boring, and competent" new executive assistant with time to spare that day. Mrs. Clarke was a kind middle-aged woman with a sharp intellect and frighteningly exacting standards. Cleo unashamedly lured her to the Dark Side from her nice, safe position as personal assistant to the accounts manager with the promise of a flattering introduction to the middle-aged and supposed lifelong bachelor Mr. Peter Whitman, to whom, it seemed, the widowed Mrs. Clarke had taken a shine. After that it had just been a matter of stepping back and watching Mrs. Clarke do her thing. The woman very quickly arranged a competent replacement to fill her own position for the next six months, managed her own immediate superior beautifully (the man seemed a little frightened of her, to be honest), and then all that was left was introducing her to Dante.

Dante, however, proved to be frustratingly elusive for the rest of the day. He had left the office soon after their ill-advised little liaison that morning and hadn't returned. His phone kept going to voice mail, and he wasn't responding to any of his messages. By the end of the day, she shrugged, leaving him a succinct memo detailing the pertinent facts regarding Mrs. Clarke's temporary transfer from accounts to his office.

A quick glance around confirmed that she hadn't forgotten anything, and with not even a twinge of regret, she powered down her computer, gathered up her things, and left.

CHAPTER FIVE

"Dante, my man, you've been scarce. I figured you were probably busy after your trip to Tokyo last month." Dante grimaced, keeping the phone pinned to his ear and grateful that his longtime friend couldn't see the guilt on his face. Being busy had nothing to do with the reason Dante had been scarce.

"Lucius, great to hear your voice. I've been thinking about you." Not a lie. He *had* been thinking of the man, wondering if Cleo had let anything slip about what had happened between them. In truth, he'd been a little reluctant to call his friend because he'd feared that the other man's reception would be cool or hostile. And that would have been . . . disappointing. He enjoyed Luc's companionship. He didn't have many other friends to do "guy" things with, and even though he and Luc came from completely disparate backgrounds, they'd become fast friends.

While they rarely saw each other these days, Dante still valued the friendship they'd forged in college when Dante had been new to the country. Most of the other so-called new friends he'd made in that first year had started hitting him up for loans, making him pay for drinks and food almost immediately upon discovering that his family was one of the wealthiest old families in Spain, and if not for Luc's undemanding, steady friendship, Dante would probably have become a complete recluse.

"Yeah? Have you been thinking about that beer you owe me?" Luc asked, his voice alive with humor. Dante's brow lowered.

"Beer?"

"Rugby match, two months ago?" Luc prompted.

"You're actually serious? I know nothing about rugby. I never stood a chance of winning that bet, and you knew it," Dante protested, grinning like a kid. He was just so damned relieved everything seemed normal with Luc, and if Cleo kept her end of their agreement, it would remain that way.

"Easy pickings," Luc agreed smugly. "But you should never have taken me up on it. Look, come over for dinner tonight, and we can watch the La Liga game afterward. Barcelona versus Real Madrid. You bring the beer."

"Blue doing the cooking?" The woman was a fantastic cook.

"Yep."

"Then it's a deal." Football, food, beer, and a good friend with whom to enjoy it all. Dante couldn't think of a better way to spend the evening.

"So, do you enjoy life in the HR department?" Blue asked Cleo, efficiently chopping up onions and peppers.

"It's only been a month, but I'm finding it quite rewarding. I'm learning a lot." Cleo sat at the ancient kitchen table as she watched her brother's fiancée slice and dice her way through the dinner preparations. Blue was incredibly efficient at cooking. She was efficient at a lot of things, but Cleo—who was useless at cooking—particularly envied the other woman's prowess in the kitchen. She had popped into the ramshackle, sprawling old Knight family home in Hout Bay after work, hoping to score an invitation to dinner. She'd been feeling a bit under the weather lately and hoped that some of Blue's good home cooking would help her feel better.

She had timed it just right. Luc wasn't home from work yet, and Blue had just started with the dinner preparation.

"Do you think you could build a career out of it?" Blue asked as she scraped the diced onions, peppers, and garlic into a pot. They immediately sizzled as they hit the hot oil at the bottom of the pot, filling the kitchen with a delicious aroma.

Cleo fiddled with the handle of the coffee mug in front of her while contemplating the hot chocolate swirling around inside.

"Maybe." She shrugged. "I'm not sure. I was hoping . . ."

Blue glanced at her sharply when her voice trailed off.

"Cleo," she said softly, ever perceptive, "it's been three years."

"I know, but every time I go to the dance studio and put on my pointe shoes, I feel like it's still in there, like I can still dance the way I used to. I keep thinking if I stay fit and keep dancing, keep doing my pointe routines, just keep going, I'll wake up one morning and just *know* that it's back. But with this job . . . there's not enough time to spend on my dancing. I have to devote my attention to either the job or dancing. I can't do both."

"You can dance in your spare time."

"As a hobby, you mean?"

Blue hesitated, before nodding, and Cleo ignored the stab of pain in her chest as she thought about what her friend had said.

"That would mean giving up on the only real dream I've ever had," she whispered.

Blue said nothing for a long time, keeping her hands busy and her eyes averted as she began meticulously peeling potatoes. "Cleo, maybe it's time to find another dream?" Blue finally whispered, and Cleo's heart stuttered in her chest.

"What's for dinner?" Cleo asked, changing the subject clumsily.

"Nothing fancy, just beef stew and mashed potatoes, with bread pudding and custard for dessert."

"Ooh, perfect for a cold, rainy day," Cleo enthused, eyeing the buckets collecting water in the corner. The damned roof leaked like a sieve, and Luc had already set aside some money to have it fixed when the rain eventually stopped, which didn't seem like it would be anytime soon. The old house was right on the beach and had a rustic charm that could possibly have passed for shabby chic, if things were a little less shabby and a lot more chic. Its location made it prime property, but the fact that it had been in their family for generations turned it into a burden that desperately needed fixing up. Cleo was a lot less sentimental than Luc and had urged him to sell it, since he couldn't afford to get married with the damned thing hanging around his neck like an albatross—but her brother had a little more respect for familial obligations than Cleo did.

"Are you staying for dinner?" Blue asked, and Cleo brightened at the invitation she'd been hoping for.

"For your gorgeous beef stew and pud?"

"It's really plain fare. If I'd known Luc was going to be asking Dante around for dinner, I would have planned something with a little more flair. He's not exactly the type of guy you serve beef stew to. Although, he's not at all a snob, is he? The last time he came around to dinner, he schooled your brother in proper manners and cleaned up the kitchen after we ate. He even helped me fix dessert. Seemed to enjoy it, really."

Cleo hadn't heard anything beyond the revelation that Dante Damaso was coming around for dinner and was immediately thankful that she hadn't already agreed to stay for the meal.

"Well, thanks for the invitation, Blue, but—much as I'd love to—I really can't stay. I've been feeling a little under the weather lately. I'm worried I'm coming down with something."

"But you drove all this way. I thought . . ."

"I was in the area for . . . uh." She ground to a halt as she comprehended that there really was no good reason for her to be so far out of her way. "Well, I wanted to see you. I haven't seen much of you since getting back from Tokyo, what with the job change and all. But I underestimated how ill I was feeling. I should go home and get into bed."

"What are your symptoms? Maybe I have something here that can help with them?" Blue was a nurse and had first met Luc eight years before, while he'd still been taking care of their ailing grandparents. Blue had been one of the junior nurses in the oncology ward, and while nothing romantic had flared between them at the time—what with Luc being so preoccupied with the stress of having two extremely ill, elderly people to take care of—he had appreciated the young nurse's kindness and concern. Their relationship had bloomed after the elderly couple had passed away.

Luc was completely smitten with the tall, doe-eyed, caramel-skinned, brown-haired woman and had asked her to marry him a few years after they'd started dating. But he wanted her to have a fantastic wedding, so the wedding date kept getting pushed back due to financial reasons. They'd been engaged way too long, and while Blue was infinitely patient and understanding, Cleo sometimes wanted to give her brother a swift kick in the butt for being so stubborn on the matter of the house.

"Some tummy issues and just general listlessness. Cal was sick last week, and I think I probably caught this from him."

"Okay, then stay hydrated and eat as much broth as you can manage. And get a decent night's sleep tonight," Blue said, stepping into her caregiving role with complete ease. Cleo smiled warmly at the woman before nodding toward the pot sizzling away behind Blue.

"Your onions are burning," she pointed out, and laughed when Blue swore and dashed for the pot.

"Give my brother a hug from me, and tell him I'll see him soon," Cleo instructed as she got up from the table, eager to leave before Dante and Luc showed up. How weird was it that after years of friendship between the two men, she'd nearly run into him in their family home for the first time *ever*? Then again, before her accident, Cleo had hardly been a regular visitor to the house. She'd always been miserable here. She hated how strict her grandparents had been, how she and Luc were never allowed out past seven on a weeknight and nine on a weekend, even when they were in their late teens. Luc had been the ever-obedient good boy, while Cleo had been a rebel—receiving constant censure from their grandparents.

Cleo had left home as soon as she was eighteen and had moved in with a small commune of fellow dancers while attending the University of Cape Town School of Dance, earning the elderly couple's disapproval. Every time she visited home—usually at Luc's behest—she had always wound up arguing with her grandparents, so she regularly made excuses not to visit. Which was something she would regret for the rest of her life.

Cleo moved to hug Blue, who was still cursing over her charred onions, and made her escape before the other woman could offer any further protest.

Dante parked his Jaguar in front of his friend's huge, rather creepy old house at exactly the same time as Luc drove up in his serviceable old Ford sedan. He felt his lips settle into a relaxed grin as he caught the other man's eye. Luc's face lit up with a huge smile as he got out of his car and rounded the trunk to greet Dante as he leisurely climbed out of his own car.

"Hey, howzit?" Luc called, and grabbed Dante's hand for a brief shake before tugging him in for a one-armed hug. "Good to see you, Dan. Ready for tonight's match? Barcelona's going to wipe the floor with Real Madrid."

"Oh, amigo, stick to rugby; you clearly know nothing about soccer."
Dante laughed dismissively at Luc's—frankly ludicrous—prediction,
and just like that it was as if they'd seen each other only yesterday.

Their banter continued all the way into the house and then into the
kitchen, where Luc greeted his gorgeous fiancée with a sweeping kiss,
and Dante followed it up with an only slightly *less* sweeping kiss. This
was the closest thing he had to a proper home in this country, and he'd
always guarded these relationships jealously. The knowledge that he'd
nearly completely fucked it up with everything that had happened with
Cleo was chilling, and he considered himself lucky that he'd managed to
get through that entire sordid situation with this important friendship
still intact.

Beer in hand, he settled back, ready to enjoy his meal and the
companionship for the rest of the evening.

"So what the hell has been going on with you lately?" Luc demanded
of Cleo a month after she had narrowly escaped running into Dante
Damaso in this very house. Thankfully she hadn't seen the man at all
since then. "We've hardly seen you since your return from Tokyo."

"I've been busy with work, and I can't seem to shake this damned
bug. I feel like I've been sick forever," she groused. They were having
dinner around the kitchen table, and delicious though it was, Cleo was
having a hard time keeping it down.

"You *do* look a little paler than usual," Luc said, concerned.

"Do you have to say 'than usual'? You make me sound like Morticia
or a zombie or something."

"She's definitely looking a bit vampirical, isn't she, babe?" he asked
Blue, who nodded somberly despite the laughter dancing in her eyes.

"Is 'vampirical' even a word?" Cleo scoffed.

"If it isn't, then it should be." Luc shrugged.

"I'm just tired and a little depressed because it just never stops raining." They all simultaneously glanced at the ever-present bucket in one corner of the room, which was rapidly filling with water. It had been raining almost nonstop for nearly a week now, and aside from being depressing and cold, it had caused floods, accidents, and illness. Cleo couldn't remember any other winter being this desperately grim before.

"Is this still the same bug as last month?" Blue asked, her pretty brown eyes warming with concern, and Cleo nodded.

"Yes. It's so irritating. It's nothing serious, just a dodgy stomach and a bit of dizziness. It comes and goes."

"There is a stomach bug going around," Blue said. "You can consider yourself lucky if all you're suffering from is dizziness and a bit of nausea. We've practically been swimming in vomit at the office this week."

"*God*, Blue." Luc grimaced, and she grinned unrepentantly. She'd left the hospital a couple of years before and now worked for a private practitioner. The job offered better hours and a much better salary.

"Sorry." Blue grinned, and Luc rolled his eyes, unable to even pretend to be mad at her when she flashed those dimples at him.

"Well you *have* lost some weight over this past month." Blue was all seriousness again as she gave Cleo a critical once-over. "Weight that you can't really afford to lose. Have you been throwing up a lot?"

"Right, I'm done." Luc tossed aside his napkin and got up, collecting his and Blue's empty plates along the way and dumping them in the sink.

"Not that much," Cleo said, ignoring her brother, who was pointedly clearing the table and piling more dishes in the sink. "Just a couple of times a day, really."

"Headaches? Fever?"

Cleo shook her head. Blue gave her a speculative look before glancing over at Luc, who was now doing the dishes.

"Hey, I wanted your opinion on this dress I bought the other day." Blue changed the subject abruptly, and Cleo raised her eyebrows in surprise. Luc glanced up.

"What dress?" he asked.

"It's a surprise. You don't get to see it until our anniversary dinner next week." She gave him a sexy little look over her shoulder, and he practically frothed at the mouth in response. Which was an exchange Cleo would rather not have witnessed. Blue grabbed Cleo's hand and dragged her from the kitchen, up the creaking staircase, only to let go once they were in her and Luc's huge bedroom, which was also filled with brimming buckets and pots. She shut the door firmly behind them.

"This better be one hell of a dress, Blue," Cleo warned, rubbing at her shoulder. "I think you've just about dislocated my shoulder."

"Never mind the dress." Blue waved her hand dismissively. "How do you feel after the dinner we just had? Any nausea?"

"Not right now," she replied, still massaging her shoulder.

"Any other tummy issues? Maybe down at the other end?

"Gross. No."

"No fever, no headaches, just nausea and dizziness?"

"What, is there some delayed echo in here?" Cleo asked sarcastically, and Blue glared at her.

"I'm working up to something here, okay?" she hissed. "Let me do my thing."

"Get to the point, will you?"

"Fine! But don't snap my head off when I ask my next question."

"Oh my God, you're so dramatic," Cleo teased. "How did my practical brother wind up with such a drama queen? Just ask the question."

"When was your last period?"

All thought fled Cleo's mind as her knees buckled and she sank down onto the bed. Blue's question hit her like a ton of bricks, and she finally understood what her friend was leading up to.

She did some frantic calculations and came to the realization that she couldn't even remember when she'd last had her period! She'd been so preoccupied with the new job, her weird illness, and the fact that she stupidly missed seeing Dante Damaso more than she had ever expected. Dante bloody Damaso, who may well have knocked her up!

"Cleo? Is it possible that you're pregnant?" Blue asked quietly, and Cleo raised a hand to her mouth, her eyes wide with absolute fear.

"It's possible," she whispered. "But not likely. I mean, we used condoms."

"They're not a hundred percent effective," Blue murmured, and sat down beside Cleo to wrap an arm around her narrow shoulders. "It's just a theory. You could still just have a stomach bug."

No, now that Blue had raised the possibility, Cleo didn't see it being anything else.

"I haven't had my period in a while," she confessed.

"If you don't mind me asking . . ." Oh, Cleo knew what was coming next and braced herself for it. "If you *are* pregnant, who's the father? You haven't been dating anyone. *Have* you?"

"That's not important," she whispered. God, she felt completely sick. "If I am . . . if there is—" She shook her head, unable to formulate the words. "He won't be involved."

"Well," Blue said after a moment, "before we get ahead of ourselves, we should probably confirm that you're actually pregnant."

"Right," Cleo whispered. She felt . . . numb, with an underlying sense of dread and confusion. How was she supposed to cope with this? She would make a terrible mother. She would be a complete failure at it, just like her own mother had been. And to do it on her own, without a partner to support her . . . she would totally mess up the kid.

"Oh my *God*, Blue," she finally said, a sob escaping from behind the hand over her mouth. "How can I be a mother? How do I support a baby? What if I forget to feed it? Or if it gets sick and I can't tell that something's wrong? My salary only barely covers the rent and food for the month. How will I afford nappies and clothes and other baby stuff? Babies need a lot of stuff, don't they?" She could hear her voice rising hysterically with each question, and Blue's other arm came up to enclose her in a warm and comforting hug.

When she stepped into the tiny flat she shared with Cal in Newlands, her slender shoulders drooped beneath the crushing weight of depression. A quick glance around was enough to nearly send her to her knees in despair. How could she bring a baby into *this* place? It was a tiny one-bedroom flat with an open-plan kitchen and living room. Cal slept in the living room, but he never bothered to put away the bedding, and the sleeper couch was strewn with his clothing. There were empty takeout cartons scattered about; the half-eaten bowl of popcorn she'd made for a movie three nights ago still stood on the coffee table where she'd left it. The sink was piled high with dishes, and the place smelled stale and a little damp.

Cal wasn't home and she hoped he was out job hunting if he wasn't auditioning somewhere. She knew an audition was probably highly unlikely because, knowing Cal, he would have been talking about it for days before it actually happened. But Cal had developed a reputation within their small dancing community of being problematic. It was getting harder and harder for him to dance with independent groups because word had gotten around about him. He'd once had a position with a contemporary dance troupe and blew it when, after one lead, he started making impossible demands. Cleo wished that he would stop sabotaging himself, but it was difficult to talk to him about the situation. He got ridiculously defensive and would storm off in a sulk for hours—sometimes *days*—on end.

Cleo sighed, not in the mood to further speculate about her roommate's possible whereabouts, and wearily made her way into her tiny bedroom. It was a total wreck. The bed was unmade and buried beneath a mound of clothing; her wardrobe was open, with even more clothes spilling out of it. At least there were no weeks-old cartons of food in here; Cleo never ate in her bedroom.

She pushed some of the clothing aside and sank down into the space she'd just created, buried her face in her hands, and cried for what seemed like the hundredth time in the past twenty-four hours. After getting it out of her system, she trudged to the bathroom for her shower, determined to be a little less mopey. She probably wasn't pregnant and her period was just late, due any day now, which would explain the mood swings and the weird bouts of crying.

Just PMS, that was all.

⁓

"You're definitely pregnant." Cleo stared at the OB/GYN in dismay, her hand gripping Blue's so tightly it actually hurt. "Early days yet, just heading into the eighth week, I'd say. That would place the delivery date somewhere in March. Sound about right to you?"

She nodded dumbly, her eyes blurring, and Dr. Klein's gaze sharpened. "I take it this news is . . . unexpected?" When Cleo nodded again, the doctor reached into her desk drawer, removed a few colorful pamphlets, and handed them over to Cleo. "Then you undoubtedly have a great deal to consider. You have options ranging from adoption to termination. Should you decide to keep the baby, there are single-mother support groups, which would help you feel less alone. In the meantime, until you decide what to do, you have to take care of yourself. Prenatal vitamins are essential, and so is the correct diet. You're quite small and definitely underweight. I want you to start eating three meals a day."

"I would if I didn't keep throwing up at random times," Cleo muttered bitterly, and the doctor smiled.

"Morning sickness can be exceedingly draining," the doctor said sympathetically. "Eat slowly. A few crackers can work wonders. There are a few effective methods to reduce the nausea, which are covered in one of the pamphlets I gave you. If natural remedies don't work to alleviate the symptoms and the nausea is persistent throughout the day, come back and I'll prescribe a safe antiemetic. Don't purchase over-the-counter medicines, as they can be harmful to the baby." The doctor rambled on for a bit longer, talking about the changes Cleo could expect in her body, suggesting reading material, and finally warning that if she opted for termination of the pregnancy, she shouldn't wait too long.

The doctor eventually stopped talking long enough to give Cleo a *very* thorough physical exam, with a urine check, blood test, a PAP smear, and so many other invasive little pokes and prods that Cleo eventually stopped listening to the doctor's explanations about what she was doing and why. She just wanted to go home and pretend this day had never happened.

When the lengthy prenatal exam ended, the doctor sat them down once again.

"Vivian, my receptionist, will schedule your next appointment—we'll do a dating ultrasound just to make sure we have an accurate idea of the baby's due date. After that ultrasound, I'll expect to see you once a month," she said. "But once you've recovered a little from the shock, please consider contacting one of those single-mother groups I spoke about earlier. It could help you with your decision making."

Cleo kept her eyes on her plate throughout the late lunch Blue had dragged her to. She was vaguely aware of Blue calling her boss to say that she would be late back to the office, and Cleo felt a pang of guilt for keeping the woman away from her work. But at the same time she felt wholly incapable of functioning in any normal capacity.

"I don't know what I'm going to do," she whispered, after half an hour of staring at her healthy green salad going limp in its bowl. Blue reached across the table and gave her hand a reassuring squeeze.

"Luc and I will always be here for you, Cleo," she said, and Cleo groaned.

"Luc is going to be so disappointed." Her brother loved her and would support her through whatever decision she made, but he would want more for her than this. Twenty-seven years old and accidentally pregnant? This was what they would have expected from her during her rebellious teen phase, not now that she was finally getting her life sorted out. Despite still desperately clinging to her dancing, she did enjoy her new job—she found it challenging and interesting. Mr. Whitman was worlds away from Dante as a boss, and he was happy to train her as they went along. He was also exceedingly grateful for the introduction to Mrs. Clarke. The two had now been on three dates and were already talking about the next one.

She hadn't seen or heard from Dante Damaso since that last day in his office. Well . . . she had seen and heard *of* him. Seen him in magazines and newspapers with a different leggy beauty on his arm in every picture, and heard chatter about him around the office. But it was like she had never really known him, never spent hours in his bed, never experienced absolute sexual bliss in his arms. It had started to take on a fairy-tale, dreamlike quality in her mind, like it hadn't really happened, but now this baby proved it *had* happened and it had very real consequences.

"So the dad is definitely out of the picture?" Blue asked hesitantly.

"Very much so," Cleo responded in a voice that encouraged no further questions. But Blue had known her too long to be put off.

"Are you going to tell him about the baby?" she pushed.

"I don't know. It depends on whether I decide to keep it or not."

"But if *you* don't want it, he might," Blue pointed out. Cleo considered that for a moment before thinking about Dante's jet-setting lifestyle and the constant stream of women parading through his life, and knew that the last thing he would want was a baby to cramp his style.

"He won't want it," Cleo said definitively.

"How do you know that?"

"Look, he and I may not have been serious, but I know him better than you do, Blue. He won't want this baby."

"So which decision are you leaning toward?"

"I don't know," Cleo admitted miserably. "I just don't know."

"You still have some time to think about it, Cleo," Blue murmured. "You don't have to decide right at this moment."

"I feel so stupid."

"It was an accident. These things happen."

"To teenagers, not to grown women who should have their crap together by now. I've failed at everything else, Blue. Imagine how spectacularly I'd fail at motherhood. This poor baby doesn't stand a chance with me as its mother."

"That's nonsense," Blue dismissed, showing rare signs of anger. "You're kind, considerate, loving, generous with your affection, and while things haven't always gone your way, you found ways to cope. You have always bounced back and found a way forward. You'll do the same this time."

"I've been completely directionless since I stopped dancing," Cleo confessed quietly. "I've felt so lost and I've tried to hide it, but even though it has been years, I still haven't found anything to fill the void it left in my life. I've even considered becoming a dance instructor, but I don't know if I can stand to teach others to do what I no longer can. How pathetic is that? To think that I could be jealous or resentful of some talented young dancer just because I lost my opportunity to be the best at it. It makes me feel petty and small and ugly. How could I ever be a good teacher if I don't want my students to soar higher than I did?"

"Cleo, I love you, but sometimes you frustrate me so much," Blue said. "I can't talk to you when you're in this mood. I can't listen to you beat yourself up over things that are completely beyond your control. Eat your lunch and tell me how the living situation with Cal is going."

Cleo grimaced, the change in subject adding to her depression.

"That bad, huh?"

"Sometimes it's so draining to have him around." And it would be worse now with all this on her plate. His self-centeredness was so frustrating. He hadn't even noticed how ill she'd been feeling recently. Cleo knew that she had once been as egocentric as Cal and was grateful that she had developed enough self-awareness to appreciate that the world did *not* revolve around her. Cal, at thirty-two, had still not come to that realization, and Cleo doubted he ever would.

"Have you considered asking him to move out?" Blue asked tactfully.

"He has nowhere else to go."

"Cleo, sometimes you have to think of your own needs," Blue pointed out, and Cleo scoffed.

"I spent most of my life being selfish and thinking of my own needs, to the detriment of others. When I look back on how I was, how much I took my grandparents and Luc and everything they sacrificed for me for granted, I'm so ashamed. When you met Luc, he was taking care of my grandparents 24-7, he only ever took time for his studies. He used to *beg* me to come home, to come and visit my grandparents." Cleo kept her eyes downcast as she spoke. She knew that Blue had probably heard all of this from Luc, but knowing her brother, he had sugarcoated the facts, and right now, Cleo wanted her friend to hear the ugly, unadorned truth about her. "And I never did. I was always too busy, having too much fun, practicing too hard. I made excuses not to visit because I didn't want to deal with their constant disapproval. I always felt like nothing I did was right.

"So I stayed away and left Luc to deal with it all, and only toward the end did I finally relent and visit them." She choked back a sob. "And they were *so* old and so obviously dying, but they were so *grateful*." Her voice broke on the word as tears seeped down her cheeks and dripped into her salad. "Just so grateful and happy that I'd come to visit them. There were no recriminations, only warmth and love and pure happiness. And I felt like such an imposter: their beautiful little ballerina who was so *ugly* on the inside. All those years I spent resenting them when all they ever wanted was my happiness. I can't go back to being that awful person. Cal did a lot for me after my accident, and I won't turn my back on him when he needs me."

Blue reached out to squeeze Cleo's hands. They were silent for a while, Blue patiently waiting for Cleo to gather herself before changing the subject to her and Luc's upcoming anniversary, and about the dress she was thinking of buying. It was a welcome change in topic, but it didn't take Cleo's mind completely off her problems.

After Cleo returned home, she went into her bedroom, pushed the pile of clothing off the bed, and curled up in the center of it, trying to make herself as small as possible. She placed her palm over the flat expanse of her abdomen and gently applied pressure, trying to feel this tiny presence, which had made such a huge impact on her life. She felt nothing and it was hard to imagine anything in there, yet it was there. It existed.

At nearly eight weeks—according to the literature Dr. Klein had given her—it was smaller than a kidney bean but was developing tiny little webbed fingers and toes and eyelids. It was alive and moving even if she couldn't feel it. She lifted her hands to her face and found it wet with tears. Her baby was alive and it needed her. It depended on her for food, for oxygen, for its very *existence*, and she couldn't make the decision to snuff out that tiny life.

And just like that, terminating the pregnancy was no longer an option.

If she were younger, who knows what her decision would have been. But she was twenty-seven and—despite all her dreams to the contrary— realistically speaking, she didn't have a dance career to think of anymore, and she was no longer the same selfish Cleo she had been years ago. She still didn't know if she would keep it or put it up for adoption, but now that the immediate decision of having or terminating had been taken care of, the pressure of making any other urgent decisions had been relieved a bit. She had time to figure that out. She still didn't think she would make a good mother, but there were so many other women out there who would die for the opportunity to have a baby to love and take care of.

Cleo fell asleep clinging to that positive thought.

⁓

When she woke up a couple of hours later, it was early evening, and the light was starting to go. Cleo immediately called Blue and told her that she planned to have the baby.

"I know it couldn't have been an easy decision to make, but Luc, your friends, and I are all here for you." Blue's warm voice washed over her, soothing her and making her feel so much better about the choice she'd made.

"How do I tell Luc?" Cleo wondered miserably.

"Your brother will understand. He's not entirely unreasonable, you know?" the other woman teased, and Cleo made a sound that was half laugh and half sob.

"He'll be gutted."

"He'll get over it."

"I'm coming to see you guys; I think it's best to get this over and done with," Cleo decided.

"No. We'll come to you. I'd just feel better if you weren't driving in these conditions while you're so distracted," Blue said firmly, and hung up before Cleo could protest.

She got up from bed slowly, alarmed when her head spun and her stomach roiled in protest at the movement.

"*Morning* sickness, my butt," she muttered beneath her breath. The term was a complete misnomer. She sat quietly and breathed deeply to try and regain her equilibrium. When she felt steadier, she made her way to the door and peeked into the living room. Cal was sitting on the couch, making out with some guy Cleo had never seen before.

They didn't even notice when Cleo stepped into the room and only—leisurely—ended their kiss when she cleared her throat pointedly.

"Hi, hon," Cal greeted cheerfully. "This is the guy I told you about. Greg."

"Oh, Greg, yes. Cal never stops talking about you," she lied. Greg—a good-looking guy about ten years Cal's junior—smiled sweetly. He had stars in his eyes as he looked at Cal. Poor kid.

Cleo turned toward the kitchen and was gratified to note that Cal had tidied up a bit while she was asleep, probably in anticipation of Greg's visit. Cal left Greg on the couch and joined Cleo in the kitchen.

"Hey, hon, I hope you don't mind us chilling here for the evening," he said casually, clearly not really concerned with Cleo's response. "But Greg still lives at home, so we couldn't hook up there."

"He lives at home? How old is he?" She looked at Greg again and reevaluated her initial assessment of his age.

"Nineteen? Twenty? Something like that." Cal waved a dismissive hand. "Isn't he adorable, though?"

"Cal, he's a baby," Cleo hissed impatiently. She was getting a little fed up with her friend's casual hookups. "When are you going to stop messing around with these little toy boys and find a decent—age-appropriate—guy?"

"Age-appropriate guys aren't fun and lack stamina," he whispered smugly. "What Greg lacks in experience, he makes up for in enthusiasm."

"Look, you and young Greg are going to have to go someplace else tonight. I'm expecting guests," she said, and Cal's eyebrows rose. "Guests?"

"Luc and Blue are coming," she explained, and Cal rolled his eyes.

"They're hardly guests. They won't mind if Greg and I are hanging around."

"Cal, I have something really important to discuss with Luc; I just need a bit of privacy."

"Since when do you have secrets from *me*?" he teased.

Cleo's patience just snapped. "Since *now*, okay?"

Cal took a step back and his face froze over.

"No need to lash out," he said icily. "Keep your precious secrets. Greg, babe, we're going out. We're not *welcome* here."

The passive-aggressive comment was *so* typical of him.

"Cal," she said miserably, and he held up a hand, still not looking at her.

"It's okay, Cleo. This is *your* flat, and you have every right to want it to yourself sometimes. I'm sure Greg and I will find someplace to go in this weather. Right, babe?" Greg's pretty blue eyes were wide and confused, but he nodded.

"It's just for a couple of hours," she explained. "I'll text you when they leave."

"Whatever." He shrugged, grabbing his coat. She tried her best to shove aside the guilt as he and the hapless young Greg left. She really didn't need Cal's drama right now, but that's how he always was, and she continually made excuses for him.

"Who's the father?" Luc asked. He had been grim and silent when Cleo told him about her pregnancy and had remained that way for nearly five minutes after she had stuttered to a halt. She had never seen her normally amicable brother so quiet and unreadable before. Blue had filled the silence with slightly nervous chatter about the weather and the new leaks they'd discovered in the roof, all the while darting uncertain glances at Luc like he was a ticking time bomb about to go off. And now, when he finally spoke, his voice was cold enough to freeze the air around him.

"His identity is unimportant," Cleo said, trying to keep her voice from wobbling.

"You *do* know who the father is, right?" The question was designed to wound, and Cleo felt the impact of it like a blow to her sternum. She gasped and folded in on herself defensively.

"Lucius Knight!" Blue barked, angrier than Cleo had ever seen her before. "You should be ashamed of yourself."

To his credit, Luc looked immediately contrite.

"I'm sorry, Cleo, that was unfair of me," he mumbled. "I'm just angry and frustrated. I hate to see you in a situation like this, with the loser who got you pregnant having zero accountability."

"It's my choice, Luc."

He nodded curtly, his jaw tight. He still looked angry and disappointed, and it killed her to have put that look on his face.

"So you're having it but not sure if you're keeping it?" he said after a long pause, during which he'd done nothing but stare at her intently and stroke his thumbs restlessly across the back of her hands.

"Yes."

"When do you think you'll know?"

"I'm not sure. I have no feelings about this baby one way or another. I just feel trapped and confused and scared and so *stupid* right now." Her voice was thick with tears.

"Oh, Pattypan," Luc sighed, and dragged her into his arms for a comforting hug. The childhood nickname—one he'd come up with because she hated her full name—brought tears to her eyes, and she sobbed into his chest, suddenly feeling years younger than her age. "We'll figure this out. I promise you that."

Cleo allowed herself to lean on him for a second longer, knowing that her big brother would always have her back. She had never loved or appreciated him more than in that moment.

CHAPTER SIX

Cal was still pointedly ignoring her when he returned to the flat, sans Greg, much later that night.

"Hey," Cleo greeted tentatively, even though she found his wounded air annoying.

"Oh. Hey," he replied, as if he'd only just noticed her sitting on the lone chair in the living room, an overstuffed monstrosity that she'd purchased at a thrift store.

"So . . . I'm pregnant," she blurted, and he froze on his way to the bathroom. He turned to face her, his mouth gaping and his eyes just about popping out of his skull.

"Shut *up*. You're shitting me, right?" He always got so American teen when he was surprised by something. It was equal parts endearing and exasperating. "Oh my God. No wonder you've been such a *bitch* lately."

"Wow, thanks," she said with a grin. She couldn't help it; his irreverence and honesty always made her smile.

"Well, you have." He forgot all about his need to go to the bathroom and sank down onto his sleeper couch opposite her chair. "Are you keeping it?"

"I don't know."

"Are you thinking about terminating the pregnancy?"

"I *was* thinking about it, but decided against it. It's not a choice that sits well with me, not at this point in my life."

"Fair enough," he said. "So adoption is still in the cards?"

"Yes."

"Have you considered telling the da . . . *Ohmygod*, is Dante Damaso the father?" His voice rose dramatically on the last syllable, and she winced.

"What do you think?"

"I think you should keep the kid and let baby daddy fork out loads to take care of you both," he said, as if she were crazy to even consider any other option.

"Yeah. No. I'm not that mercenary."

"Did you get pregnant deliberately?" Cal asked pointedly.

"Of course not. It was probably a stupid faulty condom."

"And who, pray tell, took care of the condoms?"

"He did."

"Then *why* are you stressing about this? You didn't ask to get pregnant; this is as much his fault as it is yours—*more* his than yours, in fact. You trusted him to take care of your protection. I mean, you could have caught all kinds of nasty diseases because of that one dodgy condom." Cal *would* be the one to think of gritty realities like that. But Cleo didn't think she'd caught anything other than a bad case of pregnant from Dante—the man was too fastidious.

"The doctor tested for those today," she said listlessly, remembering Dr. Klein explaining what some of the blood draws were for. She wasn't particularly concerned that they would find anything untoward.

"So, you're going to be like those impractical chicks in the romance novels, all super strong and independent: 'I don't need no stinking man and his stinking money to take care of me and my stinking baby'?" Cal asked after a while. "And while their men are rolling in dough, they're living in poverty—because they're good girls and taking his money would seem greedy, right?"

Cleo didn't respond. When Cal was off on a tangent, it was best to let it run its course.

"Because that's just plain *bollocks*. The guy was there when this kid was made; he should damned well own up to that and help you out."

"I don't even know if I'm keeping the baby," Cleo said weakly.

"Hmm. Just don't be a fool, Cleo. False pride never helped anybody."

"Look, I only learned about this pregnancy today, Cal," she said, exhausted. "I need time to think about some things."

"Yeah, and one of the things you need to think about is the fact that this baby's father isn't exactly impoverished, and if you wanted to keep it, there's no reason he couldn't support his child."

"Enough." She held up a hand and rubbed her forehead with the other hand. She was developing a splitting headache. "I'm going to bed. Good night."

For the next couple of weeks, Cleo felt like someone who was swimming in ether. She couldn't get her head together. She felt like she was living in a weird otherworld where nothing made sense—up was down, left was right, and she was carrying Dante Damaso's baby. She kept expecting to wake up and heave a huge sigh of relief because of the outrageous dream she'd had, but that never happened. Every day she faced the same crazy reality. Worse, her pregnancy made itself felt in all the nastiest ways: constant morning sickness; a severe lack of energy; lack of sleep; bloating; tender, swollen breasts—just about every symptom she'd read about, she had. It was crazy, annoying, and more than a little unbearable.

Every Sunday night she picked up her secondhand copy of a handy week-to-week pregnancy guide she'd bought at a bargain bookshop and read up on what she could expect over the next week. She found it fascinating how fast the baby was developing every week, but she found the changes in her body slightly less fascinating.

Cal was still pressuring her to tell Dante, while Blue and Luc's stoic refusal to ask about her decision had the opposite intended effect. She felt more pressured by their unwavering, silent support.

She put all of that out of her mind and focused on her book, wanting to see where the baby was this week. The most exciting news was that it should now have perfect little fingers with fingernails starting to grow in. Her hand rubbed her flat abdomen in wonder as she pictured those tiny fingers with their soft, brand-new little fingernails. If it was a girl, someday—years from now—she might take an interest in manicures and want pretty painted nails. If it was a boy, he might like working with his hands and getting dirt under those nails. Or maybe vice versa. Who knew?

Cleo fell asleep thinking about those tiny perfect hands.

It was the fingernails that did it. Cleo could not stop thinking about them. She fell in love with those fingernails and their tiny fingers on their equally tiny hands. And over the course of the next week, she stopped thinking of it as "the baby." It had become "my baby."

It was a seemingly trifling change in thinking but it had major implications. The baby was now *hers*, and she couldn't imagine anyone else loving it or taking care of it. There was no longer a choice. She was keeping it.

And Dante was entitled to know about the baby.

But first she would have to think about how she would go about this. She had to make it perfectly clear that his responsibility began and ended with the baby. She wanted what was best for her baby, and what was best was for the father to provide some kind of financial support.

She wasn't looking for some huge payday, even though she knew he would think otherwise.

⁓

Two weeks later, during her twelfth week of pregnancy, Cleo was sitting in the waiting area of Dante's office, smiling nervously at Mrs. Clarke. The woman—currently sporting a gigantic diamond on her ring finger courtesy of Mr. Whitman, who had proposed after just a month of "courting"—had happily agreed to help Cleo sneak in a visit with Dante. Cleo didn't want him to know she was coming, didn't want him to speculate about the purpose of her visit, so here she was . . . ready to turn his carefree bachelor existence upside down.

"He'll be done with that conference call in about ten minutes, dear," Mrs. Clarke informed her. "Would you like a cup of coffee or tea while you wait?"

"No, thank you, Mrs. Clarke, I'll be fine." As much as Cleo would have loved a cup of herbal tea to settle her nerves, her bladder had become ridiculously small over the last few weeks. She couldn't trust herself not to need a bathroom within minutes and miss her window of opportunity.

She was nervous about seeing Dante again, not just because of the news she had, but because she couldn't help wondering if that crazy chemistry would still sizzle between them. She didn't understand this attraction they had for each other. How could you want someone so desperately while disliking them so intensely? It was bizarre. Well, whether the chemistry still existed or not was a moot point; this baby would take care of any lingering desire soon enough. Dante was about to regret the day he'd met her.

She was nervously twiddling her thumbs when Mrs. Clarke looked up at her.

"You can go in now, Cleo. And please bring this to Mr. Damaso."
She handed Cleo a folder. Cleo straightened her skirt before taking the
folder with trembling fingers.

She halted outside of those intimidating walnut oak doors, straightened her shoulders, and, after a cursory knock, let herself in. His dark
head was bent as he focused on his phone, and he didn't so much as
glance up while she hovered awkwardly just inside the doors. She was
so enthralled by the sight of him that when he spoke, she nearly jumped
out of her skin.

"Just leave the folder on my desk, Mrs. Clarke," he said irritably,
head still down. When she made no move to obey him, completely
unable to unstick her frozen feet from the floor, he glanced up with
an imposing frown. The frown deepened into a scowl when he saw her.
That scowl certainly didn't bode well for the future of this meeting. At
first, he just stared at her, making her wonder if he'd forgotten her name
again, but after a few excruciatingly long moments, he finally spoke.

"What are you doing here, Knight? I'm busy."

"I'm aware of that, but I need to speak with you."

"I don't have time for idle chitchat," he said dismissively. "And quite
frankly, I don't care what this is about. If you have any grievances about
Whitman or your new position, take them up with Whitman's second
in HR. Just because we happened to have a *thing* at some point doesn't
entitle you to special privileges."

"I don't want special privileges," she said automatically and then
hesitated because she kind of *did* want special privileges. That slight
hesitation put her on the defensive, and she grappled desperately for a
way to regain momentum. She walked toward his desk and sat down in
the same chair she had once sunk down into in a postcoital blaze. The
memory of that morning was enough to stain her cheeks red, and
the dilation of his pupils and tightening of his jaw told her he knew
exactly why she was blushing. They both took a moment to lose themselves
in that raunchy memory before Dante snapped back to reality.

"You need to leave."

"Not before I say what I came here to say," she maintained stubbornly.

"I told you, I'm busy."

"I don't care," she snapped, and then regretted her tone when he tensed and his eyes narrowed with temper. "Look, I'm sorry to intrude, but I really have something important to tell you."

"I can't think of anything you'd have to say that could possibly be of interest to me," he growled, and settled back into his chair. He positioned his elbows on the armrests and steepled his hands just in front of his face. It made him look like a movie villain, which—she supposed—was the point. "But if you *really* think it's that important, make an appointment. My time is precious, and I have no room in my schedule for you today. That will be all. Good day."

She watched as he unfolded his tall frame and leaned forward to grab his phone and the folder she had dropped on the desk. She was so shocked by the rude dismissal that all she could do was gape at him as he got up and started to round the desk, clearly intending to leave the office.

She jumped up and moved into his path. When he casually stepped right past her, she did the only thing she could think of. She ran to the door before he could get there and pinned her back against it with her arms spread out. He stopped directly in front of her; there wasn't much more than a foot between them.

"Knight, I won't hesitate to call security," he warned. "You're starting to get on my nerves."

"I'm pregnant," she blurted, and the look of horror on his face would have been comical if Cleo wasn't so damned anxious about his response.

"*Qué?*" He exploded hoarsely. "*Qué dijiste?*"

"I'm sorry. I don't . . ."

"What did you say?" he repeated in English, his voice brittle.

"You heard me," she said, keeping her chin up and defiant. "I'm pregnant."

"I wish to know what you think you will gain from telling me this news. Is this some kind of joke?"

"It's no joke; I'm pregnant."

"Very well. Let us play this game." He shrugged. "Who is the father of this child you carry?"

"You are."

"*Sé que mientes! Te conozco muy bien.*" The frigid outpouring of Spanish told her more than anything else how much she had rattled him and how angry he was. He turned away from her and strode back to his desk, probably in an effort to put as much distance as possible between them.

"You're lying to me," he grated after he had the length of the office and a desk between them. "I like being lied to even less than I like being blatantly manipulated."

"I'm not lying." She tried to sound calm even though she felt far from it on the inside. This was exactly the reaction she'd been expecting. She warily—and on unsteady legs—made her own way to the desk. She sank back into the chair simply because her legs could no longer support her.

"This is so much bullshit. I suggest you leave this office before I call security, and I want you to vacate the building in under an hour. You're fired."

Her knees shook so badly they were practically knocking together, and her teeth were rattling in her head as shock caused her to quiver.

"You can't fire me," she whispered. "That's completely unethical."

"Not as unethical as what you're trying to do right now. Don't bother to work out a month's notice either. We'll pay you a month's salary in lieu of notice. Using our past intimacy in this way is a complete betrayal. I no longer trust you to work for this company, I no longer believe that you are an ethical person, and I cannot have someone like you employed here."

"I'm pregnant, with *your* baby," she said adamantly, and he swore before picking up his phone and punching in a number.

"Send security up to my office, *immediately*," he barked at whoever happened to be at the other end of the line.

"You need to hear me out, Dante," she said earnestly. This wasn't at all how she had expected this meeting to go. She'd known he would be upset, but this reaction was extreme even for Dante.

"I am Mr. Damaso to you," he flared arrogantly, and she snorted.

"*Fine.* Mr. Damaso, one of your condoms failed, and one of your overambitious little soldiers found its mark and left me knocked up." She spoke fast, aware that time was a limited commodity. He moved away from the desk and turned his back on her, staring out the window and refusing to acknowledge her words. But Cleo kept talking. "I'm keeping my baby. I don't want you to be a part of his life, and I don't want you to give me a huge amount of money." He swiveled back to face her at that pronouncement, his expression insultingly skeptical.

"Not a *huge* amount, but some, right?" He mocked.

"Well, yes. Of course."

"Of course." There was a world of sarcasm in those two words.

"Not a lot, a monthly allowance that will go only to this baby's health and well-being. I didn't ask for this, I didn't intend to get pregnant, but now that the baby is here, I can't do anything else but keep it and love it. But I can't afford to take care of a child without some sort of support from you."

"If you don't leave my office immediately, it will be rather embarrassing for you when security drags you out," he said coldly.

"Dante . . . Mr. Damaso, look—"

He held up a palm, and it shut her up immediately.

"*Mierda!* Enough! Enough of this now, Miss Knight. It was a good attempt to fleece me but hardly very original. I suggest you go back to the real father of your child—that blond giant, perhaps?—and hit him up for some cash. Unless the two of you hatched this scheme up together?"

He thought *Cal* was her baby's father? She would have laughed at that if this whole situation weren't so damned tragic.

She pulled an envelope from her shoulder bag and dropped it on his desk.

"Please read these documents I've had drawn up when you have the time. I understand that this has come as a complete shock to you, but maybe after you've calmed down, you'll be able to approach this situation in a more rational and calm manner."

"I am more than *rational* and *calm*, Miss Knight. I can see quite clearly what's happening here."

"Nonetheless, I'll leave these here."

Two burly uniformed security guards finally stepped into his office, and he glared at them.

"Your response time is appalling," he gritted. "I could have been murdered up here while you dawdled over your coffee and doughnuts."

The two men apologized profusely, and he shut them up with a wave of his hand.

"See Miss Knight back to her desk, wait while she packs her personal items, and escort her out of the building. I want her gone within the hour."

"Yes, sir," one huge guy responded curtly while the other slanted her a sympathetic sideways glance.

They approached her chair and flanked her, and one of them dropped a hand on her shoulder.

"Do *not* touch her." Dante surprised them all by snapping out the command.

"Sorry," the security guard mumbled awkwardly.

"You need to come with us, miss," the other guy said, and Cleo nodded, feeling defeated and exhausted. Her hand dropped protectively to her flat abdomen; the gesture was unconscious and seemed to draw his eye and darken his expression even further. She pushed herself up tiredly and grabbed one brawny guard's arm for support as she swayed slightly. She held on to him as they both escorted her out of his office. She could feel Dante's eyes boring into her back as she left, but she refused to look back. If this was how he wanted it, then so be it. She would find a way to look after her baby without his help. Dante Damaso be damned.

 ⌒

Dante dragged both hands through his hair and gulped in a deep, semicalming breath. The nerve of her. The goddamned, absolute *gall* of her.

Who the hell did she think she was? Who did she think *he* was? Some naïve fool who would fall for such a ridiculous and obvious ploy? He was absolutely livid. He wanted to wring her duplicitous little neck with both hands.

He leaped into action, jumping out of his chair and striding determinedly toward the doors. Halfway there he turned back and grabbed the envelope she left on his desk. He didn't even want to look at it, but he'd need to show it to Mike Grayson, his personal attorney.

He glared at Mrs. Clarke on his way out.

"You and I will have words later about the type of riffraff you allow into my office, Mrs. Clarke," he snapped, and the woman paled in response to his words. He was too furious to take even the mildest satisfaction in that reaction.

 ⌒

Two hours didn't do much to calm his temper. He found himself sitting across from Mike Grayson, still wearing the glare that felt like it had taken up permanent residence on his face. Mike had been startled to see his biggest client walk into his office earlier. Mike usually came to Dante, never vice versa. The fact that he had stormed into the man's office defying their usual protocol spoke to Dante's current frame of mind. He felt completely . . . discombobulated. He was annoyed with himself for not seeing this coming. Surely he should have sensed this mercenary streak in her? He usually had a better nose for these things. When she had signed that nondisclosure agreement without much protest, he had considered himself in the clear. But he had completely underestimated the lengths some women would go to for a little bit of his wealth.

"I have to say, it's a pretty fair deal," the other man said. Exactly what Dante did *not* want to hear.

"She wants a monthly stipend from the baby's birth right up until its eighteenth birthday or until she marries, whichever comes first. She asks for only enough to take care of basic necessities: food, clothing, and medical bills—for the child, not for her. She asks for an increase to cover school fees and other necessities when the child is old enough. There is, of course, interest applied commensurate to whatever changes take place in the economy. And she wants these only if a paternity test proves that you are indeed the child's father."

Dante's jaw dropped. Why make that stipulation unless she was absolutely certain he was the child's father? Had she sabotaged his condoms somehow? He immediately discounted that possibility. They had never left his possession, and he was always the one to don them, without exception. Ever. He couldn't chance an accidental fingernail through the latex. He had learned that lesson the hard way, when he had caught one of his former lovers blatantly trying to break a condom while supposedly "fumbling" with it as she tried to sheathe him. Having escaped that particular trap, Dante had never allowed for the possibility again. No woman ever got her hands on his condoms.

Which meant, if this baby was his, it was because his method of protection had failed. He had always known condoms were not 100 percent foolproof, but he had considered the risk negligible. Until now.

He shook his head, disgusted with himself, with her, with the whole bloody world.

"I don't want to be a dad," he growled. "Is there any way to get her to . . ." He couldn't verbalize it. It made him feel like a louse.

"Well, she's got you covered there too," Mike said, sounding almost admiring. "All you have to do is agree to these terms, sign this paper, and she's happy to forget you were even there at its conception. All financial transactions will be done through your attorney and hers. The baby will have her name, and the father shall remain undisclosed. And the existing nondisclosure agreement ensures that she will never speak of your relationship in Tokyo."

"It wasn't a relationship."

"Very well, your sordid encounter, then."

"Careful, Mike," Dante warned. He had known Mike for years and they had a fantastic professional and personal relationship, but Dante's mood was too uncertain at the moment to cope with the man's irreverent sense of humor.

"Hmm," Mike hummed noncommittally. "Well, I think this is all pretty aboveboard. She doesn't want a cent from you until you're satisfied that the baby is yours, and even then she won't expect payment to start until after the birth."

Okay, so Dante was willing to concede that maybe she wasn't as mercenary as he'd first thought, and he was also willing to accept his culpability in the matter if, indeed, she did turn out to be pregnant with his baby. But she'd better be serious about not expecting anything more from him because he for damned sure wanted nothing to do with her or the baby. If he ever decided to have kids someday, the mother he chose for those children would be as far removed from Cleopatra Knight as night was from day. He would do his duty and pay whatever money she needed to raise her child. But that was it. No emotional commitments were required or expected of him, and he was satisfied with that.

Cleo sat at her kitchen table staring at the damp stain on the wall above the refrigerator with a tub of melting ice cream forgotten in front of her. The front door opened and Cal stepped in, bringing with him the fresh smell of wind and rain.

"Hey." He removed his coat and tossed it carelessly over the back of the couch and grabbed a spoon from the drying rack on the sink before sitting down opposite her and helping himself to her softening chocolate-mint ice cream. "I don't know how you can eat this stuff in the middle of winter. It's freezing out there and you're sitting in here eating ice cream."

She shrugged listlessly, barely hearing him. She sat with her cheek resting in the palm of one hand, one foot tucked beneath her butt and the other swinging in circles above the floor. She looked like a cranky child.

"How did it go?" Cal asked softly, displaying more sensitivity than she would ever have given him credit for.

"I got fired."

"*What?*"

"You heard me." She shrugged again.

"Aw, man. Hon, I'm so sorry to hear that. What a complete dick that guy is! How could he *fire* you?"

"He thinks I'm some . . ." She heard her voice thicken with tears. "I don't know. Some opportunistic, mercenary, money-hungry bitch or something." She shoved the ice cream aside and folded her arms on the table before burying her face in them and giving way to the tears that had been threatening all afternoon.

Cal rubbed a hand up and down her back as she cried, her sobs quiet and her tears plentiful.

"I don't know what to do," she confessed after a few long moments of cathartic crying. "I don't know what to do."

"We'll figure it out, Cleo."

"I have no job, no savings . . . how can I take care of this baby? I can't move in with Luc and Blue. It would be so unfair. Just when they're starting to get their lives sorted out, along comes the family failure with another setback for them."

"Don't think like that," Cal said. "Think solutions. Not problems."

"What the hell does that even mean?" she asked, her voice seething with frustration. "How am I supposed to 'think solutions'? What solutions? There are no solutions right now, Cal. So how about just letting me wallow for a few lousy moments?"

"Wow." He sat back and took another spoonful of ice cream. "I'm going to assume that's the pregnancy talking."

"It's not the pregnancy," she denied, as even more tears threatened. Where was this endless supply coming from? Surely she should have run dry by now. "It's everything. You've never really grown up, Cal. You don't know how to *deal* like an adult. So all you have are these preppy teen words of advice that don't mean squat in the real world."

"And *this* is mature behavior?" he fired back, waving his spoon up and down in her direction. "This crying-fest, while you lash out at someone who cares about you instead of at the real object of your frustration."

"And how am I supposed to lash out at him? He had me kicked out of his office before I even had a chance to properly talk to him."

"What, like, *literally* kicked out?" His eyes widened.

"Called security and had me escorted out of the building," she confirmed, and his jaw dropped.

"Seriously?"

"Yes. I felt so . . ." The tears overflowed again as she remembered the mortifying moment she was marched out of his office and back to her own desk. "Humiliated."

"That guy needs his ass kicked! Tell your brother about it."

"No." She could hear the panic in her own voice. "No, Cal. Luc doesn't hear about this. He's not to know who the father of this child is." She was too embarrassed to let Luc know what a colossal mistake she'd made with Dante, and she couldn't ruin a friendship he held dear.

"But what will you tell him about your job?"

"I'll tell him I quit or something. It'll be easy enough for him to believe of his loser sister."

"Come on, hon," Cal said. "That's hardly fair. This wasn't your fault."

"Please just leave it for now."

Cal nodded reluctantly and Cleo reached over to squeeze his forearm gently.

"I'm sorry I snapped at you, okay?"

"Yeah." He shrugged. "I'm sorry I wasn't grim enough to suit the occasion."

She giggled wetly at the lame joke, and Cal grimaced before reaching into his pocket for a handkerchief.

"Jesus, blow your nose," he said. "Look at the state of you. You're such an ugly crier, Cleo."

"Shut up," she laughed, and blew her nose gustily. At that moment she just appreciated his presence so much that she couldn't hold back an impulsive hug.

"Thank you. Sometimes I just don't know what I'd do without you."

By ten the following morning, Cleo was still lounging around in her robe and pajamas. She had no real desire to do much. She felt *flat*. She'd spent the better part of the morning hugging the toilet bowl, vomiting, and now she felt completely wrung out. Her stomach still uncertain, she gingerly padded to the sleeper couch that Cal had, for once, made up before traipsing off to parts unknown earlier that morning. He always disappeared for hours on end doing God knows what, God knows where. Cleo had been relieved to see the back of him that morning because his relentless and oblivious good cheer was driving her up the wall.

She was thinking about attempting to eat some food when a knock sounded on the front door. She frowned, not used to being here during the day and not at all sure who it could be. They had an intercom security system, so knocks at the door without advance warning were extremely rare.

The knock sounded again, and she pushed herself up from the couch. She paused for an instant to get the nausea under control, before making her way to the front door. There was no peephole, so she'd have to go the other route.

"Who's there?" she called through the door. There was a long moment of silence during which she wondered if the person had moved on to a different apartment.

"Me." The voice, only slightly muffled by the thin wood of the door, was instantly recognizable, and Cleo froze. When she didn't respond for a full minute, the knock sounded again, loud and authoritative and so damned like him she wondered how she hadn't guessed who it was from the sound of the knock alone.

"It's me, Damaso!" he growled. "Open the damned door."

"No."

"What?"

She could practically feel his incredulity through the wood.

"I said no. Go away."

"I will not leave until we have settled this matter." He sounded pretty adamant, and she chewed on her lip indecisively.

"I didn't think there was anything to settle. You've made your mind up."

"I refuse to discuss this through the door. If you do not open it, I will kick it down. I don't imagine it will take too much effort, the wood is so thin."

"We can't all have fancy walnut oak doors," she said with a sneer, and he was right: the wood *was* pretty thin if she could hear him sigh through the door.

"I will count to three. If you do not open the door, I will—"

She clicked her tongue irritably and snatched open the door. Only after she stood facing him in his bespoke-suited splendor did she remember that she wore fleecy, polka-dot pajamas with a fuzzy pink robe and pink-and-white bunny slippers. Her hair was a mess, and she probably looked pretty washed out after that morning's puking session. And the way he stared at her told her everything she needed to know about how truly awful she looked.

"Your hair . . ."

She stared at him in complete bewilderment. Why would her *hair* be the first thing he noticed about her? And then she remembered. She reached up a trembling hand to run a hand through her short, sleek bob, trying to recall if the pink she and Cal had applied to the bleached tips of her hair the night before was particularly vivid.

"I figured I didn't have to look like a corporate drone anymore," she said, shrugging slightly.

"It's pink."

"Only the tips."

He finally dragged his horrified gaze from her hair down the rest of her body.

"Did I disturb your sleep?" he asked, looking truly confused.

"I didn't see the need to get dressed when I don't have a job to get ready for."

"And you did not consider going out to look for a new job?"

Jeez, rich people really had no clue how the real world worked. He sounded way too judgmental for her liking, and she bristled defensively.

"I just got *fired* from my previous position yesterday. I haven't had time to sit down with the classifieds to job-hunt yet."

He nodded and shoved his hands into his coat pockets as his gaze roamed around the small, slightly dingy, and far-from-tidy interior of her apartment.

"This place has lousy security. A student type in baggy jeans and a Rastafarian cap simply *let* me in. Held the door open and waved me through."

"Oh."

"I think he might have been on something," he said, voice ripe with disapproval.

"If it's who I'm thinking of, then he was very definitely on something." Young Isaac from down the hall was always high. Cleo didn't know how he managed to get any studying done. Dante's brow furrowed in response to her words.

"And you feel safe in this dump?"

"Why are you here?" she asked, refusing to answer any more of his questions.

"May I sit?" After a brief hesitation, she nodded. He glanced around the room again before heading toward the kitchen table and turning to wait for her there. Once she joined him, he dragged out a chair, ushered her into it, and took his own seat. A little flustered by the gentlemanly gesture, she waited for him to speak. But he didn't say anything for a long time and merely stared at his loosely folded hands resting on the table in front of him.

She shifted uncomfortably before he lifted his eyes and trapped her with that intense gaze of his. She froze beneath that stare, feeling like a butterfly pinned to a board.

"You're pregnant."

"I know."

"How far along are you now?" he asked. She couldn't help it; she allowed her hand to drop to her abdomen, still in awe that there was a life in there.

"Twelve weeks," she whispered. "This week her eyelids started to grow in properly."

"'Her'?" he asked gruffly, and she shook herself out of her reverie to focus on him again.

"The baby's a 'she' this week. Last week a 'he.' Last week was exciting; she—or he—started making fists. Can you imagine this little life, barely the size of a prune, with tiny hands that can make fists?"

"Can you feel it doing all that? Making fists and stuff?" he sounded fascinated despite himself.

"No, I can't. I've been reading this week-by-week pregnancy book. It's really good."

There was another long, awkward silence as Cleo tried to figure out if she could say or do anything to convince him to leave. "I wish I had security guards too," she said wistfully, and he glanced up at her in surprise.

"So that you can kick me out?" He sounded amused rather than offended.

"I want you to leave," she admitted. "I don't like having you here in my home."

"I came to tell you that I agree to your terms. I've signed your documents. *If* I am the father of that baby, I will pay an amount toward its support."

"You won't try to take her from me?" Cleo verbalized her worst fear on a whisper.

"No. Your baby doesn't interest me. *You* don't interest me. I want you both out of my life as quickly and quietly as possible."

Well, she'd always known that was how he would feel, but the rejection still stung. She felt the pain more for her baby than she did for herself. She'd known the stakes going into this thing with Dante Damaso, but the baby was an innocent in all of this, and now would never have a father to love her and protect her. Still, he was cold and ruthless and would undoubtedly make a lousy father. She'd grown up without a dad, and while she was a mess at times, she'd turned out mostly all right. Luc barely remembered their father either; the man had stuck around for five years and had skipped out on his family less than a month after Cleo's birth. Their mother, never the most stable of creatures, had gone on a downward spiral after that, and five years later had dumped her children with their grandparents and swanned off to Asia. None of them had seen or heard from her again, and Luc and

Cleo had received word of her death soon after their grandparents had passed. Luc flew to Nepal, where she died, and took care of the funeral arrangements. He returned with a few boxes of her personal items, and that had been that. A sad and lonely ending to a sad and lonely life.

"Why didn't you send your attorney to take care of the matter?" she asked Dante. "You didn't have to come in person."

"I wanted to make it perfectly clear that this is all there will ever be between us, just a financial agreement benefitting the child should it happen to be mine."

"Got it," she murmured. As if she needed that obvious fact spelled out to her.

"And I wanted to add that perhaps I was a little . . . *hasty* in firing you."

"Hasty? Try unfair," she corrected. "And harsh. You treated me like a criminal. Do you have any idea how humiliating it was to be escorted out by your thugs? I didn't get to say good-bye to anybody, and I heard rumors that *maybe* I'd been caught stealing."

He looked uncomfortable and his broad shoulders shifted restlessly.

"It was not my intention to humiliate you."

His words infuriated her and opened her eyes to the fact that she was a lot angrier about the embarrassing experience than she realized.

"Is that an apology? Because if it is, it needs work."

"Look, this is not getting us anywhere," he deflected. "I would like to offer you another position."

"Back in HR?" she asked, allowing the subject change. For now.

"No, there would be too many uncomfortable questions. I want to move you to the Joburg office."

Oh, he wanted to move her to an unfamiliar office, in a strange city miles away from her family and friends, did he? And far, far away from him. Wouldn't that just make his life a whole lot easier? Not that Cleo was interested in making it difficult; she just wanted to move on with her own life and forget she even knew Dante Damaso.

"I can't move to Johannesburg," she stated, her voice brooking no argument.

"Look, be reasonable. You can hardly raise a kid without some form of employment to bolster the financial aid you'll be receiving from me."

"*You* be reasonable. If I take you up on this offer, I may have the benefit of an added income, but I won't have the emotional support I would need from my family and friends. This is my first pregnancy, I'll be going it solo, and I'll want my brother, Blue, and my other close friends around. I'll want familiar surroundings. The *last* thing I want or need right now is to move to an unfamiliar city."

He was quiet for a long time before conceding the point with a very brief dip of his jaw.

"Give me time and I'll try to arrange something else," he said.

"I don't need any favors from you, *Mr.* Damaso." He looked almost embarrassed by the honorific he had insisted she use just the day before. "Just child support. You are in no way responsible for any other part of my life."

"Nonetheless, I am the reason you no longer have a job. I acted hastily and would like to make amends for that."

"A glowing reference would do just fine, thank you," she said, while the inner voice that had tried to warn her on that first night in Tokyo protested again. As before, she didn't listen to it, and Cleo hoped she wouldn't wind up—once again—paying for her refusal to heed her common sense. But she had *some* pride, and depending on him for child support was bad enough; she didn't want to depend on him for her very livelihood too, not after he had so unceremoniously fired her the day before. Yet another thing, she noted, that he had not yet apologized for.

"So how does this paternity-test thing work?" He changed the subject rather abruptly and looked remarkably uncomfortable with his own question.

"Well, you're the one who wants proof that the baby is yours, so you're going to have to arrange for that."

"They have prenatal tests, right?"

"I will accept only noninvasive testing. Anything else could potentially harm my baby." He grunted, a sound she assumed meant assent. "And *you're* paying for it. I'm not paying for some stupid test I already know the answer to."

"I have to protect myself," he said almost defensively. "You're not the first woman to ever accuse me of fathering her baby."

"Oh God, you mean you have other illegitimate kids running around out there?"

"Of course not! Those other women weren't even pregnant." He looked so disgusted that Cleo almost felt sorry for him. It couldn't be easy to be the target of so many gold diggers—no wonder he had them all sign nondisclosure agreements. Then again, how many good, decent women had he scared off with that stupid document? His personal life was crazy and a little messed up, and she was happy enough to stay well away from it.

"Maybe you should consider limiting yourself to—I don't know— one or two serious relationships a year, with nicer women. You may find life a lot easier in the long run."

"The thing with you wasn't a relationship and it wasn't—" She held up a hand to shut him up. Surprisingly enough it worked.

"Spare me. I've heard it all before. Blah, blah, 'you're not my usual type' blah, blah, 'it wasn't serious' blah, blah, *blah*. You're like a broken record, Mr. Damaso. It gets tedious after a while. Now would you please mind leaving me alone? I have stuff to do."

"For God's sake, call me Dante," he commanded, and she sighed before crossing her arms over her chest.

"I prefer 'Mr. Damaso.' It keeps things businesslike and impersonal. Besides, I hope never to see you again after this, so does it matter what I call you?"

"I suppose not." He levered himself up from the table and stood towering above her for a few long moments before she scrambled to her feet to feel less small. The hasty movement immediately sent her stomach into turmoil, and she clapped a hand over her mouth and pushed past him to the bathroom, where she was violently ill.

When she eventually came back to her miserable senses, it was to find Dante Damaso on his haunches beside where she was hunched wretchedly over the commode, one of his large hands stroking her back soothingly. Appalled that he had seen her like that, she shrugged off his touch and moved away from him shakily, ignoring him when he reached down to help her stand.

He allowed her that small, defiant move and stood back and watched while she splashed water on her face—soaking the front of her robe in the process—and gargled some mouthwash. She pretended he wasn't there and exited the bathroom to return to the living room with her spine straight and her chin up.

"Maybe you should lie down or something," he suggested, and she swallowed down her irritation as she glanced over her shoulder to find him watching her from the bathroom door.

"*Why* are you still here?" She trudged the short distance to her room, shrugged out of her wet robe, and hung it from a hook on her wall to dry. Unfortunately, he followed her. Could the man not take a hint?

He shoved his hands into his trouser pockets and glanced around her bedroom, taking in the clothes that were draped over every surface, the posters of ballet and contemporary dancers that adorned her beige walls, and the ragged pointe shoes that were hanging from one of the posts of her gorgeous, antique, queen-size four-poster bed. She loved that bed, had brought it with her from her old bedroom in the house when she moved out. It cost the earth to transport it every time she moved, but she would never sell it or leave it behind.

"I can't figure out if this room is a teen dream or nightmare," he mused, and leveled that killer gaze on her again. "A bit juvenile, isn't it? Do you plan to move out of this dump before you have the baby?"

"None of your damned business. Please leave," she demanded wearily. He sighed impatiently and turned to walk the short distance to her bedroom door.

"Mike Grayson, my attorney, will be in touch." He threw the words over his shoulder as he reached for the front door. She trailed him back into the living room and was startled when he unexpectedly turned around again to look at her. "Eat something. You look like hell."

And with that parting shot, he was gone, leaving Cleo feeling absolutely drained in his wake. Her legs turned to liquid as she finally allowed herself to relax, and she sank down onto the sleeper couch.

The door opened again seconds later and surprised the hell out of her. She jumped—instantly back on alert—when his head popped through the opening.

"And lock the damned door!" he ordered before leaving again. She stared at the closed door in complete disbelief, before forcing herself up to do just as he'd commanded. More as a deterrent against any more unwelcome visits from him than out of any real fear of an intruder.

CHAPTER SEVEN

Ten days and one simple cheek swab later, Dante sat in his office and stared at the discreet, still-closed envelope he held in his hands. He knew what it would say; he'd known since that first meeting with Mike. A mercenary woman would have demanded far more from him than Cleo had.

"It doesn't matter," he said aloud. And it didn't. It couldn't. This kid wouldn't be his in any way except biologically, and he could live with that. He could quite *happily* live with that. Why should he sacrifice his freedom for what amounted to a stupid mistake? Cleo chose to keep the baby, and Dante chose not to know the child. They could both live with that.

And someday—when it was old enough—the kid would have to live with that too.

He would have to live with the knowledge that his father had chosen not to know him. Or love him.

Dante noticed, almost impassively, that his hands had started to shake, and he dropped the envelope onto his desk and clenched his fists to control the tremble. He picked it up again seconds later, took in a huge gulp of air, and tore it open—the violence of the gesture akin to ripping a Band-Aid off a wound.

He unfolded the slip of paper carefully, reading through the scientific jargon before getting to the most relevant bit.

Cannot be excluded as the father of the child . . . probability of paternity 99.9992%

Right.

He refolded the paper precisely along the original lines and noted that his hands were trembling again. He meticulously placed it back into its envelope and then smoothed it carefully flat on the desk's surface before tucking it away into the breast pocket of his jacket. Once there, it felt like it was burning a hole into his chest, so he removed it again and shoved it into his desk drawer. He locked the drawer and tucked the key into his breast pocket.

He had anticipated this; he had known it was coming, so now he could continue with his life as planned. This matter was already taken care of; Mike had only been waiting for confirmation of the child's paternity before he made the financial arrangements. It was out of Dante's hands now. He could get back to business. He could build more hotels; go out with gorgeous, glamorous women; and one day—years from now—even marry one of them. *That* woman would be the mother of his children. Simple and uncomplicated, that's how he liked his life. And the woman he chose to be his wife would have to be equally simple and uncomplicated. Someone who could make his life easier without needing constant attention and validation. Cleo and the baby were just obstacles to overcome before he could get back out onto the open, uncomplicated road of his life again. He need never think of them again.

Only . . .

He couldn't help but recall the last time he'd seen Cleo, and he wondered if she'd found another job. And if she'd moved into a better, more secure apartment yet. Were the tips of her glossy black hair still that horrendous shade of pink?

Did she still suffer from morning sickness?

What wonders did week fourteen hold?

Mierda!

He *had* to stop thinking about this. He picked up his phone and thumbed through his contacts before finding the name he was searching for.

"Nicki, *querida*, this is Dante. Do you want to meet for a drink later?"

He was going to get this situation out of his mind in a time-honored tradition. With booze, babes, and lots and lots of sex.

Cleo read the test results, laughed, then cried a little and laughed again before tearing the paper up and tossing the pieces in the bin. She would probably hear from Grantley Bingham, her grandparents' really ancient attorney, soon. Mr. Bingham had kindly offered to help her out for a fraction of his usual fee because he felt he owed it to her grandparents. He'd been dealing directly with Dante's attorney and had informed her that things were going along swimmingly at the moment.

The old man was sweet, and despite knowing her for her entire life, had remained completely nonjudgmental and professional throughout their proceedings. He had merely congratulated her on her pregnancy and kept giving her unwanted advice on everything from morning sickness to baby names.

Cleo rested a hand on the still-flat surface of her abdomen. She still suffered from morning sickness, but luckily it wasn't too debilitating anymore. Even though her book told her that her energy should be returning, she continued to feel lethargic, which she put down to a mild case of depression. She didn't have a job yet, and once she started showing it would be even more difficult to find anything. Luc and Blue had been pressing her to move in with them, and it was becoming the likeliest scenario for her.

Luc had been seriously pissed off with her when she'd told him that she'd quit her job, and he'd put it down to "Cleo being her usual irresponsible self." Cleo had said and done nothing to correct him.

Cleo was scared and felt alone and lonely, despite Cal's constant and overbearing presence and Luc and Blue's smothering. Most nights she woke up in an absolute panic, with cold sweat dripping down her body—terrified of screwing up her baby's life—and she had absolutely no one to talk to about that.

She had her first dating ultrasound coming up in a couple of days and hadn't even told Blue about it. The appointment was for midday, and she didn't want Blue to take off any more time from work to go with her. Luc managed a small IT company in a rundown industrial part of town, and the place always seemed to fall completely apart when he wasn't there. She could take Cal, but quite frankly, she'd rather go alone; he tended to irritate her when she felt even remotely stressed.

She looked around her flat and sighed. She'd been cooped up in here for too long. She hadn't ventured out much due to a lack of funds and a lack of desire to do anything remotely social. But she was unaccustomed to going so long without any form of exercise, and it was starting to give her a dose of cabin fever.

She resolutely went about collecting her leotard, a gauzy crepe wrap skirt, tights, and pointe shoes and stuffed them into a tote bag. She tied her short hair up into a small, tight ponytail and grabbed up her coat on her way out the door.

It was midspring, but the air still had a bite, and it had been an unseasonably rainy October. A fine, misty rain fell outside, and as she walked the short distance to her favorite dance studio, the light precipitation frizzed her hair and dampened her face. The air smelled clean and she inhaled deeply. She would have to pay for her entry into the studio, and she couldn't really afford to spend the money, but she really needed this.

"Cleo, we haven't seen you in months," Susan Killian, the owner of the studio, enthused when Cleo entered the place. She was all smiles and came around the reception desk to give Cleo a hug. The woman was short and comfortably plump, she had unnaturally brassy red hair—always up in a messy bun—wore too much makeup, and had glasses perched on the tip of her nose. She had a habit of staring over the top of them when she was speaking to someone, which made her look like an aging librarian. She was still hugging Cleo—who was only an inch or two taller than the other woman—to her ample chest, enveloping her in an overpowering cloud of Red Door by Elizabeth Arden. Susan had been a pretty decent dancer back in her heyday, before retiring and opening the dance studio. Now she taught ballet to girls ranging in age from just three to fifteen as well as an adult beginner's class in the evenings. She had often tried to enlist Cleo's help with a couple of the classes, but Cleo was resistant to the idea. She felt that taking the step toward teaching would be the final nail in her dancing dream's coffin, and as she'd told Blue, she honestly didn't think she had it in her to genuinely want her students to succeed. Which just made her feel like a terrible person. Even though she hadn't danced professionally in more than three years, she'd never felt like it was completely lost to her. Now with the pregnancy, she knew that she'd have to finally face reality. Time to grow up.

"I've had a few personal issues to deal with," Cleo said, explaining her absence. "Can I book some time at the barre?"

"Of course you can." Susan waved a hand carelessly. "I'm between classes right now, and the studio's practically empty."

"Thanks, Susan."

Ten minutes later, as she was going through her stretching routine, she could feel the stiffness working its way out of her joints and muscles. The familiar routine felt like a comfortable blanket settling over her, and she cleared her mind entirely and focused only on her body. She moved on to her barre routine soon afterward, her intention to do a slow, easy workout in deference to her pregnancy and the lethargy she still felt. She'd brought her own CD along, and as the soothing strains of the piano solo flowed over her, she started slowly and gently and dropped into her demi-pliés. Simple and smooth. This was home to her.

By the time she'd progressed to her en pointe exercises, she was starting to feel a bit of strain in her knee, but she worked through it. She'd definitely encourage her child to dance, and hopefully he or she would derive as much joy and freedom from it as Cleo did. If not, she hoped they found *something* they loved as passionately.

She released the barre and moved into a fluid, easy arabesque en pointe on the left leg and held it for a couple of seconds longer than she normally would have, just to prove to herself that she could do it. When she moved to do it on the right leg, her knee immediately buckled, and she fell out of the arabesque with a frustrated cry. She grabbed hold of the barre with both hands and bowed her head in defeat.

"Stupid, stupid, stupid!" she admonished herself. And it *had* been stupid; she'd known it would happen. It always did, and yet, even three years after her accident, she kept trying. She was too stubborn for her own good sometimes. And dumb, definitely dumb.

She regained her composure and started her cooldown exercises, cutting her routine short because she felt disheartened and seriously exhausted. A telling sign that, even though it wasn't showing yet, her pregnancy was already changing her body. She could usually push herself twice as hard at the barre.

Susan was reading a romance novel behind the reception desk when Cleo limped her way out of the studio, and she frowned in concern.

"Have you been silly again?" she asked, giving Cleo a disapproving glare over the top of her glasses.

"No more than usual." Cleo shrugged and slung a towel around her neck. She hadn't bothered to change—merely pulled on a sweat suit to keep her muscles warm. She could be at home and under the shower in less than ten minutes, the studio was so close to her apartment. That was one of the reasons she'd found the apartment so appealing in the first place, despite its many other faults.

She walked home, thankful that the drizzle had stopped even though the wind had picked up and she was walking against it. She was huddled beneath her coat, hands in her pockets and head down as protection from the wind, and didn't see the huge figure looming ahead of her at the entrance of her building until she was almost on top of him.

She yelped in fright and jumped back with her hand on her chest, prepared to scream or run, when she looked up and saw Dante Damaso peering down at her as if he didn't recognize her.

"Miss Knight?"

God, why did he still insist on calling her that?

"What do you want?"

"I wanted to inform you that the paternity test result came today."

"I know."

"And I want to assure you that you and the child will be provided for."

"Just the child," she corrected, and his brow lowered.

"What?"

"You will be providing for only the child. I don't want your money for myself."

"But the medical costs alone will—"

"Don't worry about it."

"Do you have a job yet?" His critical gaze swept over her body, and Cleo recognized what a mess she was and had to use every ounce of willpower not to touch her untidy hair self-consciously.

"Not yet."

"The longer you remain unemployed, the less likely you are to find a job in your"—he made a vague gesture at her stomach region—"uh. Your condition."

"I'll work something out. It's not your concern." She brushed past him dismissively, hoping he'd take the hint and leave, but he followed her up the stairs to the entrance.

"Perhaps we should discuss these terms of yours," he said, and she turned to face him, savagely satisfied to note that because she stood several steps above him, she could meet his gaze head-on.

"There's nothing more to discuss. For a man who likes to keep his personal life clutter free, you're making a total nuisance of yourself."

"You know nothing about me," he grated.

"And you know even *less* than nothing about me," she hissed, sticking her face right up to his until they were almost nose to nose.

"I know that you're stubborn, pregnant, and unemployed. I know that you're living in a hovel and are financially ill equipped to deal with this pregnancy."

"Yeah? Well, what's my name then, smart-ass? Why do you keep calling me Miss Knight?"

"Not because I've forgotten your name, *Cleopatra*," he murmured, his voice dropping an octave as his eyes fell to her mouth. She cleared her throat, feeling hot and uncomfortable, and she stepped back, but her heel caught the edge of the next step and she lost her balance. She windmilled as she struggled to regain her footing, but his hands dropped to her elbows and steadied her. "I've got you. You're fine."

Her own hands dug into his forearms as she fought her shock and tried to regain her breath and her equilibrium. One of his hands released its grip and moved up to cup her cheek.

"You've gone remarkably pale. Are you okay?"

She started shaking as her fear of falling subsided.

"I'm fine," she said through chattering teeth. "Just a bit shocked, is all. I mean there wasn't even the slightest possibility of falling, was there?"

"No," he agreed. "And if there was, you would probably have landed on me. So you would have been fine."

"The thought of falling terrifies me a bit," she confessed. Something she did only because she still felt so off-kilter.

"The scar on your knee?" he asked perceptively. She didn't respond, merely stared at him mutely.

"I have to go," she said. "Let's *not* do this again sometime."

"Can I come up?"

She gave him a disbelieving look.

"What? No! You cannot come up."

"Then I suppose we'll have this discussion out on the steps, in public?"

"Go right ahead," she invited, calling his bluff. "You're the one who doesn't like his business aired in public. I'm quite comfortable with public scenes. I was once a performer."

That made him pause, but not for the reason she would have thought.

"You *were*? What kind of performer?"

She shrugged, uncomfortable with his interest.

"Look, I won't take up more than five minutes of your time." He took a step down to give her some space, as if sensing that his presence was making her feel claustrophobic. He held his hands palms up in a gesture of surrender. Cleo looked over his shoulder, noting for the first time that his massive black car was parked next to the curb and that one of his hulking personal protection guys—who often doubled as drivers for him—watched them silently from beside the car.

"Hey, James," she called, and waved at the huge, tattooed, dark-suited bald man. He wore sunglasses, despite the gloom of the day. He lifted one of his hands to wave back at her.

"How's your new puppy?" Cleo asked. "Still leaving surprise puddles on the floor for you?"

"He's getting better," James replied with a thumbs-up.

"Have you decided on a name for him yet?"

"Piddles." Cleo laughed, aware of Dante's incredulity at the bizarre exchange between his bodyguard and former assistant. He focused a glare on James, who refolded his hands loosely in front on him and shifted his stance slightly, until he stood with his legs shoulder-width apart. That quickly, James went from personable and friendly to forbidding and formidable.

"Do you *mind*? I would like to have a serious conversation with you," Dante said through clenched teeth, and Cleo sighed.

"I suppose you can come up for five minutes," she said begrudgingly. "But you're starting to make a nuisance of yourself."

"Noted."

Dante trailed behind Cleo as she led the way to her fourth-floor apartment. He kept his eyes on her narrow, straight back, once again noting her grace and elegant carriage. She really carried herself beautifully, and it was one of the things he'd found so appealing about her.

He didn't know why he was here, but despite arranging to see Nicki Unwin—one of his regular on-again/off-again lovers—later that evening, he hadn't been able to get Cleopatra Knight out of his mind today. He had found himself standing at her doorstep for reasons that remained completely unfathomable to him.

As he followed her upstairs, he started to take in his surroundings a bit more. The place was a complete mess. It reeked of mold and damp, the wallpaper was peeling, the light in the stairwell flickered, and the stairs themselves were old and rickety. He couldn't understand why she lived here. Why didn't she move in with Lucius? Her brother had that huge old house. It wasn't ideal, but it was better than this place.

"Why not use the elevator?" he asked as he noticed her starting to limp. Her hand, which had previously glided over the banister with barely a touch, started to grip it with each step up.

"Out of order," she grunted.

"Of *course* it is." He couldn't bite back the sarcasm and immediately regretted it when her back straightened. He had put her even more on the defensive than she had been before. When she finally reached her front door, she was slightly out of breath.

"This won't get easier, you know," he said, striving to sound gentle.

"It's none of your business," she snapped. Her hair was starting to fall out of the absurd little ponytail she had it in, and he noted that the pink tips had been replaced by pale blue ones. A few of the blue strands were peppered through her bangs as well.

She unlocked her door, and when she stepped aside to allow him entry, he waved her forward. He followed her in and immediately spotted the huge blond guy from the airport seated at the kitchen table, digging into a bowl of cereal.

Instantly beyond furious and feeling absolutely gullible, Dante's first thought was that she'd duped him. This was, as he had initially suspected, an elaborate ploy to make him believe some other guy's kid was his, and he'd caught her red-handed. How was she going to explain this guy away?

He turned to face her, ready to give it to her with both barrels, when the annoyed—not guilty, not defensive, not even scared— expression on her face gave him pause.

"You're eating my Frostees!" Cleo screeched, and Cal dropped his spoon guiltily.

"It was just a taste, I swear, hon. You know I'd never eat too much of the stuff; it's hugely calorific. Well, *hello*." His gaze drifted behind her, and Cleo became aware of the man standing so close by.

"Cal, this is Dante Damaso, my ex-boss. Mr. Damaso, my roommate, Callum Faris." Cal got up and sauntered over to them where he presented his hand to Dante, who gave it a firm shake.

"You can call me Cal," her shamelessly flirting roommate invited. "Or just call me *anytime*."

"Cal," she hissed, and he rolled his eyes. "Do you mind giving us some privacy? Mr. Damaso and I have a few things to discuss."

Cal pouted before grabbing up a denim jacket and heading toward the door.

"Be good to my girl, Mr. D," he said on his way out. "I know about five different forms of martial arts, and I'm not afraid to use them." Cleo felt a spurt of affection for her friend who, while a flirtatious lech, still knew exactly where his loyalties lay.

They watched him leave, and silence reigned for a few seconds before Cleo darted a quick look at Dante. He had a bemused expression on his face. She grinned.

"You totally thought he was my baby daddy," she said, and he had the grace to look completely uncomfortable.

"For a moment there, I thought I'd been . . ."

"Conned?" she guessed, and when he flashed her an annoyed look, she remembered that he didn't like it when she finished his sentences.

"*Duped,*" he corrected, and she snorted.

"Come on, you've got to give me that one, they mean the same thing," she groused, and he cleared his throat but didn't respond. "Anyway, I'm offended your sordid little mind went there immediately despite the paternity-test results you got today. You have a seriously low opinion of me."

He kept his gaze impassive.

"What? No apology?" she challenged, and his jaw clenched but he remained stoically silent. She shrugged, letting it go because the sooner he was out of here, the better for her.

"What did you want to talk about that couldn't be handled by our attorneys?"

"I wanted to inform you that I would pay for *your* medical costs as well," he explained, and she started shaking her head before the words were even completely formed.

"No."

"You wouldn't need any medical care if you weren't pregnant, and you wouldn't be pregnant if not for me. Therefore, the medical bills should fall to me."

"I don't want anything from you," she said as she shrugged out of her jacket and unzipped her fleecy, gray hoodie.

"Why the hell not?" he asked angrily. "Everybody else does. Why don't *you*?"

"Because I'm not everybody else," she said quietly. In that instant she felt her heart break a little for him. How did that feel? To know that people cultivated relationships or friendships with you solely because of what it might get them. She was starting to understand why he'd become such firm friends with Luc. Her brother was one of the least materialistic people she knew. Sure, he wanted the finer things in life, like everybody else, but he would work his heart out to obtain those things and never expect them to be handed to him on a plate. "And FYI, you seem to know some seriously shitty people."

"Look, I'll leave you alone if you let me do this one thing for you, okay?" he promised. "Just let me take care of the medical bills."

"*If* I need any additional procedures that would cost more than I'd anticipated, if I need to stay in the hospital, or if there are complications that require additional medical treatment, I will happily accept your financial assistance," she stipulated, but he still didn't look happy.

"All of it, Cleo," he maintained. "Give your doctor's details to Mike, and he'll take care of everything. I've already added the clause to our agreement. If you don't cooperate, I will make an educated guess as to the possible costs incurred and have Mike transfer the funds into your account on a monthly basis. Once transferred, it cannot be returned. You can then do whatever the hell you want to with the money."

She crossed her arms, drawing his attention to her chest, and sighed in defeat.

"Fine. Okay, consider your conscience clear and our association at an end."

"You will accept the money?" His eyes lit with satisfaction when she nodded. "Good. Now, maybe you can tell me what the hell you're wearing."

"What?" Cleo glanced down at herself and realized that with the hoodie unzipped, he could see the top of her leotard. "Oh. It's a leotard."

"Leotard? For dancing or gymnastics?"

"Dancing."

"That explains it," he murmured beneath his breath, and she tilted her head curiously.

"Explains what?"

"Nothing. It's nothing. What kind of dance?"

She hesitated as she debated whether to encourage this conversation any further.

"Ballet."

"Seriously?" He sounded so shocked that she was a little affronted.

"What were you expecting?"

"I don't know, with your personality I was expecting something more modern and quirky, perhaps. Ballet is . . ."

"Refined?" she snapped, on the defensive again.

"*Not* what I was going to say."

"Elegant?"

"Damn it, Cleo!" It was the first time her name had ever flowed from his lips so naturally, and it startled her into silence. He didn't seem aware that he'd used it and was still glaring at her. "I told you not to do that. I was going to say *stuffy*. Ballet is so stuffy. It's beautiful, but it has so many rigid lines and rules. It doesn't seem to match your personality."

"You don't *know* me, Mr. Damaso," she reminded again.

"I know enough," he disagreed almost gently.

"Your five minutes are up."

"Indeed they are." He walked toward the door, and she watched him from the center of the room. Once at the door, he turned to face her.

"I was wondering about week fourteen," he confessed, his voice so low she barely caught it. He kept his eyes downcast, as if embarrassed to meet her gaze.

"Week fourteen?" she repeated, buying time, not sure if she should answer him or not.

"What happened after the fists and the eyelids?" He sounded like a wistful little boy wanting to know the end of a fairy tale, and it would have taken a stronger person than Cleo to resist the appeal of that little boy.

"Last week he started urinating," she said, wrinkling her nose, still a bit creeped out by the idea. "It's kind of gross to imagine him peeing away in there. Oh, and he has his own fingerprints now. This week he's starting to make little faces."

She grinned at the thought.

"Squints and frowns," she giggled. "He's probably paying special attention to getting that frown just right, considering who his father is." The words gave her pause as she remembered that her baby wouldn't know who his father was. She kept her eyes averted as she tried to keep her sadness at bay. She'd also grown up not knowing her father and had always wanted more for her children.

"Anyway, this is all guesswork. We could be a week off. I'll know for sure on Wednesday when I go for an ultrasound. They'll be able to give me a more accurate estimate of when he was conceived and when his date of birth will be."

"Will they be able to tell you if it's a girl or boy?" he asked, and she shrugged.

"I don't think so. Some of the articles I've read indicate that they can tell by twelve weeks, while other sources state that sixteen weeks is standard practice. I don't think I'd want to know, though."

"I suppose Lucius will be going with you?"

"Luc and Blue are working," she said unthinkingly, and his eyes narrowed.

"Callum, then?"

"Sure. Cal will go," she said airily, and his eyes narrowed suspiciously. "Anyway . . . I have some stuff to take care of. So I'll say good-bye now. I'm sure Mr. Grayson has my lawyer's number."

She reached out a hand, and he enveloped it with his. She shook his hand in one decisive up-and-down movement, but he refused to release his grip afterward.

"Good luck with your hotel in Tokyo. I'm sure it'll be beautiful." She didn't really know what else to say and wished he'd free her hand, but he didn't seem to have any inclination to do so.

"Does Lucius know the identity of your child's father?" he asked unexpectedly.

"No. And I'd rather he didn't know," she said.

"Why not?"

"Because he values your friendship, and even though *I* can't see what he finds so appealing about you, he doesn't have many friends, and I wouldn't want to deprive him of one."

"You once found me *very* appealing," he reminded huskily.

"What are you doing, Dante?" she asked in a helpless little voice, and he looked as confused as she felt. It was the most vulnerable she'd ever seen him look.

"I don't know," he admitted quietly. "I have *no* clue what I'm doing."

He stepped closer and tugged her toward him until her chest was flush against his torso. He *finally* released her hand, only to cup her face in his palms, as if she was the most precious thing he'd ever beheld.

"Maybe just a good-bye," he whispered. "Can I say good-bye?"

"No." The word carried no weight and floated between them as light as a feather, and he caught it on her lips before it could properly float away. His kiss was gentle and felt alarmingly reverent, and Cleo was floored by it. He shouldn't be doing this, and she shouldn't be allowing it. It complicated things.

She captured his wrists in her hands, intending to tug his hands down, but she couldn't find the strength to do so. In the end her hands merely rested there, her thumbs caressing the warm, hair-roughened skin of his wrists as that one, tender kiss rewrote their entire relationship and took it from antagonistic and familiar to *this*. Whatever this was.

Cleo finally found the strength to jerk her head back, breaking the contact between them. Her breath came in gasps, and her body was shaking badly. A quick glance at him confirmed that he was as shaken and shocked as she.

"That was . . . it was . . ." She shook her head, frustrated with her inability to verbalize her thoughts. "It shouldn't have happened."

"I know," he said.

"I'm serious, Dante."

"Me too." He ran a shaky hand through his hair. "It shouldn't have happened. Don't worry. I'm leaving. Take care of yourself, Cleo."

He was gone seconds later.

In the end, Dante called Nicki and canceled their date. He wouldn't have been very good company anyway. He didn't know why he was being so *weird* about the situation with Cleo. They had reached an amicable agreement. She was happy enough; he didn't have to worry about being held accountable for a mistake that neither of them could possibly have foreseen. After one slight hitch, his life was smoothly on track again.

Dante's phone buzzed as he stepped into his apartment, and he groaned when he saw the message—in Spanish—that had popped up onto his screen:

Must Skype immediately, Papa

Great, just what he needed after an already difficult day. He headed up to his study and set up the Skype call. He had other, more efficient means of making face-time calls, but his father couldn't quite grasp the technology involved. This was the easiest method for the older man. Dante really only used this program to contact his father, and as such, the man was the only contact on his list. Which made it easy to spot that Enrique Damaso was already online. As soon as Dante was logged in, the familiar ringtone came up. His father really *was* in a rush to speak with him tonight. The last time they'd Skyped had been months before.

"Ah, Dante. It's good to see you, son," his father said in Spanish as soon as they were connected. "You are good? You look good."

Dante was so far removed from good that it was actually quite funny, but he merely nodded.

"All good here, Papa," he lied. Their relationship wasn't one that encouraged confidences.

"Ah. Wonderful," the man said jovially. "Listen, Dante, I have someone I want you to meet." He ushered someone off-camera to join him, and a stunning young brunette stepped into view and sat down on his father's lap. Dante sighed inwardly, already knowing where this would lead.

"Dante, this is Carmen, your new mama-to-be." Dante tried not to wince at the introduction; the girl looked a full decade younger than Dante's own thirty-two. "Carmen, this is my boy, Dante."

He planted a kiss on the giggling woman's cheek and did something—thankfully out of the camera's view—to make her squeal.

"We're getting married," he announced unnecessarily. "Carmen is the one, Dante. She makes your papa so happy." And the sixty-three-year-old man was probably going through shedloads of little blue pills and truckloads of pretty trinkets to keep her equally happy.

"Congratulations," Dante said woodenly, knowing from experience that trying to talk his father out of making yet another colossal error would simply end in failure—much like the marriage itself inevitably would. His father's marriages never ended amicably, and each divorce had involved protracted and ugly legal battles. But it was useless reminding his father of past mistakes; it was easier to just make polite noises, buy a gift, and stay the hell out of it.

The old man was both cynical and a hopeless romantic. He hated all his exes with a bitterness that had easily poisoned Dante's own mind against women, and yet he loved every new opportunistic bitch that flitted her way into his life with a passion that was borderline obsessive.

"Will you come to the wedding?" his father asked eagerly. "Carmen and I are having a beach wedding in Tenerife. Carmen wanted the most romantic destination. And I will give my beautiful Carmen everything she wants. Also, I think it's closer to you, right? Off the African coast?"

"That's northwest Africa, Papa. I'm in *South* Africa. Pretty far away." Dante tested his acting skills by pulling the most regretful expression he could muster out of the bag. Clearly, geography was not his father's strong suit. But the old man had never understood *why* his only son had chosen to move so far away, and because he was still waiting for Dante to "come to his senses," he hadn't really bothered to learn much about the place that had become Dante's adopted home.

"I sometimes regret sending you to that university when you were a boy, Dante," his father said with a shake of his head. It was a familiar refrain. "But I thought, let the boy go, he can learn to be a man far away from his home and comfort. But then you had to go and *live* there."

Enrique Damaso felt that Dante going to college in another country, far away from everything familiar to him, would be a good character-building experience. And the old man had happily handed over the reins of the company immediately after Dante received his MBA, but his father *hadn't* counted on Dante staying in that country and forging a completely new life. Worse, Dante had "rebooted" the Damaso hotel brand in Cape Town and had completely distanced himself from his father's influence.

"Now you're so far away you can't visit your old papa regularly. All because I wanted my boy to have a good education and some valuable life experience," he said despairingly, but Dante remained unmoved by the theatrics. It was a little act his father liked to put on for the benefit of his future brides. The old *Look at how devoted I am to my ungrateful and uncaring only child* shtick.

"I don't think I'll be able to make it to the wedding, Papa," Dante interrupted firmly, knowing his father could go on for ages about what an ungrateful son he had. Best to nip it in the bud now. "I'm completely swamped with work."

"You don't even know when it is," his father pointed out, and Dante suppressed a scowl at the rookie mistake. But he was happy to have diverted the conversation away from his own shortcomings, at least.

"I'm sorry I assumed it was soon," he backpedaled quickly. "I'm tied up with the Tokyo build, and you know the Dubai project is starting to gain momentum. Now wouldn't be a great time to take a vacation. But, of course, if you're talking about months down the line, I'd be happy to attend."

"Aah, no . . . we're in love, we cannot wait months. The wedding will be in two weeks," his father said with a regretful sigh. "I really wanted you there, son. I was hoping you could be my best man."

"I'm sorry, Papa," he repeated. Carmen pouted prettily. "And Carmen. I would come if I could."

"It's okay, Dante," she giggled, her voice painfully shrill. "I'm sure there'll be plenty of time to get to know each other in the future."

Yeah, right. Dante wouldn't bet on that. His father would be on to wife number next in no time. Dante had lost count of how many—progressively younger—stepmothers he'd had so far, and he had no interest in even trying to keep track of them. His father never kept mistresses or lovers, he kept *wives*, and out of the many he'd had after Dante's mother had died of leukemia, one had committed suicide, another had died of an accidental drug overdose, and the rest had all divorced him.

Thankfully, Dante didn't have dozens of half siblings scattered all over Europe, as his father had had a vasectomy after Dante's tenth birthday. Which was a mixed blessing, since Dante wouldn't have minded a brother or sister. It would have made his childhood a little less lonely.

He watched his father neck with his child bride for a few minutes longer before deciding that he'd done his familial duty.

"Well, congratulations again. Please send me the wedding pictures."

"Okay. It was great talking with you, son. We should touch base more often," his father said. The man ended every call with the same words, and Dante always agreed that they should, but they both knew they probably wouldn't talk again for months. They were both okay with that.

After ending the call, Dante wandered from room to room in his vast penthouse apartment, which overlooked the yacht basin at the V and A Waterfront in Cape Town. It was the perfect bachelor apartment and offered a less impersonal way of life than simply staying in one of his hotels, which was the way he'd lived up until his thirtieth birthday. That was when he bought himself this multi-million-dollar gem just a stone's throw away from both his office and his flagship hotel in Cape Town.

But the Waterfront wasn't exactly a peaceful environment; it was trendy, noisy, and bustling with sightseers. The property values were through the roof, and it had been a sound investment to purchase this apartment. The glossy finishes, marble floors, slick glass walls, and minimalist interior were designed by the same team that did all of his hotels. The décor was beautiful but left the place feeling sterile and cold. He often felt as if he was still living in a hotel or one of those places they use for interior-design catalog shoots. It didn't feel like home. Not that he'd ever known what one of those felt like.

When he'd been a child living at home with his father, he'd never felt a sense of permanence or place. Not with the interchangeable "mamas" traipsing through Dante's life from his sixth or seventh birthday onward.

Because Enrique Damaso believed that each new wife was the Real Thing, he'd never seen the necessity of a prenup. For a wealthy man, Dante's father could be incredibly stupid. He thought prenups were unromantic and set the wrong tone for a marriage, and with each ex-wife he lost sizable chunks of money. Only one of those ex-wives had remarried and no longer received alimony from him; the others still enjoyed their lavish lifestyles, thanks to his father's gullibility.

Dante had given up thinking that his father would ever learn his lesson, and had proceeded to protect himself against a similar fate. He'd seen what loving a woman could lead to, and he wasn't going to allow himself to be used like that. He would choose his future wife with care; she would come from a background of wealth and privilege and would comport herself with grace and dignity in public. There would be no mad, passionate love involved in his choice. It would be an intellectual process, not an emotional one.

He wandered out onto the balcony and stared down at the yachts neatly lined up in the bay beneath his apartment, their masts pointing up at the purple-and-pink dusk sky like accusatory, skeletal middle fingers. His own fifty-foot sloop was berthed down there, but from this distance, in the fading light, it was difficult to spot the *Arabella*, which he'd named after his first dog.

He could smell the faint scent of fried food drifting toward him on the breeze, hear distant laughter—carried to him on the same breeze—and see people wandering around on the dock. Just living their lives. Some happy, some not. Husbands and wives, lovers, families.

He sighed, trying to shove aside the uncharacteristic surge of melancholia. He needed to shake this off. He needed a beer and time with a friend. The only person who sprang to mind was probably the last person he should contact. How the hell was he supposed to look

Lucius in the eye after learning that Cleo was pregnant with his baby? She had inexplicably attempted to preserve his friendship with her brother, and Dante supposed he could be grateful for that. Still, facing Lucius on the same day he'd received the paternity-test results wasn't something Dante was prepared to deal with just yet.

He mixed himself a strong drink, indulging himself with a couple of fingers of twenty-year-old single-malt scotch on the rocks. He carried his tumbler out onto the balcony and sat down in one of his comfortable patio chairs with his bare feet propped up against the railing. The sky had gone a deep, velvety blue, with just a few hints of magenta still bleeding into the ocean on the horizon.

He dug his phone from his pocket and scrolled through his messages and e-mails, and after replying to a few of the semi-important ones, he gave in to temptation and Googled week-by-week pregnancy guides.

He was fascinated to learn that peeing and making faces weren't all that week fourteen had to offer. The baby had also developed a pelt of hair all over its body. Dante couldn't help but visualize a weird simian-looking thing curled up in Cleo's womb. He shuddered and continued to read. He wondered if she could see any difference in her body yet? She still looked exactly the same to him, and the top of that leotard had been quite form-fitting, so surely he would have noticed any swelling in her midsection. Maybe her breasts had been a little bigger? He couldn't be sure; the leotard had unfortunately flattened them a bit too much for his liking.

And why had he even been looking at her breasts in the first place? Why was he thinking about them now?

His thoughts drifted to her ultrasound and wondered what the baby would look like.

He tilted his head back and imagined a little girl with black hair and snapping emerald eyes like her mother's. He had no experience with kids, and for some reason he couldn't quite picture an infant. In his mind the child was a toddler, two or three, wearing a little pink tutu and white leggings. He could see her clumsily twirling until she got dizzy, and when she inevitably lost her balance, he was there to . . .

He sat up abruptly, feet hitting the deck and drink nearly spilling.

Mierda! What the hell was he doing fantasizing about some kid who would have no place in his life?

He tossed back his drink and hurried inside to change into his loose training shorts. He needed a good workout. He needed to straighten his head out.

He padded, on bare feet, into his private gym and warmed up with a vigorous jump-rope session and a few stretches before dragging on his boxing gloves and proceeding to beat and kick the hell out of the heavy punching bag suspended from the ceiling. Less than half an hour later, he was too mentally and physically wrung out to think about anything other than the abuse he was putting his body through, and after his workout was complete, the only things on his mind were shower and sleep.

Not Cleo and her inconvenient pregnancy.

He was done with that.

CHAPTER EIGHT

"Heeey!" A super chirpy voice screeched into Cleo's ear and she cringed slightly. "Guess who's back in town?"

"Hi, Coco," she said faintly, one eye still defensively squeezed shut as her brain tried to adjust to the sugar rush Coco's high-pitched, syrupy voice always sent screaming through her bloodstream. "When did you get back?"

"Last night! Did you miss me?"

"I did." And she meant it. Coco had been one of her best friends throughout dance school, and even though they'd drifted apart after Cleo's accident, she always made a point of visiting whenever she was in town. She was a member of a well-known dance troupe and had even been doing a few solos on their international tours. Cleo had always been a better dancer than Coco, and they both knew it, so Cleo couldn't help feeling envious of her friend, which made things awkward between them, so it was probably a good thing they rarely saw each other these days.

"Well, I'm back, and so's Gigi," she squeaked, while Gigi's equally high-pitched voice screeched a hello in the background. Gigi was another former classmate of theirs, a ditzy girl who was happy just being in the corps de ballet. She simply wanted to dance and receive a regular paycheck. She was also one of the nicest people Cleo knew. "Want to come out for a drinkie?"

"How long will you guys be in town?" Cleo asked, glancing at the clock. It was nearly eight in the evening, and she had her ultrasound in the morning. Not the best time to be going out.

"For a couple of weeks," Coco replied.

"Great, then can I take a rain check? I really can't make it tonight. I have an important appointment tomorrow," she said, genuine regret deepening her voice.

"What about tomorrow night?" Coco asked.

"That'll be cool. Sure."

"Yay! I'll text you the deets! See you then!" Coco always spoke in exclamations; it was a little draining chatting with her sometimes, especially without any forewarning.

Cleo headed into the living room, where Cal was stretched out on the sleeper couch. His glasses, which he was too vain to let anyone but her see him wear, were perched on his nose as he read one of the gory thrillers that he loved. He peered up at her over the top of his glasses as she went to the kitchen to get herself some juice.

"Coco and Gigi are back in town," she said after sitting down at the kitchen table and taking a sip of her drink.

"Great," he muttered. "Don't forget to take an insulin shot before you go out with the Saccharine Sisters."

She giggled. "Stop it," she admonished, her laughter belying her words. Cal and Coco didn't get along, not since they'd both fallen for the same guy a few years back. To make matters worse, the guy had gone for Coco despite the fact that Cal was still convinced—all evidence to the contrary—that the guy batted for his team.

Cleo's laughter faded as she continued to stare at her longtime friend. She had to tell him about her decision to move in with Luc and Blue; he would need time to make other arrangements.

"Cal?" she whispered, hating the necessity of what she had to do but not seeing any other way. He dropped his book to his chest and smiled at her sadly.

"I know, hon." Her eyes flooded with tears at the understanding on his face, and she sat hunched at the table, silent sobs shaking her shoulders.

"I'm so sorry. I don't know what else to do."

"You have to do what's best for you, Cleo. And right now, you can't afford to live here supporting my lazy ass and coping with a pregnancy too. But on the positive side, having to move out might light a fire under said lazy ass and get me motivated to find work again. I've been getting a little too comfortable here, you see? Living a life of leisure, like the kept man that I am."

They both glanced around the tiny apartment and laughed at the thought of living any kind of "life of leisure" in the place.

"How long do we still have before we leave this pleasure palace?" He got up and stretched lazily before sauntering over to give her a casual hug and hand her a sliver of paper towel, the last bit on the roll.

"We're out of paper towels," he noted, and she giggled messily as she blew her nose.

"Well, we're not replacing this roll. Our life of lavish spending has come to an end, my friend. We can no longer afford luxuries like paper towels."

He laughed and sat down at the table opposite her.

"Jeez, girl, I'm getting sick of seeing you cry. Cheer up, will you?" She bravely presented him with her best smile. "Better. But not by much. Now when do we move out?"

"I'll be speaking with the landlord tomorrow. So probably thirty more days before we have to vacate the premises."

"A lot can happen in thirty days," he observed.

"Not *that* much." She traced a crease on the plastic tablecloth with her finger. "Do you want to come with me to my ultrasound appointment tomorrow?"

"I'd love to."

⟶⟨⟩

"Well, well, well, two's company but three is most definitely a *party*," Cal observed the following morning as they climbed out of her car. Cleo was happy with the prime parking spot they'd found directly outside Dr. Klein's office and was grinning like an idiot when she glanced up to see what Cal was talking about. The smile immediately dropped from her face when she saw what he was referring to.

"What the *hell*?" she whispered beneath her breath. "Why is he here? *How* is he here?"

"Take a deep breath, Cleo," Cal advised softly. "You're never at your sharpest when you're pissed off."

"What the hell are you doing here?" She marched up to Dante and put her face right up to his. "How did you know where to find me?"

"You sent your OB/GYN's details to Grayson, and with that information in hand it was easy finding out the time of your appointment," he revealed insouciantly. Her jaw dropped at that blatant invasion of her privacy. Those details should never have been used to spy on her! "I thought I'd come along and see what I'm paying for."

"I didn't ask you to pay for it," she reminded.

"Look, I know I was an arrogant asshole before," he said evenly.

"Was?" she asked, her eyebrows rising. He merely gave her one of those long, level looks that made her feel completely chastised. She hated that. "Dante, I don't see what else we need to discuss. We had an agreement. *Two*, in fact. Remember? I signed yours and you signed mine. That makes us even."

"I've recently come to appreciate that our previous agreement might not be exactly what I want."

No, he was *not* doing this to her right now. Cleo tried not to panic as she kept her voice firm and her words succinct.

"Well, it's what I want," she said curtly. "Discussion closed."

"Do you have to be so damned stubborn and difficult all the time?" he seethed.

"*Yes.* Look where being easy got me. Knocked up and alone!"

"You don't have to be alone. I have decided that I would not mind sharing this experience with you."

"*Tough!* We don't get convenient do-overs in life, Dante. This has been settled before, and just because you suddenly developed a latent paternal instinct doesn't mean I have to accept that. You have absolutely no right to insert yourself in here like you have some kind of stake in all of this. Stop stalking me and get the hell out of my *life*."

"You know what?" he growled, taking hold of her arm firmly. "No."

"What?"

"You heard me. I said no. You've been calling the shots from the beginning. You sprang this on me, and I barely had time to think about what it all meant before there were papers being shoved at me to sign. Sure, it all sounded great at the time—just sign on the dotted line and for a small fee you and kid disappear as if neither of you had ever existed. No fuss, no mess."

"Legal documents being shoved at you without warning? That sounds remarkably familiar," she said pointedly. "It's no fun when the shoe's on the other foot, is it?"

"So what's this, some kind of warped revenge? Punishment because I had the nerve to treat you like every other woman in my life? Because you're so special, right? Not like all the other—"

She held up a hand to stop him, and it worked, because his mouth clamped shut.

"Let me stop you right there, Dante. I don't have to hear any more of this. Stop trying to make yourself sound like some kind of victim. I presented you with the ideal solution to a problem I knew you didn't want." She backed away and folded her arms belligerently across her chest. Her eyes were challenging him to deny her words.

"No, you presented me with a fait accompli. And why would I argue? I could continue to live my life as if none of this ever happened. But I can't. This baby exists and I can't ignore that."

His words were so eerily similar to the thoughts that had prompted her to have the baby that they made her pause and then panic. Her stomach plummeted to her feet and then back up into her throat until it took everything she had not to vomit on his stupidly expensive shoes.

"You can't have him," she whispered. "He's mine."

"He's mine too."

"No, you signed those papers. He's not yours; he'll never be yours." Her hand dropped to her abdomen defensively, and his eyes darkened at the movement.

"I don't want to take him from you, I just . . . I want to be there. I want to see him. I want to know him, and I want him to know me."

"What changed? How could everything just change *overnight?*" Her voice rose almost hysterically, and she felt Cal's arm curl around her shoulder protectively.

"Maybe you'd better get going, bud," Cal warned.

"This has nothing to do with you, Mr. Faris. It's between Cleo and me."

"I want to know what's changed!" she screeched, demanding to be heard and uncaring of the bystanders who paused on the street to glance at the unfolding tableau. If Dante Damaso insisted on doing this in public, then he would damn well get a scene.

"*I have!*" he snapped. "*I've* changed. I can't stop thinking about this baby. In my head she's a dark-haired, green-eyed little princess in a pink tutu and white leggings, and she's been toddling in and out of my dreams since Monday."

That made her pause and look at him. Really look.

His tie was crooked, she noted absently, one white cuff stuck out slightly longer than the other, one of his shirt buttons wasn't fastened, his hair looked like he'd repeatedly run his fingers through it all morning, and he'd cut himself shaving that morning. Dante Damaso looked . . . undone. He looked like a man who no longer had a handle on his life.

"In my mind he has dark hair, your golden eyes, as well as your mouth and jaw, and he's wearing the world's smallest little sheriff's uniform. He can't walk yet, but he's grinning a big, droolly, toothless grin."

They were both silent for a moment, and her shoulders dropped.

"What do you want from me?"

"I don't know," he admitted, which was quite a confession for the usually self-assured Dante Damaso to make. "I don't think I'd be a great dad. In fact, I'm pretty sure I'll be lousy at it."

It so closely resembled her own fears about the type of mother she'd be that she was staggered by the lack of self-confidence from a man who always seemed to know exactly what to do.

"But I was hoping to be . . . someone she knows?"

"This is such a huge change of heart, Dante, and it isn't at all what I want."

"I know that. I'm just asking that you allow me to properly take care of her, and that I get to see her sometimes."

"What does 'properly take care of her' entail?"

"Trust fund, private schools, decent living conditions."

"No. You're trying to dictate my life and the way I raise my child."

He just stared at her and kept his face frustratingly blank.

"Does this have to be done right now?" Cal asked pointedly, and they both looked at him in surprise, having completely forgotten his presence. He rolled his eyes. "It's starting to rain. And you, miss, have an appointment that you're going to be late for."

"Oh, crap," she muttered, before tossing a sideways glance at Dante, who stared back at her with an uncharacteristically hangdog expression.

"Dante, you can't show up here, tell me you've had a change of heart, and expect me to just be okay with that," she said. "I don't want you at my ultrasound. I don't think I want to share something so . . . *intimate* with you."

"You're having my kid, lady," he reminded, and Cal snorted. "It doesn't get much more intimate than that."

"Cal's going in with me," she maintained.

"I don't have to." Cal shrugged. He kept his eyes on his nails and ignored the murderous glare Cleo threw at him. "I'm squeamish. Blood makes me nauseous."

"Blood?" Now Dante looked a tad green, and Cleo wanted to scream in frustration.

"There's no blood involved. Cal, you're coming with me." She pointed an assertive finger at Dante. "You can wait for us, I'll . . . I'll see if they can make you a copy of the DVD or something."

"You'd do that?"

"Maybe."

What the hell am I doing here? Dante sat hunched in a small, uncomfortable plastic chair, surrounded by women in various stages of pregnancy. They were all openly staring at him, probably wondering why he was lurking about in an OB/GYN's reception room without a pregnant woman nearby. He didn't understand the thought process that had brought him here this morning. All he knew was that at random times over the past forty-eight hours, that tiny, toddling ballerina with the charming smile and sparkling green eyes had crept into his thoughts and had made him wonder, fantasize, and aspire to be more.

But he wasn't sure how *much* more he could, or wanted to, be. He and Cleo were strangers now forever bonded by circumstance. He couldn't pretend that there was anything more than that between them. What he knew about the woman could fill a thimble, and he really had no wish to get to know her, but he had discovered a weird desire within himself to know that baby. As a result, he would have to find a way to work out an amicable arrangement with Cleo.

He had closed more difficult deals than this in the past. Every problem had a solution, and he was confident he would find the solution for this problem too. He just had to find a way to convince Cleo that his way was the best course of action.

If only he knew what the hell his way *was*.

~

"He drives me crazy," Cleo complained to Cal as she lay down on the examination table as per the ultrasound technician's instructions.

"Don't think about him now," Cal said. "You're about to see your baby for the first time. Where's your sense of awe and occasion?"

Her eyes misted over at Cal's words, and she felt guilty for her initial reluctance to have him join her for this. He sometimes said and did the perfect thing at the perfect time. She should be excited, she should be awed, she'd been waiting for this moment since she'd decided to keep her baby, and Dante Damaso was not going to ruin it for her.

She reached for Cal's hand, offering him a watery smile as the technician applied the cold gel to her abdomen and stomach. She sucked in a breath at the unpleasant sensation.

"This is the transducer," the technician, Julia, explained as she held up the wand. "I'll run it over your tummy to capture the images. I'll measure the fetus's size today so that we can more accurately estimate the due date. We'll check Baby's heartbeat, make sure everything's in order and . . . do you want to know the sex?"

"No," Cleo said, decisively. "I want to be surprised."

"No problem." Julia smiled.

"Don't push down too hard with that thing, okay?" Cleo warned, and the other woman chuckled. "My bladder's about to burst." She wasn't feeling very comfortable at all, thanks to all the water she'd had to drink over the last hour in preparation for the test.

"You have no idea how often I get that warning," Julia replied. "Are you ready?"

"Yes." Cleo nodded and watched as she lowered the wand. "Wait."

Julia's hand stopped its descent just an inch away from her belly, and Cleo sighed. She was such a sucker.

"Cal," she whispered. "Maybe we should . . ."

"You want me to fetch him?" Cal asked.

"Would it be okay if we got someone else in here?" she asked Julia, whose eyebrows rose before she shrugged and nodded. "Cal, tell him he doesn't get to speak. He gets to stand quietly at the door while I pretend he's not there."

"Mature," Cal muttered.

"Shut up," she responded without heat. It didn't feel right to leave Dante sitting out there, even though she still didn't want him involved in her pregnancy. She was so confused and really just acting on a gut instinct right now. After all, her own reaction upon learning of her pregnancy had also been disbelief followed by a complete and utter rejection of the very idea of a baby, but she'd changed her mind and nobody had judged her for it. Was it really so inconceivable that perhaps Dante also, after getting over the initial shock, now had similar feelings?

He had signed papers basically renouncing his right to this child, but would it be fair to enforce that document? It wasn't just Dante she had to consider. She had to do the mature thing and think about her baby as well. Surely having Dante around would do more good than harm?

The door opened and Cal came in with Dante trailing meekly behind him. Cleo heard Julia's breath catch slightly at the sight of him and felt a little sorry for her. Dante Damaso's overwhelming physical presence was hard to take without advance warning. Just standing there, trying desperately to look timid and unassuming, he exuded sexual magnetism and supreme self-confidence. Seriously, it was like someone had set a leopard in among the house cats, and it turned Julia into a giggly girl.

"Okay," Julia squeaked, self-consciously pushing a strand of hair behind her ear. "Are we ready now?"

"Yeah, go ahead."

"Right." Julia was all business again, despite the flush highlighting her cheekbones. "Let's see what we can see."

She shifted the wand about, pausing in some places, skirting over others, and Cleo, Cal, and Dante all stared at the monitor in fascination as the grainy image began to form right in front of their eyes.

"Ah, there we go, beautiful . . . Look at that little heart beating away." She pointed to a blurry, twitching smudge on the screen and smiled, taking a couple of notes before looking back up. "There's the forehead. And down here's where the nose is forming. Look at that little jaw and mouth."

It looked like nothing human to Cleo, and much as she squinted and twisted her head this way and that, the picture made no sense to her.

"Looks like an alien." Cal shrugged, unimpressed.

"Are those arms and legs?" He Who Should Have Remained Silent asked.

"Yes." Julia pointed to a couple of white blobs on the monitor, and suddenly the image took shape and made sense to Cleo. She gasped and her hands flew to her mouth as she really saw her baby for the first time.

"Oh my God." The shaky exhalation came from Dante, who was staring at the monitor as an expression that could only be described as absolute wonder lit up his handsome features. His eyes drifted to Cleo's and held them. He seemed to be telling her something, and in the midst of all the joy and awe, a distinct chill settled in Cleo's chest. He looked determined. As if seeing the baby's image had served to strengthen an unknown resolve. And for the first time, Cleo knew that if Dante decided he wanted this child, no force in heaven or hell would stop him. All her precautions and cleverly worded legal documents meant nothing to a man with his resources.

She felt like a complete fool for allowing him back into her life again.

"She's moving," Dante was saying, his voice trembling slightly. "*Jesus,* look at her wriggle. I never imagined her moving around in there."

"Hey, look at the ribs! Are those ribs?" Cal asked, sounding a little more enthused now that he could see more.

"*Cristo,*" Dante swore shakily. "It's so much clearer than I'd imagined."

He had moved a lot closer and was standing right next to the bed, his eyes glued to the monitor and his face rapt.

"Can you determine the gender from this scan?" Really, for someone who should have stood silently in the corner, he was starting to take over the appointment a little, and the only reason Cleo didn't warn him to back off was because she was interested in the answer.

"Sometimes we can tell at this age," Julia said. "But with this one it's a little hard to tell for certain."

"And everything's okay?" he asked, his attention still riveted to the monitor. He barely bothered to glance at Julia while asking the questions.

"Perfectly fine, from what I can tell. That right there is a beautiful, healthy, thirteen-and-a-half-week-old fetus."

"Thirteen and a half? Not fourteen?" he asked, and Julia nodded.

Which meant that the baby had likely been conceived on their last or next-to-last night in Japan. He glanced up at Cleo, who caught his eye and shrugged.

"So maybe she *hasn't* been practicing her frowns yet. But she has all of next week to work on those." His lips tilted upward at her words.

"I'm thinking if it's a girl, you may want to consider naming her Daisy," he said, his eyes sparking with mischief, and she went fiery red as she recalled those damned Daisy Duck boy shorts he'd been so taken with that last night.

"No comment," she replied, and his lips quirked at the corners as he looked back up at the monitor. Cleo's eyes lingered on his profile for a few moments longer, charmed—despite herself—at how very entranced he was by the wriggling image on that screen.

They spent another ten minutes exclaiming and marveling over the various features and body parts they could identify, while Julia took down the fetus's vital statistics and answered the myriad questions Dante seemed to have for her. He asked questions that would never even have occurred to Cleo.

Julia had gotten over that first fluttery reaction pretty quickly and now treated him the way she probably did most expectant fathers, giving each question a measured and intelligent response and never once showing the slightest sign of impatience.

All three of them were a little woebegone when she finally switched the monitor off and the baby's image disappeared.

"I know it's tough to say good-bye," Julia sympathized. "But I'll have a DVD and stills made for you. Well, your baby seems to be happy and healthy, Miss Knight. You can arrange next month's appointment with Dr. Klein at the reception desk. How many copies of the DVD would you like?"

"Two," Dante replied before Cleo could respond, and Julia nodded and happily made arrangements with Dante for the delivery of the DVDs. Cleo couldn't help but feel a bit sidelined. She might be carrying the baby, but her pregnancy was rapidly becoming a Dante Damaso Production, and she was petrified that if she wasn't careful, he would find a way to marginalize her completely.

"I have to pee," she whispered to Cal after she'd made her next appointment at the reception desk. "I'll meet you at the car." She handed him her car keys so that he wouldn't have to wait in the rain, and turned to Dante, who'd watched the whispered exchanged in interest.

"I'll call you later," she told him. "We have to make arrangements to meet with our attorneys present about modifying our previous agreement."

She turned away to rush to the closest ladies' room, not waiting for him to acknowledge her words.

She half expected him to still be waiting for her when she finished five minutes later, and she was relieved to see no sign of him in the reception area upon her return. She waved to Viv, the receptionist, as she dragged on her lightweight denim jacket on her way out the door. She was so preoccupied with fixing one of her jacket sleeves that it took her a while to notice her car was missing. She glanced up and stopped in the middle of the sidewalk, still absently trying to force her arm into the jacket sleeve while she stared blankly at the spot where her car should have been. She frowned in confusion before glancing up and down the road. Maybe she was mistaken about where she'd left it. There was no sign of the nondescript, faded-blue hatchback. Maybe Cal had moved it. But why would he? The spot had been ideal.

She was still trying to figure it out when a hand descended on her shoulder. She nearly jumped out of her skin in fright, and if she hadn't just emptied her bladder she would have embarrassed herself even further. She swung around to confront her accoster and only marginally relaxed when—predictably—Dante Damaso stood behind her.

"I didn't mean to scare you," he said apologetically.

"Yeah? Then stop sneaking up on me," she griped. She was still furiously trying to get her arm into the damned jacket when he took hold of her wrist and gently guided it into the errant sleeve. Dressing her like he would a small child.

"I suppose you have something to do with Cal's disappearance," she said, once she had her jacket on properly.

"You don't have to make it sound so ominous," he replied. "I just told him that we needed to talk and that I'd drive you home. Don't worry, he issued all the warnings a dutiful friend would but recognized that you and I have a few unresolved issues to take care of."

"Well, I suppose we'd better get this over with, then." Cleo couldn't help the surliness that crept into her voice. She felt defensive and had wanted time to mentally and emotionally prepare for this discussion. "Where are you parked?"

Dante watched Cleo animatedly chatting and laughing with James, his driver. They were discussing James's grandmother's chocolate fudge cake, which was apparently "to die for." Although how the hell Cleo knew that was anybody's guess. She didn't look at Dante once during the drive, didn't make any conversation, not even to ask where they were going. Not one stray smile or misplaced comment spilled over in his direction, and he wasn't sure why, but that bothered the hell out of him. It was as if he wasn't even present.

Dante was not used to being so comprehensively ignored, so he did what he always did when a situation became awkward: he took out his cell phone to check messages and make calls. When he was working, he was in charge; he was never uncomfortable and knew how to handle every scenario that was thrown at him. It was a handy way to ignore difficult social situations. Still, this time he couldn't shut them out as completely as he would have liked; part of him wanted to weigh in on the buttercream versus fondant debate. He had very definite views when it came to cake, but Cleo wouldn't know that because she thought he was boring, stuffy, and overbearing. And maybe he was, but he could damned well discuss cake with her—and anybody else—any day of the week.

He stifled his childish thoughts and managed to complete a couple of important phone calls before their short drive ended. James rolled the car to a stop in an underground parking lot, and Cleo stopped talking and peered at her surroundings curiously. She'd been so busy proving that she could ignore Dante that she hadn't really absorbed the direction they were heading during the short trip from the doctor's office.

"Where are we?" she asked, before seeing a familiar sign on one of the nearby tourist maps. "Are we at the Waterfront?"

"Close," he said, gathering his briefcase and phone while James stepped out of the car and opened the door for Cleo. Dante didn't bother waiting for the man to do the same for him and was at Cleo's side before she had properly emerged from the car.

"Close? How close is close?" Her voice was suspicious, and he stifled a smile. He liked this prickly side of her, even though it also frustrated the hell out of him.

"Close enough." He kept his responses short and cryptic, partly because he knew it would piss her off, and partly because he didn't want her freaking out before he got her where he wanted her. "I thought we could have a late lunch and talk."

She hesitated, and he sighed before gently taking hold of her elbow.

"Cleo, try to trust me, okay? What the hell do you think I'm going to do to you? We need to have an uninterrupted talk, that's all."

She just stared at him, and he sighed before steering her toward the express elevator to his penthouse apartment.

"James, I'll call you when I need you to take Miss Knight home," Dante said once he and Cleo were safely aboard the lift. James nodded, his expression serious and businesslike once again.

"What restaurant are we going to?" she asked, her voice alive with doubt, and Dante squeezed his eyes shut before confirming her suspicion.

"No restaurant. I brought you to my apartment. We can talk there."

"I don't want to go to your apartment," she screeched, and he grimaced. "Let me off at the next floor. Where are the buttons for the other floors?"

"Cleo, come on. Don't be silly."

"Oh, sure, now you use my name, when you have me trapped in this creepy one-button elevator. Is that supposed to reassure me? Are you using my name to create a rapport with me?"

"What the hell are you talking about?" he asked, trying—and failing—to keep the exasperation out of his voice.

"That's what kidnappers do, right? Try to create a rapport with their victims?" They'd reached the penthouse floor, and Dante shook his head and stepped into the elegant lobby, leaving her to frantically push at the single button in the elevator.

"It won't work," he told her after her third desperate jab. "It's coded to accept only my fingerprint."

Of course it was. She was so pissed off. Bringing her to his place was a sneaky thing to do. She would really rather speak to him on neutral ground or on her own territory. And she had a feeling he knew that. This didn't bode well for future amicable relations.

She glared at him before reluctantly stepping out of the elevator.

"I can't figure out if this is reminiscent of Hannibal Lecter's lair or James Bond's high-tech den," she muttered, and he tossed her a cynical little smile.

"Is that a retinal scan?" she asked, fascinated in spite herself as he stepped up to a discreet sensor next to the door frame. A green light switched on after the scan, and he followed it up by placing his palm on a panel below the sensor, and a second green light switched on. Just below the panel was a keypad, and he shielded it slightly with his body as he keyed in a number. There was a third green light followed by a slightly musical beep, and he opened his door and waved her in.

"Paranoid much?" she asked as she swept by him.

The place was huge, lavish, and seriously expensive, with panoramic views of the mountain, the waterfront, the yacht basin, and the ocean through floor-to-ceiling glass panes. There was gray-and-white marble everywhere, ugly stark furniture, and gigantic potted plants that looked like they belonged in a greenhouse or a rain forest. Then again, with all the glass, this place could easily pass for both greenhouse and goldfish bowl.

"Guess you don't roam around naked much," she observed, stepping up to one of the windows and glancing down at the little people strolling around on the dock.

"The windows are tinted," he said, his gravelly voice sending unwelcome stirrings of desire shuddering up her spine. "We could do all *manner* of things in here, and nobody would ever know."

"Yeah, but you can see out." Ugh. That didn't sound sexy so much as creepy.

"Hmm, it tends to bring out the closet exhibitionist in some people," he murmured.

She ignored his suggestive tone and continued to roam around the place, pausing every so often to stare out at the view or to look more closely at some grotesquely oversized vase or to gape in awe at his gigantic flat-screen TV and ridiculously complicated-looking entertainment system.

He didn't say a word, just watched as she flitted from one part of the huge living room to the next. She eventually paused at a sliding door that led out to the wooden deck with its deep blue rectangular infinity pool.

She was aware of his eyes on her as she slipped out onto the deck. The rain had stopped enough for the weak, watery spring sun to slip between the clouds and bless her with a glorious shaft of light. She lifted her face to the heat and just stood there, trying to gird herself for what was to come.

"I'm putting a couple of T-bones on the grill." Dante's quiet voice came from behind her and startled her out of her reverie. Immediately back on the defensive, she stepped out of the sun and under the eaves.

It was cold in the shadows, which kept her alert and ready for anything he had to throw at her. "How do you like your steak cooked?"

"Medium," she said, and hugged her arms around her as she tried to ward off the chill.

"Come in out of the cold," he told her as he turned to go back inside, and she followed. Once inside she wandered aimlessly from one end of the living room to the other. He was busy in the open-plan kitchen, his tie undone, jacket tossed aside, and shirtsleeves rolled up. It was the most relaxed she'd ever seen him. His kitchen was a modern masterpiece of chrome and marble, and felt as frigid and unlived in as the rest of his home.

That's what was wrong with this place! It didn't feel like anyone actually lived here. There were no personal effects lying around, no family pictures, no clothes scattered about. No remnants of any work he'd been doing spread out, not even a book he might have been reading. It was eerie.

"You can have a look upstairs if you like," he invited, and she glanced over at him in surprise.

There was another floor?

"The staircase is tucked away over there." He nodded toward a spot opposite the patio door, and she saw that the staircase was situated inconspicuously in the far corner of the room.

She meandered over to it, and before she knew it, she had her hand on the highly polished banister and was making her way upstairs. Like the living area down below, the place was a marvel of décor and architecture and was as cold as ice. Cleo hated it. There were three bedrooms, each with its own attached bath and shower, complete with a king-size bed with matching bureaus, huge walk-in closets, and a wall of those nasty voyeuristic windows. There was also a spacious, very well-equipped gym with a treadmill, Airdyne bike, punching bags of various sizes, and weight-training equipment. Considering his hard body, she figured he probably spent a lot of time blowing off steam in here.

His study was the smallest room and the only one that bore any hint of personality. It was furnished with rich oak furniture, and gorgeous floor-to-ceiling bookshelves took up an entire wall of the room. It was also the only room with wooden floors, a fireplace, and cozy rugs. Comfy overstuffed chairs and a matching love seat were situated in front of the fireplace. His large oak desk took up an entire corner of the room, which was where she saw real signs of life. Papers, a laptop, a familiar-looking iPad, and . . . was that a *ficus* perched on his desk? She shuddered at the sight of it and focused instead on several framed photographs.

The one that held her attention was an old photo of a grinning dark-haired boy of about nine or ten hugging a scruffy dog. Of course, it could only be Dante. The eyes were the same, and the boyish features held a promise of the gorgeousness to come. There was another picture close by of an older man who bore a striking resemblance to Dante, with his arm around the teen version of Dante. A smile twitched at her lips as she took in the gawky frame that would eventually fill out so magnificently, the awkward hunched shoulders, and the glare. The glare was definitely Dante's. Then there was a picture of Dante and Luc beaming at the camera in their graduation robes, both looking young and carefree as they held up their degrees in triumph. Luc had a similar picture in his study. Cleo had missed Luc's graduation; she'd been busy doing something she'd undoubtedly considered vastly more important but couldn't even remember seven years later. She sighed and tore her eyes from the photograph.

There were a few other pictures scattered about of the dog, the older man with various women, and one of a yacht, but no more of Dante. In all there couldn't have been more than ten photographs, and she found that rather sad. She might have resented her grandparents, but every aspect of her childhood and teen years had been recorded for posterity. Every report card kept, every playbill from every dance recital she'd ever been in had been meticulously filed away in a scrapbook. She had been loved, and it showed in every memento and photograph that they had kept of—and for—her.

Feeling like an intruder, she backed out of the room and headed downstairs. Dante was focused on whatever he was doing in the kitchen.

"It smells divine," she said, leaning on the butcher block in the middle of the kitchen as she watched him chop veggies for a salad.

"I hope it *tastes* divine," he said, and shrugged a little awkwardly.

"Do you often cook?" She would never have guessed it of him.

"*Sì.* I enjoy it. I have never really cooked for anyone before now, though." The confession surprised her, and her eyes widened.

"Really?"

"I don't bring women here."

"*Really?*"

"Will you stop saying 'really'? It's . . ."

"Aggravating?" she supplied without thinking.

"It's . . . ," he continued, ignoring her.

"Frustrating?"

"*Annoying.*" The word was gritted out between teeth so tightly clenched, Cleo actually feared he'd break them.

"'Frustrating' and 'aggravating' are synonyms for 'annoying,'" she pointed out.

"I wanted to use 'annoying.' Which is what you're being right now. In addition to being frustrating and aggravating."

"And you're being redundant."

"You're really difficult to talk to sometimes," he accused, his accent thickening with every word, and she shrugged a little shamefacedly.

"I know," she confessed. "It's a defense mechanism."

"I don't mean to put you on the defensive, but it seems to be your natural state."

"It's my natural state around you."

He sighed and pointed to the kitchen cabinet.

"Cutlery, tableware, place mats." He pointed at the huge dining table a couple of yards away. "Table. Make yourself useful."

"Yes, *sir*," she said snappily, and jumped to it.

CHAPTER NINE

"Whoa, this is great," Cleo enthused, after slicing off a sliver of tender, perfectly cooked steak. It was beautifully flavored and practically melted in her mouth. Dante had served it with a mushroom sauce, a baked potato with all the trimmings, and a healthy green salad. He had a glass of Pinotage to accompany his meal, and she had settled on grape soda—she thought she could pretend it was red wine until she took a sip and the sweet fizziness made a liar out of her.

"I never imagined you'd be a good cook," she said as she dug into her potato.

"I find it relaxing," he said. He seemed a little uncomfortable with her praise and quickly changed the subject. "By the way . . . kidnappers do *not* try to create a rapport with their victims. That would make them terrible kidnappers. Victims try to create the rapport. They want the kidnappers to see them as human."

"What?"

"It's just that what you said earlier was technically incorrect," he pointed out, and she laughed incredulously.

"I was making a point," she said, and he shrugged. "You brought me here against my will."

"I brought you here for a reason," he told her.

"Yes, to talk. So talk."

"I actually wanted you to see this place."

"Why?" She didn't like the sound of that. Why would he bring her to see his home? And why was he now evading her eyes?

"Look." He sighed. "This pregnancy has taken us both by surprise, and considering how much you dislike me, I can't imagine you were too thrilled when you first learned about it. Were you?"

She hesitated before shaking her head.

"I wasn't."

"Yet you decided, despite your initial reservations, to keep the baby. Why?"

"Not because I wanted anything from you," she said, hating her own defensiveness.

"I know you don't have a financial motive for keeping the baby," he admitted. "And I apologize for initially implying that you did. I'm just curious."

Implying? He had out and out accused her of trying to extort money from him.

"At first I wasn't sure if I wanted to terminate the pregnancy or not," she said, letting the whole *implying* thing slide for now. She pushed her half-eaten meal aside, appetite lost. He did the same with his meal, seemingly as disturbed by her confession as she had been to make it.

"And then I wasn't sure if I wanted to keep him or not. But then he had fingers and fingernails." She wiped at her blurry eyes and was surprised to discover moisture there. "I just felt so protective of him after that. And then I started to think of him as *my* baby. And that was it. I was going to be this baby's mother. But in order to take proper care of him, I'd need financial support, and that's why I approached you."

"Would you *ever* have told me about the baby if you'd decided to give him up for adoption?"

"I don't know. There was—*is*—nothing between us, so it just seemed like it would complicate things even more."

"I want you to know that I understand everything you've done, all the decisions you've made up till now, and I want you to recognize that I won't attempt to take this baby from you. But I also want you to acknowledge that I have some rights here too."

"You were perfectly willing to give those rights up just a few weeks ago," she reminded him, and he leveled a steady look at her.

"And *just* like you, I changed my mind."

"So, now what?"

"You can't continue living in that apartment, Cleo. The stairs are dangerous, and the mold is a health hazard. And the walls are so damp you can't tell me it doesn't leak during the winter. It can't be good for you or the baby."

"I'll be moving in with Luc and Blue next month."

"I don't want you to dismiss this out of hand . . . ," he began, his cautious tone setting off alarm bells in her mind and making her sit up a little straighter. "But I'd like you to consider moving in here."

"Absolutely not." It was a knee-jerk response, but she really didn't want to even deliberate over the pros and cons of his proposal.

"I know it seems preposterous, but my plan has merit."

"I don't think you've fully considered this plan. The baby won't be here for another six months; that's time enough to agree on some kind of joint-custody arrangement." The thought of sharing her baby's time with him wasn't at all appealing, but she *did* acknowledge that he had rights in this situation despite the documents he'd signed. She could only hope that he changed his mind again before she gave birth.

"The baby is already here, and I want her to have the best possible care even before her birth," he told her.

"I can do that," she insisted.

"I can do it better." She gasped at that arrogant proclamation, which embodied everything she had feared about his involvement. This was Dante Damaso taking charge and railroading her.

"How *dare* you? I've been taking care of myself quite fine up until now, with absolutely zero support from you. One little letter and suddenly you're ready to play dad? And what if you change your mind again next week? Or next month? Or years down the line? How do I deal with the fallout then?"

"I told you I wasn't really sure what I'd like my actual role to be, but I *do* want to be a part of that child's life."

"As what?" Frustration made her voice shrill. "His uncle? A friend of the family? Figure out what you want before you drag my baby into your life, Dante."

"I *don't* know what I want. All I know is that I would like an opportunity to work it out, and I still have six months within which to do that. In the meantime, you moving in here would help me make that decision while simultaneously solving the immediate predicament you have with your living arrangements."

"I don't want to live with you." She shook her head, still unable to believe he was suggesting such an outlandish notion. Yet his eyes were deadly serious.

"You know how much I travel. I'm hardly ever here, so you'd have the run of the place. You can make yourself at home, have friends over, live comfortably, and I can be sure that you're safe and well taken care of while you're pregnant with my kid."

It was a completely insane idea. She wasn't going to allow him to manipulate her like this. Not while she still had options.

"And what happens after the baby's born?" Her question seemed to stump him, and he ruminated over it for a few moments before replying.

"We'll work something else out. Find a suitable home for you both. I'll help with that, and if you have reservations about me helping with property, I'll be more than happy to put it in the baby's name."

"Why not just do that now?" she asked.

"By the time we find the right place and complete all the paper-work, your pregnancy would be too advanced. And where would you live in the meantime? With Blue and Luc? Do you think that's fair? Being a burden on them like that? Besides, there's no name to put on the papers yet."

Oh, he had *all* the answers today.

"It wouldn't be a good idea for me to live here, Dante." She pushed herself away from the table. "I'd like to leave now, please."

He nodded, the muscles bunching in his jaw as he fought to keep whatever emotion he was feeling under wraps. He tossed aside his napkin.

"Very well." He helped her shrug into her jacket and then lifted his phone up from one of the kitchen counters.

"James, we'll be down in a couple of minutes. Meet us at the elevator." He hung up without another word and waved her ahead of him. "After you."

The sun was just starting to set half an hour later, when Dante walked Cleo up to the security gate of her building. An unsavory-looking young man was hanging out next to the gate. He was smoking some-thing that smelled a little too aromatic to be a cigarette and jerked his chin at them when he saw them approach.

"'Sup?" he muttered and then looked away from Dante's intim-idating glare.

"Thanks, Dante," she said firmly, hoping to send him back to the car, where James stood waiting. He was having none of that, though, and lifted an unimpressed brow at her words.

"I'm walking you to your door," he said, glancing at the lurking boy with palpable distaste. "For obvious reasons."

"It's not that bad," she protested. "They're all mostly students."

"Well, that particular student"—he said with a nod toward the sinister-looking young man—"must be putting himself through college by dealing dope. And those two over there . . ." This time he nodded toward a giggling, swaying pair of young women in tight miniskirts and thigh-high boots. "Are probably hooking to pay their tuition."

Cleo peered at the girls in the gloomy light and gasped when she recognized them. They saw her at the same time and screeched in delight at the sight of her.

"OMG! *Cleo!*" Coco screamed, and Cleo caught Dante involuntarily flinching at the sound of that high-pitched voice. "It's so weird to find you waiting down here for us. It's like you *knew* we were coming."

"She did know, remember?" Gigi reminded her in an only slightly less shrill voice. And Cleo hadn't really known they were coming, since nothing definite had been arranged.

"What the hell?" Dante muttered beneath his breath, and Cleo smiled at the consternation she could hear in his voice.

"Hi, girls," Cleo greeted, and the two scantily clad women fell all over her, showering her with hugs and kisses. Coco, predictably, was the first one to notice Dante.

"Oh, hi there. I'm Coco Sibiya. Nice to meet you. Always happy to meet any friend of Cleo's." The staggeringly beautiful ebony-skinned woman grabbed his hand before he could offer it and shook it heartily. "And this is Gigi."

"Hi." Petite and pretty blonde Gigi waved shyly but didn't try to take his hand.

Dante thrust his hands in his pockets and stared at the three of them thoughtfully. Cleo tried to picture them through his eyes and realized that they were all approximately the same height—just slightly above five feet—with similar body types. Gigi and Coco were a little slimmer than Cleo, since she'd started to pick up some baby weight.

"How do you all know one another?" he asked curiously, momentarily diverted from the loitering wannabe thug, who was also watching them curiously.

"We went to dance school together. And Cleo and I danced with the same company for a year after we graduated," Coco explained. "She always was the most talented and going on to bigger and better things before Cal dropped her."

Cleo glared daggers at Coco for wording it like that. Cal still felt immense guilt over what had happened and had tried his damnedest to make it up to her. He'd taken time off from his own career to help her recuperate, and in a way the incident had ruined his career too. Cleo suspected that he was unable to allow himself to succeed.

"He *dropped* you?" There was a dangerous edge in Dante's voice.

"It was an accident." It was the first time—since it had happened—that Cleo could hear a ring of absolute truth and sincerity in her own voice. How could she have allowed one of her best friends to wallow in his own guilt for so long? How could she have steeped herself in such absolute self-pity that she'd been blind to what she was doing to him? God, she was an awful person. Shallow, selfish, and weak. She shook her head, slightly dazed by the direction of her thoughts.

She looked up at Dante, whose eyes were narrowed in concern, and hated the doubt she now felt about him, about how she was dealing with her pregnancy and his need to be involved.

"Yeah, well, his career took a hit after that too," Coco cheerfully divulged.

"This is ancient history, Coco. I'd rather not discuss it any longer," Cleo said pointedly, and Gigi, bless her soul, jumped right into the awkward breach.

"Well, we're here to take Cleo out for a night on the town. Would you like to join us, Mr. . . . ?"

"Damaso," he informed her, and held out a hand to Gigi, who shook it with enthusiasm. "And I'm not sure Cleo's feeling up to a night on the town." The last was said with a worried look at Cleo, who felt a little punch-drunk after her epiphany.

"Cleo?" Coco waved a hand in front of her dazed eyes. "What's up with you, girl?"

"Uh . . ." Cleo blinked, finally coming back to the present. "I'm a little tired. Not up to a night of partying, I'm afraid."

"Aww, come on, don't be such a spoilsport, it'll be just like old times." Coco pouted and Cleo nearly giggled at that. "Old times" had included early bedtimes, brutally long rehearsals, tired minds and bodies, and disgustingly painful feet. The few nights they had gone out to "party" had nearly always ended after only two or three drinks before midnight had effectively wiped her out. Not exactly halcyon party nights.

"I'm a little pregnant," she admitted with a smile, happy at that moment to let that old life go and excited for whatever the future held. "No drinking for me."

"Seriously?" Gigi's shriek was impressive and could rival anything Coco had in her bag of screeches. "That's awesome. I'll make a fantastic aunt, Cleo." She hugged Cleo tightly. Cleo laughed at her enthusiasm. Coco seemed a little shell-shocked but hugged her as well.

"Wow, this is unexpected news," she said.

"Yeah, I'm making a few lifestyle changes. I have to leave this place, for one. Cleo pointed to the building behind her. "I'll probably wind up moving in with the baby's dad."

She saw Dante's head swivel in her direction, and she met his shocked, questioning gaze with a shrug. After everything she'd just learned about herself, she felt that maybe giving him the benefit of the doubt would be the best thing for her baby, for Dante, and for herself. She hoped this was the right course of action. Only time would tell.

In the end, Coco and Gigi walked her up to her apartment, and Cleo managed to send Dante on his way after he extracted a promise from her that she would call him later. Cal wasn't home when the women reached the apartment, which was a blessing—in that he absolutely hated Coco and, to a lesser extent, Gigi—and a curse because Cleo was desperate to talk to him after her revelation. She figured he was probably uncertain of her mood and hiding out after "abandoning" her at the doctor's office that afternoon.

Coco and Gigi stayed for a couple of hours, eating forbidden chocolate truffles, chatting about the company's new production of *Cinderella* and Coco's role as one of the evil stepsisters, Cal, the weather, and eventually Dante.

"So, that man is gorgeous," Coco said, licking some melted chocolate off her fingertips.

"Which one?" Cleo asked evasively, and both Gigi and Coco threw her a dry look.

"Do we have to answer that?" Coco asked incredulously.

"Okay, fine. Yeah, he's good-looking."

"And he's the baby's dad?" Coco prompted. With everything that had happened, was the nondisclosure agreement still valid? Cleo had no idea how things stood between her and Dante now.

"He's my ex-boss," she hedged. "We were just going over some details involving my old job. He's a bit of a prick, actually." Most of that was technically true.

"So, who *is* the baby's dad?" Gigi asked, falling for the subterfuge like the sweet, trusting soul she was. Coco's eyes told Cleo that she wasn't buying it at all, but thankfully she didn't pursue the matter.

"Nobody you'd know," Cleo said dismissively, before asking Coco another question about her new role. As a diversion, it was pretty effective, because there was nothing Coco loved more than talking about herself.

~⑨~

Cal wasn't back by the time they left, so Cleo bit the bullet and called Dante. Luckily she still had his number in her phone. He answered after the second ring.

"Did you mean it?" he asked without preamble.

"Yes, but there are a few caveats."

"Of course there are," he said drily.

"I won't have my freedom curbed," she said, ignoring his sarcasm.

"How the hell would I curb your freedom?" He actually sounded offended. "I won't shackle you to the kitchen sink or whatever the hell it is you're imagining."

"I just mean that I'll come and go as I please. I still dance regularly at a studio in Newlands, and I'm thinking of teaching a few classes to earn some money." She'd been thinking about this option more and more after her last visit to Susan's studio. Maybe it wouldn't be so bad; maybe she could finally let go of her old ambitions and take pride in her students' achievements. It would help if said students were kids instead of teens or adults, though. She wasn't sure she'd be any good at it, but she was still excited at the thought of a fresh start.

"You don't have to work," Dante said.

"Yes, I do." There was a long silence after that firm proclamation before she heard him clear his throat.

"What else?" he asked.

"My life is my own, and where I go, what I do, and who I do it with are none of your concern."

"You mean with men?"

"I mean in general. But yeah, any relationships—platonic or otherwise—I happen to form with other men are not your business."

"You intend to get involved with guys while you're pregnant?"

"Who knows? Life is weird like that."

"Fine, and the same rule applies to me."

"Whatever." Like she cared. Okay, maybe she cared. A little. "And we'll be looking for a small—not huge, expensive, or ostentatious—place for the baby and me to move into after he's born. The place will be in his name. It will never belong to me. Any money from you will go toward my medical bills and the baby's necessities, like clothes, medical bills, and education."

"I want to set up a trust fund and a university fund."

She let him have that one, since the next one was so important to her.

"The baby's last name will be Knight, and while you will play a role in his or her life, you will *never* be named as this child's father." He was silent for so long that she feared they had lost the connection. When his voice eventually broke the silence, it was quiet and a little hoarse.

"Fine."

Cleo exhaled the breath she'd been holding and allowed herself to relax.

"I want all of that in writing and witnessed by both attorneys before I move in," she added shakily.

"Right."

After another achingly long silence, Cleo felt her eyes well up with tears. She hoped to God this was the right move for all of them. She didn't want to be unfair, but she didn't want to screw herself over either.

"Dante," she whispered.

"Yeah?"

"Thank you."

Mi placer, cielo. The Spanish startled her. Dante's English was so good that, despite his accent, she sometimes forgot that Spanish was his first language. She was starting to learn that he only ever used it when he was under emotional duress.

"I think I'll have to tell Luc about this now," she acknowledged, saddened by how the news would potentially affect her brother.

"I should do it," Dante insisted. "It is the man's duty, and I should have told him long before now."

"Dante, there's no need for this sexist BS," she said. "He's my brother. I know how to handle him."

"I'll do it." She could hear him practically gritting his teeth as he said it, and she sighed, remaining silent to avoid an argument but already planning when and where to tell her brother about the *thing* with Dante. She just needed to get to Luc before Dante did, which would be easy since Dante was a slave to his schedule.

He seemed to take her silence for tacit agreement and changed the subject by asking her when she thought she'd be ready to move in.

"I'm not sure," she said. "I have to give notice here, sort out the teaching job with my friend at the studio, and figure out what I'll be bringing with me."

"Let me know if you need help; I will arrange movers."

"I can do it myself," she protested, and he sighed loudly.

"There you go again, being needlessly difficult. It is a sincere offer of help, *dulzura*." She blinked at the endearment. She had Googled it after their return from Tokyo and discovered that it meant "sweetness." This was the first time he had used it outside of an intimate setting, and it took her by surprise.

"Thanks," she whispered, wondering how the hell this was going to work when every single offer he made to help her felt like charity and a blow to her pride. She needed to loosen up a bit.

They ended the call soon afterward, and after a quick shower, she slipped into a pair of fuzzy pajamas and sent a text message to Cal, asking where he was. It was nearly midnight when he responded.

Out with Carl. Be home soon.

Cleo stared at the screen and wondered who the hell Carl was. Last time she checked, he was dating some guy named Bryan.

She went to the kitchen and made herself a cup of cocoa, trying not to see the dishes piled in the sink. Dante's cold marble-and-chrome masterpiece of an apartment wouldn't remain pristine for long. She wasn't the neatest of roommates, and she hoped for his sake he'd meant it when he said he wouldn't be around much.

She was sitting at the kitchen table when Cal finally breezed in about ten minutes later, and she got up immediately to walk straight into his arms and hug him tightly. His arms closed around her in surprise.

"Hey, what's this? Are you okay, hon? I'm sorry for deserting you at the doctor's office, but Damaso said he'd get you home and that you guys needed to work some stuff out, which I definitely agreed with. Did he upset you? I'm sorry. I should have foreseen that . . . I should have stayed."

"No," she murmured into his chest. "You were right. We had some stuff to work out. I'm not upset about that."

"Then what's this about? Pregnancy hormones again?"

"Cal, we need to talk." She took his hand and led him to the kitchen table, where he sat down opposite her, his face etched with concern.

"I wanted to say that I'm sorry," she whispered.

"About what? Moving? Hon, we've been over this . . ."

"For never really forgiving you after the accident." His mouth snapped shut and his eyes burned into hers. He didn't say a word, and she reached over to touch one of his clenched fists where it rested on the table. "It wasn't your fault, you know. But I needed someone to blame, and all these years I've subconsciously blamed you, and *worse*, I allowed you to blame yourself. Which makes me a crappy friend and an even crappier person."

"I dropped you," he said quietly, and he turned his hand over to clasp hers.

"And my timing and balance were off," she said firmly. "You know that. How we both didn't get catastrophically injured is beyond me."

"Still, I should have held on. I was taller, stronger . . ."

"Hon," she said, using his nickname for her, and he smiled through the tears that were starting to glitter in his gray eyes. "You're only human.

When I lost my balance, you tried your damnedest to hold on to me, but you couldn't. In all this time I never really admitted that I was also to blame. I've been so selfish. I've sat back and *watched* you practically self-destruct, and I never once said anything. I just *let* you do it. And the worst is, in three years, I never even realized it until tonight. I've felt sorry for myself long enough. My dancing career is over, and it has been for years. And my life is fine without dance, and, Cal, as your very best friend who wants nothing but wonderful things for you, I want you to go out there and be everything I no longer can. Your career isn't over; you're a damned fine dancer. Stop acting like a complete ass to make *me* feel better and get your career back on track."

"Where's all this coming from?" he asked.

"I'm going to be a mother, time for me to start behaving like an adult, don't you think? I love you, Cal, and I'm going to miss you like crazy once you start working and touring, but let's face it, we do tend to drive each other crazy all the time anyway."

He laughed, and just like that, everything felt lighter and better between them. Better than it had been for years.

"Dante, good to see you, man." Lucius grabbed hold of Dante's hand and gave him one of those manly half hugs. It was a familiarity that Dante only ever allowed with Lucius; most of his other male friends were a little more tightly wound and a little less likable. After his conversation with Cleo the night before, Dante suspected that she would try to see her brother before he could have the chance to. So he'd canceled his early-morning meetings and come straight to Luc's office. Dante knew that he risked losing a friendship he valued very much. It was one of the reasons he'd given the clearly unqualified Cleo a job in such a high-ranking position in the first place—he'd felt he owed it to Luc.

"I'm sorry to spring this visit on you," Dante told Luc as the man ushered him into a seat in his dingy little office at the back of the store he managed. Dante glanced around the place. Luc had been brilliant at school, and it was inconceivable to Dante that he wasn't the business manager of some multi-million-dollar corporation somewhere. He shouldn't be working in such a tiny store in this industrial part of Cape Town.

Dante looked at his friend and saw—for the first time—the lines etched into his brow and next to his mouth. He looked older than his thirty-two years, and there was some early gray mixed into his thick black hair. He and Cleo bore a passing resemblance to each other, in the eyes and around the nose and mouth.

"How are you, *amigo*?" he asked quietly.

"Ah, you know, same old same old. Nothing much has changed since we saw you last. Blue and I are still trying to get that wedding organized, but the house is taking up our spare funds at the moment."

Dante had offered, years ago, to help out with the house, but Luc was as stubborn and proud as his sister. He could definitely see where Cleo got it from now.

"And hey, man," Luc added, "I've wanted to apologize about the whole Cleo thing for a while now."

It was the opening Dante had been searching for, even though the man's words baffled him.

"The Cleo thing?" Dante wasn't sure what to make of Luc's cryptic statement.

"Yeah, first, she didn't even know who you were when she applied for that job. I mean, I was a little irritated with her for applying, I didn't want you to think I had anything to do with it." Dante shook his head in disbelief. Unable to grasp that Cleo's job application had been sheer coincidence. But then knowing what he knew about both Cleo and Luc, how could it have been anything different? The siblings would rather chew off their own limbs before asking a friend for help. "And then to just quit like that?"

Luc shook his head in disgust.

"She's always been so irresponsible, and now with the . . ." He paused, even though Dante knew he'd been about to mention the pregnancy. Luc shook his head again before continuing. "Anyway, I just wanted to apologize about that. Her behavior was completely rash, as usual."

Something about the way Luc was denigrating Cleo rubbed Dante the wrong way, especially since it was completely unfair.

"You shouldn't be so harsh on her," Dante said, and Luc did a double take.

"What?"

"You shouldn't be so hard on her. She didn't quit. I fired her."

"You did?" Luc's brow furrowed, as he tried to process this new information. "Why? What did she do?"

"Maybe you should give your sister the benefit of the doubt once in a while," Dante said, and Luc's eyes narrowed.

"Dante," he said, his voice going dangerously quiet. "What's this about?"

"This is what I've come here to discuss with you," Dante replied, clearing his throat awkwardly.

"What? My sister?"

"Yes. And the baby."

Luc pushed himself up out of his chair and braced his clenched fists on the desk in front of him as he leaned forward to pin Dante with his fierce glare. Dante remained seated, allowing the man the position of power in this instance because, really, Dante was in the wrong.

"How do you know about the baby?" Luc asked in an uneven voice, and Dante took a deep breath and met his friend's gaze head-on before bidding one of his longest-standing friendships a reluctant farewell.

"I'm the child's father."

Luc moved so fast it took both of them by surprise. Dante was out of his chair and pinned against the thin prefab wall in seconds.

"You *bastard*," Luc hissed, his hands fisted in Dante's shirtfront. "I trusted you with my *family*!"

"Luc, take it easy." Dante tried to remain calm and nonconfrontational, but Luc dragged him forward and slammed him back against the wall, shaking it violently.

"You'll be marrying her."

"No, I won't," Dante corrected. "Neither your sister nor I want that. I will, however, be taking care of her and of the baby."

"We don't need anything from you," Luc said, the Knight pride once again coming to the surface. "Not one bloody thing. If you won't do the right thing and marry her, then I'll take care of her and the baby."

"Don't be ridiculous, Lucius. The baby is my responsibility. Cleo—while she's pregnant—is my responsibility. You have Blue and the house to take care of. Cleo will be moving in with me for the remainder of her pregnancy, and after that she'll be moving into a house that I will purchase in our child's name—as per her wishes."

"Yeah, money buys you out of every undesirable situation, doesn't it? Must be nice," Luc said with a sneer, and the man's contemptuous words stung more than they should have. Dante tried not to let them affect him, but it was hard when Luc's opinion of him had just hit rock bottom. "My sister and her child are not for sale. You can take whatever the hell deals you have made with her and shove them up your ass. Get out of my office."

"The arrangements that Cleo and I have made have nothing to do with you. I only came to tell you about our plans out of respect for you and for our friendship."

"You have so much respect for me that you used my sister like one of your little sluts? And then tossed her aside like rubbish when she turned up pregnant? And worse than that, you *fired* her? Why? Because your mistake would be staring you in the face every day as she grew bigger and bigger with your little bast—"

"Don't!" Dante finally pushed back, releasing Luc's hold on him and preventing him from saying the horrible word he'd been about to utter. To his credit, the other man looked shamefaced for a few moments, before the anger took over again.

"Get the hell out of my office," Luc seethed, and Dante, tempted though he was to leave, stood his ground.

"Luc, Cleo *will* be moving in with me, and she's going to need you."

"Don't tell me what the hell my sister needs; I know her better than you do," Luc retorted.

Dante nodded. "Just don't abandon her because you're pissed off with me," he said.

Luc seemed to consider his words before drawing back and punching him in the jaw.

Dante reeled, his hand going up to his throbbing face. His instinctive reaction was to punch back, but he knew that he owed Luc a free one and let it go. He opened and closed his jaw to test if it was broken, but luckily it was just stiff.

"I deserved that," he acknowledged, and the words seemed to infuriate Luc even more. When the man drew back for another punch, Dante felt the need to warn him, "But the second one won't be free."

The warning made Luc hesitate.

"I hope you will come to understand that I never meant to disrespect you or your family, Luc," Dante explained. "But the solution to Cleo's pregnancy isn't marriage. We'd both be miserable, and as a consequence, the child would suffer too."

"I don't want to hear any more of your pathetic excuses, Damaso." Luc refused to meet his eyes, which bothered Dante more than anything that had happened before. "You're not the man I thought you were."

CHAPTER TEN

Cleo—upon arrival at Luc's work—spotted Dante's car immediately. She brought her car to a quick stop and jumped out to confront James, who, as usual, was a stoic sentinel beside the gleaming black car.

"Don't tell me he's in there," she said, dread pooling in her stomach. James removed his sunglasses and nodded. Cleo muttered something completely unladylike before tossing her keys at James and sprinting toward the entrance of the grubby little IT store her brother managed.

"James, I'm sorry, please park that for me," she called over her shoulder, and because she wasn't looking where she was going, she ran full tilt into something hard and immovable.

"*Oof!*" She stared up at whatever it was she'd just run into and then immediately scowled.

"God, are you okay?" Dante's hands had come up to steady her, and he looked her over for potential damage.

"You just *had* to get here before me, didn't you?" she hissed, ignoring his concern. She brushed away his hands impatiently. "Is he here? Have you seen him?"

Dante nodded, the grim set of his jaw and the blankness in his stare telling her everything she needed to know.

"How did he take it?" she asked anxiously.

"Not well." His hand involuntarily moved up to his jaw, and she saw the bruise forming there.

"Oh my God, he hit you?" Her brother was usually such a pacifist. Wouldn't even harm a fly—well, okay, he'd probably harm a fly, but he wouldn't harm a small fuzzy animal like a mouse—so for him to up and hit Dante was beyond her imagination.

"Did you hit *him*?" she asked suspiciously, and a flicker of annoyance entered Dante's frighteningly blank eyes, which she much preferred to the shell-shocked expression there previously.

"Of course I didn't hit him."

"He's upset?"

"I'd say so, yes." His dry rejoinder made her attempt to push past his bulk and get into the building, but he kept sidestepping to prevent her from passing him.

"Hey, get out of my way," she demanded, exasperation peppering her voice.

"He's extremely pissed off at the moment, Cleo. I think he might say something you'd both regret, and it'll cause an unnecessary rift." The words showed more sensitivity than she'd believed him capable of, and she wasn't sure how to take it.

"And you don't think there's already a rift now?"

"Nothing that can't be fixed," Dante said. "At the moment all his anger is focused on me. If you walk in there now, it'll redirect to you . . . don't do that to yourself or to him."

She bit the inside of her cheek as she thought about his words and finally nodded. He took her arm and led her back to where their cars were parked. Or rather, where his car was parked. James was behind the wheel of her car, trying to slot it into the space next to Dante's sedan. The huge man looked ridiculous behind the wheel of her small hatchback, and they both paused to stare before Cleo sniggered, then chuckled, then burst into loud, uncontrollable laughter. Dante halted in midstride to stare at her, and the alarmed expression on his face made her laugh harder. Soon her laughter took on a desperate, hysterical edge, and before she knew it, tears were seeping from her eyes and slipping down her cheeks, and the howls became tearing sobs. Dante said something beneath his breath and dragged her into his arms and held her tenderly as she hunched into him and allowed herself to cry.

"I'm sorry," she whispered after the worst of the storm had abated, and he murmured gently in response, smoothing her hair back from her face and using his handkerchief to dab at her hot and swollen cheeks.

"Come on, you need some rest," he said authoritatively, and she nodded, heading toward her car, but his hand on her elbow stopped her. "Not what I meant. You're definitely not driving in this condition, and I for damned sure don't think you'd get any rest in that apartment of yours. James will be following in your car, and I will be driving us to my place."

She opened her mouth to protest, but he placed a long finger on her lips to silence her. The skin-on-skin contact was so unexpected that Cleo found herself momentarily diverted. It was long enough for him to hastily bundle her into the passenger seat of his luxury car and climb in next to her.

"Dante, I don't want—"

"Cleo, try to be cooperative for once in your life, okay?"

"That's almost on par with me asking you to not be bossy for once in your life," she pointed out, and he grinned. An honest-to-God *grin*. She could get used to seeing that. It was such an open and boyish expression that it was quite breathtaking to witness.

"We each have our weaknesses," he quipped.

"Stop smiling like that, for God's sake," she admonished. "People might start mistaking you for a nice guy."

"God forbid," he retorted, and she stared at him, wondering if there was a sense of humor hidden beneath that detached façade he presented to the world.

The drive back to his place was short and silent, and when he parked his car, she made one last halfhearted protest.

"James could drive me back to my place," she suggested. "I promise to rest when I get home."

"We're already here. You might as well enjoy the quiet and take a nap. I'll be heading back to the office, so you'll have the place to yourself. Help yourself to anything, and if you need something, contact James. He'll see to it."

Cleo figured it was a good trial run for when she moved in and decided not to argue any further. She was genuinely tired. The emotional outburst of that morning, combined with the overall lethargy she still felt, resulted in a powerful urge to just sleep.

Dante escorted her back into his penthouse, going through all those high-tech security procedures before they found themselves facing each other in the middle of his living room. He dug a pen out of his breast pocket and scribbled a four-digit number on the edge of a discarded newspaper on the coffee table.

"This is the code for the elevator, should you decide to go home later." He took hold of her hand and held it palm up before dropping her car keys in it. "If you choose to leave, please let James know that you're going. I've left him with explicit instructions to ensure you get home safely." She didn't say anything to that, even though she was doing some serious mental eye-rolling. She'd been getting herself home safely for years now, but this was Dante's paranoid world, and while she was in it, she supposed she'd have to adhere to the weirdness.

He was standing so close to her that she could feel his torso brush against her chest with every inhalation of breath. He lifted his hand and oh-so-tenderly brushed her hair back from her face. His fingertips grasped one tendril, and an enigmatic smile played about his perfect lips.

"Love the blue," he murmured. "I prefer it to the pink. Pink's not your color."

"I was thinking of going p-purple next," she heard herself saying inanely, and he looked at the strand he held captive in his fingertips for one long, evaluating moment.

"It might clash with your eyes a bit. The purple would have to be subtle," he announced, and she nodded, wondering why they were standing here discussing her hair. He seemed to snap out of whatever spell he was under and blinked a couple of times before shaking his head and dropping her hair.

"Anyway, I . . . uh . . . I should get back to work. Try to rest, *dulzura*," he said, his voice soft. "It'll do both of you the world of good."

The word *both* reminded Cleo that the main reason she was here and that he even wanted her close was because of the baby. He'd kicked her out of his life before they'd known about this pregnancy, and the baby was the *only* reason she was back. She'd better not lose sight of that fact, and she had damned well better not start weaving dangerous fantasies around this man. Especially now that she was starting to see other—likable—aspects of his personality.

She watched him leave and waited for a few moments before she trudged up to one of the spare rooms. She kicked off her shoes on her way up the stairs and shrugged out of her denim jacket. By the time she fell into the closest bed, she was wearing nothing but a tank top and a pair of boy shorts. She dragged a comforter up to cover her body and was asleep in seconds.

Cleo's wreck of a car was still parked in the underground garage when Dante returned home that evening. He had—uncharacteristically—

finished work at the stroke of five, leaving a lot of speculative glances and raised eyebrows in his wake. He had ignored everybody's blatant curiosity and rushed to get home. According to James, Cleo hadn't yet left, and Dante wanted to assure himself that she was okay. Considering her stubborn nature, he would have expected her to leave hours ago. The fact that she was still here was a little concerning.

He let himself in, and a quick glance around the lower level of his apartment told him that it was empty and quiet as a tomb. He could feel his heart start up a heavy bass beat in his chest as panic began to edge its way into his consciousness. He didn't know what the hell he was expecting to find, but he wasn't sure it would be good.

He headed up the stairs and told himself that he was being ridiculous, even while his breath caught in his throat. He was so focused on reaching the top of the single flight of stairs that he didn't see the shoe on the step in front of him and tripped over it. He glanced down incredulously and picked up the small white sneaker, feeling a little perplexed by its presence there. The shoe's twin lay two steps up. And a denim jacket was carelessly thrown over the banister just above the second shoe.

He picked up the items as he went along, feeling like someone following a particularly naughty trail of bread crumbs . . . denim skirt, T-shirt, and even a bra were scattered on the staircase and landing, and Dante found himself wondering if this was an attempt to seduce him.

A rueful glance down at his straining erection told him that if it *was* an attempt, it was wholly successful so far. He reluctantly acknowledged that the thought of a half-naked Cleo in one of those huge beds was more than enough to make his dick stand up and go "Yes, please." There he stood—making an incongruous picture—with an armload of decadently Cleo-scented clothes, rampant and ready for her. He glimpsed a tiny sock discarded outside the middle door and followed it blindly, knowing that Cleo was probably behind that door.

Naked and as primed for him as he was for her.

Hopefully.

He tossed her clothes aside and stumbled toward the door, opening it without knocking and without further thought. The sight that met his eyes stopped him dead in his tracks. She lay in the middle of the huge bed, curled up in a tight ball, fast asleep. He could see that she had attempted to drag the comforter up over herself, but the thing had slid half off the bed and only covered her slender thighs. She was wearing a pair of those damned boy shorts he so loved—Daisy Duck again—and a white tank top. She must have dragged the bra out from beneath the tank. She had one hand tucked beneath her cheek and the other curled over her abdomen in an unconsciously protective gesture; her knees were tucked and drawn up almost to her chest. For such a tiny thing in such a huge bed, she took up a surprising amount of space.

Asleep she presented a picture of innocence, yet that didn't dampen his desire for her one bit. Thank God she was sleeping, or Dante might have made a huge mistake. Bringing sex into this confusing situation would complicate things exponentially. He would have to ignore these baser urges, especially if she was moving in here.

He walked over to the bed, unable to take his eyes off her. Completely relaxed like this, without that challenging look in her eyes and the combative tilt of her jaw, she was goddamned beautiful. The revelation stunned him. He had never really seen this beauty before and couldn't be sure why he was seeing it now. She still had those same odd features that in no way seemed to go together. Most of the time she could probably be described as pretty in an offbeat way, but at that moment, she was nothing short of breathtaking.

He didn't want to think about that, didn't want to evaluate this change of heart, and instead dragged the comforter back over her and tucked her in securely before turning and walking out of the room.

When Cleo woke up, she was completely disoriented and panicked. Where was she? A glance around didn't help matters when she saw not one familiar item anywhere. She took a deep breath and tried to remember what had happened before she'd fallen asleep. When she recalled where she was, she groped around for her phone, which was tucked beneath the pillow, to check the time. It was just after eight in the evening, and she'd slept for nearly nine hours.

There were half a dozen missed calls on her phone from Blue and not a single one from Luc. She sat up quickly and speed-dialed Blue's number.

"Cleo? Thank God!" Her friend's voice throbbed with relief, and Cleo felt guilty for making her worry. "Where are you? And what's going on? Luc isn't making any sense. He slammed his way into his study and refuses to talk to me about whatever it is that's bugging him. All I know is that you're somehow involved."

That was unusual behavior for Luc, who always told Blue everything. Cleo tried not to think about what it could possibly mean if he refused to even talk to Blue about this.

"Dante Damaso went to speak with Luc this morning," Cleo said quietly, her voice thick after nine hours of disuse.

"Dante Damaso? Why?"

"He's my baby's father. He told Luc that I'd be living with him until the baby's born." Blue was completely silent at the other end of the line. "Blue?"

"Oh my God," Blue moaned. "Cleo."

"I feel horrible. I know what good friends they are . . . *were*."

"You could still come and stay with us. You don't have to live with him," Blue said.

"I know that, but he is this baby's father, and I think this is the best move for everyone. Most especially for my baby."

"Luc will come around, Cleo," Blue told her.

"I ruined their friendship, Blue," Cleo said, tears running down her cheeks.

"It'll work out," Blue said, always the optimist. "He's going to need time, though."

"I'm at Dante's right now, but I won't be moving in for another couple of weeks yet. Do you think I should come and talk to Luc before then?"

"Let me talk to him and try to get him over the worst of it," Blue suggested. "I'll keep you updated."

"Thank you."

"Cleo are you . . . do you . . ." Blue framed hesitantly. "Do you have feelings for him?"

"No." Cleo ignored her annoying internal voice, which had been silent for so long, as it called her a *heinous liar*.

"Okay."

"It was just something that happened." Cleo felt the need to explain the inexplicable, mostly for her own benefit. "In Tokyo. A *thing*. He was there, I was there. It happened. We used protection, but how does that quote from *Jurassic Park* go? 'Life will find a way.'"

Blue giggled, and Cleo could hear the tears in the bubbly sound.

"Only you would compare the conception of your baby with dinosaurs procreating in a fictitious park."

"It's a badass saying, you have to admit it," Cleo said with her own wet little giggle.

They chatted for a while longer before Cleo reluctantly disconnected the call and thought about heading downstairs and back home. The place was eerily quiet, and she wasn't sure if Dante had returned yet. She knew the crazy hours he worked, and with the current project in Tokyo and a new one starting up in Dubai, she doubted he'd be home before midnight these days.

She glanced around the room for her clothes before remembering that she'd discarded them on her way up the stairs. Jeez, she'd really have to curb these messy tendencies of hers if she was going to live in this squeaky-clean place. Something on the dresser caught her eye, and upon closer inspection, she saw that it was her clothes, immaculately folded and neatly placed on the dresser's smooth wooden surface.

Someone had been in here while she was sleeping! The thought gave her the heebie-jeebies. Did Dante have a maid? Could it have been James? She doubted that. Could it have been Dante himself?

She pulled on her clothes and tentatively made her way down the stairs. The lights were on, music played softly on the high-tech sound system, and when she walked around the kitchen to the living room, she found Dante sprawled out on the uncomfortable-looking couch. He was wearing faded jeans and a gray T-shirt, and his sneakers had been toed off. Cleo had *never* seen him dressed like that before. Three-piece suits and nude, that was all she knew of Dante Damaso. This was a completely different man slumped in front of her right now. He had one long leg on the couch and the other bent at the knee, with his foot on the marble floor. His head was resting on the hard, small arm of a couch that just wasn't designed for relaxation. A sheaf of papers was spread on his broad chest, pinned down securely with one hand, and his glasses were perched on his nose and dangerously close to falling off. His mouth was ever-so-slightly open, and he was snoring quietly.

Dante Damaso was a handsome man, an outstanding specimen of manhood that other men envied and most women desired, but Cleo had never found him more irresistible than at that moment. He looked young, vulnerable, and completely disheveled, and Cleo felt like she was only really seeing him now for the first time.

She felt confused and desperate to leave before he noticed her. But she wasn't even halfway to the door before she heard him sigh and the papers on his chest crinkle as he moved.

"Where are you going?" he asked, his voice husky with sleep, and Cleo's back straightened as she shot him a guilty look over her shoulder.

"I was heading home. I didn't mean to sleep for so long." She turned to face him and swallowed when he sat up and stretched, his T-shirt tightening over his chest and abs. He had stubble growing in, and he briskly rubbed his hand over his jaw as if the hair growth bothered him.

"Stay," he invited. "Have some dinner. I cooked pasta. There's some in the microwave for you."

Reluctantly charmed by the fact that he'd gone to the trouble to make a plate for her, she hesitated, and he offered her a sleepy smile.

"I would prefer it if you stayed over," he said. "Safer than driving this time of night."

"It's eight thirty," she pointed out. "Hardly midnight. I'm sure I'll manage to get home without much trouble."

"Stay." He stood up and walked toward her, and even in his socks he towered above her. "Please."

Okay, so she was a sucker, but it was the "Please" that did it. She nodded and dropped her bag in the middle of the floor before heading for the kitchen.

Sure enough, there was a foil-covered plate in the microwave for her. She removed the foil and set the timer to a minute and a half.

"There's freshly baked bread in the tin and a salad in the fridge," Dante advised, as he sat down at the island to watch her flit about the kitchen. He seemed content just to watch her and didn't have much to say.

She set her plate and utensils down on the island beside him before fetching her salad and bread and sitting down next to him to enjoy her meal. She ate ravenously. As was usually the case these days, once the nausea disappeared, she found herself eating like a horse, and Dante watched her pack it away in fascination.

"That's a hell of a lot of food for such a little thing," he observed after a long silence, and Cleo peered at him before shrugging.

"Eating for two," she reminded him past a mouthful of bread, and he grinned. She could get used to him grinning like this all the time.

"So you were a professional dancer?" She sighed. Small talk. How . . . inevitable.

"Yep," she said, mopping up some of the delicious tomato sauce on her plate with a chunk of soft, fresh bread and stuffing it into her mouth. "This is delicious."

"Thank you."

"You made the bread too?" She didn't care if she sounded like a Neanderthal, talking with her mouth full; this was a divine meal.

"I did."

"What happened when Cal dropped you?" he asked, and she glared at him, wishing he hadn't asked that question. Good thing she'd nearly finished her meal, since her appetite had completely disappeared.

"We don't have to go through these little getting-to-know-you rituals, Dante," she dismissed coldly. "Don't worry, I won't think less of you for not really knowing anything about me. That's not why I'm here."

"Okay," he said, picking up her plate and utensils and carrying them to the sink. She watched him tidy up and shook her head at how completely different they were. "So, I'm an only child."

"What?" Why did he feel the need to tell her that?

"I'm an only child," he repeated patiently. "My mother died of leukemia when I was five and a half. My father remarried soon after that. And then he divorced and remarried again. And so on and so forth. I've lost count of how many there were. And he's getting remarried to a woman about a decade younger than me in a couple of weeks' time. He always falls head over heels in love, marries without protecting himself or his assets, and then is surprised when he gets taken to the cleaners a year or two later."

"Why are you telling me this?" she asked, horrified and fascinated by the story he was telling her, but not at all sure why he would choose to divulge this to her, now or ever.

"You might not want me to know about you, but I think it's time you learned something about me."

"Why? That makes no sense," she said.

"Not yet," he said enigmatically. "Anyway, my father is an idiot when it comes to matters of the heart, and I have decided *never* to be like him."

Was he warning her off? Trying to tell her that he would always protect himself and his assets? She already knew that about him. So this warning was moot.

"Right," she nodded. "Well, you can take great comfort in the fact that you're not like him at all. You with your nondisclosure agreements and your bloodless little relationships, or whatever you call them."

"Hmm." That was his only response. "You're probably not sleepy at all. Want to watch a movie or something?" Trying very hard not to think about what that "or something" could entail, Cleo firmly opted for the movie.

"I have a lot to choose from," he informed her, following her into the living room. He picked up a tablet from the table and showed her how his system worked. "They're all digital copies, and if there's anything on here I don't have or you would like to see, you can purchase them here."

Once she had a rudimentary knowledge of how the system worked, he left her to flick through the movie choices while he went back to his work. Cleo curled up in a hard, angular, horrifically uncomfortable chair and settled back to watch.

A few bloodcurdling screams later, Dante looked up, his face pale and focused on the gigantic screen.

"What the hell are you watching?" he asked hoarsely.

"It's one of the latest horror films," she said, naming the movie, which had been a surprise hit the previous year. "Ssh. I'm trying to watch."

His brow pleated as he continued to stare at the screen, and after a while, he was leaning forward, his elbows resting on his thighs as he focused on the screen.

"Why would they play that ridiculous game in a new house?" he asked, shaking his head but never once removing his eyes from the screen.

"Have you never seen this movie before?" Cleo asked in surprise, and he shook his head, keeping his eyes glued on the television.

"A lot of the new movies are automatic purchases, but I never have the time to watch. I don't think I've even heard of this movie."

"I've heard of it, and apparently it's pretty scary," she said.

"It's a movie," he scoffed. "We know that it's fiction. How scary can it possibly be?"

"This one is based on fact," she informed him in a spooky voice, and he shot her a fleeting glance before refocusing on the screen.

"Yeah, probably really loosely based," he retorted skeptically, and Cleo rolled her eyes.

"Shush and let me watch. Go back to work or whatever it is you're doing," she demanded. His lips quirked and he dropped his eyes back to his documents, but Cleo was watching him surreptitiously and noticed him glancing back up at the screen seconds later. After a while he sat back and put his feet up on the coffee table. One major jump scare later, he was swearing prolifically and on the edge of his seat again.

Cleo was so busy watching him that she could barely focus on the movie. He was obviously freaked out but trying manfully not to show it, yet he jumped slightly with every scare. It was cute to watch the macho, unflappable Dante Damaso losing his cool over a scary movie.

By the end of the film, Cleo barely knew what it had been about, while Dante's face was grim and a little pale.

"I don't know how you can watch crap like that," he grumbled, and she grinned.

"You seemed to be enjoying it."

"I was just . . ." He paused as he considered his next words. "Scientifically curious."

"Dante you were so scared you practically peed yourself every time something creepy happened," she pointed out gleefully, and he looked so affronted that she burst into laughter. The next thing she knew he was kneeling in front of her chair and capturing her mouth with his, swallowing her remaining laughter in a kiss so scorching and intense it set her nerve endings on fire.

When he finally lifted his mouth, it was to give her a languid smile.

"Stop laughing at me," he whispered.

"I've stopped," she responded shakily.

"Good." He kissed her again, this time he added his hands into the mix, and before she knew it, he had dragged her back onto the couch with him and she was straddling his lap.

"This is a terrible idea," she protested.

"I think it's the best idea I've ever had."

"Dante, we can't resume a sexual relationship; it'll complicate things." She sounded unconvincing, even to herself. Especially since her hands were roaming beneath his T-shirt and reacquainting themselves with his gorgeous chest and abdomen.

"How about we finally finish the one we started in Tokyo? We've never gotten that out of our systems. We ended it before it ran its course." Each sentence was punctuated with a long, drugging kiss, while his hands went to town beneath her tank top. She hadn't bothered to put her bra back on, since her breasts were starting to feel swollen and painful and her bras were all getting too tight and confining. When his fingers flicked one of her nipples, she hissed and arched her back violently.

"Okay?" he asked worriedly, his hands retreating slightly.

"Sensitive," she muttered. "Very, *very* sensitive. Treat them with care."

"Always," he said, and dragged her tank up to drop a reverent kiss on the hard little nub. He followed it up with a lick and then some quick, extremely tender suctioning.

"Oh." Cleo's hands tangled in his thick hair, and his mouth left her so that he could peer up at her over the peaks of her small breasts.

"They're bigger than I remember," he said, his tone sounded bemused and a little reverent. "And the nipples are darker. Still so damned pretty."

He flipped her over until she was sitting on the couch and moved down to kiss her abdomen tenderly, right above the spot where she knew their baby rested. The gesture was so sweet and loving that it took her breath away. Dante might not have known what role he wanted to play in this baby's life yet, but he was clearly starting to fall in love with it despite himself.

He moved even lower until he was under her short denim skirt, and he peeked up at her with a grin.

"I'm glad to see my friend Daisy is back," he said as he placed his hands on her hips and dragged her down slightly. Shortly after that, "Daisy" was slowly slipped down over her thighs, then knees, before he removed her completely. He took one of her slender thighs and rested it on his broad shoulder before—with one last wicked grin at her—he bent down to taste her.

Cleo cried out at the touch of his mouth and tongue on her most sensitive flesh, and it didn't take more than a few strokes before she was lost. She was floating back down and was aware of him rearranging her until he was flat on his back on the marble floor and she was straddled above him.

"Is it okay if we do this?" he asked, the tip of him poised at her entrance. "For the baby. Is it okay for the baby?"

"It's okay," she said dazedly. This was happening so quickly. Too quickly. His face was tense as he focused on where their bodies were on the verge of joining. Cleo swallowed. Now that her orgasm had passed and she could think clearly again, her previous doubts came swamping back.

"Dante," she said, her voice filled with regret as she shifted off him. He looked at her intently before raising an arm to cover his face and sighing deeply.

"Bad idea, huh?" he muttered.

"I'm sorry." She glanced at him and winced at the sight of his angry-looking erection. "You know it's not a good idea. It just all happened so fast."

He nodded, his mouth tight beneath the arm that covered his eyes.

"I'm going to need some . . . time," he said.

"I think I should go home," she whispered.

"No!" he said sharply, and she jumped. He made an effort to soften his voice before speaking again, shifting his arm to glance at her quickly. "No. Go on upstairs. I just need to get myself under control, and having you right here, where I can still smell and taste your orgasm, is a little difficult."

"I'm sorry," she said again.

"It's okay, but please just . . ."

"Yes, of course." She leaped to her feet and vacated the area as quickly as she could. She scurried up the stairs and slammed into the room she'd already picked as her own. Once there, she crawled to the center of the massive bed, drew her legs up, and buried her face in her knees. How the hell were they going to make this work if they couldn't keep their hands off each other?

She only hoped that once she started to show, he would lose interest in her body, even though she could barely look at the man without wanting to spontaneously combust. She had seriously mixed feelings about what had just happened between them and wished she hadn't allowed it. Especially since the evening had ended with him still hard and wanting. Was this another example of Cleopatra Knight being selfish? At this point she had no clue.

She officially moved in two weeks later, bringing only her clothes, some books, wall art, and her bed. It was a sad testament to her nearly twenty-eight years that she had absolutely nothing more than that to show for herself.

Cleo and Dante hadn't interacted much since that last evening together at his place. They had exchanged telephone conversations, and he had e-mailed her snippets from articles he had read about pregnancy and what she should eat and what vitamins she should be taking. It was endearing and a little disconcerting, the level of interest he took in her pregnancy.

She, in turn, had reciprocated with week-fourteen (which they both already knew) and week-fifteen updates.

She was in regular contact with Blue, but Luc still wasn't talking to her or Dante, and it broke her heart. She had tried calling him on several occasions, but he never answered and didn't respond to a single one of her text messages. Blue told Cleo that he needed time. Cleo gave him his space, but it was difficult not having him around to talk to. She couldn't remember a single time in her life when her brother hadn't been there for her, and this was so much harder without his support.

Cal was doing well. Since their talk, he'd made a real effort to find decent work. He'd auditioned to be part of the corps de ballet for a small dance company based in Durban, and they had called him just that morning to inform him that he'd gotten the job. He would be staying for the remainder of Cleo's lease and leaving two weeks after she moved out. Cleo was happy for him, but she would miss him like crazy, especially since her relationship with Luc was so strained.

Cleo's own life was looking up too. She'd started helping Susan out with a few classes—kids between the ages of ten and twelve—and she *loved* it. More than she ever expected. Susan even offered to let her do the choreography for one of their upcoming recitals and was willing to let her do even more classes if the recital went well.

Cleo's love for dance was rekindling, but in a different way. She was thinking more and more about the technical aspects of it, how a dancer's body moved, how she could achieve certain shapes with those bodies through her choreography. It felt fantastic.

And as far as her pregnancy went, she was developing a tiny bump, which was even more exciting than her new part-time job. Once, she even thought she felt a little wriggle in there, but she'd been mistaken. She couldn't wait for the baby to start moving.

Now she stood in her new room in Dante's penthouse and took in the changes he'd made to accommodate her. Of course, the trendy king-size bed was gone and had been replaced by her four-poster bed, which would have looked out of place in the room had he held on to the old furniture. But whomever it was he employed to do these things had matched bed stands, bureau, and dresser with the warm teak of her bed, and the room looked so much more inviting. Vertical bamboo blinds, which made it feel more private, now covered the windows.

Dante was standing in the doorway as she took in her new surroundings, and when she looked back at him, she was surprised to see a flash of nerves on that handsome face. He disguised it pretty quickly, but that brief glimmer had been enough for Cleo to recognize that he was actually unsure of her reaction to the room.

"I like this room a lot better now," she said with a smile, and could see the tension around his eyes easing, even though there was no perceptible change in his expression.

"Great," he said. "I have something else to show you. Follow me."

Curious, she trailed him out of the room and into his gym. He stood aside and waved her in, and she passed him tentatively, wondering what he could possibly have to show her in here. When she looked around the room and noticed what was different, her eyes immediately flooded with irrational, stupid tears.

"Oh my God, Dante," she cried, her hands going to her mouth in shock. "This is too much."

"Do you like it?" he asked, striving to sound casual.

"How can I not?" Her voice wobbled dangerously, and she inhaled deeply as she walked toward the sprung floor that simply hadn't been there just two weeks before. He had cleared out a whole corner of his gym for the floor, covered the wall with mirrored panels, and installed a ballet barre to run parallel with the floor.

"I know it's not as big as the space you're used to, but I was hoping it would suffice. And of course I consulted a professional dancer—Callum, actually—about the type of floor that would be best. I wasn't sure . . ." She turned around and shut him up with a fierce hug and an equally intense kiss. The kiss was short-lived, and she stood back to stare into his stunned eyes through a haze of tears.

"Nobody has ever done anything like this for me before," she said. "Thank you."

"I . . ." At a loss for words, he settled for a shrug. Cleo kicked off her shoes and stepped onto the floor. She took hold of the barre and did a quick and easy series of demi-pliés.

"I can't wait to give it a go," she said over her shoulder, while he stared at her with a completely unreadable expression.

"Great," he said tightly. "I have to get back to the office. I've squandered enough of my day. James will remain to run your biometrics through the security system. He'll explain how it all works."

He left without so much as a backward glance.

Stung, Cleo reminded herself to never lose sight of the fact that he was Dante Damaso, and despite any unexpected kindnesses he might throw her way, he wasn't a very nice man. She was here only because of the baby in her belly, and she'd better not forget that. While there might be some residual desire between them, it would be dangerous to confuse that with anything more meaningful.

Her hand came to rest on the small bump of her baby, and all her joy in the room fled. She stepped off the floor and, barefoot, went in search of James.

CHAPTER ELEVEN

Two weeks later, Cleo was sitting on the horrendous couch with a huge comfy pillow shoved behind her back and her feet propped up on the coffee table. She had a bowl of warm, buttery popcorn on the stand next to the couch and was watching one of her all-time favorite movies with the intensity of someone seeing it for the first time.

Dante had been pretty much absent since she'd moved in. He left before she got up in the mornings and came home way after her bedtime. And because he was such a neat freak, he even had a maid come in to clean up his nonexistent mess every other day, so there was never any trace of him around the place. It was like living with a ghost.

Cleo, who was so used to Cal being up in her business and Luc constantly calling, felt lonely. She still had her friends from the dance studio and had befriended a few of the mothers of the girls she taught, but at the end of the day, she came home alone to this tomblike place. She wasn't unhappy, but she felt increasingly isolated. She didn't have to worry about money or work or her apartment falling apart around her ears—which was a relief—but she had no one to talk to.

Blue called her regularly, but Cleo tried to keep her sense of isolation from her friend because she didn't want Blue to feel torn between her concern for Cleo and her love for Luc.

Cleo was spending most days at the studio now, and Susan had entrusted her with two back-to-back classes in the afternoons after school hours and with choreographing the ten- to twelve-year-old group's upcoming recital performance. It was exciting and challenging, and she had so many ideas. Of course she had to consider her students' abilities, and once she had everything ironed out, they would start rehearsing the dance. She couldn't imagine anything more exciting than to see her idea come to life onstage. It felt like she had two babies due, and both of them were bringing joy, excitement, and fulfillment into her life.

Most evenings were spent working out for an hour or so at the barre Dante had installed for her—since she didn't have time to do so at Susan's studio anymore—working on the routine, and then eating some dinner and settling down to watch a movie. Tonight, after a long bath in the massive tub in her room, she had donned shorty pajamas and a pair of striped knee socks before getting comfy in front of the TV. She was so focused on the movie that she didn't even notice the front door swing open and wasn't aware of Dante's presence until he spoke.

"What are you watching?" he asked from almost directly behind her, and she nearly jumped out of her skin.

"*Crap,*" she squeaked, lifting a hand to her chest. "You scared the stuffing out of me."

"Stuffing?" He raised an eyebrow at her language, and she wrinkled her nose.

"I read somewhere that the baby can hear my voice. I don't want him to pick up any bad language before he's even born."

"He can hear us?" Dante looked completely disconcerted by that bit of news, and after shrugging out of his jacket and neatly placing it on the chair, he sat down on the couch next to her. "Seriously?"

"Yep. Shocked the shi—sherbet out of me too."

He grinned, the expression so infectious she found herself grinning back.

"How long do you think you'll be able to keep that up?" he asked, his voice wobbling with laughter.

"I don't know, but I'm going to try my damnedest not to . . ." She paused, frowned, and then her shoulders sank as she grasped what she'd said. *"Shit."*

"Yeah, that's what I thought," he chuckled, toeing off his shiny shoes and propping his feet up on the table next to hers. Of course his legs were a lot longer, so they were bent at the knees while hers were straight. She got a funny little flutter in her stomach at the sight of his long, slender feet next to her much smaller ones. How could a man's *feet* be sexy?

"I'm exhausted," he confessed, his shoulders slumped and his voice weary. "Tokyo hit another snag, and Dubai just can't seem to get off the ground. I spent the entire week bogged down in meetings."

Without seeming to think about it, he turned sideways, dropping his feet over the arm of the couch and—shockingly—his head into her lap. He tugged at his tie and unbuttoned the top two buttons in an effort to get more comfortable and then turned to face the TV.

"What are we watching?"

The "we" undid her, and she allowed the tension to leave her body at this unexpected turn of events. Her hands, which had been hovering in midair as she tried to figure out where to place them, dropped—one to his hair and the other to his shoulder.

"Uh . . ." She stared blankly at the screen as the high-resolution space marines argued among themselves. *"Aliens."*

"Oh, I know that one," he muttered, his voice sounding slurred. "What was that thing she said? 'Stay away from her, bitch'?"

"Philistine," she said with a long-suffering sigh, her hand starting to run soothingly through his hair. "You got that quote all wrong."

He twisted his head to meet her eyes with his smiling gaze.

"*Sì?* What is it then?"

"You'll see. Now be quiet and watch."

∽

Half an hour later, after pilfering half of her popcorn, criticizing a few of the choices some of the characters had made, and wondering why they didn't just leave someone on the "big ship" to wait for everybody, his big body went completely limp. A quick glance down confirmed that he'd fallen asleep. Cleo smiled, feeling an overwhelming surge of affection for him. She had *never* expected to like Dante Damaso, and yet she did. He had wormed his way into her good graces, and she wasn't exactly sure how.

The logical part of her brain told her to keep him at a distance, that feeling anything more than fondness for him would lead to pain and possible heartbreak. He wasn't the type of man one could play house with. He was like a wild animal who seemed to do better without any sentimental emotion bogging him down. Cleo and this baby were momentary blips in his lifestyle, and maybe it was the novelty of the situation that drew him. She couldn't allow herself to depend on him. Not in any emotional sense. He would keep his word when it came to supporting the child, but if she thought he could feel anything deeper than what he'd promised already, she would be fooling only herself.

But it was so hard to remember all of that when he was sprawled out on her lap like this.

She continued to run her hand through his thick, soft hair. He had a dense growth of stubble on his jaw, and she tentatively ran her palm over it, loving the burn of it on her skin. She was so riveted by the feel of him under her hand that at first the fluttering in her abdomen went unnoticed. But when it came again, she recognized that it wasn't just a tummy rumble or the popcorn unsettling her stomach. A third, faint movement had her gasping and sitting up straighter.

Her movement woke Dante, who looked at her in alarm.

"What's wrong?" he asked, instantly alert. "Are you okay?"

"I think the baby's moving," she whispered, keeping her voice low as if she were afraid a loud noise would scare the baby and stop the movement.

"He is? You're sure?"

"Yes! Oh God, there he goes again." Dante sat up and stared at the small bump fixedly. Cleo blindly reached for his hand and placed it where she'd felt the movement. His hand was so large that it just about covered the entire expanse of her stomach. "*Oh.* Did you feel that?"

"No." He shook his head, looking frustrated.

"It's very faint. Maybe you can't feel it yet."

"Is he still moving?"

She paused for a moment before shaking her head.

"No, I think he's stopped." He looked so disappointed that she covered the hand he still had on her stomach with her own.

"I'll let you know the moment he starts up again," she promised, and he nodded briskly. She moved her hand, and he was just about to remove his when the gentle flutter returned. This time he felt it, and his eyes shot up to meet hers.

"Christ!" he gasped.

"Language, Dante," she warned, tears in her eyes and excitement in her voice. "There's a kid in the room."

"Sorry," he whispered, before leaning down until his mouth was within an inch of her stomach. "Sorry, *pequeño*, don't you listen to your daddy's bad language, okay?"

Almost simultaneously, they both comprehended that he'd used the word *daddy*, and Dante froze, his eyes leaping up to meet hers. Cleo wasn't sure how to respond. What did it mean, him naming himself father to the child? How active did he now expect his role in this child's life to be?

"How does it feel?" he asked, changing the subject but keeping his hand firmly anchored on her stomach. "To have him move around like that? Does it hurt?"

"It feels strange. A little bit like indigestion. Not painful or anything, just like a tiny tummy rumble. I wasn't even sure what it was at first."

"It's amazing," he said, his tone brimming with awe and discovery. He stared down at her stomach again, obviously hoping the baby would move some more.

"I think he's done for the night," she said gently, and his eyes shadowed with disappointment.

"Thank you for sharing this with me, *dulzura*," he said as he reluctantly lifted his hand from her abdomen. She smiled and refocused on the movie that had been running unheeded while they had marveled over the miraculous life they'd created together.

He once again lifted his feet to the coffee table and folded his arms over his chest, keeping contact between them limited to occasional accidental brushes.

"So do you enjoy the teaching?" he asked about ten minutes later, as they were watching Ripley battle her way through droves of ugly aliens.

"I'm finding it quite rewarding," she replied. "The kids are enthusiastic and talented. They remind me a little of myself at that age. I was absolutely obsessed with dancing. I couldn't wait for school to finish every day so that I could get to dance classes, I spent all of my time practicing my *chaînés tournes* in the mirror, and I wouldn't stop until my grandmother forced me to do my chores. I resented her so much for that."

She could hear the sadness in her voice at that admission, and from the change in his body language, she knew that Dante could too.

"They only wanted what was best for Luc and me."

"Where were your parents?"

"I never knew our dad. Luc has a slight recollection of him, but he never talks about the man. Our mother left us at our grandparents' house—the huge old place that Luc's staying in—when we were five and ten. Told us it was for a holiday and never came back. I heard my grandmother arguing with her on the phone soon after she left us there, and for years afterward I believed that our mom didn't come back because my gran had chased her away."

Dante was silent as she sat there, her hand idly stroking the gentle curve of her abdomen.

"Of course, now I know that if she'd wanted us back, no force on earth would have been strong enough to keep her away. But I spent my entire childhood and teens resenting my grandmother for a telephone conversation that I could only hear one side of. So stupid."

She shook herself and peered up at Dante in embarrassment.

"I'm sorry. You didn't want to hear all of that."

"On the contrary . . . I found it quite insightful."

"In what way?" she asked, and he shook his head.

"I'm not sure yet. Did you ever hear from your mother again?"

"No. Not a single Christmas or birthday card. No phone calls or letters or e-mails. Nothing until we received word of her death just months after our grandparents passed. She died in Nepal, and the cost of the trip put Luc in a financial hole so deep that he's still struggling to get out of it more than eight years later. That's when I really hated her . . . all those years of misdirected anger aimed at my grandparents, who were only trying to provide a stable home life for us. They paid for ballet lessons that they could barely afford and scraped together their money to buy Luc that beaten-up old hatchback for his eighteenth birthday that I now drive. By the time I'd recognized how much they'd sacrificed to raise us, it was too late; they were sick and dying, and then they were gone."

"I'm sorry." Dante's husky voice jolted her back into the present, and she pressed the heels of her hands into her eyes, embarrassed to find them wet.

"Aargh, I should be over this by now. I just wish I had a second chance with them."

"They sound like the type of people who wouldn't have wanted you to live with all this guilt; they worked too hard to make you happy. You dishonor them by remembering them with only regret in your heart." His pragmatic words made her pause and consider. He was right; her grandparents had only wanted Cleo and Luc to be happy. And they'd had some good times too. Maybe she should start remembering those?

"My granddad insisted I learn how to ride a bike," she recalled with a smile. "I argued, at six years old, that a dancer didn't need to know how to ride a stupid bicycle. And he insisted that *everybody* needed to know how to ride a bicycle. That man spent days running up and down the road with me, catching me whenever I fell. He never once dropped me."

She stared blindly at the screen in front of her, and they were quiet for the remainder of the movie.

"I loved them very much," she said when the credits were running.

"I know," he replied and reached over to take one of her hands. He gave it a gentle squeeze before dropping it back into her lap.

And in that moment, Cleo knew that her feelings for Dante Damaso had definitely evolved into something very complicated. She wasn't able to put a name or definition on them, wasn't sure what—if anything—they would grow into, but one thing she *was* sure of was that she didn't like where they seemed to be leading. She felt much too vulnerable.

When Cleo made her way to the gym the following Saturday morning, she heard heavy breathing, grunts, and solid punches. Sure enough, Dante was positioned at one of his heavy punching bags. He was wearing protective gloves, but he was bare chested and barefoot as he punched and kicked the crap out of the bag. It was very primal and masculine and intense. He paused when he saw her standing at the door dressed in her toe shoes, a black leotard, pink leggings, and a wispy pink wrap skirt. He pushed one gloved hand into his already messy hair to get it out of his eyes—he definitely could do with a haircut—and kept his gaze trained on her as she made her way to her dance corner. He looked a little intimidating, gleaming with sweat, and his heaving breaths and rippling muscles and the way he was staring at her, like a lion eyeing a gazelle, didn't help matters much.

She hesitated, not sure if she should wait until after he was done with his workout, but he waved her in, and it was too late to turn around.

"Hey," she greeted, and he nodded.

"Hey," his greeting was curt, and he went back to thumping his bag aggressively seconds later.

"Okay, then," she murmured to herself as she put her music on. The peaceful strains of Chopin's *Nocturnes* flooded through the room, so quiet and gentle at first that Dante didn't seem to notice it above all the vigorous grunting and punching he was doing. Satisfied that she wasn't disturbing his workout, she settled into her stretches and then started her barre work. She was moving on to her en pointe exercises when she became aware of the silence at the other end of the room. She looked up into the mirror and saw that he had stopped his workout completely and was watching her again, riveted. She was in the middle of an *arabesque penché*, supported by her left leg, with her right leg lifted and extended straight behind her. It was a classical ballet pose and did an amazing job of strengthening her core and working on every single muscle in her calves and thighs. She slowly sank back into first position, and he raised his eyes to meet hers in the mirror.

"That was beautiful," he gritted out.

"So was what you were doing." And it was, in an extremely raw and primitive way.

"Yeah, well, it didn't quite match this music." His broad shoulders moved restlessly and drew her attention back to his beautifully proportioned, well-muscled body.

"The Ballerina and the Beast," he said gruffly, as if reading her thoughts. "You make that look so effortless. It's hard to believe that you're no longer able to dance professionally."

"Oh, believe it," she said, turning around to face him properly. "The way I fell? I'm lucky I didn't break my neck. Broke my leg in two places, injured my hip, and my knee." She shook her head, the memory sending a shudder down her spine even all these years later. That awful feeling of inevitability of being unable to stop yourself as the worst happened.

"I would have been able to fully recover from any one of those injuries quite easily," she said, unconsciously sweeping her right foot back and forth. "But all of them combined were catastrophic, and the knee is simply unable to bear the strain of a professional dancer's life anymore. I'd had injuries before, countless injuries, and I knew when I landed that it was the end of my career, but it took me years to accept it. Anyway . . . I was wondering how long you've been doing *this*."

"The kickboxing?" She nodded, and he rolled his shoulders before peeling off his gloves. "Since I was an early teen. I had some . . . anger-management issues. My father thought I needed to channel some of that rage."

"Oh?" she prompted, but he just nodded and went back to punching his bag, ending the conversation. A little irritated that she had told him so much about herself while receiving next to nothing in return, Cleo went back to her own workout, vowing to keep her own counsel in the future. Just because she was lonely and a chatty person didn't mean Dante was the best person to blab to about her sorry life story.

He finished before she did and left the gym without another word. She watched him leave in the mirror; he didn't spare so much as a backward glance.

She had no idea what was going on in his mind most of the time, and once again questioned her decision to come and live here. Despite the improved surroundings and financial circumstances, she was filled with as much doubt as ever and constantly worried about the future.

She finished her workout and headed to her room for a shower. When she emerged a short while later, it was to find him sitting on the deck with a mug of coffee in hand. He was staring at the yachts, deep in thought. She grabbed a glass of juice and hesitated at the sliding door leading out to the deck, not sure if she should join him or not. Maybe he wanted some privacy; she didn't know him well enough yet to tell.

She decided to play it safe and turned away from the door to wander into the living room instead. On the way, she grabbed a discarded newspaper from one of the kitchen counters and sank down onto the floor next to the low coffee table. She went straight to the crossword puzzle and picked up his expensive Montblanc pen, which was lying on the table next to his glasses. She was immersed in the puzzle within minutes.

"Why are you on the floor?" Dante's voice brought her back into the present, and she gazed back at him blankly. He stood, hands in his trouser pockets, staring down at her with a curious look on his face.

"Your couch is uncomfortable," she said, before going back to nibbling the end of his pen and giving the puzzle her rapt attention.

"More uncomfortable than the floor?"

Irritated by the interruption, she clicked her tongue and glowered at him.

"I'm trying to concentrate," she snapped, and his eyebrows shot up before he unceremoniously plonked himself down next to her.

"Try 'place,'" he suggested, pointing to the paper.

"What?"

"Fifteen down. It's 'place,'" he said with a smug smile. She peered at the paper and sighed.

"No, it's not," she said, before neatly penning the letters $VENUE$ into the blocks. His lips twisted, and he refocused his attention on *her* puzzle before grunting.

"Twelve across is . . ."

"Stop!" she commanded, placing her hand over the puzzle in an effort to block his view. "What are you doing?"

"I'm helping you," he replied, looking a little perplexed by her reaction.

"I don't need help finishing *my* puzzle," she fumed.

"It's my newspaper," he pointed out. "So I think it's *my* puzzle."

"Once a newspaper has been read and then tossed aside, it becomes public property."

"That's ridiculous," he scoffed. "I have never heard of this rule."

"Well, that's the rule in South Africa. I can't help it if you had different rules in Spain. I have an entire nation behind me on this one. Now back off and let me finish my puzzle."

"While I'm down here, I might as well help you out," he said magnanimously.

"English isn't even your first language," she rebuffed.

"That's not nice," he chastised. "I don't make fun of your shortcomings."

"Because I have none."

"You talk too much," he pointed out, and she gasped, rather outraged by that. "You have this annoying habit of finishing my sentences, and you have an odd sense of humor."

"And you have *no* sense of humor," she dismissed breezily. "Jeez, would it kill you to laugh once in a while? You really need to find a surgeon to remove that stick you have up your—"

"What do you call a fly without wings?" he interrupted, and she blinked. He was staring at her expectantly, eyebrows up and lips tilted at the corners.

"Uh . . . what?" she asked, needing some clarification.

"What do you call a fly without wings?" he repeated, his voice laden with anticipation and something she couldn't quite define.

"A walk?" The light dimmed in his eyes, and the smile that had been forming on his lips faded. She was actually sorry she had given him the right answer.

"You've heard it before?"

"Dante . . . everybody over the age of five has heard that joke before."

"I heard it in passing at work yesterday. See? I have a sense of humor, but clearly it's much too sophisticated for someone like you to possibly comprehend," he said gravely, and she gaped at him, not sure if he was serious or not. He thought the fly joke was sophisticated? Was he *joking*? But his face was expressionless, and she couldn't quite tell what was going on in that diabolical mind of his.

"Someone like me?" She latched onto that bit, and when he opened his mouth to clarify what he'd meant, she held up her palm to stop him. "No, wait, don't tell me. I've heard this before. Something about you not appreciating celebrity gossip or wanting to hear about what's trending on Twitter. Or the Kardashians."

"Why *did* you carry on about them so much while you were working for me? There are also Klingons, Vulcans, and . . . why are you laughing?" The last as Cleo literally rolled on the floor and laughed her ass off. She actually had to clutch her sides because it was the kind of belly laughter that just couldn't be contained. When the laughter died, she felt completely spent and gradually came to realize that she was lying flat on her back, staring up at a smiling Dante. How could he smile at her like that one moment and be completely remote the next? His eyes were warm and inviting, and that smile was open and tender. He reached over and brushed a thumb over her cheeks. They came away wet.

"I've never seen you laugh like that before," he muttered.

"We haven't had much to laugh about," she pointed out softly. She remained on her back, one arm curled up above her head and the other resting on the mound of their baby. "An unwanted sex *thing* followed by an unwanted pregnancy. Not exactly giggle-worthy topics of conversation."

"Baby can hear you," he warned, his tone serious. "Don't let him come into this world thinking he's unwanted."

"I'd never do that," she said. "Not after knowing what that kind of rejection feels like. He's going to know that his mother wants him and loves him."

⟨⟩

But not his father, Dante reflected. *Because that particular idiot gave him up without a second thought.*

He was having a hard time with this entire situation. Living with her and seeing the child grow inside of her. Feeling that child move. How the hell was he supposed to feel about this baby, knowing that it would never bear his name and never know him as a father? Every single decision he'd made since she'd informed him about her pregnancy had been wrong, and he was paying a harsh price for that stupidity.

He couldn't allow himself to develop strong feelings for this baby, not when he would never be able to show those feelings.

And Cleo . . .

What the hell was he supposed to do about Cleo? He told himself he'd stay away from her, but then when he came home from work he'd find her watching a movie or reading a book, and he'd find a way to insert himself into that activity. He'd ask her questions even while telling himself he didn't want to know the answers. And that morning, in the gym, God—how did she get more and more beautiful every time he saw her? How was that even possible?

And then there was the other night when he'd allowed himself to get too close. She'd been so right in calling a halt to those proceedings. He barely recognized himself anymore. He was usually much better disciplined than this. He wasn't a man easily swayed by his emotions. He would get this under control.

He had to.

"Why do you know so much about *Star Trek*?" she asked curiously, on the verge of falling asleep on the tiled floor. He glanced down into her sleepy face and had a hard time not smiling.

"Why does anyone?" he shrugged. "Why do you know so much about some celebrity family?"

Ah, so he knew exactly who she'd been talking about, which meant that he must have made that comment to make her laugh.

So, who the hell was this guy?

Before now she would have bet her life on the fact that Dante Damaso did not have a sense of humor. Yet it was there—subtle, dry, and shockingly self-deprecating.

"So you *did* know to whom I was referring?" She grinned.

"I didn't back when I told you to find a replacement assistant for me. I looked it up." He flushed at the confession.

"So the comment about the Klingons and the Vulcans just now was . . ."

"I told you I have a sense of humor," he reminded her. "Like I said, you're always finding all kinds of weird shit to laugh about, but you're relentlessly grim or sarcastic with me. I didn't think I'd ever be able to make you laugh as openly as you do with other people."

What did that mean? That he had wanted her to laugh with him? That was so . . .

"Sweet." She completed the thought out loud and he looked startled.

"What?"

"You wanted to make me laugh. That was sweet of you, Dante. Don't deny it." The last was said when he opened his mouth to comment. Her quick command made him shut his mouth again. "You wanted to make me laugh. Admit it."

"God, you really are quite obnoxious sometimes," he groused, without heat. "Fine. I wanted to make you laugh. I wanted to prove that I could. Like I said, you're always laughing with every random person you meet but . . ." His voice tapered off.

But not with him. Cleo completed the unfinished sentence. Sure, they'd had a few amicable moments together, and she'd shared smiles with him, but this was the first time she'd ever really laughed with him. She'd put up some major defensive barriers to keep him from hurting her, but she couldn't really remember the last time he had deliberately said or done anything designed to hurt her. Still, just because he hadn't, didn't mean he wouldn't, so her shields would stay up, even though they were taking some battering beneath this weird charm offensive he occasionally launched at her.

"Are you going to laze around on the floor all day, or are you going to let me help you finish this crossword puzzle?"

She sighed and unselfconsciously held out a hand for him to tug her back into a sitting position, which he did with the utmost tenderness.

"Fine, but I'm doing this under protest."

"Duly noted."

They were halfway through the puzzle when she noticed him staring at her. She lifted a self-conscious hand to her hair, wondering if it was sticking up or something.

"What?" she prompted, and he hesitated for a moment, his mouth opening and then closing. "Come on, Dante. Spit it out."

"I'm sorry." The words were hurried and a little garbled but unmistakable. She raised an eyebrow and noticed that he had trouble meeting her eyes.

"For which item on your long list of indiscretions?" she asked as she toyed with the pen.

"All of them?"

"Please. I don't do blanket forgiveness." She waved her hand dismissively and was delighted to see a grin flirt along the corners of his mouth.

"Fine. I'm sorry I had you kicked out of my office that day," he said humbly.

"And . . . ?"

"And for having security escort you out of the building."

"Hmm."

"It was wrong of me."

"It was," she agreed.

"I'm sorry it caused you humiliation and pain." An edge of desperation started to creep into his voice.

"Are you?"

"Yes. You believe me, don't you?"

"Maybe."

"Come on, Cleo . . . I'm really sorry. It was a shitty thing to do, and I've regretted it ever since."

She thought about it, savoring the moment a little longer.

"Okay."

"Okay?"

"That one has been struck off the list."

"Wait a second. How long is this list?"

"It varies. Items get added and removed all the time. Now can we finish this puzzle, please?" The rest of the morning and part of the afternoon was spent on the floor together, amicably arguing over every single answer. Cleo couldn't remember the last time she'd enjoyed herself more.

⌒

Cleo and Dante got along much better after that day. They no longer seemed like strangers forced to live together and felt more at ease around each other. They fell into an easy routine; Dante cooked when he was home, and Cleo ordered takeout for them when he called to let her know he'd be working late, which happened on average about twice a week. And for some reason, Dante *always* called to let her know that he'd be back late.

Their workouts were almost always done together, usually in the mornings before Dante headed off to work, but as Cleo's pregnancy progressed, her physical routine became less strenuous, and her en pointe exercises nonexistent. On Saturday mornings, they did the crossword puzzle together even though Dante was dismal at it, and they often watched old action or horror movies together. Dante wasn't the biggest horror-movie fan, and that's all she ever chose when it was her turn to pick a film, mostly because she loved watching him freak out.

The next couple of weeks passed quickly and peacefully. But the main source of grief and discontent for Cleo—and she sensed for Dante too—was the fact that Luc still didn't want to speak to either of them. It was going on longer than any of them had anticipated, and Blue was at her wit's end. Cleo had actually gone to see Luc at the house and at his office on several occasions. He'd asked her how she was, how the pregnancy was going and—at the house—had found a reason to exit the room and leave her with Blue. At work he'd told her he was too busy to chat. She didn't know what else to do and decided to let him figure it out in his own time.

"You're not even watching," Dante complained, his voice interrupting her thoughts, and she squinted at him before switching her attention back to the television.

"Well, it's your fault for choosing this boring movie," she retorted, waving a hand at the screen. It was some generic action movie; she didn't even think she knew the title. It was badly acted and kind of bland.

"Are you thinking about tomorrow?" he asked. "Are you nervous?"

The dance recital was the following evening, and Cleo didn't feel the kids were anywhere close to ready. She thought her choreography was lame, and she just knew that something catastrophic would happen. The building nerves and anxiety were pretty much on par with what she used to feel before performing.

"It'll be fine," she said, more to convince herself than him. "The kids seem confident."

"Then what's bothering you?" he asked.

"Luc." The name was out before she could prevent it, and he sighed heavily.

"I had no idea he could be so stubborn," he said with a wry twist of his lips. "Why is he so set against the idea of us living together?"

"Because he knows . . ." Her voice tapered off.

"Knows what?"

"He knows that there's no love between us, and he wanted better than that for me." Except that she wasn't so sure the "no love" thing was strictly true anymore. There seemed to be quite a lot of love between them.

All one-sided and all from her.

The heavy silence strained the atmosphere, and she kept her eyes glued blindly to the TV even though she could feel his gaze boring into her profile.

"We could . . ." This time it was his voice that faded away in the middle of a sentence. He reached for the touch-screen controller and paused the movie, turning his body toward her and waiting until she, reluctantly, did the same. He picked up one of her hands in both of his and turned it over so that he was tracing the lines of her palm with his forefinger. "I think we should consider getting married."

She gasped and snatched her hand back as if it had been burned.

"Hear me out," he said calmly, and she shook her head.

"Oh my God." She got off the couch and folded her arms across her chest. He got up as well.

"Just listen," he said, and tried to reach for her again, but she sidestepped him.

"What a manipulative bastard you are," she marveled. "You've decided that you want this baby, and you think that offering me *marriage* will help you get him. You still have such a low opinion of women in general that you probably genuinely believe that this is the brass ring for me, don't you? What woman wouldn't want to marry Dante Damaso? After all, you're loaded and handsome, and that's what all women want, right?"

"I just figured it would make Luc happy and fix the gap between the two of you," he began.

"How goddamn selfless of you, relinquishing your precious freedom on behalf of my relationship with my brother."

"I didn't say it was selfless." Frustration started to creep into his voice. "It's not just about your relationship with Luc. It's also about mine. And aside from that, you're right, I *do* want this baby. I want to be his dad. I want him to have my name, I want him to know who I am."

"He won't have your name," she whispered, her voice thick with loathing. "You don't deserve to give him your name."

"Why the hell not?" He finally lost his cool, and his voice rose as his temper broke. "What did I do that was so fucking wrong? I made a mistake in the beginning, I reacted in the wrong way, and I'll be paying for that for the rest of my life. And worse, the baby will be paying for it too, won't he? Because you're too stubborn to admit that maybe I'd be a good father to that child."

"And a pretty lousy husband to me," she added resentfully. "I deserve more than a man who doesn't love me and who only married me because I was pregnant. We all deserve more than that."

"So you want me to tell you I love you? Would that make it all better?" he asked, his voice steeped in bitterness and sarcasm. She uttered a hoarse cry as his words broke something inside of her. It made her want to hurt him as much as he had just hurt her.

"You're a miserable excuse of a man, Dante," she said, venom dripping from every word. "And if you came crawling to me on broken glass, professing to love me, I would never believe you . . . because you're incapable of feeling anything remotely close to love."

His jaw clenched and he went pale before he shoved his hands into his pockets and allowed the tension to leave his shoulders until he was almost slouching.

"I take it that's a no to the marriage proposal, then?" he asked with a smirk.

She gasped and whirled on her heel before heading up to her room as fast as she could. She slammed the door behind her and took childish satisfaction when the sound reverberated through his cold and uninviting apartment. She was shaking uncontrollably and didn't know how to stop it.

This is what happened when you allowed yourself to have feelings for someone like Dante Damaso—they found the most creative ways to hurt you, and God, this *hurt*. She told herself that he hadn't meant to inflict pain; in his mind it was a cold, businesslike proposition, supposedly beneficial to them both. He expected her to view it in the same dispassionate way he probably did—marriage to him meant wealth and status for her. It meant she and the baby got the protection of his name and that he got to see if he was capable of being a halfway decent parent to a child.

He didn't know that she had fallen in love with him. Why would he? It wasn't like he had given her any reason to love him, aside from his unexpected moments of sweetness, charm, latent humor, and charisma. But then he turned around and showed her the callous, calculating, and cynical side of him with what had to be the most cold-blooded, jaded proposal in history.

And how did she tell the idiot that she couldn't marry him because she loved him? Living as his wife, as the mother of his child, and not having his love would be soul-destroying. She didn't know what to do, or whom to turn to, and in the end she dragged out her phone and scrolled for Cal's number. She looked at his name on her screen for a long time before she changed her mind and tossed the phone aside.

She curled up in the middle of the bed and dragged her knees up to her chest, curving her body protectively around the mound of her baby. She couldn't leave this apartment, not with Luc still angry with her. She had nowhere else to go.

She would hold Dante to his promises, she would allow him to be a presence in the child's life, but she wasn't going to marry him, and the baby would *not* have his name. That was what they'd agreed upon, and that was what the latest—in the increasingly useless—lot of legal documents said. And this was a document she would fight tooth and nail to enforce.

"I don't know if I'm doing the right thing, Baby," she whispered. "But it *has* to be better than subjecting all three of us to a loveless marriage, right?"

She was gratified when the baby kicked, and took it as a sign of agreement.

CHAPTER TWELVE

The following evening, Cleo stood backstage in a tiny school gymnasium and felt her chest swell with pride as her young dancers took their bows and curtsies. They'd been magnificent, and she just wanted to hug every single one of her little stars.

She gave each one a high five as they trotted offstage and passed her on their way to the changing room. Every child got a word of encouragement and praise, and she couldn't resist giving the last—tiniest—girl a brief hug.

"Did you see me, miss?" the little girl asked in excitement, her face flushed and happy.

"I did. You were absolutely marvelous," Cleo said but then added, because she *was* still the teacher here, "but you have to work on your basic turns, Maisie. We'll talk about it on Monday, okay? You were fantastic."

"Yes, miss. Thank you, miss," the girl said with a grin before prancing off, her pink tutu bouncing as she moved. Cleo watched her go with a fond smile on her face, but the smile faded when she saw the man standing in the doorway Maisie had just disappeared through. Why did he always have to show up where he wasn't expected or invited?

He watched the girl go before turning back to her with a quizzical look on his face.

"Did you ever wear those ridiculous little skirts?"

"Of course I did, I was a ballet dancer," she replied before getting straight down to it. "Why are you here?"

"I came to watch the performance. The kids were great. Your choreography was fantastic."

"I have to go and talk to the children," she said. "Excuse me."

"I'll be waiting out in the reception area," he informed her, and stepped aside to let her pass.

"Don't bother, I drove myself here and I can drive myself back."

"I'll be waiting," he reiterated. Her back stiffened, and she walked off without another look back.

It took her nearly an hour to finish up. After heaping praise on the kids, she was stopped by parents who were keen to discuss their children. She was supposed to help Susan clean up after the rest of the recital was finished, but the woman, who'd come backstage to congratulate her after her group had danced, urged her to go home, overriding Cleo's protestations by reminding her that pregnant women should take it easy. Unable to argue with that logic, Cleo had conceded her point and grabbed her denim jacket, heading out of the gym, where the fourteen-year-olds were currently performing.

She had her keys in hand and her head down when she walked out of the building, but she was very aware of the fact that Dante and James were standing in the parking lot watching her come down the school steps. They were waiting by her car, so there was no way to avoid them.

She sighed—knowing it would be useless to argue—and handed her keys to James and waited for Dante to lead her to wherever his car was parked. All without saying a word. She just didn't feel like arguing, not when they were all going to the same place anyway. Dante didn't have much to say either, but he threw glances at her every few minutes, which she pointedly ignored.

"I'm not used to such silence from you," he finally said when they were about five minutes from home.

"I don't have much to say at the moment," she said with a shrug.

"That bad, huh?"

She didn't know what the hell that meant, but it just rubbed her the wrong way, and she turned to him with a ferocious scowl. "You think being *flippant* is the way forward here?" she snarled. "Because I've got news for you, buddy—"

The ear-splitting sound of screeching brakes interrupted her in midsentence, and she looked up into the driver's-side window to see a car barreling straight at them.

"Dante!" Her scream was sharp and short-lived, and mere seconds passed between impact and the cessation of all movement and sound.

She battled her way out from beneath the airbag, which had deployed with a startling pop and had knocked the breath out of her. She could hear Dante groaning and was desperate to get to him. She could see blood and started to panic. His head was bleeding and his eyes were shut, and he sounded like he was in pain.

"Dante?" she whispered. "Oh God, Dante! Are you okay? Can you hear me?"

Her door was wrenched open, and she looked up to see James—who'd been following in her car—towering above her, his face grim. He reached down to unbuckle her seat belt.

"Are you okay?" he asked, his voice harsh.

"I'm fine. See to Dante first."

"You *know* that he'd want me to help you first, Cleo." James's voice brooked no argument, and Cleo knew that disagreeing with him would only delay the time it took for him to get to Dante, so she allowed him to unbuckle her and help her out.

He ran expert hands over her, his touch telling her that he knew exactly what he was doing and what he was looking for. She batted his hands away impatiently.

"Help Dante," she commanded, and he nodded curtly before heading back to the car. They had been pushed off the road, she noticed dazedly. They were hit while crossing a T-junction, and the other car had pushed them into a field. The second car had come to a standstill a few yards away, and Cleo could see the driver staggering his way out of the car. She stood frozen, her hands to her face in horror, and her entire body went numb as shock started to set in. She turned away from the other driver and back to their car, willing James to hurry, to bring Dante out to safety. And then she heard it—the unmistakable sound of Dante's impatient voice—and the relief made her legs weak. She sat down in the middle of the field as her body started shaking from head to toe.

Cleo could hear them quite clearly: James saying that he didn't think it was wise for Dante to move, and Dante telling him to get the hell out of his way. Dante, being Dante, predictably got his way, and after pushing his way past James, he stood looking like a wild man, his head whipping back and forth as he looked for something. *Her*, as it turned out.

"Cleo!" The harsh, commanding voice had a desperate edge to it as he called for her, clearly panicking because he couldn't see her.

"I'm here," she called, sounding shockingly weak. His head snapped in her direction, and she saw him wince at the fast movement before he lurched toward her.

"Ah, *Jesus*," he cursed when he sank down to his knees in front of her. His hands cupped her face and tilted it up to peer at her closely. "You're okay. You're okay."

He sounded unsteady, and he released her face to gather her tenderly into his arms and hug her close.

"I'm sorry," he whispered into her hair. "That shouldn't have happened. I'm sorry."

"He came out of nowhere," she protested, her voice wobbling even more than Dante's. "It wasn't your fault. You're bleeding, Dante."

The quiver in her voice gave way to a sob, and he held her even closer.

"It's okay. It's okay, *nena*. Don't cry. I'm okay." He muttered similar phrases, his English liberally sprinkled with Spanish. They could hear sirens in the distance and shouting as James and the other driver argued about something, but neither Dante nor Cleo moved, or even looked in that direction.

When the emergency services showed up, James pointed them to Dante and Cleo, who still sat in the middle of the field. They had long since lapsed into silence, Dante holding her close while Cleo battled to stop shaking.

"He's bleeding," she told the paramedics as soon as they crouched down in front of them.

"And she's pregnant," Dante informed them, as one of the men applied pressure to the bleeding wound above his right eyebrow, where a shard of the shattered window had narrowly missed his eye.

Her hand went to her bump at the mention of her pregnancy—of course it would be the first thing Dante thought about in a situation like this. No wonder he'd been so worried about her. There'd be no baby without a healthy Cleo.

It hadn't even occurred to Cleo to be concerned about the baby. Her baby was fine. She'd know if it wasn't. Still, it would be wise to check. She gave the bump a reassuring pat and stood up with the overeager assistance of two paramedics and one apprehensive-looking Spaniard. One of the paramedics attempted to steer her toward the waiting ambulance, but Dante stepped between them and took her elbow, as if she were the most fragile thing in the world.

"I'll do it," he said firmly, and the paramedics exchanged glances before shrugging and smoothly moving to flank the hobbling couple as they slowly made their way toward the ambulance.

A second ambulance was just arriving, and so were the police. James left the other driver with the emergency responders and strode toward them.

"You both okay?" he asked, his sharp gaze taking in their injuries, or lack thereof, in a single glance.

"Fine," Dante replied, while the paramedics were checking their vital signs. "What about that guy?"

James made a disgusted sound.

"Drunk. And feeling confrontational even though he can barely stand upright. He actually wanted to get back into his wrecked car and drive off. I had to take his keys. The fool thought this was an intersection and blasted through the red light. If you hadn't been driving by at that exact moment, he would have wound up in this field."

"We're lucky it wasn't worse," Cleo whispered, her hand going to her abdomen as she considered the awful possibilities. It was bad enough that Dante was injured.

"You're both going to have to come to the hospital with us," one of the paramedics said sternly. "Sir, we have to rule out concussion, and we need to make sure that everything is in order with your wife's pregnancy."

"I'm not . . . ," she began.

But Dante cut her short with a terse, "Fine."

He helped her into the ambulance and climbed in after her.

"The cops are going to want to speak with you both," James said as the paramedics shut the doors. "I'll let them know which hospital they're taking you to, and I'll pick you up from there."

Dante merely nodded, and his efficient bodyguard took control of the situation.

Endless hours later, Dante was given the all-clear. No concussion, but it was still a nasty bump to the head, and he needed to call a doctor immediately if he suffered headaches, nausea, or blurred vision. He had five stitches above his eyebrow and a bruise forming on his cheek. Cleo had a tender chest from the impact of the airbag but no damage to her ribs or sternum and was treated for shock. The baby seemed fine, but they warned her to rest for the next few days and to contact her OB/GYN as soon as possible if there was any unusual cramping or bleeding.

They'd both made statements to the police and were assured that the driver of the other car would be arrested on drunk-driving charges, and since it wasn't his first offense, he would likely be stripped of his license. Happy with that outcome, the exhausted couple gratefully followed James to Dante's second car, which he'd picked up after dropping off Cleo's hatchback. Cleo eyed the gleaming navy-blue car in amusement and arched a look at James.

"Didn't you think my beat-up old Volkswagen was good enough for His Majesty over here?"

James grinned. "I thought you'd both be a lot more comfortable in the Mercedes."

"Good call," Dante said, his voice leaden with exhaustion and pain.

It was close to one in the morning by the time they finally got home. After saying good night to James, they wearily made their way up to the penthouse. Once there, Dante stumbled up to his room. Cleo trailed after him, wanting to be sure he made it to bed okay. She'd never seen him this sluggish, and it concerned her. She still worried about his head injury, even though the doctor assured them it was minor, and she knew it was probably the painkillers making him groggy. He dragged off his clothes, keeping on his black boxer briefs and black socks, and threw himself facedown on the bed without saying a word. Cleo didn't even think he was aware of her presence in his room. She tried to convince herself that he would be fine if she left and reluctantly turned to exit the room.

He said something, his voice muffled by the pillow, and she stopped, turning to look at him. He didn't appear to have moved a muscle.

"Did you say something?" she whispered, in case she'd imagined the sound. He turned to look at her. The bruise was taking on a livid, purplish hue, and his eye was swollen almost shut.

"Stay," he said gruffly, and she wavered before admitting to herself that she didn't want to leave him anyway.

"Just for a while," she conceded. She took off her jacket and pulled one of the decorative chairs over to the bed. She curled up in it, pulling her bare feet up and tucking them beneath her butt.

With only his bedside lamp providing light, the room felt cozier than it actually was. She could see him clearly in the warm, yellow glow but knew that she was sitting just outside the little circle of light and was not as easily visible to him, which allowed her to study his features hungrily. Even with the swelling, the gauzy patch above his eye, and the bruises, he was still a remarkably good-looking man. But that wasn't what riveted her—instead, it was the naked vulnerability she could see on his face that held her captive. She doubted that he was even aware of the expression; he was on the verge of falling asleep, every muscle in his body and face going limp as his exhaustion overtook him.

Cleo stayed awhile longer, watching him, enjoying the silence and knowing that despite the closeness they'd experienced tonight, tomorrow would see them back in their respective corners, facing off in the endless battlefield that was their relationship.

She waited until she was certain he was asleep, then stumbled to her own room and crawled into bed after taking off the least amount of clothes necessary for her to be comfortable. And then she fell into a thankfully dreamless slumber.

⁓

"You look awful," Cleo said with a wince when Dante joined her for breakfast the following morning. "Jeez, does that hurt?"

"Like a sonofabitch," he grunted, gingerly probing at his swollen eye with his fingers.

"Don't touch it," she admonished. "You'll make it worse."

"How are you this morning?" he asked, peering at her through his one good eye.

"Fine. I have a huge bruise on my chest from the airbag, and the entire area is a bit tender, but it's nothing serious." It actually hurt more than she was letting on because of her already sensitive breasts, but there was no point in complaining since there wasn't any pain medication she'd feel comfortable taking anyway.

Dante poured himself a cup of coffee and sat down at the table opposite Cleo, who was having a bowl of cereal.

"You're not eating?" she asked, and he made a face and shook his head.

"Do you want to do something today?"

"Something like what?" Cleo asked in confusion, and Dante shrugged, looking a little discomfited.

"I was thinking we're heading into week twenty, and Baby's about the length of a banana, so we should probably call her Nan this week." The baby had been Tom last week because he'd been about the size of an heirloom tomato. It was a silly game that had evolved between them when they'd discovered a fruit-and-vegetable-comparative-size chart to go along with their weekly growth updates. She'd been Pepper at week eighteen, when they'd first started this game. "I thought we could go do some shopping for her room."

"But we don't even know how big the room will be," Cleo said, and Dante's face became an expressionless mask.

"Cleo, you can't mean to move out as soon as she's born? You'll need help during those first few months."

"*Months?*" she squeaked. "You expect me to stay here for months after she's born? Dante, no. You said you'd help us find a place to stay; it's in the contract, and that's what I'm expecting from you."

"I'll get Mrs. Clarke started on the search for a place first thing in the morning," he said after a long silence, and her shoulders slumped in relief. She shoved her half-eaten cereal aside.

"It's Mrs. Whitman now," she reminded him.

"Yes. I'd forgotten." He stared down into his cup of coffee as if it held the key to unlocking all the secrets in the universe.

"We could go window shopping," he suggested. "And maybe get a basic idea of the stuff you'd need for Nan's nursery."

"Why are you so keen on doing this?" she asked, and he lifted and dropped his shoulders again.

"Maybe I want to feel involved," he said. "Or maybe I'm just bored and want to get out of here today. This seems to be the most productive thing to do, and it is an activity that would interest both of us."

His answer surprised her.

"You would find shopping for baby stuff interesting?"

"I've never bought baby things before. It would be educational, at the very least."

Cleo considered his words; she *did* need some new clothes, since her skirts and trousers were getting too tight in the waist. She'd been thinking of getting a few maternity dresses. But she didn't want them to be *obviously* maternity dresses. She always imagined awful, frumpy, tentlike frocks whenever she thought of maternity wear, and those were so not her style. She was hoping to find some fun, loose tops and dresses and drawstring trousers and skirts, which her changing body could grow into.

"Okay," she said. "If you're sure you're up to it, I wouldn't mind going out. I need some stuff anyway."

⤳

Their first stop was a large high-end baby store in Green Point, and the moment she set foot inside, Cleo was overwhelmed by the sheer amount of tastefully displayed products. This wasn't at all what she'd expected from a baby shop. Discreet and soothing tunes played in the background, and the place smelled like expensive wood. There were no price tags in sight, which made Cleo nervous. They were approached by several salespersons, all of whom homed in on Cleo and Dante like sharks smelling fresh blood, and Cleo felt a little intimidated by the predatory gleam in their eyes. A woman about two years younger than Cleo reached them first, and her colleagues backed off and disappeared into the woodwork, like wraiths. The saleswoman turned a hundred-watt smile onto her potential new clients.

"Good morning, ma'am, sir . . . I'm Kate. May I be of assistance?" Cleo peered at Dante, who—with his arms folded across his chest—seemed to be waiting for her to say something. Cleo was tempted to turn down Kate's offer, but another look around the bewildering array of baby paraphernalia and Dante's impassive face changed her mind for her.

"I need . . . well, *everything*," she said helplessly. She felt a little inadequate when she acknowledged to herself that she wasn't certain exactly what babies needed, aside from love, care, food, and clothing. As she watched Kate's smile transform from a hundred watts to a hundred thousand megawatts, Cleo realized it was the worst reply she could have given.

"Well, then," Kate said smugly, "you've come to the right place, because we have *everything*." She lowered her eyes to Cleo's barely protruding stomach, and her smile turned simpering. "Your first?" Cleo nodded, and Kate's smile became beatific. She certainly had an amazing variety of smiles.

"How far along are you?"

"Just on five months," Cleo replied.

"Babies are wonderful, aren't they?" Kate gushed. "So full of life."

"I wouldn't know." Cleo's response was dry. "I don't have a baby yet."

Dante made a little choking sound that Cleo was coming to recognize as his attempt at disguising a laugh. Another quick look in his direction confirmed that his lips had tilted upward, even while he kept his gaze firmly averted from Cleo's. Kate's smile faded somewhat; she clearly did not like having the obvious pointed out to her.

"Of course." The woman nodded before going into full-on sales mode. "Well, the best place to start would be with a crib. If you'll follow me, we have a fantastic variety, which I am sure you'll *adore*! Everything we have here is for display purposes, and your crib will be built to order, so we can change aspects of any design if you're not happy with something. We could even custom-build one for you based on a design you have in mind. So it's a good thing you came to us this early, because it takes time to make, especially if you're purchasing matching furniture, which will also have to be built to order."

Kate led them to the cribs in the back, and even to Cleo's untrained eye, she could tell that everything was ridiculously expensive. While Kate was lauding the merits of one of the beautiful cribs, Cleo gravitated toward a smaller, less conspicuous one tucked away in the back. While not as beautiful as the rest, it definitely looked less pricey.

"This one looks okay," she said, running her hands over the plain, unadorned surface of the crib. Actually this plain, boxy little thing was not something she had ever pictured her baby in, but if she wasn't going to feel beholden to Dante for the rest of her life, instinct told her this was the one to take.

"I rather like this one." Dante spoke for the first time since they'd entered the store, and both women looked at him in surprise. He was standing beside a crib smaller than the one Kate was gushing over but bigger than the one Cleo had been eyeing.

Truth be told, it was perfect—not too small and not too ostentatious either. She knew what he was doing; he was trying to help, without flaunting his obvious ability to buy the most expensive and best. He was allowing her some measure of pride and independence, and she was grateful to him for that. But a cynical part of her brain hissed that if he didn't want to flaunt his ability to buy the most expensive, then maybe he shouldn't have brought her to this snooty upmarket store.

She walked over to the crib while he examined its lines and tested its durability with a keen masculine eye. He asked Kate about the toxicity of the varnish they used and other technical questions that wouldn't have occurred to Cleo. The girl's answers seemed to satisfy him, because he nodded approvingly with each of her replies before turning back to Cleo.

"It's sturdy," he informed her quietly before testing the catches. "And the rail isn't likely to come down accidentally. The baby should be safe in here."

"Hmm," she murmured thoughtfully, pretending to consider, even though he'd sold her on it already. "It's pretty too. I love the little pixies and fairies carved into the head- and footboards, as well as the mobile." She touched the colourful mobile, which swayed at her touch. The mobile consisted of winged fairies and cavorting pixies and elves.

"I like this one," she told Kate, who jumped to attention and enthused over their "wise choice."

"This particular model comes in teak, oak, and pine. Obviously the price varies according to the wood you choose. Which would you prefer?"

Cleo considered the choices, while Kate pulled out a catalog to show her the difference in the wood.

"Teak." She ran her finger over the carvings in the headboard of the crib and thought of her own bed. She liked the idea of them matching, and she pictured Nan sleeping contentedly in this crib and smiled. Kate practically vibrated with excitement as she wrote down the details of the order and then took them toward the changing tables.

"That was an excellent choice, Dante. I don't know why I didn't notice it at first." He looked pleased with her praise and grinned like a little boy.

"You think so?"

"Yes. Thank you. And it has given me an idea for the nursery. What do you think of a fairy-tale motif?"

Dante hesitated, a little surprised that she'd asked for his opinion. He didn't want to do anything that could spoil what was turning out to be a pretty good day . . . but he really had to tell her what he thought of this idea of fairies.

"You want my honest opinion?" he asked. They were both ignoring poor Kate's frantic attempts to get their attention, while Cleo lowered her eyelashes and pretended to consider his question.

"Honesty would be appreciated," she said demurely.

"What if it's a boy?" he asked. "You can't seriously want to surround the kid with fairies and pixies? That's girlie stuff!"

"No, it's not!" she argued, quite affronted by this view. "Fairies and pixies sometimes have a dangerous air to them, and they're appealing to a child of any sex. If it's a boy and he wants to change his room later, that would be entirely up to him." He didn't respond; instead he gazed at her impassively.

Cleo couldn't read his expression and wasn't certain of his mood, especially since he was wearing dark glasses to hide part of his shiner. His lips thinned and he sighed quietly.

"Must you argue? You seem to forget that you asked for my opinion," he said gravely. "Cleo, sometimes you can be so damned . . ."

"Frustrating?" she supplied with a sympathetic nod.

"No."

"Annoying?" she guessed, and he gave her the Look, which shut her up immediately. He really was so super anal about her finishing his sentences.

"Cute," he said with playful smile, and shocked the hell right out of her. "Sometimes you can be so damned cute."

"Oh." Well, how else was she supposed to respond to that? "Are you flirting with me?" She really couldn't tell. Dante Damaso did nothing conventionally.

"What if I were?" he asked speculatively, and she pondered over that for a moment.

"I'd tell you to stop," she finally replied. "It's weird."

"Maybe I'm wooing you," he said.

"To what end?"

"You know what," he countered, confirming her worst fear.

"Well, stop it at once. I gave you my answer Friday night. It's not just a no, it's a *hell* no." As if she would marry a man who didn't love her.

"Okay," he said so casually that she blinked at him uncertainly. His response was unexpectedly easygoing, and it threw her a little.

"I'm assuming you have the accompanying pieces to this crib." He directed the comment to Kate, who'd been watching their exchange with interest.

"Uh. Yes. Of course." She was just way too enthusiastic. Cleo wished the woman would tone it down a bit. She was starting to develop a headache and was questioning the wisdom of coming out so soon after the accident. Her entire body ached, from her shoulders on down. She followed the other two a little sluggishly, and when Kate told them that the matching changing table and dresser were must-haves, she found herself unable to argue with the woman.

A stroller, a baby bouncer, a rocking chair, and a car seat later, Cleo—deciding new clothes could wait another day or two—pleaded exhaustion, and Dante, who was also looking a bit pale and peaked, agreed that it was best to head home. She went straight up to bed when they got home and fell asleep almost instantly.

Her sleep was restless and filled with disturbing dreams, and when she awoke hours later, it was to an even worse headache. She took a warm bath to try and relax her muscles and ease her tension, and it seemed to work to a certain extent. Her headache had definitely diminished enough for her to face going downstairs to dinner.

Dante was in the kitchen, cooking something that smelled divine. He smiled when he saw her.

"I hope you're hungry," he said, and she sat down at the island to watch him. The scene was reminiscent of that first night he'd cooked for her.

"I could eat."

"I made some paella, my second stepmother's recipe. That woman was a genius in the kitchen, which was great, since none of the old man's other wives bothered. They thought cooking was beneath them, and they married a rich man so cooking was something the chef did."

He was unusually forthcoming tonight, and Cleo rested her cheek in the palm of her hand and idly traced the pattern of veins on the marble countertop.

"Did you like any of your stepmothers?"

"That one, Stepmom Number Two? She was my favorite. Taught me a thing or two about cooking. The rest were just . . ." His voice faded as he thought about it. "I don't know, interchangeable maybe. After Number Two, I stopped trying to get to know them."

"Did you act out?" Cleo asked, thinking of her own rebellious years.

"I was a good kid, got the best grades and stayed out of trouble. I didn't have many friends. I still don't." And he'd lost one of his best friends because of her, Cleo thought, swallowing past a lump in her throat. "It was only when I hit puberty that I started getting into fights, and my father thought it best for me to take boxing classes in order to channel that aggression. It worked. One of his more sound parental decisions."

"Do you get along with him?" she asked.

"We get along *now*. He wasn't too happy when I decided to stay here. However, since I've made a success of the business, he's back in the black and able to fund his current wife-to-be, Carmen's, spendthrift ways. So he's come to accept the idea. I love him, he's my papa, but we're not friends. If we go a year or more without seeing each other, both of us are fine with that. We're both happy with a few Skype sessions a year."

"That's sad."

"I don't think so," he said with a little shrug. "It's life. Sometimes we get along with our parents, and sometimes we don't."

Her hand went to her abdomen, and she silently promised her child better than that. Dante's eyes followed her hand to her stomach, and his Adam's apple bobbed as he swallowed thickly.

"I would want a different relationship with her," he said softly. "I didn't know this at first, Cleo, but I do know it now. I want to be a real father to Nan, and I don't want her to go through the turmoil of numerous stepparents. Just us. Her mother and father."

"What you're proposing is a cold and cynical arrangement that will result in a cold and cynical environment unsuited for raising a child. Please don't bring this up again. I don't want to marry you, and I know that it's not what you want either. Not really."

"I've come to . . ." He hesitated, clearly picking his words carefully. "I've come to like and respect you, Cleo, and I do think we can have a good marriage together."

"Oh my God." She jumped up and planted her hands on her hips. "That's not enough, Dante! I don't want *good*. I want amazing; I want fantastic; I want blissful. I want *love*, and you can't give that to me."

"Who says I can't?" His handsome face was a study in frustration and building anger. Cleo gasped at his words and pinned him with a glare.

"Don't you *dare*," she whispered. "Don't you dare treat me with such condescension and downright contempt, Dante. I'm not an idiot, so don't even think about going down that road. I don't need the 'someday we might come to love each other' speech. I don't want to hear it. It's insulting."

"This isn't easy for me either, Cleo," he snapped. "I'm trying my damnedest to think of ways we can make this work for both of us, and you're not making it easy."

"I'm not talking about this again," she maintained, rolling her aching shoulders as she headed back toward the staircase.

"Where are you going?"

"I don't feel like doing this with you right now," she said. "I'm headed back to my room."

"You haven't eaten."

"I've lost my appetite."

"Cleo, you should eat for the baby's sake."

"Dante, I can't sit at that table with you and pretend that everything is just fine. I wish to God that I'd never agreed to live here with you. It was a dumb decision that has already cost me my pride, my independence, and my brother." He flinched and went as white as a sheet at the last two words, but Cleo refused to feel any guilt over it.

It was time Dante Damaso accepted that, for once, he *wasn't* going to get his way.

She was sitting on her bed, listlessly clicking through the multitude of channels available on the wall-mounted large-screen television, when a sharp knock sounded on her door. She ignored it and sighed impatiently when the door swung open despite her lack of response. Dante stepped in and placed a loaded tray on her dresser before leaving without saying a word.

Cleo couldn't ignore the heavenly aromas and got off the bed to investigate the contents. There was a small bowl of salad beside a plate laden with delicious-looking seafood paella and a slice of rich, moist chocolate cake on a side plate. He had also been thoughtful enough to include a silver carafe of cold water. Cleo's mouth watered. She dragged over a chair and sat right at the dresser and scarfed down half of the paella and salad in one go. It was absolutely perfect.

Definitely one of the perks of living with Dante was his cooking; the man loved being in the kitchen, and it showed in the meals he prepared. After polishing off her meal, she practically inhaled the cake, which was absolutely delicious, and there was no doubt in her mind that it had been baked by Dante.

After finishing, she considered going downstairs to thank him, but the thought of going another round with him was mentally exhausting, so she sent him a thank-you text instead.

`You're welcome. Glad you enjoyed it.`

His response was almost immediate. She contemplated sending him a smiley face or something in return but decided to leave it at that. Ten minutes went by before her phone buzzed again.

`Want to watch Star Trek with me?`

It was the equivalent of a white flag, since *Star Trek* had become kind of an in-joke between them, but she didn't think she could face him again tonight.

```
No thanks. Tired. Going to sleep.

Good night.
```

She decided not to respond to his "Good night" and curled up on her bed, her hand on her little bump. Nan shifted gently beneath her touch, and Cleo smiled before falling asleep with the TV still on.

CHAPTER THIRTEEN

She awoke with a gasp. The TV was on, playing quietly in the background, the light flickering in the darkened room.

Something's wrong. She tried to push herself up and nearly doubled over in pain. This wasn't right. She tried to stand again, and this time succeeded for a few seconds before her knees buckled, and she groaned as excruciating pain knifed through her abdomen.

"No," she moaned. She braced her palm on the night table and pushed herself up again, managing to keep her balance as she hugged the wall all the way to the bathroom. It was only when she got into the brightly lit room that she saw she was bleeding. The horror of the realization impacted her like a freight train, and she sat down on the commode as she tried to wrap her head around what was happening.

"Dante." His name was just a whisper, as her breath was stolen from her by another sharp pain. She gritted her teeth and clung to the basin beside the commode. After the pain had passed, she managed to inhale; Dante's name emerged on the exhalation. This time it was a scream.

Dante sat up with a frown; he'd fallen asleep while watching the movie and was still sitting in the living room. He focused his bleary gaze on his watch face and saw that it was after three in the morning. He must have been more tired than he thought. He rolled his shoulders and his neck, working the kinks out, when he heard Cleo scream.

Unnerved by the fear he heard in her voice, he was up the stairs mere seconds later and in her room in under a minute.

"Cleo?" he called, alarmed when he stepped into the room and she was nowhere to be found. He heard sobs coming from the bathroom and dashed to it only to stop at the door at the scene that met his eyes.

There was so much blood. Violent red smeared the white tiles of the floor. Cleo was bent double on the commode, clutching her arms to her middle and rocking back and forth.

She lifted her tear-stained face to his as he entered the room.

"Make it stop," she pleaded, her voice weak. "Please make it stop."

Swallowing down the fear and panic clawing its way up through his throat, he grabbed a towel and knelt in front of her.

"It's okay, *dulzura*; it's okay. I'll take care of you. It will be fine." He handed her the wadded-up towel. "Use this to stop the bleeding while I call an ambulance."

"Don't leave me," she begged as he turned to exit the room.

"Just to the next room to get your phone. I'll be back in a second," he promised. Her phone was on the night table beside the bed, and he quickly dialed emergency services, then found the number for her OB/GYN and told her to meet them at the hospital. When he returned to the bathroom, Cleo was clutching the already blood-soaked towel between her legs. He grabbed more and held out a fresh one to her.

This was too much blood. Cleo could go into shock. Feeling helpless for the first time in his life, Dante tried to think logically. He needed to keep her warm. He ran back into the room and tugged the comforter off the bed and came back moments later to wrap it around her.

"Why is this happening?" she wondered dazedly. "Am I being punished because I didn't want her at first? I want her. I want her so much, Dante!"

"I know, *dulzura*, I want her too. She'll be fine. *You'll* be fine. Just stay strong for me, okay?"

He gathered Cleo into his arms, comforter and all, and sank down onto the bathroom floor with her head tucked beneath his chin. She was trembling, a delicate armful of woman, and he just wanted to hold her close and keep her safe.

～◎～

Cleo and Dante lost their baby at six thirty that morning. Cleo stared at Dr. Klein in horror as the grim-faced woman told them the news. She heard fragments of sentences.

Placental abruption . . . possibly caused by the accident . . . early labor . . . autopsy . . . couldn't be helped . . . just one of those things.

Just one of those things.

Her baby had been taken from her, and she felt *hollow*, but it was just one of those things. One of those silly things that happened for no reason. She was empty inside now, and while she watched the doctor's lips move, she heard nothing further. She didn't want to hear.

Dante was still here. Hovering. Why was he still here? He could leave now. His sole reason for being in her life was gone, and he didn't have to be here. She didn't have the will or the energy to tell him that now. She just wished they would leave her alone. She needed to be alone.

"Cleo, do you want to say good-bye?" Dr. Klein's voice intruded into her roiling thoughts. Grateful that they were finally leaving, she nodded numbly.

"Yes, good-bye." But they didn't leave. Instead, someone else came into the room. A woman. And in her arms she held . . .

"Oh." This was cruel. This was . . . why were they doing this to her? Why were they bringing her dead baby to her? Before she could protest, the woman had placed the not-living *thing* in her arms. Just a little thing, the length of a banana.

"Oh, Nan," she whispered, and her heart broke open in her chest as she stared into that perfect little face. He looked like a tiny plastic replica of a full-size baby. He was wrapped in a blue blanket, and they'd put a minute hat on his head. She ran a trembling forefinger over his forehead, down over the bridge of his nose, to his lips and jaw.

Then Dante was there, his own finger following hers as it traced over the precious little features reverently.

"Leave me alone," Cleo hissed, not sure if she meant Dante, the doctor, or just the world in general. The doctor and nurse left the room quietly, but Dante remained standing there. She clutched her baby protectively to her breast and glared up into Dante's remote face. Tears clung to her eyelashes before they spilled down over her cheeks.

"Don't make me leave," he begged. "Please, *cielo*, I can't leave."

She didn't want to deal with him too; she was in too much agony to have to think about him, consider him . . . it was all too much!

"I can't do this alone and neither can you," he muttered as he pressed his lips to her forehead, but she barely felt the kiss; she was cold and numb and didn't think she would ever feel anything again.

"I want to name him Zachary," she whispered. "Zach Damaso Knight."

She heard a sound very like a sob torn from him, but she still refused to look at him.

"He's so perfect," she marveled. "So perfect."

"Yes." He sat on the edge of the bed, one arm around her shaking shoulders and his jaw resting on top of her head as they stared down at Zach. Cleo didn't know how long they sat there, but when the numbness finally gave way to exhaustion, Dante continued to hold her while she slipped into a restless slumber.

When she next woke up, it was to harsh sunlight streaming through the bare window. Memories flooded back, and she sat up and looked around the room frantically. There were cards and flowers on every available surface. How had people gotten word of this so quickly? Dante was asleep in an uncomfortable-looking chair, his chin on his chest and his long legs sprawled out in front of him.

"No," she muttered, panic lacing her voice when she couldn't find what she was looking for. "*No!*"

The sharp cry woke Dante, and he sat up quickly, his face etched with grief and concern as his eyes immediately flew to her.

"What's wrong?"

"Where is he?" she demanded, trying to pull the IV lines out of her arms so that she could get off the bed to search. He jumped up and put a hand over her frantically tugging fingers.

"Stop that, Cleo." His voice was rough with sleep, and she noted that his eyes were bloodshot, his jaw black with stubble, and his hair stood up in tufts. "You'll hurt yourself."

"Where did they take my baby?" she screamed. "Where is he?"

"Cleo, they had to take him down to the . . ." His words ground to a halt, as if he were physically incapable of saying the next one.

"Take him where?"

"You know where," he whispered. "Downstairs. To the . . . to the morgue."

"No! He belongs here, with me," she said, her voice anguished. "How could you let them take him away from me? How *could* you?"

"Cleo, be reasonable," he begged. "He couldn't stay here. They had to take him. To p-preserve—" Again he stumbled, and this time seemed completely unable of finishing what he'd been trying to say. She heard a high, thin wail, and for a second didn't register that it had come from her. Dante—alarmed by the sound—reached for her, trying to gather her into his arms, but she resisted his embrace, pushing him away, and his eyes flared with pain as he stepped back.

Cleo turned away from him until she was facing the opposite wall, and curled into a tight ball. It hurt to have him here. She wanted him gone.

"Luc and Blue were here," he said, determinedly disregarding the fact that she was ignoring him. "And Cal called. The pink roses are from him."

He kept talking and talking even though she stubbornly refused to acknowledge his presence. He told her that Blue and Luc had promised to return later and that they both sent their love. Susan Killian had sent flowers, as had James, Mrs. Whitman, and Coco and Gigi. But she didn't care. She didn't care about any of those people. How could they possibly understand how this felt? Zach had trusted her to take care of him, depended on her, and she had failed. Utterly failed him. Her hand went down to her abdomen, wishing she could feel him move again. Willing any kind of movement that would tell her that this was nothing more than a horrible nightmare, but it never came.

Her baby was gone. He was dead. And all the smiles, the first step, the first word, his first day of school, the long and beautiful life he should have led were gone with him. The unbearable agony that came with that gaping sense of loss was immeasurable, and the tears that finally came flooding out in no way at all helped her feel better.

She felt Dante climb onto the bed behind her and curve his body around hers. It was a tight fit, but he made it work. His arm crept over her waist, and his hand came to rest over hers on her abdomen. He held her as she cried, and while initially she tried to resist the comfort he offered, in the end she was grateful for his solid warmth and silent support.

"I wanted to hold him again," she said into the silence, her voice thick after her onslaught of tears. "The morgue is cold. It's not the place for him. He's so tiny."

"I know," he said, tightening his arm around her waist. "I didn't want them to take him either."

"This is your fault," she accused. The words seemed to come from out of nowhere, but she found herself needing to blame someone, needing to hate someone, and hating Dante right now was so much easier than loving him. She couldn't love anybody right now; love led to loss and pain.

"We can go down and see him when you're feeling a little calmer," he said, misunderstanding her. He withdrew his arm from around her waist, and she felt him get off the bed, leaving her cold and alone. But that was what she wanted. She couldn't depend on him; she refused to depend on him. Not when he would inevitably move on with his life and leave her behind. She turned around to face him.

"That's not what I meant," she corrected, amazed by how calm her voice sounded. "You did this."

"What?" He seemed to lose every ounce of blood he had; his usually swarthy skin went completely white. "What do you mean?"

"This is your fault." Her voice rose and became shrill as the nascent thought gained momentum. "The Great Dante Damaso always knows best, doesn't he? He always gets his own way! If I hadn't gotten into that car with you on Saturday night, if I'd driven myself back, this would *never* have happened. But you would never have let me, would you? Because you always know best!"

He stepped back, stumbling over the visitor's chair as he shook his head. His eyes were bright and feverish, and his face looked carved from granite.

"You can't mean that. You don't know what you're saying," he said. His voice was urgent and rough with emotion. "This wasn't my fault, Cleo; how can you say that it was?"

"From the moment I met you, every single thing in my life went *wrong*," she sobbed, and he shook his head again.

"Do not blame me for your life, Cleo. It was a fucked-up mess before I ever met you," he snapped, and then took a deep breath as he tried to get his spiraling emotions under control. He held up his hands in surrender. "You're in pain, I get that. You're hurting, but don't do this . . . not now. Let's be the parents Zach deserves; let's give him a dignified and loving farewell."

"We don't have to be together to do that." She kept her face and voice remote and cold. "I want you to leave. Go home. Please."

"I don't want you to be alone," he protested, his face clenching in frustration.

"I'll be fine. Your being here makes this worse; don't you get that?" Her voice was bordering on shrill again, and he backed away.

"I'll pick you up tomorrow." He probably sensed that she was on the verge of losing it completely and that his presence really just exacerbated her distress. He approached her again, with the extreme wariness of a man reaching out to pet a snake, and before she knew his intention, he dropped a kiss on her cheek.

"I'm doing this under protest, Cleo," he whispered. "I'd stay here all day and through the night if you'd let me. Try to get some rest, okay? I'll see you tomorrow."

She didn't reply, just watched as he picked up his jacket and left without a backward glance. After she was sure he was gone and wouldn't be back, she curled up on her side, stared out at the blue sky visible from her window, and allowed the tears to come again.

Blue and Luc showed up a couple of hours later, and Cleo burst into fresh tears when she saw her brother hover uncertainly in the doorway. His face just crumpled as he made his way to her bedside and gathered her into his arms.

"I'm sorry, Pattypan! I was such an asshole," he whispered into her hair.

"My baby died," she told him, and his arms tightened around her at the words. "He was so beautiful, Luc. I named him Zachary Damaso Knight."

"I'm so sorry," he said again, still holding her close, and she felt comforted by his embrace. But the solace she found in his hug made her guiltily think of Dante and acknowledge to herself that he didn't have anyone to offer him this comfort. She shoved that thought aside, telling herself that he would be okay, he hadn't felt the same depth of love for Zach, he'd been going through the motions, trying to do the right thing.

He would bounce back.

"Please, take me home," she begged her brother.

"Of course," he assured her. "As soon as they give you the all clear, we'll get your stuff from Dante's and . . ."

"No, take me home now! Today." She felt a pang of loss at having to leave Zach behind, and she very nearly changed her mind. Earlier, after Dante left, she had demanded they bring Zach up to her again and had sat in a rocking chair for an hour just singing to him until her voice hoarsened. Afterward, when she resisted their attempts to take him from her, they gave her a mild sedative and very gently but firmly removed him from her grasp. A grief counselor had been dispatched to her room and told Cleo that the anger she felt was normal, but nothing the woman said had helped. Nothing anybody said or did could help or make her feel better. Nothing could make this gaping chasm in her soul go away.

Dante restlessly paced from empty room to empty room, avoiding the bloodied bathroom in Cleo's room. He knew he would have to clean it up before she came home again. He didn't want her to see it. He doubted she even knew how much blood she'd lost, and the memory of the fear and panic he'd felt at the time surged back.

He had gone over it and over it in his head. Maybe if he'd done something differently he could have saved the baby. Maybe if he'd heard her cry out sooner. Or perhaps if he'd helped her apply pressure to stop the bleeding. Maybe if he hadn't *insisted* they go shopping that afternoon. He swallowed back bile as he remembered how he had pressed her. He should have used his common sense, but he had selfishly wanted to spend that time with her and hoped an inoffensive pastime like shopping would make her see him in a positive light. Would make her consider marrying him.

His mind kept coming back to her words in the hospital. Even though she voluntarily gave up her keys, she had only done so to avoid a prolonged argument with him. An argument he'd had no intention of losing, and she knew that. She was right, this *was* his fault, and he didn't blame her for hating him right now and for not wanting to be around him. He hated himself and could barely stand his own company right now.

He found a bucket, scrub brush, and some detergent, and after mentally bracing himself, he stepped into the bathroom.

Oh God. It was worse than he remembered; the blood was smeared on the white tiled floor, the side of the bath, in the basin, on the commode, even on the wall. He swallowed back his nausea and went about the solemn task of cleaning up the last vestiges of Cleo's pregnancy. Once he completed the grim job to his satisfaction, he finally allowed himself to succumb to his nausea and lost his meager lunch down the toilet. He stripped down where he stood, climbed into her shower, and scrubbed himself clean with delicately fragranced soap that reminded him of her. He stood beneath the buffeting, punishingly hot spray, with his hands braced on the tiled wall, his head tilted up toward the water, and finally allowed himself to grieve.

"Where is she?" Dante stood chest to chest with his former friend and glared threateningly at the man. He'd gone to the hospital only to be informed that Miss Knight had left against medical advice the previous afternoon. She *left* without even having the courtesy of telling him. Dante headed straight to Luc's place from the hospital.

"Dante," Luc greeted wearily. He was surprisingly noncombative as he stepped aside to allow Dante entry into the creaky old house.

"Cleo!" Dante called the minute he stepped over the threshold.

"She's not here," Luc said.

"Don't fucking lie to me, Luc," Dante snapped. "Where the hell else would she be?"

"Well, she's not *currently* here. Her OB/GYN insisted she come in for a follow-up appointment because Cleo discharged herself early against medical advice yesterday. Blue's gone with her."

"I should be there." Dante turned to head back out, but Luc's hand on his arm stopped him.

"She won't want you there, *amigo*," Luc said, looking almost sympathetic.

"She blames me for this," Dante confessed, running a hand through his hair. "We were in an accident on Saturday night, and if I hadn't been such an overbearing asshole, she would have been in her own car, safely behind us. So, she's probably right. I did this. I killed our baby."

"Shit." Luc massaged the back of his neck as he watched his usually stoic and unemotional friend unravel right in front of his eyes. "You didn't kill your baby, Dante."

"The hell of it was," Dante whispered, ignoring Luc's words, "I wanted him so badly. I don't even know when it changed. I watched her growing bigger with our baby; I listened to her chatter on about ultrasounds and week-by-week growth charts. I even felt him move, Luc, and he became so *real* to me."

Luc steered him into a large room that, like the rest of the house, was grand but shabby. It housed a couch and a couple of mismatched love seats and armchairs. Luc pushed him onto the couch and poured him a glass of something amber. He pressed the tumbler firmly into Dante's hand.

"Drink this," Luc insisted. Dante took a sip and winced when the Scotch hit the back of his throat.

"So why are you here, Dante?" Luc asked, taking a sip from his own glass. "Your responsibility to Cleo ended with her pregnancy."

"You think I can switch these emotions on and off like a machine?" Dante asked resentfully, hating that his old friend would think so little of him.

"What emotions? What you felt for the baby is unrelated to your relationship with Cleo, so you can let her move on with her life now, while you move on with yours."

Dante stared at him mutely, not sure how to respond, not sure how he felt but knowing one thing with absolute certainty.

"There is no moving on for me without Cleo." Luc's eyes narrowed at his words, and he lifted his glass in a slight salute to Dante.

"Well, you'll have your work cut out convincing *her* of that, my friend."

"Am I?" Dante asked uncertainly, a little embarrassed by the hope and vulnerability he heard in his own voice.

"Are you what?"

"Your friend."

"Yeah, man. Always."

And that was really all he needed to say.

"Cleo?" Blue's voice intruded into Cleo's darkened room. "Why don't you join Luc and me downstairs? We've ordered a pizza—with all your favorite toppings—and would love it if you'd have a slice or two with us."

"I'm not hungry," Cleo responded listlessly. She wasn't interested in eating or talking or being around people. She just wanted to lie here and stare at her favorite patch of wall.

"You have to eat something, Cleo," Blue said, her gentle voice grating on Cleo's frayed and wearied nerves.

"Please leave me alone," she begged, the ever-present tears seeping from behind her closed lids and wetting the pillow beneath her cheek.

"I'll bring you a slice," Blue said quietly, and retreated from the room.

It was a week since she'd lost the baby, and each day was harder than the one before it. The hospital had called to inform her that they had cremated Zach's remains and would keep his ashes until she was ready to collect them. But Cleo, whose body was still recovering from the pregnancy and the induced labor, couldn't deal with the thought of collecting the ashes of a baby she was still *lactating* for. Her breasts producing milk for her dead baby had been such a kick to the stomach that she was still reeling from the blow. She couldn't face the world yet; she didn't know how she would ever recover from this, didn't know how it was possible for *any* woman to recover from this.

To make matters worse, she missed Dante badly and thought about him constantly. She was still convinced that she'd made the right decision in leaving and knew that he'd probably come to that realization as well since he hadn't tried to contact her at all after that last day in the hospital. She pictured him in his office, wheeling and dealing. For all she knew, he was in Tokyo or possibly Dubai.

She told herself she didn't care what he was doing. What did it matter? He was out of her life; he would never be a part of her life again. He must be so relieved that they hadn't married, after all.

The thought brought fresh tears to her eyes, and she curled up into a tight ball, wanting to be as small as possible in an effort to shield herself from the relentless barrage of pain. This would pass. It had to pass.

⁓

Dante's initial reaction to his front door opening up unexpectedly was to hope for one wild moment that it was Cleo coming home. But when

Luc stepped over the threshold instead of Cleo, Dante could do nothing but stare at the man stupidly

"How did you get in here?" he asked after a long moment of silence.

"Your guy, James, let me in. Turns out he's a little concerned about you." Luc ran a critical eye over Dante. "And I can see why. When did you last shower?"

"Is Cleo okay?" he asked, ignoring his friend's question. Luc had advised him last week to give her some space, and Dante had reluctantly complied. After the accident and its terrible consequences, he had started to doubt his every decision, especially where Cleo was concerned. But not a day went by that he didn't want to tear over there and drag her back home with him. He slept in her damned bed every night, for God's sake.

"Cleo's about the same as you," Luc said, and Dante forced away his annoyance at the cryptic response. "From the looks of you, you haven't been eating or showering, and according to James, you haven't left the building since last week. Not even to go to work."

"I am entitled to compassionate leave, just like every one of my employees," Dante said defensively, and then immediately regretted rising to Luc's obvious baiting.

"Look, I know I told you to give Cleo space, but I take that back. She's . . . she's in a bad place."

"She just lost her baby," Dante pointed out.

"And so did you," Luc said with a nod. "And that's why I was wrong in telling you to give her space. Neither of you should be going through this alone."

"She won't want me around," Dante said quietly.

"Do you *want* to be around?" Dante gave him a look that told Luc exactly how dumb he thought that question was. "Then you should be around."

Exactly two weeks to the day after losing Zach, Cleo was wandering around the house like a wraith. Blue and Dante had both gone to work, and Cleo knew she should attempt to do something more positive than stay at home. It was a glorious summer day in mid-December, and nobody had even mentioned Christmas because her brother and Blue were both walking on eggshells around her. They had gently tried to talk her into thinking about some kind of farewell ceremony for Zach, but Cleo still couldn't bring herself to even contemplate it.

Her body was slowly returning to normal; her milk had dried up, and she'd spent a day crying over that too. She didn't recognize herself anymore. Who was this woman who could spend entire days crying, and other days just staring at a wall doing nothing? She felt like she had lost herself along with the baby and couldn't find her way back.

So today was the day she would turn it all around. She would get dressed, leave the house, and buy Christmas presents for Blue and Luc. She would go to the hospital and pick up Zach's ashes . . .

Only she couldn't.

When midday rolled around, she was still in her pajamas and still just drifting from one end of the house to the other. It was almost a godsend when the doorbell rang. She yanked open the door without considering how very unfit she was to be seen by anyone.

She became very much aware of that fact moments later when she stood staring up at Dante.

"Oh," she whispered as his eyes ran over her body wordlessly. His face was grim, and his lips thinned. "What are you doing here?"

He said nothing, just pushed his way past her and into the house. That made her angry, and it felt *wonderful*. It was the first emotion other than sadness that she'd felt in too long.

"You can't just barge in here like this, Dante." She slammed the door and turned to confront him. "I . . ." Her voice faltered when she saw his face. He looked seriously pissed off with her. His eyes had gone dark and intense, and it made her back up until she felt the door behind her.

"Okay, I know you're upset with me for just leaving the way I did," she said, trying to keep her voice level. "But you have to understand that I *couldn't*, I just couldn't, go back to your place."

The fixed, feverish look in his eyes was starting to freak her out, and it made her talk a little faster.

"I wanted to be around people who love me and understand me." A muscle was starting to tick in his jaw, and she swallowed nervously. Why was he just *staring* at her like that? She wished he would just say something. She opened her mouth to say something else, but all that emerged was a squeak when he took a purposeful step toward her, then another, and then the third bridged the gap between them completely. He was way too close to her now, and she was trapped between his chest and the door.

She tilted her jaw up and met his gaze head-on. Why did he have to look so formidable? Cleo was aware of her heart beating like a maddened, trapped animal against her rib cage and—even though she knew he would never physically hurt her—she jumped when he brought his hands up.

He palmed her narrow shoulders and with an anguished groan, dragged her into his arms.

"Dante—"

He interrupted whatever she had been about to say by speaking for the first time since entering the house.

"Just shut up for a moment while I hold you, okay?" he growled into her hair, and Cleo sighed and leaned into his embrace, relishing the feel of his protective arms around her.

"I can do that," she whispered as she wrapped her arms around his waist and hugged him close.

"This happened to me too, Cleo," he said after a long, long silence, and Cleo trembled at his words. "I lost him too and it hurts like hell.

I need you. I can't . . . I can't do this without you. And I know that maybe I'm the last person you want to be around right now because of the accident, but—"

Guilt reared its ugly head; she should never have said those words to him. He'd been dealing with the same loss, and she had made his grief so much worse by blaming him for their baby's death.

"It wasn't your fault, Dante," she said, leaning back to look up at him. There was moisture gleaming in his eyes. "It really wasn't. They did an autopsy and he had a chromosomal problem, or imbalance. The accident hastened the inevitable, but our baby would never have made it. I shouldn't have put that on you. Dr. Klein called me with the results yesterday, and I know I should have called you immediately, but I was just so *sad* and I felt so horrible for blaming you. Even when I said those things, I knew they were awful and unfair and I wanted to call you, but I—" She stopped and sobbed. "I didn't know what to say. You must have felt so terrible. I'm so sorry."

"I did," he whispered. "I do. Not because of anything you said or did, but because I wanted him. I so badly wanted to be his dad."

She was crying again, and that was okay because Dante was crying too, and Cleo no longer felt alone.

CHAPTER FOURTEEN

Dante was still there when Blue and Luc came home from work that evening. Blue invited him to stay for supper, and after a quick glance at Cleo, who nodded, he happily accepted. He clung to Cleo's hand for most of the evening, and after small talk and drinks on the veranda while they listened to the waves crashing nearby, Blue and Luc excused themselves and went to bed.

Cleo sat on her grandmother's old rocking chair. She still wore the loose pajamas she had on when he arrived. Dante was on a deck chair next to her, and he took her hand for the umpteenth time that day. They didn't speak, their silence speaking for them, and after another half an hour in the cool, briny air, Dante sighed.

"I should probably get going," he said quietly. "Thank you."

"For?" she asked, genuinely confused.

"Including me." *Oh.* The underlying vulnerability in those words hit her hard. He'd been made to feel excluded and alone at a time when he should have had a solid support base, and it was entirely her fault. Well, that would end right now.

"Stay," she invited.

"What?"

"Stay the night. As a friend." She wanted to make it perfectly clear that she was expecting nothing more than that from him. He wasn't obligated to stay with her after all this was over. She didn't want him to. But for now they each needed the other.

"Are you sure?" he asked, hopeful and hesitant. She thought about it for a moment before nodding.

"I'm sure." She took his hand and led him upstairs to her room, which was even messier than usual for her, and for the first time since she'd lost the baby, that bothered her. "I'm sorry it's a bit crazy in here."

"You should see the penthouse," he said wryly, and her head swiveled to meet his gaze. She couldn't imagine the penthouse being anything other than immaculate.

"Seriously?"

"I've been at home a lot since it happened, and I didn't want to be disturbed, so I asked Esta not to come in." Esta was his cleaning lady.

"Yeah but you're inherently neat," she reminded him, and a corner of his mouth tilted up.

"I haven't been myself these past two weeks," he said with a shoulder lift.

"And work? You haven't been to the office much?"

"I have competent people to run things in my absence. I took compassionate leave." He unbuttoned his shirt and kicked off his shoes while he spoke, and Cleo turned her back to give him some privacy, while nervously rearranging the myriad decorative perfume atomizers on her dresser.

"You did?" She wouldn't let the fact that he was stripping down affect her; she'd invited him to stay, and he couldn't very well sleep in his shirt and trousers. It was ridiculous to be nervous around him; she'd seen him in less. It wasn't like she didn't know what his body looked like. And being sexually aware of him was completely inappropriate and disrespectful considering the circumstances. "You can turn around again," he said, his wry tone making her wonder if he knew exactly what crazy thoughts had been running through her head. She turned around reluctantly and kept her eyes fixed on his face.

"I can sleep in one of the guest rooms," he suggested gently. "There have to be more than a few in this gigantic house?"

"None of them are currently habitable," she said, wrinkling her nose. "Water damage in a couple from the leaky roof, mold in the other, and the last one is being used as a storage room for generations' worth of crap. We're talking everything from spindles to World War II rifles to old-time girlie magazines."

"Why not store those in the attic?" he asked, but she didn't respond, waiting for him to figure it out instead.

"Ah," he said, snapping his fingers. "Holes in the ceiling?"

"The roof leaks like a sieve, and naturally it's worse up in the attic, so Blue and Luc moved everything into the biggest guest room. Honestly, it's only a matter of time until it starts leaking in there as well." Talking about what a train wreck the house was calmed her nerves a bit, and she felt herself relaxing by degrees.

"So I suppose you're stuck with me tonight, then. Unless you want me to go home, after all?" he asked, generously giving her the opportunity to back out.

"It's fine," she whispered. "Let's just go to bed."

"Great, because I'm exhausted, and I didn't relish the thought of the drive home." He crawled under the covers without further discussion and stretched out on his side. He eyed her with a slight smile playing about his lips and lifted the sheet invitingly.

Cleo returned the smile and slowly climbed in next to him. He sighed, the sound almost content, and brought the sheet and his arm down over her, cuddling her close. She turned onto her side so that she was spooned against him, and Dante pulled her tightly against his hard, beautiful body and tucked his arm around her waist. It was reminiscent of the way he'd held her in the hospital the day they'd lost Zach, and it was equally as tender as that particular gesture had been.

Cleo reached over and switched off the bedside lamp, and the room was plunged into darkness. The top of her head was tucked beneath his jaw, and their breathing was almost in tandem. At first they said nothing, both of them enjoying the warmth and company. The only sounds in the room were their soft breathing and the gentle rattle of the breeze against the loose pane of her window.

"I've never done this snuggling thing before," he declared. His chest rumbled against her back, and his stubble tugged at her hair.

"That's a shame," she whispered, hugging his arm to her chest. "You're a fantastic snuggler."

"I haven't been a very good guy. Terrible with women," he whispered. The darkness of the room and the fact that she was facing away from him seemed to be enough to inspire this unexpected bout of honesty. "I didn't want more than sex from them, maybe a short-lived affair here and there."

"I know," she said, her voice dry. "I was there."

"Of course I mean to settle down someday," he said, ignoring her sarcasm. He sounded driven to speak, and she was more than happy to let him air his thoughts. This whole turn of conversation took her mind off her immediate grief.

"I'm sure you had a type picked out, right?" she prompted, when it looked like he was done speaking.

"I always thought I'd marry a beautiful, elegant creature who would be the perfect wife and mother. We would have a quiet, calm marriage with mutual respect for each other. So much respect that the ugly concept of divorce would never once enter our minds. We would never argue, and we would have two children. A boy and a girl."

"Would they be as boring as their mother, or as cowardly as their father?" Cleo asked scathingly, and she felt his arm tense around her waist before it relaxed again.

"Probably a mixture of both," he said, a hint of amusement in his voice.

"Boring cowards," she said sympathetically. "Luckily you're loaded, else they'd have absolutely no friends."

"So why are you casting disparagement on my future wife and me?" he asked.

"You want someone without personality," she said. "A beautiful, empty vessel, into whom you would pour all your unrealistic expectations for the perfect marriage. The perfect Stepford wife."

"Que?"

"It's a movie. Considering how much you hate horror films, it doesn't surprise me that you've never seen it. It's about a bunch of guys who turn their wives into these perfect housewives. They all think the same and act the same. But never mind that. The point is, she'd never challenge you, and you'd be bored with her in months."

"And I'm a coward, why?"

"Because you don't *want* to be challenged. You're terrified that a woman with any personality will mess up your perfect, orderly life and that you wouldn't be able to deal, and then the fighting would start and the irritation with each other and then the inevitable divorce. Just like your dad, right?"

"I refuse to wind up like him."

"Yeah, well, your dad's an idiot." Cleo wasn't in the mood to pull any punches tonight.

"I couldn't agree more," he said, his voice wobbling a little. "But I know why *I* think he's an idiot, so I'm interested in hearing your view."

"Because he's clearly an appalling judge of character, and he *never* seems to learn from his past mistakes. Sound about right?"

"Sí."

She patted his arm smartly.

"Good talk," she said, and this time he actually chuckled.

"I like you a lot, Cleo," he said, the words sounding impulsive. "You make me laugh more than anyone else ever has."

"Oh, how . . ." She paused to think of the word. *Unexpected.* "Nice of you to say that."

"I wonder if Zach would have had your sense of humor."

"I don't want to talk about him," she said, clamming up at the sound of his name.

He squeezed her briefly in apology and dropped it. The conversation died after that, and Cleo listened to his breathing even out and become deeper. His arm grew heavy around her waist, and after a while, the comforting weight of that arm and the soft little snore that came with every third breath he took lulled her into a deep sleep.

When Cleo woke the next morning, it was to the same bleak reality that she'd woken up to over the last fortnight, but this time the knowledge didn't physically weigh her down as much as it had just yesterday. She turned over and stared into Dante's relaxed face. He was still fast asleep, and as she really looked at him for the first time in two weeks, she saw that he appeared exhausted and definitely thinner. He had lost weight and had gained a few lines on his face. It was clear that this loss had taken a physical toll on him as well. At least his bruises from the accident had disappeared; there was only the very faintest tinge of yellow left around his eye.

She watched as his breathing became shallow and his eyes started to flutter beneath their lids, and when they opened, she kept her gaze level. She watched confusion flicker in his eyes for a second, followed by what could only be described as radiant joy, which flared and disappeared so quickly that she wasn't sure if she'd imagined it or not.

"Morning," she murmured, and then wrinkled her nose and covered her mouth. He grinned in delight at the gesture.

"Come on, morning breath isn't cute," she protested. He leaned over and dropped a kiss on the back of the hand covering her mouth.

"*Buenos días, dulzura,*" he said, his voice rasping sexily. "How did you sleep?"

"Like a log," she said, still from behind the hand. He stretched with a groan and smiled at her contentedly. God, he looked so beautiful in the morning, with that stubble, the slightly crooked grin, and his hard, ripped chest uncovered. She tried—and failed—to avert her eyes.

"Me too. Best sleep I've had since it happened." His gorgeous smile dimmed somewhat at the reminder.

He got out of bed and stretched again, arms up over his head, with a massive yawn. Cleo blushed at the sight of all that toned, gorgeous flesh and at the obvious morning erection straining at the front of his white boxer briefs. The underwear left very little to the imagination. He noticed her fixed stare and glanced down at himself.

"It's nothing," he shrugged. "Morning wood. Although waking up next to you has definitely made it more impressive than usual."

It reminded her of Tokyo and how comfortable he had been with his own nudity.

"You're getting out of those pajamas today," he mandated. "And we're going out."

"Dante," she murmured miserably. She really didn't want to be among crowds of happy people when she felt like she was only half-alive.

"Trust me, *cielo*," he implored, and she bit the inside of her cheek painfully as she considered his words.

"Please, I don't think I can be around people right now."

"Nothing like that," he said. "Just us. Trust me."

To her surprise he took her to a yacht, the *Arabella*, which he proudly told Cleo was his. She recognized it from the photograph in his study.

"This is nice," she said as he helped her on board. She looked around, fascinated, and was reaching out to touch one of the intricate knots on the crossbar of the mast when Dante barked, "Stop!" She jerked back her hand in fright.

He took her hand and led her to a cushioned seat by the steering wheel.

"Sit here and don't touch anything, okay? If I need your help, I'll let you know." Bossy Dante was back. Great.

She pointedly folded her arms over her chest and stared back at him mutely. His lips quirked when he turned away from her and started untying rigging and doing the other mysterious and fascinating-looking things that boat people did. Because he hadn't brought a change of clothes with him last night, he was wearing a pair of Luc's faded old jeans, battered sneakers that her brother used for handiwork around the house, and a T-shirt that was a size too small for him. He looked scruffy and absolutely scrumptious, and it was hard for Cleo to focus on much else. While she had definitely learned to value many other aspects of Dante's character—his warmth, his sense of humor, his kindness and thoughtfulness—she still fully appreciated the packaging all that unexpected generosity of spirit was wrapped up in. The man was damned fine.

But she was soon distracted by his seeming skill around the boat. As with all things, he just looked supremely competent and confident. Cleo had never been on a boat before and had no idea how things worked. So in hindsight she should probably not have reached for that knot like a child who didn't know better. She might have broken his boat.

After he used the motor to steer them out of the harbor, he unfurled the sails and switched off the engine, leaving only the creaking sounds of the boat, the swish of water as they skimmed across the surface of the ocean, and the sound of the wind billowing in the white sails.

It was magnificent. Absolutely and unutterably peaceful.

"Got your sea legs yet?" he asked after about half an hour of not a single word exchanged between them. The silence had been enjoyable and comfortable. Cleo, who was still sitting where he'd left her, looked up, not sure what to make of the question.

"I wouldn't know. I've just been sitting here, very industriously not touching anything," she said pointedly, and he chuckled.

"Since you usually do your own thing, I had to speak a bit sharply to ensure you understood that I meant business this time," he said, and she gasped, clutching a hand to her chest.

"Oh my God, are you kind of, almost, sort of *apologizing* to me?" She squealed, and he very uncharacteristically rolled his eyes. A habit he may have picked up from her.

"Yes, I am," he acquiesced. "Kind of. Almost. Sort of. I'm still trying to work my way through that list of yours."

She laughed merrily and then immediately sobered.

"Cleo, it's okay to laugh," Dante said gruffly. "It's okay to be happy. There is no right or wrong way for you to deal with this."

"And how do you know this?" Since when had he become an expert grief counselor?

"When I went back to the hospital the next day and found you gone." His voice broke slightly on that last word, and his eyes darkened. "I immediately went to Luc's place to fetch you. Luc and I had a long conversation." That was news to her. Luc had never told her about it.

"He convinced me to give you space, and even though it went against my every instinct to walk out of that house without you, I thought it might be best. I told myself not to be selfish, that even though I needed you, I had to do what was right for *you*, not for me. So I left. But . . . I couldn't go back to the apartment alone. I couldn't face that." He cleared his throat before continuing. "The hospital offered grief counseling, and I thought maybe it would help. So I went to talk to someone. And when you're ready . . . I think *you* should go as well. We could go together."

"Yes," she said, her voice so soft she doubted he could hear her above the sound of the wind in the sails. Dante Damaso never failed to surprise her, and she wished he would stop because each new thing she learned about him made her love him more. How hard it was for a man like Dante to reveal his vulnerability, and yet he'd done it often over the course of the last few weeks. She wanted to suppress her feelings for him, but it got harder and harder with every moment spent in his company.

"Do you want to steer?" he invited, quite deliberately changing the subject, and she was happy to let him.

"I don't know. I wouldn't want to sink your precious boat."

"Wimp," he taunted, and she narrowed her eyes in mock outrage.

"Ooh, you're going to pay for that one." She got up and walked over to the wheel on wobbly legs. It certainly wasn't very easy to walk on these boats.

He grinned and stepped aside to let her take the wheel. The boat immediately listed to the side, and she squealed. He chuckled and stepped up behind her, caging her with his body when his hands dropped on top of hers on the wheel. As usual, he smelled absolutely divine, and as his scent wrapped around her, she could barely concentrate on his instructions.

"Got that?" he asked, after a whole lot of gobbledygook that she hadn't been paying attention to, and stepped back. It was a sheer fluke that Cleo managed to keep the boat upright. And this time when she squealed, it was with excitement, and when she laughed, it was without guilt.

They spent a delightful afternoon on the boat, and Dante took her to dinner at a Mexican restaurant afterward. Cleo enjoyed herself, and the evening was relaxing and stress free. Their conversation centered around the hotel in Tokyo, the cute cards and paper flowers Cleo's dance-class students had made for her, and Luc and Blue's ramshackle old house. He was sweet and conscientious, and the one little sour point in the evening was when he asked her if she wanted a glass of wine and she refused, forgetting that she was no longer pregnant. Then the memory had hit her like a ton of bricks, the pain fresh and intense. It was seeing the same flash of pain in Dante's eyes that helped her get over it, knowing that she wasn't the only one feeling the loss. Being with somebody who understood what she was going through helped immeasurably.

On the drive home, he broached the subject of Zach again.

"What would you like to do with Zach's ashes?" he asked quietly, and Cleo, who had been on the verge of dozing off after her two glasses of wine, was immediately wide-awake.

"I haven't thought about it," she said.

"Cleo, we have to lay his soul to rest. We can't leave him in limbo like this."

"I'm not ready to think about it," she said stubbornly.

"Why did you name him Zach?" Dante asked.

"I read on a few of the baby-name websites that the name meant *remembrance* or something similar. And I just want him to be remembered." She swiped at a stray tear that slipped down her cheek.

"And what made you decide to add Damaso to his name?" His voice was quiet and filled with an emotion she couldn't quite place.

"It would have been wrong not to," she said simply, and he kept his eyes glued on the road.

"Thank you. It means a lot to me."

When he pulled into Luc's driveway, he turned to face her, his eyes gleaming in the darkness.

"Cleo, I know it's tough, and I want to do what's right for you . . . but I also want to do right by our son. I can't stand the thought of his ashes remaining there unclaimed. That is not how it should be; he was loved. I thought I could keep them until you're ready to make a decision, but they won't release the ashes to me. I've tried."

"Maybe—" she started to say, and then hesitated, before swallowing loudly and plunging ahead. "Maybe we should take him out on the *Arabella* and scatter his ashes at sea? It was so peaceful out there, so beautiful, and the view was lovely. I think it would be n-nice."

He reached out with one hand, hooking the back of her neck and tugging her toward him to plant a gentle kiss on her lips.

"I think that's an amazing idea," he whispered, his own voice wobbling with emotion.

"Will you come with me to . . . to pick up his ashes tomorrow?"

"Of course."

"Are you going to stay again?" she asked, hating the edge of neediness in her voice. He ran his thumb over her cheekbone, his eyes gleaming in the dark interior of the car.

"Much as I'd love to, I don't think I can spend another day in your brother's too-tight clothes or wear his nasty shoes again. I need a change of clothes, *dulzura*. Would you like to come home with me instead?" he asked gently. "Most of your clothes are there, and I'm sure you'd prefer sleeping in your own bed, *sí*?"

"I can't, Dante," she whispered, and his hand moved to cup her cheek.

"That's okay. I can go and fetch a bag and return here later."

She was tempted to say yes to that suggestion but didn't think it would be fair to ask him to make the half-hour drive to his penthouse at the Waterfront and back to Hout Bay again.

"I can't ask you to do an hour of unnecessary driving," she said regretfully. "It's okay; you go home. I'll see you tomorrow."

⟨♱⟩

Picking up the ashes the following morning wasn't as much of an ordeal as Cleo expected. With Dante by her side, it was surprisingly easy. He took charge and was even thoughtful enough to bring a beautiful, ornate little urn along with him. They waited in an uncomfortable, sterile office while the worker took the urn away to transfer Zach's ashes into it. When he returned moments later, he handed it over with a sympathetic nod.

"I'm so sorry for your loss," he said somberly. Cleo couldn't contain the sob that escaped when she saw the urn and acknowledged what the contents were. Dante wrapped an arm around her and held her close, while the morgue worker discreetly left them alone.

"It's so stupid to be this . . . *sad* about the loss of someone who never really lived," she said, her voice muffled by his chest.

"He lived," Dante said firmly. "He lived inside you, and in a different way, he lived inside me. He lived in our hearts and in our heads; we saw him, we felt him. Don't ever say he never really lived, Cleo. He may not have had a life, but he lived."

"You know, for a guy who only ever said or did the wrong thing in the past, you're doing pretty great with the pep talks lately," she said, trying to sound a little more lighthearted even while she plucked a white handkerchief out of his breast pocket and blew her nose inelegantly. "How do you always manage to say the right thing?"

"In this instance, I'm not saying anything you don't already know." He stroked her hair back and kissed her sweetly.

She was getting used to his kisses, and it scared her because one day he wouldn't be around to give her any more. She dreaded the inevitability of that day.

They left the hospital hand in hand, Dante carrying Zach's ashes. When they reached the car, Cleo turned to him impulsively.

"Could we . . . do you think we could do it today?"

"Are you sure about that?" he asked. "Don't you want your brother and Blue to be there too?"

"They've been amazing, but they don't understand, Dante. Not really."

"Don't you think you'll come to regret excluding them?"

She thought about that and then sighed.

"I don't know," she confessed miserably. "Maybe I would." He squeezed her hand and lifted it to his mouth to plant a kiss on her knuckles.

"Let's do it properly, okay? Would you like me to take care of the arrangements?" She hesitated at his question, feeling horrible about letting him bear the brunt of the responsibility, but he stared down at her with those infinitely patient eyes, and she found herself nodding.

"Do you want it to be a religious ceremony?"

"No, something intimate but informal."

"Okay. I'll take care of it."

༄

Dante asked Cleo, Luc, and Blue to meet him at the Waterfront by seven thirty the following evening. He was waiting beside his berthed yacht, dressed all in white. Cleo was wearing a simple white summer shift dress, and Blue and Luc had also respected Dante's request that they wear white.

He helped them aboard and cast off after making sure everybody was comfortably seated. Naturally, Luc didn't remain down for long; he wandered over to pepper Dante with questions about the boat, and the two chatted amicably while Blue and Cleo sat down.

"You okay?" Blue asked, taking her hand.

"It helps to have you and Luc here," she said honestly, grateful to Dante for persuading her to include them. Her eyes drifted over to the big, handsome man who was talking to her brother. He was wearing a pair of expensive dark sunglasses, effectively shielding his emotions from all of them. But she knew exactly how he was feeling today.

"It helps to have him here too," Cleo admitted, nodding toward where the two men stood. Dante was casually winding some thick rope around his elbow and thumb.

"I've known Dante for a few years now; he's visited the house on occasion for dinner or to hang out with Luc," Blue said unexpectedly.

"Yes?" Cleo prompted, curious to hear where this was going.

"Yes, and he was . . ." Blue shook her head. "Very different from this guy."

Cleo snorted, knowing exactly what Blue meant.

"Let me guess." Cleo held up a hand to stop Blue from saying more. "He was bossy, arrogant, a little too self-assured, and a little too unconcerned with the world around him?"

"Sounds about right," Blue said with a smile. "I could never fault his friendship with Luc, though. Classic bromance if ever there was one. You don't expect them to have much in common, and yet they can talk for *hours*. I think that's one of the reasons Luc reacted so strongly to the news that Dante was your baby's father. It felt like a betrayal. His best friend had disrespected his sister, and his sister had robbed him of his best friend."

"Well, he doesn't have to worry about that anymore. After today, Dante and I will probably not be seeing much of each other again." She couldn't think of a single reason they should have any connection after this. Zach's remains were all that tied them together. Life would *have* to go back to normal, even if Cleo would never be the same.

"Why not?" Blue asked. "You guys are good for each other."

"We're helping each other get through this, Blue. After this, we have nothing tethering us to each other. We can move forward and carry on with our lives."

"Have you spoken to him about this?"

"He'll agree with me. He has to. It makes no sense to drag this out when there's nothing more between us."

The boat finally started moving, and Luc sat down on Cleo's other side and dropped an arm around her shoulder in casual affection, giving her a comforting squeeze.

"It'll be okay, Pattypan," he said beneath his breath, and she gave him a small smile.

"I know," she whispered, and dropped her head on his shoulder. She watched the Waterfront slide by and get left behind, watched the beautiful flat-topped Table Mountain recede and become flatter and flatter the farther out they went. The view was breathtaking. Once they were far enough away from other boats to be alone, Dante switched off the engines. He didn't unfurl the sails but pulled a lever that he'd told her the other day was the anchor release.

He stared off into the distance, the orange orb of the setting sun reflected in his sunglasses. He took a deep breath, and the lowered angle of his head told Cleo that he'd shifted his focus to her. He stepped away from the wheel and held out his hand to her, and she took it without hesitation, getting up to join him.

"Look at that," he said, pointing out at the horizon and the huge, shimmering globe of the sun as it sank silently into the ocean. He wrapped his arms around her waist from behind, resting his chin on her shoulder and tugging her back until she could feel his hard warmth against her. His next words were spoken directly into her ear. "I want you to always remember the beauty of this sunset when you think of Zach, *dulzura*. Can you do that for me?"

Tears flooded into her eyes, and she gulped back a sob as she nodded mutely.

"Good." He seemed to silently communicate something to Luc, who got up and went into the cabin. He emerged moments later with the urn in his hands. He came up to stand on their left, while Blue moved to their right.

"Cleo, you have to be prepared . . . there's not much in there. He was so tiny." This time her sob couldn't be swallowed back, and he gave her a squeeze when he heard the sound.

"Are you ready?" he asked as the sun disappeared completely, leaving only a bright-orange-and-scarlet sky in its wake, making the ocean look like it was on fire.

"Yes."

He released his hold on her and took the urn from Luc.

"We do this together? Okay?"

"Okay," she whispered.

"Would you like to say something?"

"Yes." Her response was so faint she wasn't sure if he heard her, so she straightened her shoulders and found her voice. *"Yes."*

She put her hands below his on the urn, and he adjusted his grip until his hands were on top of hers.

"When you're ready," he told her.

"You will . . . ," she began, but the words felt too big and obstructive to squeeze past her swollen vocal cords. She cleared her throat and tried again. "You will always be in my heart, Zach. I will love and cherish you till the end of time." The last word was so badly mangled that it actually made her wince. Dante kissed her cheek sweetly and then returned his attention to the vessel in their hands.

"Te amo, hijito. Te amo," he muttered, before lifting one of his hands from hers to take the lid off the urn and hand it to Luc. Once he had his hands over hers again, he looked at her, and this close to him she could see the faint quiver of his lips and, most tellingly, the line of moisture trickling down his cheek from behind his glasses.

"Okay?" she asked him, recognizing that nobody had asked *him* that question since they'd boarded the boat. His lips quirked slightly in acknowledgment of her consideration, and he inclined his head.

They both took a huge gulp of air, and together they upended the urn and watched as the meager contents poured into the water below. A minute portion was taken by the wind and scattered toward the distant city.

Blue and Luc scattered white rose petals into the water to mix with the ashes, and they all watched as the petals drifted away from the boat. The ash, being heavier, sank almost immediately. Cleo felt . . . hollow but at peace, grateful for the support of these three people who meant so much to her, and happy to have the opportunity to offer the same support to this man she loved with her entire being.

They all silently watched the petals drift farther and farther away, and after half an hour, when it was almost completely dark, Dante started preparing to take them back to shore. As the boat started back up, the powerful purr of the engine shattered the silence around them, and Cleo felt a moment's panic at leaving. But as the boat stirred up water in its wake, something absolutely astonishing happened, and she cried out at the beauty of it. Dante left Luc at the helm and came leaping over at her startled cry, but he paused when they saw what had caught Cleo's attention.

"It's so beautiful," Cleo whispered in awe. The stirred-up water in the wake of the boat was a sparkling electric blue, creating an otherworldly glowing path back to where they'd left Zach. It was perfect, and even though Cleo knew it was ocean phosphorescence, it couldn't have happened at a better time or had a more magical impact.

She felt a strong and familiar arm creep around her shoulder, and she leaned into Dante as they both watched the shimmering wake stream behind them.

"It looks like a path to heaven," she said, and then turned to look at him before hugging him fiercely. "Thank you for this, Dante. It's perfect. So beautiful."

"My pleasure, *dulzura*," he said, returning her hug. She took a deep breath and inhaled his wonderful scent one last time before stepping away from him.

CHAPTER FIFTEEN

Christmas would have been a lot grimmer if not for Blue and Luc inviting him over for the day. It had been almost two weeks since Cleo had simply upped and left with nothing but an unsatisfactory note of "explanation" for Dante.

He was pissed off and worried about her. He couldn't understand why she'd just gone without a warning or good-bye. It had felt like a kick to the gut, especially since she'd flown out the day after they'd scattered Zach's ashes. Dante felt a little used and a *lot* hurt. Only Cleo had the ability to make him feel such contrary and powerful emotions.

He, of course, knew exactly where she was, despite the fact that she'd kept that information from Luc and Blue just to avoid the possibility of them telling him. But all he'd really needed to know was that she was with Callum Faris, and his resources had done the rest. He had known where she was since two days after she left. But he kept waiting for her to call. Only she never did.

"Dante?" Blue's voice prompted him, her eyes concerned. "Do you want another slice of roast beef?"

"No, thanks," he said, taking a sip of red wine. He'd been drinking way too much since she'd left, and he didn't want to become *that* guy, the fool who turned to alcohol whenever things didn't go his way. Still, it was damned satisfying to get rip-roaring drunk every night. At least he didn't have to face his cold and empty apartment sober.

He was starting to hate that place more and more. Cleo had turned it into a home while she had lived there, and he resented not having that home anymore. He missed her companionship, those movie nights with those awful films she got such a kick out of making him watch. He longed for the dinners they'd shared and the conversations they'd had. He had loved cooking for her. Once his greatest passion, it had become a lackluster affair now that he prepared meals for only himself. And even though it had driven him crazy sometimes, he even missed tripping over the stuff she used to leave lying around the place. He couldn't bring himself to work out in his gym anymore and used the one at the office instead, because it physically hurt to stare at that dance floor and not see her doing her barre routines there. And crazy though it seemed, he even missed having her finish his sentences

"When did you hear last from Cleo?" he asked Luc, and watched his friend tense.

"This morning. She called with Christmas greetings."

"Is she alone today?" The thought of her being alone at Christmas bugged him, but then he told himself that she didn't *have* to be alone. She could be here with people who cared about her.

"Cal's there. They're attempting their own version of a roast lunch."

Dante grimaced at that news.

"They'll poison themselves," he grunted, shaking his head. "Especially if Cleo does the cooking."

"Yeah, she's a pretty awful cook."

"Is she happy?" Dante hated asking, but he needed to know, and Luc shifted uncomfortably in his seat.

"She's not *unhappy*, and for now I think that's all we can hope for."

A month after leaving Cape Town, Cleo was starting to feel like she had a handle on her life again. Just a couple of days after arriving in Durban, she'd gone to a local dance studio and informed them they'd be idiots not to enlist her to teach a few ballet classes. Cal and a few of her former colleagues had vouched for her. She loved teaching and had fledgling dreams of opening her own dance school. She finally felt like she had a purpose again. She also choreographed dance pieces in her spare time, sometimes inspired by a song or a piece of art or even a bird in flight. It was wonderful and stimulating. She was developing quite a portfolio but didn't know if she would ever be brave enough to pitch those ideas to any dance companies.

It was close to five in the evening, and she was just getting home to the apartment she shared with Cal after one of her new junior dance classes. She had her head down and was fumbling with her keys when she walked straight into something huge, warm, and solid just outside of the apartment door.

"You really need to start looking where you're going, *dulzura*," chastised the last voice she had ever expected to hear again. She dropped her keys, her head flying up in reaction to that voice. She was filled with such raw, unbridled joy at the sight of him that her knees could barely hold her upright.

"Well?" he prompted in that dulcet voice. "Do you have anything to say to me?"

"What are you doing here?" she asked shakily. He snorted and shook his head in disgust before bending down to retrieve her keys.

"I think the more accurate question is, what the hell are *you* doing here?" He unlocked the door and steered her inside before following her in and slamming the door behind them.

"I live here," she replied defiantly.

"No, you live with *me*," he gritted out. "You never moved out!"

"I seem to recall moving out after I lost our baby," she said pointedly.

"That was always going to be a temporary thing."

"How can you say that? I was only living there because I was pregnant."

"Cleo, tell me what the hell happened? We had Zach's memorial, we said good-bye at the Waterfront, I told you I'd see you the next day, and you just left! How could you *do* that?"

She had boarded the first plane out of Cape Town the next morning, telling Luc and Blue only that she would be living with Cal, but not telling them exactly where that was, because she didn't want to put them in the position of lying to Dante. They'd protested, of course, said that she was making a mistake, and begged her to stay for Christmas. But Cleo hadn't been able to face the holidays and had firmly believed that she needed to get out of the city and as far away from Dante as possible in order to cut him out of her life completely.

"I left you a note," she reminded him.

"Which said absolutely *nothing*. 'Thank you for everything you've done. I cannot express how much it has meant to me but I think we both deserve a fresh start'?" He sounded incredulous, but Cleo was more shocked that he could recite her note verbatim. "What the hell was that supposed to mean?"

"It meant exactly what it said, Dante. Everything that tied us together is gone, and there is no need for us to be in each other's lives anymore."

"*Bullshit,*" he growled. "There is every reason!"

"I didn't want you to stick around because you felt guilty or whatever. I wanted you to go on with your life, and I tried to pick up the pieces of mine. It's for the best. There's just no reason for us to ever see each other again."

"Stop saying that!" he snapped. "No reason for us to ever see each other again? Well, what about *this*?" He framed her face and planted an angry, bruising kiss on her lips, and she was so shocked at first that she didn't react, but when the shock wore off and she started to struggle against his hold, his kiss gentled. His mouth opened and his tongue traced the seam of her lips. It was an invitation she couldn't resist . . . not when she'd spent the last month missing him every single hour of every day. She welcomed him in, and he groaned, the sound smothered against her mouth. He deepened his kiss, taking just that little bit more before ending it and stepping away from her, leaving her reeling.

"There's that," he said triumphantly, pointing a finger at her, and she shook her head to clear her befuddled senses.

"We know we have chemistry," she said. Her tongue flicked out to taste him on her lips, and he groaned at the gesture. "We'll probably always have chemistry, but let's face it, that's all we ever had, all we'll ever have. It's not enough."

"I'm getting sick of you leaving me, Cleo."

"I didn't leave you, Dante."

"Why do you have to be so damned unreasonable?" It was a familiar refrain, one she had heard from him in various forms of exasperation before. "Sometimes I don't even know why I bother."

"I don't know either," she said, her absolute confusion showing in her face and in her voice.

"So you're living with Callum again?" he asked, changing the subject.

"It's just temporary."

"And how have you been? After everything?"

"Fine," she said. "Some days are harder than others, you know?"

"Yeah. I know. I got a call from that baby-furniture store the other day." His eyes took on a shimmer. "I forgot to cancel the order, and they wanted to know . . . to know when I wanted them to deliver it."

"Oh *God*." Her hands flew to her mouth as she imagined how awful that must have been.

"That was one of the bad days. I left work early and went home and wished to hell I could talk to you about it! Only you weren't around, and I got sick of giving you time to come to your senses, so I came to fetch you home."

"Wait, are you saying you knew where I was?"

"*Dulzura*, please, you forget that I am Dante Damaso. I have wealth, power, and influence at my fingertips."

She rolled her eyes, old habits surfacing in his presence.

"Also ego," she added. He sent her a quelling glance before continuing.

"I knew you were with Callum. It was just a matter of finding out which company he danced for, and there aren't many options in Durban. Once I figured that out, a quick phone call told me exactly where he was staying. I've known since almost the beginning. But I wanted to give you time to figure this out by yourself. Then I got sick of giving you time, because I missed you like hell."

"W-what?"

"I spent Christmas with your brother and Blue," he said. "Because they felt sorry for my pathetic ass. I was always calling them and asking if they'd heard from you and wanting to know if you were okay."

Cleo knew that; Blue and Luc had both told her stories of how Dante kept questioning them about her well-being. She had thought it was just polite concern, but looking at him now, she could see it was far from that.

"Damn you, Cleo! You gave me a home and family, and then you just took it away from me," he hissed. "We lost Zach; we didn't have to lose each other too."

"Okay, back up a second," she said. "You're making no sense, Dante. Before I lost the baby, we had an arrangement. I'd move out with Zach and set up house in an apartment you provided, and you would play the role of his glorified uncle or something. *That* was the extent of our relationship. We were living together for convenience, and you never once hinted at anything different."

"I asked you to *marry* me," he reminded her, his nostrils flaring with irritation.

"Because you wanted Zach!" she said.

"No, you idiot." He was practically yelling now, and she blinked at the spectacular emotional explosion she was witnessing from the famously cool Dante Damaso. This was just . . . fascinating. "Because I wanted *you*!"

She stumbled backward and sat down on the hard couch with a thump. "What?"

He sighed and sank down on the couch next to her. "I mean, of course I wanted the baby, but I wanted you too. No, let me rephrase, I wanted you *especially*."

"I . . . *how?*"

"I'm not great at talking about things like this," he said with a wince, keeping his gaze straight ahead while she kept hers fixed on his stark profile.

"Give it a go."

"When we first slept together in Tokyo, that was just sex, but I couldn't stay away from you for the entirety of that trip, despite trying my damnedest to leave you alone every night."

"You didn't seem to try very hard." She sniffed.

"No, you're wrong. I tried exceptionally hard, and yet every night we just wound up in bed together. Maybe I should have known then, but I wouldn't see it. I told myself I just needed to get you out of my system; we had some crazy chemistry, and it would eventually fade. Only it didn't. It got worse. I mean we had sex on my desk! On my *desk*." He sounded mildly astonished by that fact. "I stepped over a line that day, and I didn't even care. I transferred you out of my office and figured that was that. But it wasn't. Every day, Cleo. I thought about you every bloody day."

"Well . . ." She wasn't sure how to respond to that. He was now facing her, his eyes glowing with a powerful emotion.

"Then you came to my office and told me you were pregnant. And with all the confusion that followed, with the craziness, the disbelief and doubt and all those hurtful, angry words we exchanged, I just never . . . I never saw it. I didn't recognize you." He sounded completely confused, and Cleo shook her head, not understanding.

"What?"

"I didn't know who you were." His voice bordered on desperate, and the intensity in his eyes deepened as he struggled to verbalize his emotion. "Do you understand?"

"No," she said regretfully. She wished she did, because she sensed that this meant a lot to him, and his inability to explain it was frustrating to both of them. "I'm sorry, Dante; I don't."

He glanced upward as if seeking answers from the heavens and then brought his gaze back down to hers.

"When we first met, I saw a pretty woman. One who immediately set off my internal alarms. 'Instant dislike,' I told myself. 'Stay away from her; she'll annoy the ever-loving hell out of you!' But I couldn't stay away. Before Tokyo you were in my space day in and day out. I kept farming you out to other people just so that I could get some work done. Because you *did* annoy me, aggravate me, shatter my concentration, and you made me feel damned uncomfortable in my own skin! I couldn't wait to get rid of you, even while I couldn't seem to stay away from you. But back then I didn't know who you were, not even after we made love."

Made love? What had happened to his other—cruder—term for it?

"Even after that, I didn't recognize you."

"Dante, I don't understand." And she desperately wanted to understand.

"You're *it*, Cleo," he snapped, clearly annoyed with himself for losing his grasp on the English language so completely. "You're her. You're my she. My other. *Mine.*"

"What?" she whispered in disbelief. Even with his incoherence and his accent thickening on every syllable, Cleo was starting to understand. And what she thought she understood was utterly unbelievable.

"You're mine. The one who was put on this earth for *me*. And I'm so damned sorry I didn't recognize you immediately. I was stupidly prepared to let you walk out of my life forever, but fate stepped in and gave us Zach," he said, his voice breaking as he dashed at the tears in his eyes. "And Zach gave me a chance to *see* and finally recognize you."

"Dante," she said, her voice wobbling slightly, "take a deep breath and tell me in easy English so that I know I'm not going out of my mind here. What are you trying to say?"

"I'm trying to say that I'm an idiot! A blind fool. And that I already lost Zach, and I don't want to lose you too. Because my life is shit without you! I'm saying that I adore you. I revere you. I cherish you. I fucking *love* you, Cleo."

Her hands flew up to her mouth to stifle her gasp, and she simply stared at him in shock.

"I love you and you keep leaving me," he said angrily.

"Well, it's not like I knew you loved me," she said logically, and he glared at her.

"I know I've been an asshole," he said, his voice earnest. "And that it's probably hard to imagine yourself ever caring for me or loving me, but I'm trying to change and—"

"Dante," she interrupted him firmly, "let's get two things straight. You haven't been an asshole for a very, *very* long time. But I couldn't trust you with my heart because I thought all you wanted was the baby, and I didn't want a marriage like that."

"Would you trust me with your heart now?" he asked tentatively, one finger reaching out to stroke the back of her hand in a feather-light touch.

"That was the second thing. It's pretty easy for me to imagine myself in love with you."

"*Sí?*" he asked, hope blooming in his dark eyes.

"Yep."

He edged closer, crowding her back against the sofa and twisting until his hands were braced on the back of the sofa and his torso was hovering above hers.

"Care to elaborate on that?" he asked.

"I think *I've* been the asshole," she said, and he made a protesting sound. "Even after you showed me what a good guy you could be, starting with your immediate refusal to allow me to pay for my own medical bills, right up until Zach's farewell, I still doubted that you could really care for me. Now maybe that's just me lacking a whole lot of self-confidence, but it's also in part because I never really believed in you. And I'm so sorry, Dante."

"I'm sorry too," he whispered against her lips. "I didn't give you much reason to trust me."

"So, now what?" she asked.

"A couple of things," he said, digging into his jacket pocket and tugging out a long black jeweler's box. "Your Christmas present."

She took the box from him and held it in her hands, a little overwhelmed by everything that was happening. A Christmas present. How did she always keep underestimating him, despite all the evidence pointing to the fact that he was a good man? Cleo had never felt more foolish or more humble than she did in that moment.

"Open it," he urged, and she cracked the box open and gasped when she saw what was nestled inside. It was a tiny, heart-shaped gold pendant, with a minute off-center diamond catching the light. The pendant hung from a delicate chain.

"It's lovely," she said, smiling.

"I don't know how you're going to feel about this, but it seemed like the right thing to do at the time," he said quietly, and she peered up at him curiously.

"What do you mean?"

"I removed a small portion of Zach's ashes from his urn the night before we scattered them and had this pendant made for you. I thought that maybe after you've had time to think about it, you'd like the idea of carrying part of him close to your heart at all times."

"Are you saying the ashes are in here?" she asked in disbelief. The heart looked boxy but absolutely seamless except for the small holes running through the top for the chain. As she inspected it, she noticed the curling script on the back of the pendant.

"They, uh . . . they seal it after they place the ashes inside. There's a little indentation close to the bottom of the heart where they inserted the ashes."

"Oh, Dante!" she cried, not really hearing his nervous words, as she read the script. "It's beautiful."

Zach, remembered forever.

"You don't mind?" he asked, and she flung her arms around his waist and hugged him close.

"No, I don't mind," she said as she put the beautiful pendant on, turning slightly for him to fasten it for her. "It means so much. Just *so* much."

"I have one too." He tugged on a leather cord around his neck and dragged out an infinitely more masculine silver hoop. It wasn't very big, and again she couldn't see how it could possibly contain the ashes, but it was beautiful and had the same sentiment engraved on the outer loop.

"And the . . . the second thing." He sounded really nervous, and she leaned back, her joy at the gift momentarily forgotten as she stared at him in fascination. He fumbled around in his jacket pockets again and this time produced a square box.

"So, I'm going to ask you again. I've asked you a *million* times already, Cleo, and I'm probably not asking again after this. Probably. So you'd better consider my question carefully." He was rambling, and Cleo could only stare at him with what she knew was a besotted grin on her face. She had never really seen him this nervous before, and it was absolutely adorable. A word she wouldn't previously have associated with Dante Damaso. He smoothed down his hair, straightened his tie, and then, quite unexpectedly, dropped to one knee in front of her.

"So, Cleopatra Pandora Knight . . ." She winced at the use of her full name. "Will you marry me? Because like I said before, my life is shit without you, and I love the hell out of you."

"You going to show me the ring, champ?" she asked pointedly. "My answer may well hinge on the size of the rock you got me."

"Mercenary woman," he said without heat. He flipped open the box, and Cleo gasped.

"It's beautiful," she said reverently. It was a deep square-cut emerald bordered by smaller diamonds.

"It matches your eyes almost exactly," he said, removing the ring from its velvet cushion.

"I love you so much," she said, feeling completely overwhelmed by the depth of her feeling for him.

"So you'll marry me?"

"If I must," she said, striving for casual even though her eyes were heavy with tears. She held out her hand, and he kissed her ring finger before sliding the ring onto it.

"No more running away from me, Cleo," he warned. "Talk to me next time."

"I left because I loved you so much," she said seriously, and he cupped her face in the palms of his hands.

"Next time stay because *I* love you so much."

"There won't be a next time, Dante."

"That's all I ask for." He kissed her deeply, and by the time he ended the kiss, she was straddling his lap, his tie was undone, and his shirt was unbuttoned halfway down his chest.

"I've missed you," she said, and leaned in for another drugging kiss, which he happily reciprocated, his hands cupping her butt. "I'm sorry I left. The first time you proposed, I thought you wanted to marry me because of Zach, and I never wanted you to feel trapped or obligated to marry. After he died, I thought we were just helping each other cope with the grief."

"No more talk. I've missed more than your weird sense of humor and your appalling taste in movies, you know," he said seriously.

"Oh?"

"Yep, I've missed tasting this mouth," he growled, before leaning up to do just that. It wasn't nearly long enough or satisfying enough. "And I've missed this highly cuppable little bum." Again, action to match his words. Cleo squirmed with excitement and wondered where he was going next. "Oh God, and these sensitive little beauties have haunted my dreams." Her breath quickened in anticipation, and she wriggled on his lap, excited for what was to come. "My mouth has been empty without them to . . ."

"Well, *hello*." The masculine voice coming from such close proximity shocked the hell out of both of them. Cleo squealed and tried to jump off Dante's lap, but his palms flattened against her hips and kept her in place.

"You stay *right* there. At least until after I've managed to lose the hard-on," he warned under his breath, and she collapsed against his chest in a fit of giggles, hiding her face from Cal, whom neither of them had heard come home.

"Nice to see you again, Mr. D," Cal said in a voice that sounded wholly insincere.

"You might as well call me Dante, since you'll be seeing so much more of me in the future."

"And why would that be?" Cal asked.

Keeping her face buried in Dante's chest, not so much because of embarrassment but because it smelled so wonderful there, Cleo held up her left hand for Cal's inspection.

He gasped and grabbed her hand.

"Now that's a serious rock," Cal said. "'Bout time you made an honest woman out of her." His tone changed, going deeper and more serious. "I wanted to tell you I was sorry to hear about the baby. It just about broke my heart. You have my sympathies."

"Thank you, Callum," Dante said sincerely. "That means a lot."

"So, look . . . this is a onetime deal. I'm gonna take some clothes and head over to a friend's and stay the night. Knock yourselves out, but do not, for the *love of God*, have sex on my bed!"

Cleo sniggered, and after an experimental wiggle, figured it was safe to climb off Dante's lap. She launched herself at Cal and hugged him fiercely.

"Thank you," she said. "For everything."

"Anytime, hon. Anytime."

A couple of hours later, sated and exhausted, Dante and Cleo lounged on the sleeper couch, completely naked.

"I've never made love on a sleeper couch before," he said bemusedly, and Cleo giggled. She felt absurdly happy.

"It's called slumming it."

"I mean, we could have gone to the Damaso International Hotel on the Golden Mile," he said, referencing Durban's famous beach strip. "But the thought never even occurred to me."

"So . . . some stuff to talk about," she said, toying with his pendant as she sat on his lap.

"Hmm." He looked and sounded exhausted.

"I hate that penthouse; we're getting a real house."

"Bossy," he said on a yawn.

"And we're having a proper wedding with a big white dress and a tux and everything, but you're paying for it because I'm totally poor." He snorted as his hands roamed absently up and down her slender back.

"We're honeymooning in Japan," he added. "And going to each and every page marked off in your travel guide."

"How do you know about that?" she asked, stunned. As far she knew, he'd never even noticed her guide.

"Please, you were poring over that thing every time we were in the car with Daisuke, asking him questions about places that interested you in the book. Most evenings, I had Daisuke drive by some of those places so that, even though we didn't have the time to properly visit them, you could have a sense of what they were like."

"I wondered if that was your doing," she said. It had been a kind and considerate gesture, to say the least.

"I also happened to leaf through the book one day while you were in the bathroom."

"Sneaky," she tut-tutted.

"Hey, it was just lying there, in full view at the top of your handbag," he joked.

"I also wanted to discuss children," she said, and he went still, obviously bracing himself for something. "I'd like to hold off on another baby for a couple of years, if that's okay."

"That's fine with me, *dulzura*. I get to have you all to myself for a while." He looked so relieved by her comment that she was curious.

"What were you expecting me to say?" she asked.

"I was concerned that maybe you never wanted another one."

"What would you have done if that were the case?"

He considered her question carefully.

"I would have left you to think it over a little longer, and in a few years' time I would have asked you to reconsider. If you were still adamantly against it, I would have tried steering you toward adoption."

"You wouldn't have minded?"

"I would have minded very much, but your happiness is my happiness," he said simply, and she cupped his stubbled jaw between the palms of her hands and kissed him.

"I also want you to draw up a prenuptial contract," she said quietly, and he went still beneath her. Every muscle in his body froze.

"We don't have to."

"We do," she said. "You're not your father, Dante, so don't be stupid. Draw up the contract."

"But I'm happy to share everything I have with you."

"And that's fabulous, but I want you to approach this union as you would have approached marriage to your boring dream woman. Draw up a contract that you know we'll *never* use because we love and respect each other too much for the ugly notion of divorce to ever enter our heads. Do it for me. Make sure I don't take you for every penny you own."

"You're a weird and wonderful woman, Cleopatra Knight."

"God, I wish you'd *stop* calling me that! And don't you *ever* use my middle name again, Dante Aloysius Damaso," she said, and he scowled. "Remember, I can dish the dirt too."

"I have some rules for you too," he said. "They're pretty simple. You allow me to finance a studio for you so that you can start teaching on a more serious basis."

"But that's . . ." He held up his forefinger and tilted his head.

"Shush. I'm not done talking yet. You *always* share a workout space with me, because you're seriously sexy when you're doing that whole ballerina thing."

"So are you when you're doing the boxing thing."

"Once we get a house, we're getting a dog. Not one of those snappy, fiddly little things. A proper dog."

"Sir, yes, sir," she saluted sarcastically.

"This last rule is negotiable," he said, tilting his hand in a "so-so" gesture. "You walk around naked all the time and tell me you love me at least twice a day."

"That's a hell no on the first, and an amendment to three times a day on the second."

"Spoilsport," he pouted.

"I love you," she said, and he grinned.

"That's one," he said, and she wrapped her arms around his neck.

"Who's counting?" Then, leaning down until her mouth was right next to his ear, she whispered, "I love you, I love you, I love you, I love you . . ."

EPILOGUE
FIVE YEARS LATER

Cleo stared at her reflection in the mirror with a critical eye, tilting her head this way and that as she swung around to look at her butt. Dante stepped into her line of sight, and she gave him a perturbed frown in the mirror.

"This kid is making me fat," she pouted, and he grinned, coming up behind her to wrap his arms around her. He could barely fit them around her huge stomach.

"You look beautiful and you know it," he told her, dropping a kiss onto her shoulder.

"Everybody's here," he murmured. "You ready for this?"

She covered his hands with hers and looked at the picture they presented in the mirror. Both were wearing white—Dante, a simple shirt-and-trouser combination that looked devastating on his lean form, and Cleo, a pretty maternity sundress with shoulder ties.

Every year on the anniversary of his birth and death, they celebrated the life of the son who had brought them together. During their first two years of marriage, they'd gone out on the *Arabella* to the same spot where they'd scattered his ashes and watched the sunset. They never saw the phosphorescence again, and that made the memory of it so much more special to Cleo.

On the third anniversary they changed things up a bit as their daughter, Tamara, had been only a couple of months old, so they commemorated the day differently, planting an oak tree in their garden instead. Afterward, they worked together for months to create a beautiful little remembrance garden around the tree. Dante had a stone bench placed in the garden, and they would often sit there together, or sometimes alone, and think about their lost baby. He also commissioned a discreet engraved memorial stone to be placed at the base of the tree, and like their pendants, it simply read

ZACH, REMEMBERED FOREVER.

After that, they started having the anniversary in the garden and included Blue and Luc, Cal and Tami. And this year, Enrique Damaso, who was between wives at the moment, had joined them too. A doting grandpapa, Enrique visited and Skyped regularly, but he had never been there for Zach's memorial before.

The day had become one of celebration as they remembered their baby with joy rather than sorrow. And sometimes in the privacy of their bedroom, when it was just the two of them, they would wonder aloud what he would have been like.

Dante's hand moved up to toy with her pendant.

"Cal is trying to convince Luc that he's the better *braai* master, and the two will be having some kind of cook-off later. As if I'd let either of them anywhere near my grill," he snorted, the corner of his eyes crinkling attractively. The man just got more gorgeous with age; the sprinkling of gray in his hair and the fine lines forming around his eyes and on his brow just added to his disgusting good looks. It was something she often complained about, protesting the fact that she was getting a bit saggy in the boob area and a little thick around the middle, while he just improved like fine wine. He usually shut her up by making love to her until she couldn't speak, and telling her that he loved her, "saggy boobs, stretch marks, and all."

"Jeez, why don't Blue and Kyle put a leash on their men?" Cleo asked in exasperation, stepping out of his hold and moving toward the bedroom door at a fast waddle. Kyle was Cal's longtime boyfriend, and they were talking about tying the knot. They'd been together for nearly four years. Cal, who was now the principal male dancer in his company, had never been happier, and Cleo was ecstatic for him.

"Blue's too busy trying to stop Adam's crying, and Kyle's teaching Tami and my father a magic trick," Dante replied. Adam was Blue and Luc's two-week-old son, their first child. After Dante finally convinced them to take a loan from him four years before, Luc and Blue had, at long last, been able to fix the house and get married. Dante was still trying to convince Cleo's proud brother to work for him at Damaso International, Inc., but Luc was being stubborn about accepting.

Dante sauntered out of the room after Cleo and caught up with her at the stairs. He took her elbow as she moved down the stairs, adding his support.

He was holding her hand as they walked into the chaotic living room. Cal and Luc were still arguing good-humoredly, Adam was screeching at the top of his lungs, Kyle had abandoned the magic tricks and was chasing an excited and squealing three-year-old around the room. Titan, their two-year-old Chihuahua, was chasing after both of them and yapping at the top of his lungs, while Enrique futilely tried to call the tiny dog to heel. Titan and Dante had been inseparable since the dog had been just two months old. It was ridiculous to see them together. And all of them, down to little Adam, were wearing white. Even Titan was wearing a little white T-shirt. The scene filled Cleo with great love while simultaneously making her want to run screeching in the opposite direction.

None of them spotted Dante and Cleo, who paused in the doorway.

"Want to make a run for it?" he whispered in her ear, and she looked at him and grinned.

They quietly backed away from the crazy room and, by unspoken agreement, walked to the kitchen of the beautiful two-story beach house that she and Dante had chosen together. It was situated close to Luc and Blue's home. They made their way into the sprawling backyard, wandered to the bench in Zach's garden, and sat down together. Cleo rested her head on his shoulder, and they kept their fingers entwined as they sat quietly together, enjoying the beautiful summer afternoon in silence.

"Still love me?" he asked, and she angled her eyes up to look into his face. He was looking down at the forget-me-nots, which were in full bloom, and the smile flirting around the edges of his lips told her he wasn't particularly concerned about her answer.

"Yeah, I suppose I love you," she said casually, and watched as the smile blossomed on his lips.

"That's one," he counted.

"Who's counting?" she murmured. This had become one of their favorite little daily rituals. "I love you, I love you, I love you. *So* much."

He tilted his head toward her.

"I love you too, *dulzura*."

ACKNOWLEDGMENTS

Thanks to Maritza for being such a patient Spanish tutor.
And thanks, Nicola, for the dance chats.

ABOUT THE AUTHOR

Photo courtesy of the author

Natasha Anders was born in Cape Town, South Africa. She spent nine years working as an assistant English teacher in Niigata, Japan, where she became a legendary karaoke diva. Natasha currently lives in Cape Town with her opinionated budgie, Sir Oliver Spencer, and her temperamental Chihuahua, Maia. Please feel free to contact her, Oliver, or Maia on Twitter at @satyneɪ; on Facebook; or on her website, www.natashaanders.com. They would all love to hear from you.